612

THE
FIFTH
VIAL

.

ALSO BY MICHAEL PALMER

THE
FIFTH
VIAL

MICHAEL
PALMER

**Doubleday Large Print
Home Library Edition**

St. Martin's Press **ℳ** *New York*

THE FIFTH VIAL. Copyright © 2007 by Michael Palmer. All rights reserved. Printed in the United States of America. No part of this book may be used or reproduced in any manner whatsoever without written permission except in the case of brief quotations embodied in critical articles or reviews. For information, address St. Martin's Press, 175 Fifth Avenue, New York, N.Y. 10010.

Grateful acknowledgment is made for permission to reprint from the following:
"Fish and Whistle," written by John Prine. © 1978 Big Ears Music (ASCAP) and Bruised Oranges Music (AS-CAP) administered by Bug. All Rights Reserved. Used by Permission.

ISBN-13: 978-0-7394-8007-6

**This Large Print Book carries the
Seal of Approval of N.A.V.H.**

To

Zoe May Palmer, Benjamin Miles Palmer,
and Clemma Rose Prince:
May you grow up in a world of peace.

And, as always,
to Luke

ACKNOWLEDGMENTS

The friends, family, and resources set down on this page are not listed in order of importance . . . except for the first two.

Jane Berkey, founder of the Jane Rotrosen Agency, has been the guiding force in my writing for more than twenty-five years.

Jennifer Enderlin, my editor at St. Martin's Press, has shepherded *The Fifth Vial* through its creation, evolution, and publication without ever losing sight of my vision for the book.

Thanks also to:

Sally Richardson, Matthew Shear, George Witte, Matt Baldacci, and everyone else at St. Martin's Press.

Don Cleary, Peggy Gordijn, and the gang at the agency.

Eileen Hutton, Michael Snodgrass, and their crew at Brilliance Audio.

Matt Palmer, Daniel James Palmer, and Luke Palmer. It would be sweet someday for all of us to meet on the *Times* list.

Drs. Joe Antin and Geoff Sherwood, readers Robin Broady, Mimi Santini-Ritt, and Dr. Julie Bellet, private investigator Rob Diaz, and firefighter Cindi Moore.

Bill Hinchberger of BrazilMax.com, "the hip guide to Brazil," and humorist Alexandre Raposo.

Professor Nancy Scheper-Hughes, founder of Organs Watch and director of the medical anthropology program at the University of California, Berkeley.

Various experts in organ donation, who have asked to remain anonymous.

Bill Wilson of East Dorset, Vermont, and Dr. Bob Smith of Akron, Ohio. I suspect that you fellows know why you're being included here.

THE
FIFTH
VIAL

.

PROLOGUE

The beginning is the most important part of any work.
    —PLATO, *The Republic,* Book II

Hold still, now. This won't hurt a bit.

Those were the only words Lonnie Durkin had heard for hours.

This won't hurt a bit.

Vincent always said the same thing just before he stuck the needle into Lonnie's arm and drew blood.

Vincent lied. The needles didn't hurt much, but they did hurt.

"Take me home! Please take me home! Please, please, please."

Lonnie leapt up from his bed, jammed his fingers through the metal wire fencing, and kicked the locked gate. He knew what a nightmare was. His mother had explained bad dreams to him when he was a boy and had begun waking up every night screaming. But he could tell that the cage was no nightmare.

The cage was real.

"Please!"

At that moment, the van swung a turn that threw him hard against the wall, banging his head and his shoulder. He cried out, fell, then crawled back to the bed.

The van was a house on wheels, like the one Uncle Gus and Aunt Diane had. But instead of a cage in the back, theirs had a nice room and a big bed and some closets. Five years ago, for Lonnie's sixteenth birthday, they had taken him to Yellowstone in the van and had let him sleep in that bed at night for the whole trip. The bed in the cage was too small for him, and the mattress was too hard. Beside the bed there was a chair, a pitcher of water in a holder on the wall, and some paper cups. On the chair there was a magazine called *MAD,* which had lots of weird cartoon drawings, but way too many words for him to read. And finally, there was the clicker for the TV that was attached to the wall outside the cage. That was everything.

Lonnie couldn't stop thinking about his mother and father, and the men who worked on the farm. The guys knew how much he loved M&Ms, and always had some for him when he walked down to the fields to visit them, and sometimes even help them out.

"Let me go! Please don't hurt me! Just let me go!"

Three sides of the cage were the walls of the van. The fourth side was the fence, made of chicken wire, just like the coop behind the barn at home. It completely filled the opening to the rest of the van and had a gate with a lock on the other side. There was a light in the ceiling just outside the cage, but no windows. Beyond the fencing was the bathroom, and just past that was a folding wall that pulled across the passageway to where Vincent and Connie were.

Frustrated, Lonnie rose and kicked at the fence. He guessed that he had been in the cage for three days, maybe four. The van had been moving almost the whole time.

He wasn't really cold, but he felt that way—cold and frightened and lonely.

"Please! Please take me home!"

His voice was almost gone.

Except for the needles when they gave

him a shot or drew blood, neither Vincent nor Connie had hurt him so far, but Lonnie could tell they didn't like him, either. They looked at him just like Mr. and Mrs. Wilcox in the house down the road from the farm looked at him, and once, while he was on the toilet, he had heard Vincent call him a fucking retard.

"Let me go! I want to go home! Please, please. This isn't fair."

The van slowed and pulled over to a stop. Moments later, Vincent opened the door beyond the bathroom. He was a big man with yellow curly hair—not fat the way Lonnie was, just big. He had a tattoo of a battleship on each of his arms, right above his wrists. Vincent had been so nice to him at first. Connie, too. They had stopped the van where Lonnie was walking to the rec center, and had asked him directions to the farm. Cousins of his mother, they had said they were. Otherwise he would never have gotten in the van with them. His mother had taught him about going with strangers. But these weren't strangers. They were cousins, who knew his name and his father's and mother's, but had just never been up to the farm.

His hands on his hips, Vincent stood by

the bathroom door. Lonnie could tell he was angry before he even spoke.

"What did I tell you about yelling?"

"N-not to do it."

"Then why are you doing it?"

"I-I'm scared."

In spite of himself, Lonnie felt his eyes filling with tears. Just the other day, his mother had said she was proud of him for not crying so much anymore. Now, here he was, about to cry again.

"I told you that you didn't have anything to be frightened of. One more day and we'll let you out."

"P-promise?"

"Okay, I promise. But if there's any more hollering or you give us any trouble at all, the promise is off and I'm going to take away the TV remote."

"The TV doesn't work good anyhow."

"What?"

"Nothing. Nothing."

"No more noise. I mean it."

Vincent spun around and left before Lonnie could say any more. After wiping his eyes with the back of his hand, Lonnie pulled the blanket over himself and drew his knees up, facing the back wall. *One more day and we'll let you out.* Vincent's promise played over and over through his head. He should have made him do a pinky promise. *One more day.* . . . For a time, the tears came even though he tried to stop them. Then, gradually, Lonnie's sobs gave way to a troubled sleep.

When he awoke, the van had stopped moving. His shoulder hurt from where he had fallen, and there was a sore lump just over his eye as well. He rolled over slowly, aware that he had to return to the bathroom soon to pee. A woman was standing outside the fence, looking at him. She was wearing the kind of blue hospital clothes that the doctors who fixed his hernia wore, and over them a white jacket. Her hair was pulled back and covered with a blue paper hospital hat. Vincent was standing behind her, tapping a short, black club against his hand. The door behind him was closed.

"Hello, Lonnie," the woman said, adjusting her glasses and looking down at him. "My name is Dr. Prouty. Did Vincent or Connie tell you I was going to be here?"

Lonnie managed to shake his head no.

"Well, then," Dr. Prouty went on, "you needn't be afraid. I'm going to take your temperature under your tongue, and check you over the way doctors do. Do you understand?"

This time Lonnie nodded. Despite the doctor's quiet voice and smooth skin, there was something about her that seemed to make it impossible for him to speak. Something cold.

"Good. Now, I want your word that if I open this gate and come in there with you, you'll be cooperative. . . . *Cooperative,* Lonnie. Do you know what that word means? Lonnie, answer me."

"I . . . know."

"Good."

Dr. Prouty nodded to Vincent, who unlocked the gate and pulled it open, all the time keeping the club where Lonnie could see it.

"Okay, now, Lonnie," Dr. Prouty said, "I'm going to give you a shot and then I'm going to examine you. First I want you to get undressed and put this gown on with the strings in the back. Do you understand?"

"I have to go pee."

"Very well. Vincent will help you, then he'll help you get changed. First, though, let me give you this shot."

"Then I can go pee?"

"Then you can go," Dr. Prouty said, somewhat impatiently.

Lonnie only moved a little when the needle was jammed into his arm. Then he went into the tiny bathroom and peed. When he had finished, Vincent took him by the arm and led him back into the cage to change into the gown. Even with it on, he felt naked. The fear that had been building inside him tightened like a band around his chest. Dr. Prouty returned from the front of the van, closing the door behind her. As she examined him, he began to feel his eyelids grow heavy.

"He's going out," he heard Dr. Prouty say. "Let's get him up front while he can still hold most of his own weight."

Vincent helped him to stand. Then Dr. Prouty opened the door. It was the first time Lonnie went to the front of the van since the day it had stopped for him. Things there had completely changed. A bright saucer light was attached to the ceiling, and beneath it was a narrow bed covered with a green sheet. Beside the bed stood a tall doctor, wearing a blue mask over his mouth and nose.

"Get him up there while I scrub in," Dr. Prouty said.

Lonnie looked toward her voice and saw that she, too, had a mask on. He felt wobbly, barely able to stand. Vincent helped him to lie facedown on the bed and pulled a strap across his back. A sheet was lowered over him. Then the tall doctor put a needle into his arm and left it there. Lonnie's eyes closed and refused to open. His fear subsided.

"Now, Lonnie," the tall doctor said, "I'm going to put a special breathing mask over your face. . . . Perfect. Okay, just breathe in and out. In and out. This won't hurt a bit."

"The body is that of a well-nourished white male in his twenties. Height five feet nine inches; weight one hundred ninety-seven pounds. Hair brown, eyes blue. No tattoos or . . ."

Pathologist Stanley Woyczek used a foot pedal and overhead mike to dictate as he worked. He was in his second term as medical examiner for Florida District 19, which included St. Lucie, Martin, Indian River, and

Okeechobee counties, all located north and west of West Palm Beach. He loved the intricacies and puzzle-solving that went along with the job, but was still not at all inured to the human tragedy. Cases often stayed with him for weeks, if not years. He had no doubt that this would be one of them. A young man, carrying no identification, had run out of a grove of trees and onto a sparsely populated stretch of Route 70, where he was blasted out of existence by a tractor-trailer. The driver of the semi estimated he was going sixty-five when the man suddenly appeared as if out of nowhere, right between his headlights. Gratefully, Woyczek reasoned, the pain of the impact couldn't have lasted more than a second or two.

Preliminary screens for alcohol and drugs of abuse were already back, and were negative. Assuming the more extensive toxicology was also going to be unrevealing, there would probably still be two glaring questions when this postmortem was completed: Who? And why?

"There is a well-healed scar over the left inguinal canal, presumably from the surgical repair of a hernia. There is a seven-inch laceration and compound fracture of the skull above the left ear, and a twelve-inch-long vertical tear through the left chest, through which a severed portion of the aorta can be seen."

Woyczek motioned to his assistant that it was time to turn the victim over. They did so with care.

"Posteriorly, there is a deep abrasion across the right scapula, but no other—"

The pathologist stopped speaking and peered down at the top of the man's buttock, just above his right hip . . . then at an identical area on the left.

"Chantelle, what does that look like to you?"

The assistant studied both areas.

"Puncture wounds," she said.

"No doubt about it."

"No, Dr. Woyczek. There are six on each side, maybe more."

"We'll do a microscopic on some of them to set the age, but these punctures are recent. I'm sure of it. I think we have something here." He stepped back and stripped off his gloves. "Hold the fort for a couple of minutes, Chantelle. I want to get the detectives to come over. I might be wrong, but I don't think so. Sometime in the last day, two at the most, John Doe here was the donor for a bone marrow transplant."

CHAPTER 1

The partisan, when he is engaged in a dispute, cares nothing about the rights of the question, but is anxious only to convince his hearers of his own assertions.

—PLATO, *Phaedo*

Go ahead and sew him up, Ms. Reyes."

Natalie stared at the slice down Darren Jones's forehead, across his eyebrow, and down his cheek. Until this moment, the largest knife wound she had ever seen was one she had accidentally inflicted on her own finger. Treatment then had been a couple of Band-Aids. She forced herself not to make eye contact with Cliff Renfro, the surgical senior resident in charge of the ER, and followed him out to the hallway.

In her three years and one month as a medical student, she had sutured countless pillows, several varieties of fruit, some ragged stuffed animals, and recently, at what she considered great peril, the seat of a pair of her favorite jeans. Renfro's order didn't make much sense. She was only two hours into her second day on the ER rotation at Metropolitan Hospital of Boston, and although Renfro had checked her diagnostic skills out on several patients, he had yet to see her sew.

"Dr. Renfro, I . . . um . . . think maybe I should go over things with you before—"

"Not necessary. When you're finished, write a scrip for him for some antibiotic—any one. I'll sign it."

The resident turned and was gone before she could respond. Her classmate and good friend, Veronica Kelly, who had already finished her surgical rotation at Metropolitan, had told her that Renfro was in his final year before taking over as chief surgical resident at White Memorial, the flagship of the medical school's many famous teaching hospitals. After years of training, he had the air of one who had seen it all and was burnt out on what he considered the lowlife patient population of Metro.

"Renfro's smart and damn competent," Veronica had said, "and he'll take the really messy trauma cases. But he couldn't care less about the routine stuff."

Apparently he considered a black teenage loser in a gang fight to be routine. Natalie hesitated outside the boy's room, wondering what the fallout would be if she chased Renfro down and asked for a demonstration of his skill.

"You okay, Nat?"

The nurse, a gravel-voiced veteran of years in the ER, had given a portion of yesterday's student orientation, including the tradition that in a hardscrabble place like Metro, almost all the staff used first names. Hers was Bev—Bev Richardson.

"I asked for this rotation because I heard the students got to do a lot of procedures, but sewing up a kid's face on my second day is a bit more than I had expected."

"Have you sutured before?"

"Nothing that was ever alive, except a few unfortunate oranges."

Bev sighed.

"Cliff's a darn good doc, but he's a little immature at times and can be hard on people. And the truth is, I don't think he cares all that much for our clientele."

"Well, I do," Natalie said, stopping short of

a litany of the many times earlier in her life when she had been wheeled or carried or dragged into this very ER.

"We like having people working around here who care. The patients have it hard enough everyplace else. Their hospital ought to be something of a sanctuary."

"I second that. Well, Dean Goldenberg has told me that he's heard I'm going to be accepted into the White Memorial surgical residency. Maybe Dr. Renfro has heard the same thing and he's just testing me."

"Or maybe he senses that you're not like him and he wants to see if you'll back down from the challenge."

"He wouldn't be the first," Natalie replied, already setting her jaw and mentally ticking through the pages of the plastic surgery text she had reviewed during the week before this rotation.

"You're the runner, aren't you?"

The question didn't startle Natalie in the least. Her tragic accident during the Olympic trials was chronicled on the local and national news and the cover of *Sports Illustrated.* From the day she started med school as a thirty-two-year-old first-year student, people knew who she was.

"Past tense," she said, her terse response requesting a change in subject.

"Think you can do this boy's face?"

"At least he'll have someone working on him who gives a hoot, if that means anything."

"It means plenty," Bev said. "Go ahead in there. I'll get you set up with some six-oh nylon suture. Even though most of them aren't, we assume everyone down here who is bleeding is HIV-positive, so best wear a gown and plastic face shield. If I think you're going wrong in any way, I'll clear my throat and you can come away and we can talk. Keep your fingers away from the needle. Straight instrument ties, double overhand knots about an eighth of an inch apart. Don't pull them so tight that the skin edges bunch, and don't shave his eyebrow because they never grow back right."

"Thank you."

"Welcome to the ER," Bev said.

"You doin' a good job, Doc?"

Natalie looked up at Bev Richardson, who nodded proudly that she was. From the moment Nat had numbed up the skin edges, Darren Jones had been talking nonstop. Nerves, she guessed. If he only knew that he was hardly the only one. The procedure had taken probably three times what it one day would, and Natalie was still just through the forehead and eyebrow, with the cheek yet to go, but the repair looked quite decent.

"Yes, I'm doing a good job," she replied matter-of-factly.

"'M I gonna have a scar?"

"Every time skin is cut there's a scar."

"Women like scars. They're mysterious. Besides, I'm tough, so why not announce it. Right, Doc?"

"You seem pretty smart. Smart is more important than tough."

"Tough men like me scare you?"

"The guy who cut you would probably scare me," Natalie said, smiling beneath her mask. "You still in school?"

"I have a year to go, but I quit."

"You should think about starting up again."

"Fat chance." Darren laughed. "You wouldn't know about such things, Doc, but where I come from, the only thing that matters is being tough."

Again, Natalie grinned. Matched up against this boy in almost any measure of toughness, she would win hands down. She reminded herself that it wasn't the first person who had suggested *she* get back into school that had led her to the Edith Newhouse Academy for Girls, or even the second. But somewhere along the line, thanks to those who had tried before, someone had finally been able to breach the ramparts of her own toughness.

"Tough is swimming against the stream and having the courage to be different," she said, tying off the last of the sutures. "Tough is realizing that this is the only life you're going to have, so you might as well do what you can to make the most of it."

"I'll keep that in mind, Doc," the teen said with little sincerity.

Natalie glanced over her shoulder at Bev, who gave her technique a thumbs-up and mouthed the words, "Steri strips," motioning at the packets of paper stitches she had placed on the instrument tray. After ineptly fumbling several of the strips into useless balls, Natalie figured out how to cut and place them across the incision to reduce scarring by taking the tension off of her suture line.

"Five days," Bev mouthed, holding up one open hand.

"These stitches will probably be ready to

come out in five days," Natalie said, grateful for the hedge inherent in the word "probably," at least for the time being.

"You got soul, Doc," Darren said. "I can tell."

Natalie stripped off her face protector and gloves. Another milestone, she was thinking. It was a huge advantage to be thirty-five and a med student—especially one who had seen more than her share of life. Decisions came easier to her than to most of her classmates, many of whom were a decade younger or, in a few cases, even more. Her perspective was often more finely honed; confidence in her convictions was stronger.

"Don't sell yourself short, my man," she replied.

"Stick around, Darren," Bev said. "I have a tetanus shot, some instructions, and some medication for you."

"Pain meds?" Darren asked hopefully.

"Sorry, antibiotics."

"Hey, you claim you're tough," Natalie said, heading out the door. "Tough guys don't need no steenking pain medicine."

She wrote her note at the nurses' station, feeling very pleased with the way she had performed under pressure. Renfro had issued the challenge and then had walked away, but she had more than measured up. She had set high school, college, and national records on the track, and had made it to within one unfortunate step of being on the Olympic team. Along the way, she had dealt with any number of Cliff Renfros, bent on feeding their egos off the insecurity of others. Well, she was still the same woman who had run 1,500 meters in 4:08.3. Let this particular Cliff Renfro keep trying. She hadn't knuckled under to any of the others, and she wasn't going to be intimidated by him either.

Bev materialized at her elbow.

"Saralee just came over from room four. You know what that is?"

"Yes, for the alcoholics."

"And other street people," Bev added. "Patients are put there when they're particularly . . . um . . . grimy."

"I know. I worked in there for a while yesterday. It wasn't so bad."

"Well, apparently the ER got a little backed up while you were off suturing and a code was going on in the other wing. So, much to his chagrin, Cliff is holding down the fort in room four. He wants you to take over in there as soon as you're done."

"I'm done now."

"Good. You handled that kid well, Nat. I think White Memorial made a good choice. You're going to make a fine doctor."

"That hospital may be the best of the best, but they're still a decade or two behind when it comes to accepting women into their surgical programs."

"So I've heard. Well, like I said, you'll do great. Take it from one who's seen them all come and go."

At that moment, they turned toward the sound of a commotion coming from down the hallway.

"I'm telling you, Doc, you're wrong! There's something the matter with me. Something bad. Right here behind my eye! I can't stand the pain!"

A man was being escorted out of room 4 by an orderly. Even at some distance, there was no doubt that he qualified to have been there. Grizzled and worn, he was in his forties, Natalie guessed, or maybe even his fifties. He had on a tattered windbreaker, stained chinos, and sneakers without laces. An oily Red Sox cap with its brim pulled low still failed to hide the sad hollows of his eyes.

Hands on hips, Cliff Renfro appeared in

the doorway and glanced to where Natalie and Bev stood before addressing the man.

"What's wrong with you, Charlie, is that you need to stop drinking. I would suggest you get yourself over to the Pine Street Inn and get them to show you to the shower. They'll probably have some clothes for you, too."

"Doc, please. This is serious. I've got lights flickering in this eye and the pain is killing me. Everything keeps going black."

Clearly irritated almost beyond words, Renfro ignored the man and stalked down the hallway past where the two women were standing.

"You've got to move faster down here, *Dr. Reyes*," he paused long enough to say. "Now, please take over in four. I'm going to get washed up and," he muttered, "maybe fumigated."

Natalie caught the briefest spark of anger and frustration in the patient's eyes before he turned and allowed the orderly to lead him toward the waiting room, and beyond that, the street.

"I'll bet Renfro didn't even examine him," Natalie whispered.

"Possibly, but he usually—"

"There's something seriously wrong with

that man, I just know it. Horrible pain, flickering lights, lost vision. I just finished six weeks on neurology. That guy has a tumor, or maybe a leaking aneurysm, or even a brain abscess. These people deal with pain and discomfort every day. If his symptoms are bad enough to have him drag himself in here, something's the matter. Did Renfro order any tests?"

"I don't know, but I don't think—"

"Listen, Bev, I want to check that guy over and then get a CT scan. Can you arrange that?"

"I can, but I don't think it's such a good—"

"And some bloods. A CBC and Chem-Twelve. I've got to catch him before he gets away. Believe me, if he were a well-dressed businessman at White Memorial, he'd be over having a CT scan right now."

"Maybe, but—"

Before Bev could finish the sentence, Natalie was off. She checked the waiting room, then hurried out the doors to Washington Avenue. The man was a dozen yards away, shuffling slowly toward downtown.

"Charlie, wait!"

The derelict turned. His eyes were bloodshot, but he held his head erect and met her gaze evenly, perhaps even with some defiance.

"What is it?" he growled.

"I'm . . . Dr. Reyes. I want to check you over a little more and maybe order a test or two."

"Then you believe me?"

Natalie took his arm and gently led him back toward the ER.

"I believe you," she said.

Bev Richardson was waiting just inside the door with a wheelchair.

"Room six is empty," she said in a conspiratorial whisper. "Hurry. I have no idea where Renfro is. Lab is on the way. Hopefully we can get his blood drawn and get him over to CT without anyone seeing."

Natalie helped the man out of his clothes and into a blue johnny. Renfro was right about one thing, she was thinking, Charlie really did smell. She did a modest neurologic exam, which disclosed several definite abnormalities in strength, eye movements, hand-eye coordination, and gait, any and all of which could be due to a brain tumor, abscess, or leaking blood vessel.

A technician had just finished drawing blood when Bev backed into the room hauling a stretcher.

"I pulled some strings," she said. "They're ready for him in CT."

"He has some clear-cut neurologic abnormalities. I'll get him over there, and then get to work in room four."

"I'll clean up in here."

Natalie wheeled the stretcher into the hallway.

"Thanks, Bev, I'll be right b—"

"What in the hell is this?"

Cliff Renfro, livid, stormed toward her from the nurses' station.

"I believe there is something seriously wrong with this man," Natalie said. "Maybe a tumor or a leaking aneurysm."

"So you chased him down after I had discharged him?"

Renfro's voice was raised to the point where staff and patients alike stopped and stared. Several people emerged from the examining rooms, several more from the nurses' station.

Natalie held her ground.

"I wanted to do the right thing. He has some neurologic findings."

"Well, this isn't the right thing. The findings, like everything else about him, are the result of alcohol. You know, I had heard from a number of people that you were too arrogant and hard-edged to be a good doctor. Just because you had fifteen minutes of fame doesn't mean you can step in here and act as if you're in charge of the place."

"And just because you like to keep your clinic coat from getting soiled doesn't mean you can brush off patients like this man," Natalie shot back.

Bev Richardson quickly inserted herself between the two combatants.

"It was my fault, Cliff," she said. "*I* was worried about this man, and thought it would be a good learning experience for—"

"That's nonsense, and you know it. Don't protect her." He stepped to his left to get a clear line of sight at Natalie. "There is no place in medicine for anyone as self-absorbed and conceited as you are, Reyes."

Natalie's jaws clenched. She was furious at being rebuked so publicly, and anxious to have all the witnesses know why Renfro's prejudices had led him to do an inadequate job in evaluating this down-and-outer.

"At least I care enough about people like Charlie here to do a complete evaluation on him."

"Five years as a doctor have made me

perfectly capable of deciding what is and is
not a complete evaluation. I intend to make
sure that anyone at the medical school who
will listen learns about you and what's happened here."

"Well, I think before you do that, you
should see what this man's CT scan shows."

Renfro's glare could have melted block
ice. He looked as if he were going to say
something else, then turned and stalked off
toward X Ray. Two exquisitely tense minutes
later, a CT tech came and wheeled Charlie
away. Natalie sighed her relief.

"Whew. I was certain he was going to cancel the test out of spite," she said, as she and
Bev walked back to the nurses' station.

The seasoned nurse looked at her and
shook her head.

"I'm sorry I couldn't get him to calm down,"
she said. "There was probably a better way
to have done this."

"Renfro could have admitted he was
wrong," Natalie said. "The fact that he went
ahead with the scan says as much. When
they find a tumor behind poor Charlie's eye,
he's going to be grateful I saved his bacon."

Tumor, abscess, leaking aneurysm. In her
mind, Natalie was already projecting the re-

actions of Renfro and the staff when her approach to the man was vindicated. Hopefully, whatever the poor guy had would be operable. She thought about how her mentor, surgeon Doug Berenger, would react to her coup. Midway through her undergraduate years at Harvard, well before the incident that tore her Achilles, he had sought her out and offered her a position working in his lab—a job she still held. Later, he had brought together the best sports medicine people around to aid in her recovery, and still later, he had talked her into attending med school.

Berenger, perhaps the foremost cardiac transplant surgeon in Boston, if not in the country, was already talking about a fellowship in his department when her surgical training was complete. He had a framed sampler hung on the wall behind his desk chair: BELIEVE IN YOURSELF. He would be damn proud of the way she had believed in herself and held her ground against Renfro's unnecessary onslaught, especially when Charlie's diagnosis became known.

Natalie went into room 4 and worked up the three patients waiting there. Her pulse continued to race—in part fallout from the acrid exchange with Renfro, and in part from the excitement of soon getting the results of the lab work and scan on her patient. Finally, through the doorway of room 4, she saw Renfro pass by, wheeling Charlie on his stretcher. A manila X-ray envelope was tucked under the thin mattress. Moments later, the resident called out her name.

"Dr. Reyes, staff," he said quite loudly. "Could I have you all out here, please?"

A group of perhaps a dozen stepped quietly into the hallway. Renfro waited until it seemed there would be no more, and then continued, holding up the envelope with the CT scan for emphasis.

"You were all here a little while ago for the . . . um . . . discussion about patient care that occurred between Ms. Reyes and myself. Well, I have all the lab work and the CT back on our patient. I would like to inform you that there is nothing abnormal on any of them. *Nothing.* Charlie here has just what I said he had—just what he *always* has, *Ms. Reyes*—an alcohol-induced headache. He had a blood alcohol of one hundred and ninety when he came in, and I don't suspect it's much lower now, since he just managed to get at the pint of Thunderbird in the jacket in his clothing bag. Bev, please discharge this man for the second time. Be sure to fill out an incident report.

"Ms. Reyes, go home. I don't ever want to see you on my service again."

CHAPTER 2

**Until philosophers are kings . . . cities will
never have rest from their evils, no, nor
the human race.**

—PLATO, *The Republic,* Book V

Early afternoon was clearly one of the better
times to shop at the Whole Foods Market.
Natalie would have had no reason to know
that fact until today. With her mother's grocery list in one hand and hers in the other,
she made her way up and down the un-
crowded aisles in no particular hurry. It had
been three hours since she was booted out
of the Metropolitan Hospital ER by Cliff Renfro, and for the moment at least, she had
more time on her hands than she had things
to do.

Tomorrow she would make an appointment with her advisor, and maybe with Doug

Berenger, and together they would straighten things out. It wasn't as if anyone had gotten hurt. Compared to a hemostat being left in an abdomen, or a lethal medication error, or the wrong leg being amputated, the events in the ER were small potatoes. If she was guilty of anything, and in truth she didn't believe she was, it was a crime with no victim. As Bev Richardson had said, even though Renfro was well along in his training, he was still immature. For the time being Natalie and he were destined to be enemies, at least until she got the chance to prove to him what a dedicated, driven, caring physician she was. At the worst, she would have to complete her ER rotation elsewhere. Ideally, after a day or two of cooling off, perhaps the two of them could meet and patch things up on the spot, and with her promise not to repeat what she had done, she could resume the rotation where she left off.

The foods Natalie picked up for herself were the freshest and healthiest. Whole Foods Markets, noted for their produce and seafood, were the only places she would shop. The ridiculous hours of medical school were unavoidable, but in her soul, she was still an athlete. She worked out as much as possible, often at absurdly early or late hours. Her repaired Achilles tendon would keep her from ever coming close to the world-class times that were once routine, but as she got older, she could see the day approaching when her times for various distances in her age group would be competitive, if not among the leaders. Goals. Always goals. Having them, pushing toward them, reinventing them—along with the care she gave her body, never being without well-defined goals was the secret to her success in school and in sports.

She grimaced as she scanned down her mother's list, dictated to her last night over the phone. Steak, frozen fries, pecan rolls, Cherry Garcia ice cream, trail mix, hot dogs (and buns), whole milk, whipped cream, Pringles . . . half of the items, Whole Foods wouldn't even deign to carry. Hermina Reyes was a piece of work—beloved by so many, yet as abusive of herself and her body as Natalie was meticulous. A bigger concern for Natalie, however, was her niece, Jenny. Hermina was responsible for most of the girl's meals. With that fact in mind, she added some broccoli, yams, cheese, and salad to her mother's order.

At the bottom of the list Natalie had reluctantly penned in *Winstons—one carton.* After
it, she had written a note to herself: *optional.*
She laughed ruefully. More often than not, in
what she knew was a futile gesture of
protest, she refused to buy her mother's cigarettes. It didn't matter. Hermina had a car,
and didn't hesitate to leave Jenny at home
for brief periods. Plus, there were others the
woman could call on, plenty of them, who
knew an unbreakable bond when they saw it.
They also knew that if there were ever justifi-
cation for smoking, the death of one's child
was it. Hermina would be wedded to her Winstons until the day she died, more than likely
at the hands of her beloved cancer sticks.

Natalie spent a leisurely half hour selecting her own fruits and vegetables. With the
vast summer selection, she felt especially
fortunate to care about such things, particularly today, with a few hours of unexpected
free time on her hands. She really had to try
harder to be more tolerant of people like
Renfro, she was thinking as she squeezed,
then tapped, then shook a honeydew, testing for ripeness. First thing in the morning
she would do whatever was necessary to
straighten things out with him.

Whole Foods was far too responsible to sell cigarettes, so after loading eight plastic bags of groceries into the trunk of her Subaru, Natalie trotted across the street to a pharmacy. It wouldn't be a problem showing up at her mother's place earlier than expected. The time when Hermina knew the details of her life and schedule had passed long ago, so there wouldn't be any but the most cursory questions about why she wasn't in the ER. Nor was there much chance that Hermina would be out. With Jenny to care for, she tended to stay pretty much close to home when the girl wasn't at school.

Dorchester, a rapidly aging, gritty community directly south of the city, was just a few miles along Route 203 from Natalie's quaint Brookline apartment, but sociologically and demographically the two towns were widely distant. Small pockets of elegant, well-maintained homes still survived in Dorchester, but they were islands in a sea of poverty, immigrants, drugs, and too often, violence. Natalie pulled to the curb and popped the trunk in front of a peeling, gray clapboard duplex with a small dirt lawn and a sagging front porch. She had left home shortly after her mother's move to this place, but her younger sister Elena, who was eight at the time, had grown up there, and until the accident, lived there when she wasn't in detox or rehab.

Natalie doubted there was anyone in Dorchester who didn't know that Hermina Reyes kept her house key under a withered potted plant by the door.

"There's an advantage to having nothing to steal," her mother liked to say.

As always, the pungent odor of burnt and burning cigarettes hit Natalie the moment she opened the door.

"Health inspector, ditch the butts!" she called out, hauling five bags at once down the hall and into the kitchen.

The flat was, as always, neatly kept and clean, including Hermina's decades-old Fenway Park ashtray, which she ritually emptied and washed down after every second or third smoke.

"Mom?"

Hermina was usually ensconced at the kitchen table, with a cup of half-consumed coffee, a box of vanilla wafers, her Winstons, the ashtray, and a book of Sunday *New York Times* crossword puzzles. In fact, all of her accoutrements were in place, but not the woman herself. Natalie set the groceries on the floor and hurried to her mother's room.

"Mom?" she called again.

"She's taking a nap," Jenny called out.

Natalie followed her niece's voice to her prim and feminine room—lace curtains, pink walls. Jenny, dressed in shorts and a floppy sweatshirt, sat in her wheelchair, a book propped up in the apparatus that made it easier for her to turn the pages. The ankle braces that enabled her to walk with crutches lay on the floor by her bed. Jenny's official diagnosis was mild cerebral palsy, but Elena had used and drank and smoked throughout her pregnancy, and now that Natalie knew what fetal alcohol syndrome was, that diagnosis had taken the top spot on her list of the possible causes of the girl's disabilities.

"Hey, babe," Natalie said, kissing her on the forehead. "What's happening?"

"Staff day today, no school." Jenny had the creamy skin and wide, engaging smile of her mother. "Gram was awake for a while doing her puzzle, then she just went to bed."

"If I ever *ever* catch you with a cigarette—"

"Let me try, let me try this time. You're going to break both of my lips."

"Actually, I like the sound of that. What are you reading?"

"*Wuthering Heights.* Have you read it?"

"A while back. I think I loved it, but I also think I had some trouble following it. You're not having trouble with the way time and the scenes bounce all over the place?"

"Oh, no. It's so romantic. I would love to visit the moors someday if they're still there."

"Oh, they're still there. We'll go. I promise." Natalie stepped to where her crippled niece couldn't see the sadness in her eyes. "Jenny, you make everyone around you a better person, including me."

"Now what's that supposed to mean?"

"Nothing that serious. Listen, you want to come in and help me wake Gram?"

"No, thanks. I want to read a bit more. Heathcliff isn't very nice to people."

"As I recall, when he was young, people weren't very nice to him, either."

"It's like a vicious cycle."

"Precisely. Are you sure you're ten?"

"Almost eleven."

Hermina, wearing a print housedress, had dozed off on the bed. A cigarette, burnt down to the filter, was still smoldering in a saucer on the bedside table. The kitchen was still her favorite spot, but more and more over recent months, this was the scene that greeted Natalie—either here in the bedroom or on the sofa in the living room. The cigarettes were taking their toll on her mother's oxygen levels and stamina. Before too much longer a green oxygen tank on a roller would be accompanying her wherever she was.

"Hey you," Natalie said, gently shaking the woman awake.

Hermina rubbed at her eyes and then propped herself on one elbow.

"I expected you later," she said somewhat dreamily.

Natalie was bothered by the unnatural depth of her sleep when she had been awake enough to light up a cigarette that was still burning. At fifty-four, this once vibrant and entrancingly beautiful woman was aging rapidly, and growing more leathery-skinned with every butt. Her cocoa complexion was much darker than Natalie's—understandable, given that Natalie's father, whoever he really was, was white—but unlike her deteriorating skin, Hermina's wide, hazel eyes were playful, intelligent, alluring, and virtually identical to Natalie's.

"Ma, you've got to stop smoking in here," Natalie said, helping her up and into the kitchen.

"I almost never do it anymore."

"I can tell."

"You're not attractive when you're cynical."

Hermina was Cape Verdean. She was brought to the States by her parents when she was Jenny's age, and still retained more than the hint of a Portuguese accent. By the time she was nineteen, she had graduated from high school and was a certified nurse's aide with plans to go to nursing school. That was when she became a single parent for the first time.

"Jenny seems okay."

"She's doing fine."

"That's good."

There was a brief, uncomfortable silence. To Hermina, Jenny *was* Elena, and no matter how many rehabs had given daughter number two the gate, no matter how fast the police said she was driving when she slammed through the guardrail, Hermina always considered her to have been the victim of external circumstances.

Daughter number one, who had run away from home at fifteen, was another story. If

Hermina Reyes knew nothing else, she knew how to harbor a grudge, and in this household, Elena was still and always would be the child of choice. The grocery shopping, the monthly checks, the trophies, the Harvard degree, and soon the one from medical school, still didn't balance off the hurt Natalie had brought on her mother.

"So, help me out here," Hermina said, picking up her pencil and pointedly turning her attention to the crossword puzzle in front of her. "Eight-letter word for nervous?"

"No idea. I'm never nervous. Ma, it's wonderful that you're taking care of Jenny the way you are, but you've got to try not to smoke when she's in the house. Secondhand smoke is no different than firsthand when it comes to—"

"So what about you? You seem tense."

There were many, including Natalie and her late sister, who equated Hermina's remarkable intuitiveness with sorcery.

"I'm okay," she replied, putting the groceries away. "Just tired is all."

"That doctor you were seeing hasn't worked out?"

"Rick and I are still on good terms."

"Let me guess. He wanted a serious relationship, but you just didn't love him."

Sorcery.

"The demands of the surgical residency
I'm about to start make it hard to be available to someone else."

"What about that Terry who you brought
over for dinner? He's so nice and so very
handsome."

"He's also so very gay. That's why I like
him so much. He doesn't want anything from
me except my friendship and my company.
There's never any talk about commitment
and moving our relationship to the next level.
Ma, believe me, almost every one of my
friends who is married or living with someone is miserable over it a good deal of the
time. Just trying to make their relationship
work absorbs ninety percent of their energy.
In this day and age, love is temporary and
marriage is unnatural—the product of Madi-
son Avenue advertising executives and television producers."

"Daughter, I know you're long past listening to me, but you've got to break through
that hard shell of yours and let love in or
you're going to be a very unhappy woman."

Let love in. Natalie kept herself from speaking too soon or, worse, laughing out loud. With two children born of different swains, both long gone, Hermina Reyes wasn't exactly the poster child for true love. In her case, at least from Natalie's viewpoint, physical beauty had proven to be a mortal enemy. Still, her enduring sense of romance, trust in men, and unflagging enthusiasm for life were as unfathomable as her inability to put away the Winstons.

"Right now I don't have time to be unhappy."

"You sure you're okay?"

"I'm fine. Why do you keep asking that?"

"No reason. Sometimes, when I came to watch you run, you would hold yourself before the race in a funny way—an awkward, uncomfortable way. Almost always, when you did that, you didn't run well and you lost. You're sort of doing that here."

"Well, nothing's the matter, Ma, trust me."

At that moment, Natalie's cell phone announced a call. The caller ID displayed a number she didn't recognize.

"Hello?"

"Natalie Reyes?

"Yes?"

"This is Dean Goldenberg."

Natalie stiffened, then walked into the front hallway, out of earshot from her mother.

"Yes?"

"Natalie, I wonder if you're free to come over to my office to discuss the incident this morning at Metropolitan Hospital."

"I can be there in twenty or twenty-five minutes."

"That will be fine. Please call my secretary when you are ten minutes away."

"O-okay."

Goldenberg waited until Natalie had a pencil, then gave her the phone number of the medical school and his extension. Throughout their brief conversation, she had tried unsuccessfully to get a read on his voice, and now was stifling the urge to ask for the details of why she was being called in. Over the years, Dr. Sam Goldenberg had expressed any number of times what a fan he had been of her running, and also of her performance as a medical student. Whatever was up now, they could work out. She felt certain of it.

"Trouble?" Hermina asked as she returned to the kitchen.

"Nothing that drastic. Just some problems with my schedule at school. But I do have to rush off. Sorry."

"That's okay."

"I'll be back to see you both before long."

"That would be wonderful. Take care of yourself."

"You, too, Ma. Jenny, I'll see you again soon."

"I love you, Aunty Nat."

"I love you, too, babe."

"Panicked," Hermina said.

"What?"

"That eight-letter word for nervous. It's 'panicked.'"

Natalie's teenage years had been written up in a number of publications. Her tumultuous struggles on the streets of Boston ended after almost a year when workers at an agency called Bridge Over Troubled Waters managed to convince her and the Edith Newhouse School for Girls in Cambridge that the two of them were potentially a good match. It then took many months in the school before an uneasy truce with the teachers and administration enabled her to discover her talent for track—and for academic success. Three and a half years later, she started at Harvard.

After her graduation from college, in addi-

tion to training and racing, Natalie worked in
the laboratory of Dr. Doug Berenger, then
and now a huge booster of hers and of Harvard track. By the time of her injury at the
Olympic trials, she had her name as coau-
thor on half a dozen papers for research
work performed with the cardiac surgeon
and his team. She had also taken all of the
required courses for medical school admis-
sion. Sooner or later, she probably would
have applied anyhow, but the accidental
step onto her Achilles tendon by the woman
running in second place definitely sped up
the timetable.

For as long as Natalie had been affiliated
with the medical school, Dr. Sam Goldenberg had been dean. An endocrinologist by
trade, he was as kindly and concerned a
man as he was brilliant—clearly dedicated
to the principle that getting into medical
school should be much harder and more
stressful than staying there.

As requested by Goldenberg, Natalie had
called his office when she was ten minutes
out. Now she sat in his comfortably appointed waiting area and tried to work out
phrasing by which she could underscore
that no one had been hurt by her ordering

the tests she did, but that she understood there might have been better ways she could have handled the situation. All she wanted now was to make things right with Cliff Renfro and get back to work.

She had been there just a few minutes when Goldenberg came out, shook her hand with an uncharacteristic lack of warmth, thanked her for being so prompt, and escorted her into his office. Standing by chairs at his conference table, their faces grim and troubled, were her closest allies on the medical school staff, Doug Berenger and Terry Millwood, and her friend, Veronica Kelly, cherubic, exceedingly bright, and often more intolerant of pompous, self-important professors than even Natalie herself.

The sudden chill through Natalie's spine had nothing to do with the temperature of the office. Both surgeons shook her hand formally. Veronica, with whom she had traveled to Hawaii and once to Europe, smiled tensely and nodded. The two of them enjoyed Boston together as often as busy med students could manage, and Veronica's stockbroker boyfriend was responsible for fixing Natalie up whenever her resistance slipped below the "I'm fine, really, I am" level.

Goldenberg motioned everyone to sit, and took his place at the table. Natalie's expectations of charming the dean and making whatever reparations were necessary toward Cliff Renfro began to evaporate.

"Ms. Reyes," Goldenberg began, "I want you to read the notarized statements submitted to my office at my request by Dr. Clifford Renfro and Mrs. Beverly Richardson, the nurse who was present at the time of this morning's incident. Then I would ask if your account of the events would differ substantially from theirs."

Still astonished that things had moved forward so swiftly and forcefully, Natalie read through the statements. Aside from a word here and there, both were in concordance and were accurate. Bev Richardson did her best to explain what she felt Natalie's mindset was at the time. However, she also stated, nearly verbatim, the clash with Renfro. On paper, the statements were cold and damning. Natalie felt the earliest grip of fear, and flashed momentarily on the eight-letter word in her mother's crossword puzzle.

"Both of these are substantially accurate," she managed, "but I don't think they capture the motivation behind what I was trying to do."

"Nat," Berenger said, "I promise you that we understand that there was nothing overtly malicious in your motives."

Seated next to Berenger, Millwood nodded his agreement.

"I'll be more than happy to admit that what I did was wrong, and to apologize to Dr. Renfro."

"I'm afraid it's not that simple, Ms. Reyes," Goldenberg said. "Dr. Schmidt, who as you know is Dr. Renfro's chief of surgery, has insisted that you are unfit to be a physician and he has demanded that you be expelled from the medical school."

The words were a dagger thrust into Natalie's chest.

"I can't believe this. My grades have been honors level, and as far as I know, my clinical work has been strong."

"Actually," Goldenberg said, "while there has never been anything negative reported about your work with patients, there have been several complaints suggesting a consistent lack of respect for authority, an intolerance for some of your residents, and even some of your classmates, and an arrogance that one faculty member has suggested could be a source of serious problems in the years to come."

"I just can't believe this," Natalie said again. "My only incident with a classmate that I know of was when I refused to partner with him because he was throwing cadaver parts around the anatomy lab."

"Excuse me, Dean, for breaking in here," Veronica said, "but I feel as if I need to back Natalie up on this one. When Dr. Millwood called and told me what was happening, I asked him to find out if I could come. I appreciate your allowing me to. The student Natalie was speaking of was totally inappropriate, and deserved her response. Natalie and I have been close friends since before we started med school. I wanted to make sure you knew how well-liked and respected she is among almost all the students, men *and* women, and also how difficult Dr. Renfro can be at times. He and I clashed more than once during my surgical rotation."

"But you never ended up being reported to me," Goldenberg said.

"No," Veronica said, clearly deflated. "No, I didn't."

"Thank you, Ms. Kelly."

"Nat," Millwood said, "didn't you stop to think about the trouble you were asking for by bringing back a patient that a senior resident had discharged without even consulting him?"

Natalie shook her head. "I know now that it was wrong, but I was upset with Dr. Renfro, and all I was thinking about was the patient, a poor old drunk whom I felt was being booted out of the hospital without a complete evaluation of his problems."

Millwood turned to Goldenberg, as did Berenger. Natalie watched her future unfold in an unspoken three-way conversation, battling back the knee-jerk urge simply to say, "Oh, screw this! I quit." Veronica, probably sensing that, subtly raised a calming hand. Finally, Goldenberg nodded that he had reached a decision, and turned to Natalie.

"Ms. Reyes, there are a number of faculty members, including your two biggest boosters here, who have written glowing evaluations about your potential to be an exceptional physician. I also appreciate the effort your friend Ms. Kelly has made to be here today, as well as the things she has had to say. I know for a fact that you are being seriously considered for selection into the Alpha Omega Alpha medical honor society. I can assure you now that will not happen. You are an unusual person, with many fine qualities, but there is an edge to you—call it hardness, call it arrogance—that will contribute nothing toward making you the sort of physician we want to graduate from this school. With the help of your supporters here, I have decided that expulsion is too severe a punishment for what you have done—but not by much. As of today, you are suspended for four months. If there are no further incidents after that, you will graduate with the next class after yours. Other than a legal challenge in court, there is no mechanism in place for reconsideration of this decision. Do you have any questions?"

"My residency?"

"Nat, we'll go over the possibilities for you later," Berenger said. "I can tell you that your place in the surgical program at White Memorial will be filled by someone else."

"Jesus. What about my work in your lab?"

Berenger got tacit approval from Goldenberg before responding.

"You can still work for me, and even attend grand rounds and any other conferences you wish."

"Making this decision doesn't please any of us," Goldenberg said.

"It seems too harsh to me," Natalie said coolly, much closer to an angry outburst than to tears.

"Possibly, possibly so. But it is the hand you have dealt yourself."

"Tell me one thing, Dean Goldenberg. Would we still be sitting here if the CT scan I ordered on that poor man had shown a large clot pressing on his brain?"

Across from her, Terry rolled his eyes and sighed. Veronica shook her head.

Sam Goldenberg seemed almost ready for the question. He fixed some papers in front of him, then leveled his gaze at her.

"Since part of the issue here is your assault on Dr. Renfro's clinical judgment, I feel the need to remind you that there was no such clot. The CT scan on which you staked your medical school career was normal, Ms. Reyes. Absolutely normal."

For nearly ten seconds after the final passage of Beethoven's violin sonata in F had drifted through Queen Elizabeth Hall, there was absolute silence. Then, as one, the audience erupted, leaping to its feet, drowning out the quivering echo of the last note with shouts and applause.

"Bravo!"

"Huzzah!"

"Wunderbar!"

The seventeen-year-old beauty, cradling her two-hundred-and-ninety-year-old Stradivarius as if it were a newborn babe, beamed as she gazed out across the throng. She looked too small for the stage, but everyone who knew music, and that was most of those in the hall, knew she was a titan. Her accompanist took his bows and then left the stage so that she might bask in her return to performing—the moment many had felt might never come.

Standing in the tenth row center, an Indian man, resplendent in his tuxedo, continued applauding as he turned to his taller companion.

"Well?"

"I am very proud of her, and very proud of us," the other man, square-jawed and elegant, said. "The scar down her chest has barely healed, and yet there she is."

"Beautiful. Just beautiful. I don't think I've ever heard the 'Spring' sonata played with more feeling or technical brilliance."

As was the Guardians' policy, the men never spoke one another's names in public, and even on their frequent conference calls used only Greek pseudonyms, which each of their members was required to commit to memory.

The tumultuous applause continued, and the young virtuoso, destined now to enthrall the world for decades to come, took one curtain call after another.

"Those roses she is carrying are from us," the Indian said.

"Nice touch."

"I agree, thank you. You know, it is amazing what the minor addition of a new heart and lungs can accomplish in the right body."

CHAPTER 3

The unexamined life is not worth living.
—PLATO, *Apology*

Nailed.

Ben Callahan set the stack of five-by-seven glossies on his desk, then popped two Zantac antacid pills into the back of his throat and washed them down with his third cup of coffee of the morning. *Another shitty beginning of another shitty day.* Maybe it was time to give his friendly neighborhood career counselor a try. Outside, a chilly, vertical rain was snapping against the grime on his office window. Yesterday it had reached 101 with a humidity of, like, a thousand. Today, fifty-five and pouring. Summer in Chicago. You just couldn't beat it.

Ben spread the photos across the desk in two rows. God, but sometimes he detested earning a living this way. He would have detested it even if the living he *was* earning amounted to anything substantial, which it most certainly did not. Well, at least Katherine de Souci would be happy. She had demanded that Ben "nail the bastard," and now Robert de Souci had, in fact, been nailed, although not quite in the way Katherine had expected.

So what if Robert was active on the board of a dozen or more charitable foundations? So what if he was, from all Ben had been able to ascertain, a terrific father and enlightened corporate CEO? Katherine, whom Ben had come to think of as something of an amalgam of Lizzie Borden and his ex-wife, had her suspicions of infidelity, and now, thanks to crackerjack private detective— make that private *eye*—Benjamin Michael Callahan, she had her proof. And soon, she would have her gazillions in settlement, as well as her husband's surpassingly handsome head on a platter.

There were just two problems.

Robert's secret lover was a *he*, not the *she* Katherine had expected, and the significant other in question was a man Ben knew well. Caleb Johnson, a pillar of the black community, was arguably the finest, fairest, most intelligent criminal judge in the region. It was possible the judge could survive this looming scandal, but not without a significant reduction in his influence on the bench and around the country. And this was a man who had earned and deserved all the influence he possessed.

Ben flipped the edge of a small stack of unopened bills with his thumb. Katherine de Souci's check would make every one of them disappear like David Copperfield, with enough cash left over to actually buy something.

He slid the photos back into their manila envelope and prepared to call Katherine. Who in the hell cared what the fallout might be? He had been given a job, he had taken it, he had spent the advance and most of the per diems, he had done the work. Case closed.

Admittedly, this career had been something of a miscalculation on his part, but when he chose it, he was legitimately excited about becoming a detective in the mold of his fictional heroes—knights-errant like

Mike Hammer, Travis McGee, and Jim Rockford. He knew he'd have to start slow at first, taking whatever cases came in. Unfortunately, those cases—chasing bail jumpers, philandering spouses, and deadbeats of one kind or another—remained his primary source of income, and with few exceptions, had never amounted to anything approaching noble. Not a single, mysterious, alluring dame-in-distress in the bunch.

Now he was about to take a pile of money from someone he didn't like in exchange for ruining the lives of two men he respected.

De Souci and Johnson should have been more discreet, he tried to reason. There were all those underfunded charities and all those African-American kids looking for role models who were counting on them. They should have thought things through a little more. There were ways the guys could have stayed undetectable, or at least *more* undetectable, but for whatever reason, maybe just the blindness of love, they had chosen not to take them.

Now there were photos.

Ben picked up the phone, dialed Katherine's number, and as usual went through her private secretary to speak with her.

"You have something for me?" the socialite asked without even deigning to say hello.

Her voice grated over the phone. Ben flashed on her perfectly made-up face—so proud, so tight, so haughty. In a life already boringly full of possessions, privilege, and victories, he had uncovered the evidence that would make her day. *Katherine de Souci, come on down! You're a winner and you're next on* The Price Is Right!

For several moments there was only silence.

"Well?" she persisted.

"Um . . . actually, I don't have anything, Mrs. de Souci. Nothing. I think your husband's clean."

"But—"

"And the truth is, I don't think I can take any more of your money. If you want to keep pushing this matter, I would recommend you find someone else."

"But—"

"Goodbye, Mrs. de Souci."

Please be more careful, Judge. Robert's wife is vengeful, he wrote on a blank piece of paper. Then he signed it *a Friend,* slid it in with the photos, addressed the envelope to the judge with no return address, marked it PERSONAL AND CONFIDENTIAL, and set it aside until he left for whatever would pass today for lunch. Just in case, he decided, he would send it by registered mail. Outside, the rain continued pelting the city. Within minutes, any glow Ben felt at so gloriously disappointing Katherine de Souci had given way to his usual, baseline state of numbness and ennui. It was hard to believe a life once marked by enthusiasm and a spirit of adventure had come to this. It was even harder to believe that he really didn't care.

The phone had rung five or six times before he noticed and picked it up.

"'Lo?"

"Mr. Ben Callahan?" a woman's voice said.

"Yes."

"The detective?"

"Yes. Who is this?"

"This is Professor Alice Gustafson's office calling."

"Okay."

"Department of anthropology at the University of Chicago?"

"Okay."

"Mr. Callahan, you had an appointment to

meet with Professor Gustafson fifteen minutes ago."

"I had what?"

Ben shuffled through the papers on his desk until he found his appointment book, optimistically containing a full page for each day of the year. The name Alice Gustafson, an address, office number, and the time fifteen minutes ago were written in his uneven scrawl on the page for today. Beneath the time were two words: Organ Guard. Only now did he remember taking the call, a week or so ago, from a secretary who didn't exactly bubble over about the wonderful opportunity the job presented for him.

He had agreed to the appointment without bothering to tell the woman he still had absolutely no idea what it was about. Now, it appeared, he had missed it. After four or five years in college, and a stretch as a high-school social studies teacher, he had rolled the dice and decided on life as a private detective. Now it seemed it was time for something else. Perhaps he would learn that he was better suited for life behind a hot-dog pushcart or maybe his true calling was as an animal trainer.

"I . . . I'm sorry," he said. "Something came up and I've been delayed."

"I guess," the woman replied. "Well, Professor Gustafson says that if you'd like to reschedule the interview, she can see you at one today."

Ben scratched at the reddish brown stubble of five o'clock shadow that seemed to be appearing on his face earlier and earlier of late, and stared down at the words in his book. Organ Guard. Still no bells. He really had to start paying more attention.

"This appointment," he said, "can you refresh me a little?"

Even over the phone he could hear the woman sigh.

"You responded to an ad we placed in the papers about a year ago, requesting your services for Organ Guard. At the time we informed you and those others who responded that we were putting together a database of investigators for future jobs. You encouraged us to include you."

This has to be bullshit, Ben was thinking. He couldn't remember the last time he had encouraged anyone to do anything.

"So, what is this interview about?"

Again a sigh.

"Mr. Callahan, I believe Professor Gustafson has some work for you."

"And money to pay for it?"

"I believe so, yes. So, will we see you at one?"

Ben pulled his keyboard over and moved to go online to search for Organ Guard, then remembered that his browser service had been disconnected for the usual reason. Well, at least this didn't seem to be another stalk-and-gawk infidelity job. After Lady Katherine de Souci, he might not have another one of those left in him.

"One o'clock," he heard himself say. "I'll be there."

Ben was certain he had an umbrella someplace, but never used it. After checking the closet off his small, deserted waiting room, he gave up looking. A cab was a possibility, but also an expense, and one of the remaining spoils of his years as a teacher was a decent trench coat. Head down, wearing the belted coat and a Cubs cap, he pushed twelve blocks through a penetrating rain, ducking into entryways for relief every minute or two. Haskell Hall, on Fifty-ninth, was an expansive, powerful stone building with deeply carved openings, anchoring a well-maintained, tree-lined quad.

ALICE T. GUSTAFSON, Ph.D.
MEDICAL ANTHROPOLOGY

was on a small, brass-embossed plaque beside the door of her third-floor office. Beneath it, a smaller plaque—letters mechanically carved in white into black plastic—read ORGAN GUARD INTERNATIONAL. The door was locked. Ben knocked softly and then a little louder.

It was just as well, he thought. What he really needed to do at this point was to hunker down in his apartment with his cat, Pincus, and figure out what he wanted to do with his life if, in fact, he wanted to do anything at all. What about sales? Everybody needed a Mazda or a vacuum cleaner. He moved to knock again, then thought, *The hell with it,* and turned to go. A woman, arms folded, was standing just a dozen or so feet away, appraising him. Her plaid, long-sleeved shirt was tucked into carpenter's chinos and cinched around her narrow waist with a broad leather belt and heavy silver buckle. She was sixty or so, with gold-rimmed glasses, a narrow, intelligent professor's face, and graying dark hair, fixed in a short ponytail. Ben's take on the woman, especially after three weeks of Katherine de Souci, was decidedly positive.

"Mr. Callahan, I'm Professor Alice Gustafson," she said. "Sorry if I startled you."

"Only a little. I guess I just flunked the catlike-senses part of my professional evaluation."

Ben shook her narrow hand which, it was sadly easy to tell, had the firm swelling of chronic arthritis in the knuckles.

"Years of walking places where I didn't want to disturb the people or startle the wildlife have given me a fairly soft tread," she understated, opening her office with a key, and, Ben noted, with some difficulty.

The space was surprisingly roomy, but also cluttered and cozy. One wall held two eight-foot-high windows, and opposite them were floor-to-ceiling bookcases, piled to overflowing with academic tomes, bound and loose journals, and even a few works of fiction. In one corner, a tall, glass-enclosed case held dozens of artifacts of various kinds, unlabeled and arranged in no discernible order. On the back wall were a number of framed photos of people, mostly men, and all of them brown- or black-skinned. Most of the men were displaying scars on their sides, and none of them looked either prosperous or happy.

"Coffee?" Gustafson asked, gesturing to a Mr. Coffee in the corner as she settled in behind a busy, massive, antique oak desk, and in front of a six-foot-wide world map festooned with pushpins.

Ben shook his head and took the chair opposite her. There was an odd, appealing mix of intensity and serenity in the woman's face.

"I . . . I'm embarrassed to say that I don't really remember answering your ad," he said.

"So Libby, our department secretary, told me. Well, no matter. You're here."

Ben looked about.

"I'm here," he said.

"But you have no idea where here is. Is that right?"

"I suppose you could say that."

The professor studied him for a time, and Ben sensed that she was close to thanking him for coming and sending him back to whatever rock he had crawled out from. He wouldn't have blamed her in the least, and sadly, it wouldn't really have mattered to him.

Was he in a depression? Midlife crisis? Probably both. But that didn't matter either. Maybe instead of the friendly neighborhood career counselor, he should pay a visit to the friendly neighborhood psychopharmacologist.

"I think you should know," Gustafson said finally, "that you're not the first detective I've interviewed for this job. You're the third."

"Why did you reject the first two?"

"I didn't. Neither of them wanted it."

"Not enough money?" Ben asked, knowing from his experience with others in his clan that there was little likelihood of any other possibility.

"A year or so ago it looked like we were going to get a grant to expand the investigative, enforcement-oriented portion of our work. That's why I placed the ad I did—to try and line up the right people for the job. Then the source of our grant decided to spend their money elsewhere. Now another foundation actually has delivered. It's not much, but it is something."

"Congratulations."

"Would you like to hear what this is all about?"

That's okay. Whatever it is, I'm not up for it, Ben was thinking.

"Go on," his voice said.

Gustafson took a small pile of twice-folded pamphlets from her drawer and handed one over. It was entitled "Underworld Organ Trafficking," and subtitled "The World's Problem."

"Trafficking in human organs is illegal in most countries in the world," she began, as Ben scanned the pamphlet, "yet it continues to happen at an alarming rate. The donors of these illicitly procured organs may be dead, in that 'dead/not quite dead' middle ground, or very much alive. But what almost all of them have in common is that they are impoverished. There are buyers, sellers, brokers, hospitals, clinics, and surgeons involved. And believe me, Mr. Callahan, the amount of money changing hands in this secret, outlaw world is considerable—millions upon millions of dollars."

Ben set the pamphlet aside.

"Tell me something, Dr. Gustafson," he said. "An impoverished person is desperate for money, and a person with means is desperate for a kidney or liver or whatever."

"Yes?"

"If it is a crime for someone to broker the

exchange of an organ for cash, who is the victim of the crime? And perhaps just as importantly, does anyone care?"

"I'll answer the second of your questions first, Mr. Callahan. *We care.* Seldom do any of the donors end up with what they expected. As usual, they are the needy, taken advantage of by those with more. If you need an analogy, think of a poor young woman who is encouraged by a pimp with money to sell herself as a prostitute. Organ Guard is one of just two watchdog agencies of its kind, but our membership is steadily growing. Countries around the world are beginning to see the need to commit some of their resources to this problem. And as you will see, even here in the States situations are arising."

"You say governments are committing resources to the problem," Ben said, "but I have this feeling there may be at least some exaggeration in that claim."

Again, Gustafson studied him.

"Progress in this area is slow," she acknowledged grudgingly, "I'll give you that. But it is happening. When we provide authorities in any number of countries with hard evidence of illegal organ trafficking, arrests are made."

"Congratulations," Ben said again, not knowing what else to say, and hoping he didn't sound cynical or insincere.

In a world rife with disease, terrorism, dictatorships, drugs, prostitution, political corruption, and corporate vice, Alice Gustafson's cause was fringe. She was Doña Quixote—an idealist tilting against the injustice of a crime in which there were no victims, and aside from an occasional investigative article in the *Times,* precious little interest.

"If you don't mind my asking, Mr. Callahan, what made you become a private investigator?"

"I'm not sure I know anymore. I used to teach school, but the principal thought my classes were too unstructured and I didn't discipline the kids enough. The kids loved me, and I loved them—well, most of them—but he said that really didn't matter."

"Nice."

"I never read his reference letter, but the results of my search for another teaching job suggested it wasn't exactly glowing. Reading detective novels was always a passion of mine, so I thought I'd give it a try. I sort of saw myself as the best parts of each of those guys."

"That would be quite a man. John D. Mac-Donald is my personal favorite author. I think I've read almost everything he ever wrote."

"His Travis McGee was *the man* as far as I was concerned."

Gustafson's laugh was natural and uninhibited.

"Well, who wouldn't want to live on a houseboat in Florida and rescue beautiful women in distress?"

Ben flashed on Katherine de Souci.

"The problem is I forgot that all of my role models and their beautiful women were fictional."

"Living in the real world is often a daunting task for all of us." The professor leaned back in her chair, tapping her fingertips together, clearly trying to decide if it was worth continuing or whether she should simply move on to detective number four. "So," she said, the decision apparently made, "speaking of Florida, are you still interested in learning about the job? Because that's where we would be sending you."

"Professor Gustafson, I would be lying if I said I have any real interest in your cause."

"I admire your owning that, Mr. Callahan. Candor is always appreciated here."

"There's a fine line between candor and just not caring, Professor."

"I see. . . . Well, take a look at these photos. They were sent to me by a coroner in Fort Pierce, Florida, named Stanley Woyczek, who used to study medical anthropology with me. He knows all about Organ Guard. You may be right about illicit organ trafficking being a victimless crime, but then again . . ."

Over the years, Ben had seen a number of coroner's photos, in black and white and, as these were, in color. Still, these images caused him to inhale sharply. The cadaver, a man in his twenties, had been bludgeoned to a pulp.

"He was wandering across a largely deserted highway at three in the morning, when he was hit by a tractor-trailer," Gustafson explained. "According to Stanley, death was instantaneous."

"I imagine so."

"When you're ready, take a look at the bottom three photos."

"His buttocks?"

"Actually, the area just above the buttocks. Stanley writes that he is absolutely certain this man was a bone marrow donor within a day of his death."

"So?"

"So he's called every hospital and clinic and hematologist in the area, and as far as he can tell, this man was a patient of none of them."

"Identification?"

"None."

"Fingerprints?"

"No match."

"Goodness. And there is no doubt in the coroner's mind about him being a marrow donor?"

"For the moment, you can make that *unwilling* marrow donor."

"I'll bet there's a simple, logical explanation."

"Perhaps. But take a look at this."

Gustafson passed across a file folder with a single word, RAMIREZ, handwritten on the tab. The contents included a tape cassette, typed transcript, several photographs, and two newspaper articles, one carefully cut from the *Hallowell Reporter* in Hallowell, Maine, and the other from the *National Enquirer*. Both articles were from about fourteen months ago. Ben chose to start with the more spectacular of the two.

VAMPIRES SUCKED MY BODY DRY
Modern-Day Vampires Use RV to Scoop Up Victim, Needles to Suck Out Blood

The brief article, complete with photos, recounted the claim of Juanita Ramirez, a fifty-year-old motel housekeeper, that she had been drugged, blindfolded, kidnapped, held prisoner in the back of a mobile home, then experimented on by vampires claiming to be doctors. A physician who examined Ramirez after the alleged abduction found evidence that her bone marrow had been sucked out through large needles twisted into the bone of her hip. One of the photos from the paper, allegedly a shot of the skin just above her buttocks, bore a striking resemblance to the one sent by Gustafson's former student.

"Stanley Woyczek didn't know anything about this other case when he sent me the photos," Gustafson said.

"How on earth did *you* learn about it?" Ben asked.

Gustafson's smile was enigmatic. "Some people read newspapers when they're not working, some watch television, some play around on eBay. I Google things. Lots of things. It relaxes me. That other article—the smaller one—quotes an osteopathic doctor in the north woods of Maine as saying that this woman's bone marrow may have been taken. I went up and interviewed both Juanita and the doctor. She describes a big gray mobile home with some sort of dark decorations on the side. Even before this packet from Stanley, I believed someone had, in fact, kidnapped this woman, aspirated her bone marrow, and subsequent to her procedure, blindfolded her and dropped her off someplace."

"But why?"

"That, Mr. Callahan, is why we need a detective. I would do this myself, but I have courses to teach. And besides, my arthritis is giving me a devil of a time. Sneaking in disguise into hospitals in Turkey or Moldova or South Africa in order to expose organ traffickers may be a thing of the past for me."

"I truly hope not, Professor."

"Why, thank you."

"So why Florida? I thought your interest was focused on Third World countries."

"Mostly because that's where the action is

right now. If we can come up with something organized in this country, anything at all, I suspect we wouldn't have to worry nearly so much about funding. And even though having bone marrow taken might not be as debilitating as losing a kidney, or liver, or heart, it's still organ theft."

The woman's story and flimsy evidence didn't leave Ben any more taken with Organ Guard or its mission, nor did he believe there was anything more sinister surrounding the young man's death in Florida than the grille of a tractor-trailer, but he was absolutely impressed with Alice Gustafson, and in truth, jealous of her passion as well.

"I'm afraid the foundation grant we have is not very large, Mr. Callahan."

"That sounds ominous."

"Would you be willing to go to Florida and see if you can find the identity of the unfortunate man in that photo, and perhaps piece together what happened to him?"

"I'm not licensed in Florida."

"That shouldn't get in your way. I'm sure at one time or another, you have followed people into other states."

"I have."

"Besides, my former student, Stanley, knows the police in his area well. He has promised to put me in touch with them. I don't think he'll have trouble doing the same for you."

"Haven't the police been working on the case?"

"Technically, there hasn't been a crime committed, so I don't think they are devoting too much energy to identifying the victim. Besides, they have many cases going on at the same time. You will have only one. Are you interested?"

Ben was about to say something about how busy he was, but there was nothing about this woman that suggested she'd believe him in anything but the truth.

"How long do I have?" he asked instead.

"We can afford your plane fare—coach—and eight days at one hundred and fifty dollars a day, plus expenses. Make that *reasonable* expenses."

Ben tried to keep his black humor in check. Katherine de Souci had been paying him a hundred and fifty *an hour.*

"I understand why you're having trouble getting someone," he managed. "I would think that anyone who would work for that little wouldn't be someone you'd want."

"*You* are someone I want," Gustafson said. "You have the honesty to tell me you don't care for our cause and the intellect to have succeeded, at least by my standards, as a teacher."

"What if I need more time?"

"I doubt the Organ Guard committee on enforcement would authorize any further expenditure on you."

"Who's the committee on enforcement?" Ben asked.

Alice Gustafson grinned modestly.

"That would be me."

CHAPTER 4

There can be no doubt that the elder must rule the younger.
—PLATO, *The Republic,* Book III

The St. Clement's High School track, a quarter-mile banked cork oval, was Natalie's favorite in the city. Because it was neither near her apartment nor the medical school, she didn't run on it as much as she would have liked. Today, though, reexperiencing the pleasures of working out on such a near-perfect surface, she promised herself that situation would change.

From as far back as she could remember, she had known that she could run fast, and at times over the year before she entered Newhouse, when she was putting herself in one unsafe situation after another, the ability was lifesaving. A gym instructor at the school timed her at several distances, and quickly referred her for training to a friend who just happened to coach track at Harvard. By the time she was accepted into the college, she had broken several high-school records, and had established herself as a star at the middle distances.

Sometime in her junior year, following publication in the *Globe* of an article about her, Doug Berenger came to watch her train. He had been a decent runner at Harvard, though far from a record-breaker. After lunch together the following week, he invited her to work in his lab, provided she could do so without interfering with her running. The two of them had been a team of sorts ever since.

At eleven in the morning the air was warmer than she would have preferred, but the track seemed to absorb the heat and hold it at bay. After just ten minutes of easy jogging, her Achilles was already thanking her for the relief from running on the roads. Wearing maroon warm-up pants, a narrow-strapped tee, and a white sweatband around her forehead and ebony hair, she loped effortlessly through a turn, searching for Terry Millwood.

She was almost three weeks into her four-month suspension from school—an unmerited punishment, she believed, that effectively moved her back a year from the class with which she started, and ended her residency appointment at White Memorial. Not a day had passed without recurrent sparks of anger directed at Cliff Renfro, his surgical chief at White Memorial, or Dean Goldenberg. At thirty-five she had precious little time to waste getting to where she wanted to be professionally. Now, thanks to them, she had no choice but to hurry up and wait.

Up ahead, Millwood slipped through the gate and onto the track, waving when he saw her. At six feet, he was four inches taller than she was, but whereas her physique was willowy—wiry, many would say—his was burly and almost overly muscled. Millwood was a better than decent tennis player, and good at most other sports as well. But what he really excelled at was surgery. At Doug Berenger's urging, Natalie had begun hanging about the OR even before she entered medical school. Her mentor was urbane and composed in almost every circumstance, and was respected and revered as a cardiac transplant surgeon.

But during especially tense times in the OR, he could be a madman—hyper and quite tough on the surgical crew.

Millwood, Berenger's protégé on the transplant team, was quite the opposite—calm and positive even in the most critical, gut-wrenching crises. Natalie's first case observing the man was the twelve-hour replacement of a leaking aortic aneurysm and dysfunctional aortic valve. He sang opera softly throughout the grueling, eventually successful procedure, not once raising his voice or losing his composure. In her heart, Natalie knew she wanted to emulate Millwood when—make that *if* now—it was her turn in the number one position at the table, but in her head, she suspected she would be more like the flamboyant, volatile Berenger.

"So, how goes it?" Millwood asked, moving in next to her midway down one of the straightaways.

"Ever had road rage?"

"Maybe once."

"Well, I have it all the time now, whether I'm in a car or not, and it's directed at virtually everybody. It's a wonder I haven't ground my teeth down to nubs."

"Have you seen someone?"

"You mean like a dentist?"

"At least you're still funny."

"I love that you appreciate that I'm funny. You're like the only one. If you mean am I seeing my therapist, Dr. Fierstein and I are having mini-appointments almost every day. Ten or fifteen minutes. They're all the same. I tell her I feel like I'm going to kill someone, anyone, and she tells me that would probably only make matters worse. Sadly, I'm not sure she's right."

"When it's appropriate, Doug and I will go to bat for you with one of the other surgical programs. I promise you that."

"But first I've got to come to peace with what I've done wrong in school, and what I did wrong in the Metro ER." She held up her hand to keep him from reiterating that, in fact, if she had done nothing wrong she would still be in school. "I know. I know," she said.

"Used together like that, those are two of my least favorite words," Millwood said.

"I know."

"On your left!" a voice from behind called out.

Two boys, wearing the purple and white of perennial track powerhouse St. Clement's, flashed past them on the inside, forcing them to move to the right. Then, in unison, the youths glanced back, their expressions scornful condemnation of the policy that would allow just anyone onto their track.

"Easy," Millwood muttered. "They jail people for what you're thinking of doing. You don't have a weapon anyhow."

"Don't be so sure."

"So, Doug tells me you're spending quite a bit of time in the lab."

"What else do I have to do? The other techs want to kill me for making them look bad by being the first one in and the last one out, only they don't appreciate that I don't have anything else to do. They also don't know that just on general principles, I want to kill them more."

"What time did you say your shrink appointment was today?"

"You think I'm too angry?"

"I wouldn't be much of a friend if I just kept telling you that you were right all the time. You know I adore you, Nat, but I have to agree with what Goldenberg said about that hard edge of yours getting in the way."

"I am who I am. You of all people should appreciate that."

"You mean because I'm gay? That's *what*

I am. I wouldn't want to change that even if I could—which I can't. The kind of person I am is another story, and as wonderful as you are, you have a chip the size of Minnesota on your shoulder that's getting in the way of—"

"On your left!"

Once again, the St. Clement's runners rudely forced them to the right.

"Hey, guys!" Natalie called.

"I don't think I want to see this," Millwood muttered.

Up ahead the boys stopped and turned. They were older than Natalie had first thought—probably juniors or seniors. One of them, curly blond hair, some residual acne, kept trotting effortlessly in place, while the other, swarthy and utterly self-assured, took a step back toward them, hands on hips, head cocked. Natalie had no doubt that this was hardly the first time the youths had asserted themselves this way with recreational joggers. She felt Millwood's mute plea to forget the whole thing, but there was no chance. He was right that she didn't have a gun to shoot them with, or a knife with which to carve them up, but she did have her legs.

"Why didn't you just go around us?" she asked.

"Because we're serious runners in training, and you're joggers who could be running anyplace."

Wrong answer. Natalie saw Millwood step back, arms folded.

"Is that so?" she said. "I'll tell you what, serious runners, if either of you can beat this old, broken-down lady jogger back around to this spot, my friend and I will leave and go trot about someplace else. But if you can't beat me in a quarter mile, we'll keep our spot here, and you two can move way to the outside—or better still, go sit down on the grass and watch until we're finished."

The youths exchanged looks and smiled knowingly. They were both good, Natalie realized, maybe very good. But hopefully not good enough. She was a distance runner, and a quarter mile was a sprint, but at that moment, she needed nothing more than to beat them. No, she needed to *crush* them.

Natalie stepped out of her warm-ups as Millwood moved aside.

"I'll call the start," he said, helpless to alter history in advance.

As she lined up on the outside of the two

teens, Natalie felt the familiar, fierce rush of competition course through her. *You are not going to beat me. . . . You are not going to beat me. . . . You are not going to send that man out of the ER without a CT scan. . . .*

"Ready . . . get set . . . go!"

The youths were fast and arrogantly warm to the challenge of a race—especially against an older woman jogging on the track with a middle-aged man. Still, within the first twenty yards, Natalie knew that unless they each had rockets strapped to their legs in reserve, they were in for a rude surprise. The two of them seemed about equal, and ran that way—shoulder to shoulder. For a time, Natalie stayed back, drafting in the twin shadows. But a quarter of a mile was just that, and she was in no mood to nip these rivals at the finish. They both needed a profound attitude adjustment. Nothing close. The blond was Cliff Renfro, the darker one Sam Goldenberg.

"Hey, fellas," she called, "on your left!"

The two looked back, clearly startled that she wasn't far behind. It took only that instant for her to burst between them and accelerate away. Whether or not the teens could have run better had they known how fast she was didn't really matter. In a hundred races they would lose to her a hundred times, only perhaps never again as badly as they did this day.

Millwood had started the race halfway down one of the straightaways. Now he watched in some amusement as Natalie pounded around the final curve and sprinted in, not letting up until she had passed him. The St. Clement's boys were just finishing that last turn. Without looking back, and battling not to show that she was even breathing hard, Natalie took her friend by the arm and led him down the track in a brisk jog.

"Happy now?" Millwood asked.

"Less miserable," she said.

It was early afternoon when Natalie finished dropping off groceries for Hermina and Jenny and at her own apartment, and arrived at the lab. Jenny, upbeat as always, had finished *Wuthering Heights* and started in on *Oliver Twist*. As far as Natalie was concerned, unless her niece suddenly leapt out of her wheelchair and ran to play with the other kids, God had some serious ground to make up.

Even with Berenger's lab to go to, empty

time was weighing heavily. The latest of what passed for a romantic relationship for her had ended quietly nearly three months ago, and in truth, she really hadn't missed it—until now. Berenger and Millwood had promised to help her land another residency spot, but so far, what preliminary inquiries she had made had produced nothing. She had signed up for more time at the women's shelter where she had volunteered since college, and had even enrolled in a knitting course at Boston Adult Ed. Still, having been forced to shift in an instant from fourth gear down to first, her life felt as if it were moving in slow motion.

In addition to the track and the roads, the lab was a godsend—a place she could stay productive. She was one of a team of three, assigned by Berenger to a project examining the side effects of a new immunosuppressant drug still in the early phases of animal testing. If the evaluations were encouraging, somewhere down the line, the drug might replace or augment one of the toxic medications currently in use to reduce the frequency and severity of transplant rejection.

Natalie changed into light blue scrubs and a lab coat, and took the elevator up to

Berenger's impressive research suite on the ninth floor of the Nichols Building. The two other members of the team, Spencer Green and Tonya Levitskaya, greeted her with their typical lack of enthusiasm. Given Berenger's intellect, charisma, variety of interests, and superb surgical skill, it was a wonder to Natalie that either of them was still on the payroll.

Green, a cadaverous, dour Ph.D. who had never mastered the knack of getting grants, had been with Berenger for ten years, and Levitskaya, a Russian-schooled resident on the transplant service, now doing a six-month research fellowship, seemed to have a deeply ingrained opinion on almost everything— usually negative. Married, in her late thirties, and absolutely humorless, Levitskaya almost certainly had a crush on their mentor, and so treated Natalie as a rival. Berenger, himself, seemed oblivious to the continuously smoldering acrimony among his research team.

Entering the lab, Natalie checked to be sure that the small animal procedure room was available, then went to the holding area and returned with a cage of twelve specially bred white mice.

"I'm using the animal room," Levitskaya said, her dense accent vintage Count Dracula.

Not already, Natalie sighed to herself. The little lift that remained from putting the St. Clement's boys in their place vanished.

"I just stopped by there, Tonya," she said with artificial cheer. "The room's empty."

"Well, I am about to use it."

"Tonya, I'll be done in twenty minutes."

"Just do it later."

"Tonya, please don't do this. I'm having a very tough time and—"

"Or better still, do it tonight while you're in here working until midnight and making the rest of us look lazy."

People skills, Natalie reminded herself. That's what the dean and Terry had said she needed to work on. *People skills.*

"Tonya," she said, smiling sweetly, "if you don't back off and stop giving me a hard time, I'm going to flatten your nose across your face."

There, how's that for people skills?

Levitskaya stepped forward. She was a stocky woman, a little taller than Natalie, and heavier by thirty pounds or more. Her

crooked smile suggested she had faced
challenges like this one before, and wasn't
even considering backing down.

Damn, Natalie thought. *Well, what's the
worst thing that can happen?*

The last time she had been in a fistfight
had been in her junior year at the Newhouse
School. She had come away with fractures
of her nose and one knuckle, loudly claiming
victory over the other girl, who was virtually
unscathed. Would she ever learn to pick
fights with people she actually had a chance
against?

"How about in the hallway where we can't
wreck anything?" she said, resigned to taking a pounding.

"Ladies," Spencer Green called out from
across the lab, ignoring the conflict he
couldn't have helped but hear, "that was
Doug on the phone. He says both of you are
supposed to be in the follow-up clinic with
him right now."

Levitskaya's eyes narrowed as if she were
calculating whether she could finish Natalie
off and still make it to the clinic with minimal
delay. Finally, with a shrug that said some
other time, she headed out the door. Natalie
debated staying with her mice, but then put

them back and followed. Berenger clearly considered her part of his service regardless of her standing in the medical school—a gesture that was worth respecting.

The clinic space, used by various services on different days, was four examining rooms, a consultation office, and a small waiting area on the sixth floor of the Hobbs Building. This afternoon was given to Berenger's transplant patients, probably five or six of them. He was averaging about two transplants every three weeks, but the number would have been much higher had there been more donors. As things were, the number of people dying for want of a donor heart far exceeded the number saved by a transplant.

By the time Natalie arrived at the clinic, Levitskaya was already in the consultation room mooning at Berenger. Natalie was surprised to note that the woman's respiratory rate was normal, knowing she had to have sprinted over from the lab.

Seated behind his desk, Berenger was every bit the med school professor of cardiac surgery, square-jawed and steely-eyed, with wonderful, long fingers. Respected by patients, students, and faculty alike, he was a world-renowned lecturer and researcher, yet most of the time as humble as such a man could be. Natalie had met his wife and teenage daughters on several occasions, and knew enough to believe that if Berenger cut any corners in his remarkably complex existence, it was with them.

"So," he said, "there was some misunderstanding in the lab?"

Green.

"We have straightened things out," Levitskaya said quickly, smiling around nearly clenched teeth.

"Ready to go," Natalie added with exaggerated cheer. "I appreciate being included."

"You both know this is all about teamwork, right?"

"Right," the two women answered in unison.

"Well, Mr. Culver is in the next room. He's three months postop. Tonya, you know this man, so brief Natalie and bring her in to observe your evaluation. Natalie, let's talk afterward."

The cardiac surgical resident led Natalie to the hall, then gave a thirty-second, totally unenthusiastic presentation of a forty-seven-year-old truck driver who had developed cardiomyopathy—heart swelling of unknown cause—and managed to get a lifesaving transplant after two years of progressive cardiac failure with profound shortness of breath and massive fluid retention. Medically, he had done quite well since the surgery.

Culver, first name Carl, was a husky, swarthy man with thick brows, a wide pancake face, and disconcertingly small eyes. But there was something even more unappealing than his appearance—he reeked of cigarettes. In her presentation, Levitskaya had made a point of saying that he was once a heavy smoker, but had kicked the habit as his breathing deteriorated and he was made to see that his continued smoking would all but eliminate him from the transplant list. Clearly, he had fallen off the abstinence wagon.

Without so much as a greeting or a handshake, the Russian exploded.

"Goddamn it, Carl," she said in a near shout, "you stink of cigarettes!"

"Well, I got laid off and my daughter got sick, so—"

"No excuses. Do you have any idea how many hours and how much money went into putting that new heart into your chest, to say nothing of the poor man who gave it to you or the many, many others who did not get a chance at it? And here you are, smoking like a chimney, doing your best to destroy it."

"But—"

"No buts. I am going to see if Dr. Berenger even wants to speak with you. If not, then I want you to get out and only come back when you have stopped smoking again. What a waste this is of a heart that could keep a nonsmoker alive for years."

She brushed past Natalie and stormed from the room, leaving Carl Culver bewildered, frustrated, and angry.

"I'm sorry about your job, Mr. Culver," Natalie said.

"Thanks. I'm sorry about the cigarettes, Doc, I really am. But it's hard, especially when things aren't going well."

"Is your daughter very ill?"

"She had a seizure. They thought she might have a brain tumor, but it turned out to be migraines. Honest, Doc, I'll try to stop, I really will."

"You really need to keep trying," Natalie said, moving forward and putting her hand on his shoulder. "Your daughter needs you more than ever now. I know it's hard, but you've really got to keep trying."

At that moment, the door opened and Berenger entered, followed by a still crimson-faced Levitskaya. Over the ten minutes that followed, Natalie's mentor put on an instructional clinic on how to be a doctor, making constant, honest eye contact with his patient, reasoning, not chastising, asking about his family and his situation at home, calming him down, touching him reassuringly on the arm, yet all the while counseling him on the dangers of continued smoking. Quiet, stern, concerned, empathetic, understanding, unwavering.

"I hear some wheezes, Carl," he said after examining the trucker. "That's bad—very bad. Now it's time for you to go to work on this problem. I'm going to refer you to our SSN program—that's Stop Smoking Now. But the doctors and social workers there can only go so far. You've got to do the rest."

"I will, Dr. Berenger. I promise I will."

"You need to exercise more. Do you have a Y near you?"

"I . . . I think so."

"I want you to stop at cardiac rehab on your way out of the hospital. I'll call and have them go over your exercise program again. If there is a Y, they'll call the people there and sign you up. If money is a problem, talk to the SSN people. They have some funds available. Now I did a beautiful job on you. No more messing it up."

"Thanks, Doc. I'll do better. I promise."

"Your family needs you."

The two men shook hands warmly, and then Berenger left Culver in the room as he made calls and wrote out referrals. Finally, he sent Levitskaya back with the paperwork and instructions to move to the next patient when she was finished.

"Tonya's a very good surgeon," he said when he and Natalie were alone.

"I believe she is."

"Did you really threaten to flatten her nose across her face?"

"I wasn't using my people skills. Sorry. This isn't the time for me to act smart. It was my fault. I was feeling angry at the world and sorry for myself, and I goaded Tonya into fighting."

"I see. Well, you're both too valuable to my work to have you duking it out. I'm paying you to do battle with the mysteries of science, not with each other. No more incidents."

"No more incidents," Natalie echoed.

"Besides, I suspect ol' Tonya would be a real brawler."

Natalie grinned.

"I was thinking the same thing."

"So, how would you like to get away from all this for a while?"

"Excuse me?"

"Away."

"But not away as in I'm fired?"

"You're going to have to do a heck of a lot worse than threaten Tonya to get me to fire you. How's your Portuguese?"

"Third grade, maybe. Possibly fourth. I'm half Cape Verdean, but I was infamous for never doing anything that might have pleased my mother, and she desperately wanted me to speak the language."

"You probably won't need it anyhow. There's an international transplant meeting next week in Brazil—Rio to be exact. Have you been there?"

"I raced in the University Games in São Paulo, but I never made it over to Rio."

"Well, I was planning to go and deliver a version of our graft versus host paper, but my disc has been giving me a devil of a time, and Paul Engle, my neurosurgeon, has rec- ommended against long airplane flights or car rides. I thought maybe you had some things you might want to get away from for a while, and that was even before I caught you about to mix it up with my research fellow."

"You want me to go to Rio?"

"Business class."

"You're not just trying to keep me and Tonya from killing each other?"

"Firing you would be a lot less expensive."

Natalie felt a surge of excitement. The past three weeks had been worse even than those following her injury in the Olympic trials. Her unnecessary humiliation of the high-school runners and the angry encounter with Levitskaya were symptoms of her unraveling. She was a pressure cooker, plugged up and about to blow. There was nothing she could use at the moment more than a change of scene.

"When do you need to know?" she asked.

"When can you let me know?" Berenger responded.

"How about now?"

CHAPTER 5

The true physician is also a ruler having the human body as a subject, and is not a mere money-maker.

—PLATO, *The Republic,* Book I

The child was failing. Her name was Marielle, and despite the antibiotics and the IV fluids, the oxygen and tiny feeding tube, the six-year-old was slipping away. Malnutrition was fanning the flames of infection in her abdomen, and now her nervous system as well. Dr. Joe Anson brushed some flies from her parched, cracked lips and looked up helplessly at the nurse. Working in his hospital in an impoverished area thirty miles north of the capital city of Yaoundé, Anson had seen more than a few children die. Each one pained him worse than the last, and even though there had been many victories, they never seemed to balance off the defeats.

At that moment, though, four o'clock in the morning, the frail, malnourished girl was not the only thing upsetting Anson. Over the past hour there had been a steady increase in his own air hunger. The sensation—at its worst a horrible, strangling claustrophobia—was never completely gone anymore. After almost seven years, his primary pulmonary fibrosis—progressive lung scarring—was nearing the end of its course. PPF—cause unknown, course inexorably downhill, effective treatment none. It was a rotten, debilitating disease, and sooner or later, Anson knew, a transplant would be his only hope.

"Claudine," he said in fluent Cameroon French, "would you please get me a tank of oxygen and a mask?"

The nurse's eyes narrowed.

"Perhaps I should notify Dr. St. Pierre."

"No. Let Elizabeth sleep. . . . I will be fine with the oxygen."

He had to pause between sentences for an extra breath.

"I am worried," the nurse said.

"I know, Claudine. So am I."

Anson strapped the polystyrene mask to

his face and leaned forward so that gravity would pull his chest wall down and help expand his lungs. He closed his eyes, willing himself to calm down as he waited for the oxygen to banish the dreadful hunger. Five interminable minutes passed with no change, then another five. The situation could not get much worse. The episodes of breathlessness were occurring more frequently and taking longer and longer to abate.

At some point, some point soon it seemed, the oxygen simply wouldn't be enough. At some point, unless he consented to a lung transplant, and of course unless an appropriate donor could be found in time, his heart would be unable to force enough blood through the scar tissue in his lungs. Medications would work for a short while, but then his heart would weaken even further and he would begin, quite literally, to drown in his own fluids. By then, even if an appropriately matched donor could be found, the transplant would almost certainly be a waste.

Breathe in. . . . Slowly. . . . Don't stop. . . . Lean forward. . . . Let gravity help. . . . That's it. . . . That's it.

Though a self-proclaimed agnostic, Anson

began praying for relief. He still had work to do here—great, important work. Clinical testing of Sarah-9 was well under way, with astounding results. The drug he had created from a soil yeast unique to this area was still experimental, but it was clearly at the forefront in the field of neovascularization—the rapid development of life-giving new blood vessels. The new circulation had already shown the potential to cure conditions as diverse as battlefield wounds, infection, heart disease, and various forms of cancer . . . but ironically, not pulmonary fibrosis.

It took more than fifteen minutes, but finally Anson began to draw in more air. Moments later, though, just as he felt the attack was over, a slight tickle in his chest led suddenly to a racking, painful cough. *Damn it!* In the minute or so it would take him to gain control of the cough, the air hunger would again take over. He had once been able to play hours of rugby without slowing so much as a step. It was hard to believe that half a thimbleful of sticky mucus in one bronchial tube was now enough to bring him down.

On the narrow bed beside him, Marielle breathed sonorously. Anson stroked her forehead. Their battles were painfully similar.

Would either of them win? He flexed his neck and savored a few blessed gulps of air. Although he was beyond exhaustion, and hadn't had more than a few catnaps for almost twenty-four hours, he wasn't even considering sleep. His patients were what mattered. Sleep, as always, was secondary.

Born and educated in South Africa, Anson had once been handsome and dashing enough to have run with some of the most beautiful women in the world, and unfocused enough to have forsaken all but the most superficial connection to medicine. But that was long ago.

Another fifteen minutes of oxygen and Anson sensed the insufferable band around his chest begin to loosen. Claudine, unable to stay and witness his anguish, had gone off to check on their twenty or so inpatients, many of whom—children and adults—were suffering from the complications of AIDS. Thanks to the London-based Whitestone Foundation, and their appointed administrator, Dr. Elizabeth St. Pierre, the small hospital was well maintained and equipped with almost anything that Anson and she could think to ask for.

Fearing another relapse, Anson waited

before setting the oxygen aside. The effort of pulling in enough air had left him light-headed and nauseated. It wasn't supposed to have come to this. In nearly fifteen years he had never taken time away from work, nor had he ever wished to.

After a particularly exhausting and de-pressing weekend on the party circuit, en-meshed with people he no longer cared about, doing things he more and more ab-horred, Anson's life as a dilettante and play-boy ended abruptly. He used his legacy and whatever else he could borrow, and brought his vibrant wife and child into the jungle on a mission to save the people of his continent.

Now, at fifty-five, he was physically a specter of the man he once was, and con-stantly frightened of having his work taken from him before it was ready, but even with diminished oxygen levels, his mind still pro-cessed information and solved problems at a torrid pace. There was no way he was sup-posed to stop now. As long as there was work to do, there was no way he could ex-pose himself to the vagaries of a lung trans-plant and the antirejection treatments surrounding it.

Silently promising that as soon as Sarah-

9 was perfected, he would relent, Anson fit his stethoscope in place and did a careful reevaluation of his patient. The child might last a day or two, but without some sort of divine intervention, three days was a stretch. *Divine intervention.* The words went right to the heart of the matter. Anson did not acknowledge the power of God, but he totally embraced the power of Sarah-9, named after his only child in the hopes that someday, she would understand the choices he had made. Even though Marielle didn't fit into any of the current clinical protocols, she might well benefit from treatment with the wondrous drug.

There was, however, a major problem in doing that.

Elizabeth St. Pierre, controller of the purse strings supporting the Whitestone Center for African Health, was also in charge of the clinical testing of the drug. She had vehemently forbidden random use of Sarah-9 before the researchers at the Whitestone Foundation had completed their evaluation. The edict restricting use of the drug seemed unreasonable on the surface, but Anson knew the problem was one strictly of his own making.

Until he relinquished his total control of its

manufacture, Sarah-9 would be in precious short supply.

Anson felt his pulse quicken at the notion of stealing his own drug. He was doing everything possible for the girl, but her disease was deeply entrenched. He needed to increase the circulation in the area of the infection in order to deliver more oxygen and more antibiotics. Sarah-9 was just the ticket. Perhaps he could broker some sort of a deal with Elizabeth, he wondered now—his secret notebooks and cell cultures in exchange for enough Sarah-9 to treat his patient.

No, he decided. They could call him unreasonable or even paranoid, but he simply wasn't ready to turn over his research to Whitestone. At this juncture, it would be better to ask forgiveness than permission.

The bamboo and cinderblock research facility, a series of laboratories and sleeping quarters fifty yards north of the hospital, was impressively outfitted, with state-of-the-art incubators, two mass spectrometers, and even an electron microscope. With refrigeration units and both yeast and tissue culture lines to protect, there was also a phalanx of mammoth generators automatically backing up the power that had been brought out from Yaoundé through the towering trees along the Sanagra River.

Doing his best to mask the weakness and uncertainty in his steps, Anson caught up with Claudine as she and the other evening nurse were medicating the patients. In addition to Anson and St. Pierre, two physicians from Yaoundé and several residents worked at the hospital. They rotated nights on watch, but in truth, Claudine and the other nurses were experienced and competent enough to handle most problems.

"So, how is our flock doing, Claudine?" he asked, subtly bracing one knee against a wall.

The woman appraised him.

"You are feeling better?"

"Much, thank you. I am going to go back to my quarters to wash up and change. Then I will return."

"You should stay there and get some sleep."

"Later this morning, after the others arrive, I will catch up on sleep. Believe it or not, I am quite wide awake at the moment."

"We worry about you."

"I appreciate that, Claudine, and I need you to. Please hold down the fort. I will be back shortly."

Anson paused to assure himself that his little patient was stable, and then left the hospital. A uniformed security guard was waiting outside the door.

"Good evening, Jacques."

"Good evening, Doctor. Long night."

"Sick child. Listen, you can stay there if you want. I am just going to my apartment to wash up."

"Sir—"

"I know, I know."

Unaccompanied walks at night were forbidden. Where there was poverty, there was inevitably crime. The security force—each armed and former military—was there primarily to thwart kidnappings and any form of industrial espionage. The commercial potential of the formulas and notebooks protected in Anson's massive safe was quite literally unlimited.

The dirt and stone path between the hospital and the research compound was weakly illuminated by ground-level lighting. It wound through lush jungle growth, and ended at a bamboo vestibule off of which there were five

wings—three of them containing research facilities, and the other two, residential quarters. Posted by the doorway to the vestibule
was another security guard—well over six
feet tall, broad-shouldered, and quite impos-
ing in his starched khakis.

"Good morning, Doctor," he said formally.
"Good morning, Jacques."

"Francis," the other guard replied with a
curt nod. "The doctor wishes to wash up before returning to the hospital."

"Then so he shall. Thank you, Jacques. I
can handle things from here."

The guard hesitated, clearly trying to recall if there was a regulation covering the
transfer of hospital personnel from one security guard to another. Finally, he shrugged,
nodded at the two men, and headed back
along the path. Before Anson could speak,
Francis Ngale nodded minutely at the security camera, mounted in a waterproof hous-
ing midway up a palm tree facing the door.
There was no need for such a reminder. Anson was well aware of the electronic security
throughout the compound. The system had
been put in place by Whitestone once their
deal with him was finalized.

With Ngale at his side, Anson started

down the corridor to his two-room apartment. Halfway there, at a spot safe from the cameras, they stopped.

"Pardon me for this observation, Doctor," Ngale said, "but your breathing seems quite labored tonight."

"It was bad a little while ago, but now it is better. I have been battling to keep a little girl alive."

"Nobody fights that battle better than you."

"Thank you, my friend. I was quite relieved to find you on duty tonight. I need to get at the medication."

"For the girl?"

"Yes. You know the rules prohibiting this?"

"Of course."

"And you are willing to risk helping me?"

"That question does not need asking."

Like almost everything else at the Whitestone Center for African Health, the security force was hired and supervised by Elizabeth St. Pierre. Now, although she and Anson were still as close as ever, there were times when she was forced to remind him that according to the pact he had made, it was the Whitestone Foundation that paid the bills, and the Whitestone Foundation that made the rules.

St. Pierre had brought Francis Ngale on board, but she was unaware that Anson had once saved the man's father from a nearly fatal episode of meningitis. Of all the security guards, Ngale was the only one Anson could completely trust.

After a brief stop in his apartment to shower and change into a fresh set of scrubs, Anson met Ngale back in the corridor. The first blush of dawn had begun to dispel the dense night. Side by side, the two men crossed the vestibule and proceeded toward the cinderblock room containing two vaults—both set in four feet of concrete. The timing was as good as it could be. The security man assigned to the banks of video monitors would be half-asleep and easily distracted. Anson checked his watch.

"Five-oh-two," he said.

"Five-oh-two," Ngale agreed.

"I will need three minutes. No more. Begin at five-oh-seven."

"Three minutes. I will get you that. My friend, Joseph Djemba, is on watch. He loves nothing more than talking Cameroon Indominable Lions football."

"The team is very good again, yes?"

"They must play to their potential, Doctor."

"As must we, Francis," Anson whispered, pointing at his watch and motioning Ngale down the hall to the security office. "As must we."

Access to the vault room was by keypad. The combination to the vault on the right, containing Anson's notebooks and other research materials, was known only to him and an attorney in Yaoundé. In the event of his sudden death, the contents of the vault would be turned over to St. Pierre along with the information to break the code in which they were written.

The other vault—the one to the left—was refrigerated, and contained vials of Sarah-9, each carefully labeled, numbered, and catalogued. It seemed bizarre that he was forced to steal a drug that he had developed, but the process of synthesizing it from viral packets and yeast was complicated and extremely slow, and until Whitestone was allowed by him to develop mass production, it would always be in preciously short supply.

Anson stayed back just inside the entryway until exactly five-oh-seven, then approached the vault. Just thirty feet away, in the security office, was a bank of twenty-four monitors—three rows of eight. Hopefully, at that moment, Francis was seeing to it that Joseph Djemba was looking somewhere other than at the screens.

Anson fished a folded piece of paper from his pocket, knelt by the safe, and whispered the combination as he dialed. He exhaled audibly when the tumblers clicked into place and the heavy door swung open. Through a waft of cold air, he could see that there were eight vials of medication—the product of two or three days of laboratory work. Each vial, sealed with a rubber stopper, contained enough Sarah-9 for a week of intravenous treatment. In many instances, though, positive results were apparent in as little as two or three days. Hopefully, he would be able to keep his patient alive that long.

As he slipped one of the chilly vials into his shirt pocket, Anson wondered how closely Elizabeth kept count. Knowing the woman as he did, it was doubtful the missing vial would go unnoticed. *Deny, deny, deny.* That would have to be his strategy. If he was firm enough, Elizabeth would at least have to consider the possibility she had miscounted. With a minute to spare, he silently closed the vault door and returned to the corridor. A few seconds later, Francis left the security office and joined him.

"You are safe, Doctor," he said.

"At least for the moment."

"The security video is a loop that erases itself every twenty-four hours. If you can keep Dr. St. Pierre at bay for that length of time, the proof you were inside the safe will be gone."

Anson returned to the hospital, his breathing much easier than when he left. Whether it was changes in blood flow to his damaged lungs, mucous plugs, or a bronchial spasm, it was unfathomable even now how much better he could feel from one hour to the next—or sometimes even from one minute. He used the increasingly rare periods of minimal symptoms to convince himself that there was still time—plenty of time—before drastic measures would be called for.

Marielle was as Anson had left her, although her spiking temperature was, for the moment at least, down to near normal. She could respond to a loud voice, or to being moved about in bed, but otherwise remained almost motionless. Her mother, from a village on the river to the north of the hospital, had lost two of her three children to the fall-

out from malnutrition. Hospital social workers had been doing all they could to prepare
her for Marielle's return, but the one time Anson had met her, it was clear that although
she was hoping for the girl's recovery, she
was expecting the worst.

It was five thirty when Anson slid the vial
from his pocket, and drew up the first of ten
doses, which he would administer over a
week. If the child managed to survive, he
might have to find a way to get a hold of another vial. The clinical trials were progressing
so well that the optimum dose and administration schedule for several conditions had
been worked out. Pinching off the child's IV,
he slid the needle into one of the rubber
ports and injected the bolus of Sarah-9. He
was flushing the medication through with the
IV fluid when he became aware of another
presence in the four-bed ward. The instant of
warning kept him from a major shock.

"How's she doing?" Elizabeth St. Pierre
asked.

She was standing behind Anson and to
his right. There was no way for him to be certain how long she had been there, but he
gauged the angle to where he had held the

vial of Sarah-9, and knew there was a possibility she could have seen.

"She's in bad shape," he said.

"I suddenly went from deep sleep to being wide-awake, so I decided to drive out here and see how you were doing. Want me to take over so you can get some rest?"

St. Pierre, a native of Yaoundé, had returned home after receiving her MD degree and training in London. She worked with Anson and his team for two years in the hospital and in the lab, and then brokered the agreement with Whitestone to exchange the rights to Sarah-9 for their unrestricted support of the Center for African Health.

Through the dim light, St. Pierre studied Anson with undisguised concern. She was a full-figured woman in her early forties, with aquiline features and smooth, ebony skin. Her tortoiseshell glasses always seemed too wide for her face, but somehow managed to underscore the sharp intelligence in her eyes. She was fluent in half a dozen languages in addition to several tribal dialects of her homeland.

"I have a full day scheduled in the clinic," he said, searching for some hint of whether she knew what he had just done, "but perhaps I could sleep for a couple of hours before then."

Considering the years of their association, Anson knew surprisingly little of the woman's personal life, other than that she had been married briefly to a businessman in Yaoundé, and still had a home on a hill overlooking the city. He also knew that she was a dedicated, incredibly well-read physician, certified in renal diseases, and an acknowledged expert in the medical aspects of kidney transplantation.

"Joseph, do you wish to tell me what is going on?" she asked, switching from French to English.

Anson froze.

"Pardon?"

"Earlier this morning. Claudine tells me you had quite a difficult time of it for a while."

Anson's jaws unclenched. He swept his hand across the pocket of his scrub shirt to ensure the vial was not obvious.

"I have a little bronchitis," he said.

"Nonsense, Joseph. This is the natural progression of pulmonary fibrosis, and you know that as well as I do."

Anson became aware of some renewed tightness in his chest—just what was not needed. He gripped the seat of his chair and willed himself to breathe slowly. St. Pierre was a sharp clinician. It wouldn't take too long for her to discern that he was in trouble once more.

"I'm not ready yet for a transplant," he said with determination.

"Joseph, you'll be as good as new once you have the operation."

"I'm doing fine most of the time as is."

"Is there nothing I can say to convince you?"

"Not at this moment. Listen, Elizabeth, I really could use a little sleep . . . before the morning clinic. Do you think you could take over for me here? Marielle has gotten all of her meds."

"Of course."

Still battling the surging air hunger, Anson pulled himself to his feet, thanked St. Pierre, and with a posture of accentuated dignity headed off to his apartment.

"Joseph?" St. Pierre called out as he reached the doorway.

He spun quickly.

"Yes?"

"Use some oxygen for a while. Your respirations have sped up to twenty-four, air movement is down, and you're stopping to breathe between sentences."

"I'll . . . do that. Thanks."

Elizabeth St. Pierre made brief rounds on most of their hospitalized patients, then repaired to her office and placed a long-distance call to London.

"This is Laertes," a man's deep, cultured voice said.

"Laertes, this is Aspasia. Is it safe to speak?"

"Please go ahead, Aspasia, I hope you are well."

"Things with A's health are getting worse," St. Pierre said. "I don't know how much longer he can last like this. Even if we had his notebooks and could translate them, the project would be terribly delayed if he should die. I think we must find a way to break through his fear and move forward with a transplant."

"The council agrees."

"Then I will do what I must to convince him."

"Excellent. We know we can trust you."

"Just remember, Laertes, it must be a perfect or near-perfect tissue match, no worse than eleven out of twelve. I don't want to proceed with anything less."

"We have word there is such a donor."

"Then I will proceed."

"Very well. We will get the details to you shortly."

"Please extend my warmest regards to the rest of the council."

CHAPTER 6

The justice of the State consisted in each of three classes doing the work of its own class.

—PLATO, *The Republic,* Book IV

Mrs. Satterfield, what do you mean Pincus is gone?"

Bracing the receiver between his shoulder and ear, Ben bunched the thin pillow beneath his head.

"He wanted to go out, dear, so I let him go out, and he hasn't come back."

Ben groaned and stared up at the ceiling of room 219 in the Okeechobee Motel 6. It was just after eight in the morning of yet another day that was going to be cloudless and hot. The motel, fifty-two dollars a night for a single, was just off the highway, twelve miles from where Glenn had been hit face-on by a

speeding tractor-trailer. Although Ben had
no more idea of the man's identity now than
he had when Alice Gustafson first presented
the case to him, he found it easier to moti-
vate himself with a name than Unknown
White Male, or even John Doe.

He chose Glenn because of the vanity
plate GLENN-1 on a black Jaguar convertible
that cruised past his rented Saturn as he left
the Melbourne International Airport on
Florida's Atlantic coast. Perhaps *that* Glenn
won the Jag in a raffle. Maybe he had won
the lottery. Whatever the case, the man had
to have had some good luck along the way,
and Ben knew he was going to need more
than a little of that. So far, though, over his
five days in Okeechobee County, and several counties surrounding Okeechobee,
good luck had been in depressingly short
supply. Dogged by a lack of enthusiasm, he
had nevertheless worked long hours every
day. Still, he had come up with absolutely
nothing that would shed any light on who
Glenn was or what had happened to him.

The unpleasant conclusion persistently
nagging at him was that despite some modest successes in stalk-and-gawk domestic

cases, as a real private eye, he left much to be desired.

And now, his cat had gone missing.

"Mrs. Satterfield, remember what I said about Pincus being an indoor cat and not having any claws, and how he couldn't climb trees to get away from things like dogs?"

"But he wanted so desperately to go out, dear. He was crying."

Ben sighed. Althea Satterfield, his next-door neighbor, was Pop-Tart sweet and as kind as St. Francis, but she was also on the north side of eighty, and a little shaky on details. Her voice reminded him of comedian Jonathan Winters doing ancient Maudie Frickert.

"It's okay, Mrs. Satterfield," he said, "Pincus is a really fast runner. Besides, it's my fault for letting his claws be removed in the first place."

And, he reflected ruefully, it was. He and Dianne were still a few years from the big split when she caught his longtime pet having its way with the hem of one of her slip-covers. *All right, Ben, either that cat of yours gets declawed, or I'm out of here!* As always, the memory of her words brought a bittersweet smile. It could never be said that she hadn't given him a chance to take the initiative.

"So, how is your latest investigation going, Mr. Callahan?"

My only investigation.

"I haven't cracked the case yet, Mrs. Satterfield."

"You will."

I won't.

Alice Gustafson's former student, coroner Stanley Woyczek, had been as helpful as he could be, but the police in Port St. Lucie and Fort Pierce, as well as those in the sheriff's office and, for that matter, the state police, had a serious resentment against a private investigator whose very presence suggested they were not able to do their job. There wasn't a single question he could ask nor a single way to ask it that didn't sound condescending or patronizing. After five days of repeated visits to the various stations and substations, attempts to chat about the Marlins, Devil Rays, Buccaneers, Jaguars, and Dolphins, and several dozen doughnuts, he had failed to cultivate even one dependable source of information. Ultimately, he was forced to conclude that, had he been one of the policemen, he would probably have reacted and sounded just like they did.

"Mrs. Satterfield, don't worry about Pincus. I'm sure he'll come back."

"I wish I shared your optimism, dear. Even your plant is sad."

"My plant?"

"It's the only one in your whole apartment."

"I know that, Mrs. Satterfield."

"It used to have such a big, beautiful pink flower."

"Used to?"

"I'm afraid it's fallen off."

The plant, an Aechmea, was a gift from a violinist in the philharmonic, his significant other for ten weeks before she took up with a French horn player, claiming, quite correctly, that Ben simply had no direction to his life. Not surprisingly, over the intervening two years, a replacement significant other for him had simply failed to come forward.

"Mrs. Satterfield, you have to water that plant every d—" He stopped himself mid-sentence, imagining Jennifer Chin stretched out naked on red satin sheets with her French horn blower. "You know what, Mrs. Satterfield?"

"What, dear?"

"Just give the cat's food to the plant and everything will be fine."

"Anything you say, dear. And don't worry about your case. You'll solve it."

"I'm sure I will."

"Just start with what you know."

"What?"

"Pardon?"

"Never mind, Mrs. Satterfield. You're doing great, I'll be home in a few days."

"I'll see you then, dear."

Start with what you know.

With Althea Satterfield's oddly cogent words roiling about in his brain, Ben pulled up in front of a modest beige stucco house on a quiet side street in Indrio, just north of St. Lucie. A small red neon sign in one window read simply, READINGS. The door was opened by a tall, slender woman in her forties with bronze skin and straight, jet-black hair down to the small of her back. A colorful, artfully done zodiac was tattooed inside a half-moon across her forehead, the arc extending from the ends of her brows to just below her hairline.

"Madame Sonja."

"Well, Mr. Callahan," she said in a dreamy voice, "come in, come in. I couldn't remember if you were to be back this morning or tomorrow."

"You could have just read the future," Ben said, careful not to stare at Libra, his sign, which he knew from his last visit was just above her left brow.

It took a few seconds for Madame Sonja to gauge his expression. Then she grinned.

"That was funny."

"I'm relieved you think so. Sometimes, most of the time, in fact, I say things that are meant to be funny, but I'm the only one who thinks they are."

"That *is* a curse."

She led him past a heavily draped reading room, complete with a card table, tarot deck, teacups, and nearly as many arcane artifacts as were in Alice Gustafson's office, into a cluttered den with overfilled bookcases, several computers, scanners, banks of electronics, and a professional-grade artist's easel. Except for a computer workstation and a small desk chair, there was no furniture, but in one corner was a potter's wheel, well used and splattered with dry clay.

"Any luck?" he asked.

"Perhaps. I'm quite pleased with what I have for you."

"As I mentioned, Dr. Woyczek spoke very highly of your work."

"He knows I appreciate his referrals. I only wish that his regard for me carried over to his friends, the detectives at the police department. I'm afraid they think I'm something of a quack. They have their own artists, and even with numerous examples of my superior accuracy, they refuse to send their business this way."

Woyczek had understatedly described Madame Sonja as something of an eccentric, who used the latest in computer graphics to create or re-create faces, but often then modified her renderings with something she just saw in her mind. Three days before, Ben had brought the hideous photos of Glenn's nearly obliterated face to her. For a time, she sat across the table from him in her reading room, studying the pictures, sometimes with her eyes totally closed, sometimes open just a slit. He sat patiently, although he considered her actions a complete charade. Despite Woyczek's glowing endorsement of the woman, Ben had confessed his heavy, cynical bias against clairvoyance, mental telepathy, telekinesis, fortune-telling, and the supernatural.

"I've done one set of renderings in color, and one in black and white," Madame Sonja said. "As you will see, the sets are somewhat different from one another. I can't explain why." She sat down at her computer with Ben studying the screen over her shoulder. "Here is your man."

The first image, face-on in full color, materialized on the screen. It was essentially three-dimensional, done by a remarkable program, and clearly drawn by a woman with talent. The man depicted had a round, youthful face; pudgy, ruddy cheeks; rather small, widely spaced eyes; and somewhat low-set ears. There was little about the face that Ben found interesting, but it did have a certain childlike aura. Madame Sonja rotated the electronic bust 360 degrees.

She allowed Ben a couple of minutes to study her handiwork and then put the black-and-white drawing on the screen. Few would have said the drawings were of the same man. The face was narrower and more intelligent, the eyes fuller.

"How do you explain the differences?" Ben asked.

"I don't try to explain anything. I draw what I see—on the photos and up here." She tapped a long, scarlet fingernail against Gemini. "I wonder if this man has—make that *had*—diminished intelligence. Perhaps I have drawn him as he was at the time of his death, and then as he might have been save for some accident of birth."

Another strikeout, Ben was thinking. Woyczek might be right about this woman, but as far as he could tell, her uniqueness began and ended with the zodiac on her forehead. He wondered how many customers had paid how much money for her "wisdom."

"I have hard copies of five views in each of these envelopes. My charge would usually be a thousand dollars per set, but because Dr. Woyczek sent you, I'll give you both of them for five hundred."

Shocked, Ben hesitated, about to refuse, when the woman added, "As you are thinking, you can refuse to pay and leave these here. But I tell you, Mr. Callahan, these renderings are what you are after."

Ben's eyes narrowed. Anyone could have known what he was considering, he finally decided. It was logical and obvious—pure deduction from his hesitation and probably his expression. Anyone could have known. Reluctantly, he took his checkbook from his briefcase.

"I'm afraid I only take MasterCard and Visa," she said with no sheepishness whatsoever, "and, of course, cash."

An entrepreneur with a tattoo across her forehead. What happened to the simple, carefree antiestablishment types he had hung out with in college? A little grass, a little beer, a little rock and roll. Ben checked his holdings and handed over the cash. It was extremely doubtful that Alice Gustafson and Organ Guard would reimburse him in full for this one, but what the hell.

Then, in a move that totally surprised him, Madame Sonja reached out and took his hand.

"Mr. Callahan, I'm sorry you feel as uncomfortable about me as you do. You have a wonderfully kind face, and I can tell that you are a good man. If you will, please come and join me for a cup of tea."

Ben wanted nothing more than to hit the road. He had visited every hospital within twenty-five miles of the accident site, as well as every police station. Now, as long as he had sprung for these pictures of Glenn, he might as well use what time he had left before returning to Chicago to show them to some people—perhaps starting with the hematologists. But there was something compelling about the woman's touch. Reluctantly, he followed her into the den and took a seat. A minute later, she was pouring a rust-colored, aromatic tea into two Oriental cups, each with a different Asian symbol on the side.

"Please, drink it down," she urged. "I assure you there is nothing in it but tea. When you have finished, please pass your cup over to me."

Ben did as she asked. Madame Sonja stared into the cup for a few seconds, then wrapped her hands around it and looked intently across at him. Finally, she closed her eyes.

"I'm not getting much," she said.

Since when is five hundred dollars not much?

"I'm sorry," he replied.

"I keep hearing the same words over and over, though."

I've got to get out of here.

"What words?"

"Just start with what you know."

Ben stared across at her in stunned silence. Althea Satterfield's words precisely.

"A . . . a friend in Chicago just said those exact words to me not an hour ago."

"They did come in loud and clear."

"I don't believe this. Anything else?"

Madame Sonja shrugged and shook her head.

"Nope. Some days are better than others for me. This one isn't much."

"You think that was just . . . luck? Coincidence?"

"Do you?"

She led Ben to the door.

"Well, thanks for your drawings and your help," he said, shaking her hand and heading down the walk.

"I hope you find your man," she called after him.

"So do I."

"And I hope you find your cat, too."

With no feeling for where he was headed or what he was going to do, Ben found himself on a small road that dead-ended at a grassy patch overlooking what his map said was the Inland Waterway. Madame Sonja's parting reference to Pincus's disappearance had shaken him, as had her reiteration of Althea's odd suggestion.

Start with what you know.

The phrase wasn't all that unusual, he reasoned, and maybe the words weren't precisely the same ones his neighbor had used. And as for Pincus, he was focused on his failure as an investigator and on handing over five hundred dollars in cash, but in addition the disappearance of his strongest connection to the world of the living was very much on his mind. He must have said something about the cat. That had to be it. In all likelihood, he had said something in passing and just couldn't remember having done so.

There was no other explanation for what had happened—no other explanation, of course, except the obvious. Was it possible that a woman with a zodiac tattooed on her forehead, living in a tiny house on an undistinguished street in Florida, had somehow tapped into his thoughts? If there were people running about with that ability, why didn't everyone know? How many times had he walked right past a tent at a county fair offering readings for five dollars?

He remembered talking with Gilbert Forest, a physician friend whose foundation of medical beliefs had been badly shaken by a traditional Chinese doc, who had cured an inoperable cancer in one of Gilbert's patients using only acupuncture and what he called "vitamins." Since Ben believed in very little at this point in his life, the biggest danger posed by Alice Gustafson and Madame Sonja was to those many things he *didn't* believe in.

Start with what you know.

As the sun rose higher and the wet heat grew more intense, Ben set his case file on the ground beside him, and started going through it a page at a time, searching for some angle he had missed. Perhaps the renderings of Glenn would stir some memory in one of the hematologists, he mused. Not likely, he quickly decided.

Okay, okay, Callahan. Aside from the fact that you're not much of a detective, what else, exactly, do you know?

Ben's gaze drifted out over the glistening water. When it returned to the papers in his lap, he was looking down at the article about the woman, Juanita Ramirez. The three photographs accompanying the text, typical of the tabloids, were grainy. There was one of the woman, one of the puncture wounds

above her buttocks, and one of a likeness of
the mobile home in which she had been kidnapped, held prisoner, and operated on. The
mobile home . . .

Ben pulled out the transcript of the interview Gustafson had with the woman. The
parts he considered important were high-
lighted in yellow. The part he needed at that
moment was not.

AG: Can you describe the mobile home
     where you were held prisoner?
JR: I only saw the outside once, when
     they stopped to ask me directions,
     and then pulled me inside. It was big.
     Real big. Most of it was gray or silver,
     and there was like a maroon or pur-
     ple design on the side, sort of like a
     swirl pattern, or a wave.

The woman's description wasn't much,
Ben acknowledged, but it was something.
He had done the police stations and the
hospitals and the hematology offices and
the surgicenters, all the while searching for
the man he called Glenn. His plan, now that
he had Madame Sonja's renderings, was to
make the loop once again, hoping against

hope that someone might connect with the face. *Insanity is doing the same thing over and over and expecting different results.* Who had told him that?

"All right, Callahan," he muttered, "you've been calling yourself a detective. So detect."

Two hours and four mobile-home dealerships later, he was losing faith. Beaver, Alpine, Great West, Dynamax, Road Trek, Winnebago, Safari Simba. The list of RV makers seemed endless. Damon, Forest River, Kodiak, Newmar Cypress, Thor Colorado. Almost every one of them had a model or more with a design on the side that could have been the one described by Juanita Ramirez.

By midafternoon, his feet and back were aching, and the super-stuffed burrito he had eaten at Taco Bell, usually a staple in his diet, was making more encore appearances than the Rolling Stones. A hundred and fifty dollars a day—maybe ten dollars an hour for the time he had put in. He had done quite enough. Alice Gustafson should have found some other way to spend Organ Guard's money. Even though he didn't care much about her miniscule organization and its arcane mission, he really had tried his best. Now it was time to give up and go home.

Three hours later, through lengthening late-afternoon shadows, he swung the Saturn up the short driveway to the Schyler Gaines Mart and Gas, the fifteenth gas station he had visited since deciding to quit the case and return to Chicago. He had managed to add a pounding headache to the persisting miseries in his feet and back. Callahan's Syndrome, he decided to call it— CS for the purposes of fund-raising.

The brainstorm that kept him on the road long enough to develop the syndrome was a circle he had drawn on his map, ten miles around the spot where Glenn had been killed. Armed with catalogues from the RV dealers and the pictures of Glenn, he had decided to go down fighting, visiting every gas station he could locate within the circle. Given the single-digit miles per gallon of the largest RVs, the one he was searching for had to spend as much time at the pump as in the trailer parks. Perhaps, he decided, pigheadedness should be added to the symptoms of CS.

The station, three miles off the highway in Curtisville, might as easily have been on the other side of a time portal. It was a rickety-looking red clapboard structure with a peaked, shingled roof, and a small porch, complete with two rocking chairs. The hand-painted sign over the door was faded and peeling. Out front was a single gas pump that, while modernized at some point from the glass-topped Esso pump standing off to one side of the tarmac, still looked outdated.

It was to the good that the active pump was a fair distance from the porch, because the man Ben assumed was Schyler Gaines was seated in one of the rockers smoking a pipe. With his bib overalls, plaid shirt, dirt-stained Caterpillar cap, and gray beard, he might have been teleported to the mart from Li'l Abner's Dogpatch. Ben pulled the Saturn to a stop not far from the corner of the porch and approached the man, who eyed him with some interest, but said nothing. The smoke from Gaines's pipe was cherry-scented and not at all unpleasant.

"Good afternoon," Ben greeted him with a half-wave, mounting the first step to the porch and leaning on a rail that he guessed was a fifty-fifty bet not to hold him.

Gaines pulled out a gold watch on a chain and checked the time.

"S'pose you could still say that," he replied, sounding exactly as Ben might have predicted.

"My name is Callahan, Ben Callahan. I'm a private detective from Chicago, and I'm looking for a man who was run down and killed on Route Seventy, south of here."

"He 'uz killed an' yer still lookin' for 'im?"

"Let's try that again. Actually, I'm trying to learn *about* him. No one even knows his name, let alone what he was doing out on Route Seventy at three in the morning."

"Big Peterbilt three-eight-seven hit 'em head on—back cab sleeper, contoured roof cap."

"You know the truck?"

"Stops by here for gas from time t' time. I got a diesel pump out back. Charge a dime less than the stations on the turnpike, but it adds up when yer pumpin' a hunnert gallons. Guy named Eddie's the driver."

"Eddie Coombs. I spoke to him. He's still pretty messed up over what happened."

"I'll bet. It's a crackerjack rig he got. Six-hunnert horsepower Cummings engine. Fella who got hit couldn't a had much time to knowed it happened."

"I think that's the case," Ben said. "Well,

here are some computer drawings of what the guy might have looked like."

He passed the renderings over, suddenly feeling strangely foolish and impotent. What was he doing here? What could he possibly expect to learn from this laconic old man? Why had he ever said yes to Alice Gustafson in the first place? Rocking and puffing, Gaines studied the pictures for a time, then handed them back, shaking his head.

"Don't mean nothin' t' me."

"I didn't think they would," Ben said. "You got some cold Coke in there?"

"I do. Just short a havin' ice in the can if you know what I mean."

"Oh, I know exactly."

Ben used the back of his hand to wipe a sheen of sweat from his forehead.

"Cans are in the cooler. Jes leave a dollar on the counter. I'm enjoyin' this bowlful too much t' git up."

The Coke, icy as advertised, washed away a bit of Ben's consuming feeling of futility. He left a five by the antiquated register, took Madame Sonja's renderings, and headed back to his car. Would Alice Gustafson accept *oh, well, I tried*? Doubtful. More likely, she'd want her money back.

Just start with what you know.

Ben opened the driver's side door, then stopped and returned to the porch with the brochures and his absurdly long list of RV models.

"Mr. Gaines, I'm also looking for a mobile home," he said.

"A what?"

"A mobile home. You know, like an RV. Would have been here somewhere around the time this fellow was killed. Maybe from up north, maybe really big, maybe gray with darker gray or maroon markings. Here are some brochures of possible candidates."

"That would be a thirty-nine-foot Winnebago Adventurer," Gaines said matter-of-factly, without bothering with the brochures. "Oh-four or oh-five, I would guess. Ohio plates. Pulled in fer a fill. Took more'n seventy gallons."

Ben felt his heart skip a beat.

"Tell me about it."

"Not too much t' tell. The couple drivin' her didn't seem like the RV type."

"How so?"

"Oh, you know. Too young, not country enough, movin' about quicker'n most RV owners move. Bought three sandwiches and three chips even though there 'uz only two of 'em."

"Can you describe them?"

"I got a memory for cars 'n' trucks. Not people. She 'uz quite pretty, though. I do remember that. Cute bottom on her. Pardon me for sayin' that. I may be old, but I ain't dead."

"It's perfectly okay, Mr. Gaines. Is there anything else you can remember about the RV or the people?"

"I didn't notice until it was pulling away, but I don't think there 'uz windows in the back. As you'll see from them brochures, that ain't the usual."

"No windows. Are you sure?"

"If'n I said it, then I'm sure. What is it? You deal with people that sez what they don't mean?"

"I've been known to, yes."

Ben was aware of his pulse snapping in his fingertips. This whole business about the Adventurer could be nothing, but in every fiber he believed it was the RV described by Juanita Ramirez. He began rapidly processing ways he might use the limited information he had just gathered. How many people in Ohio buy a thirty-nine-foot Winnebago mobile home? Did the manufacturer keep records? How far would seventy gallons have taken such a beast? The questions weren't much, but after nearly a week of abject frustration, they were palm trees in the Sahara.

"Mr. Gaines," he said, "you've been very helpful. Is there anything else you can think of about this RV? Anything at all?"

"Nope. Except—"

"Except what?"

"I s'pose it might help if'n I gave ya the license plate number."

"The what?"

"They paid for their gas an' supplies with a credit card—a Visa, I think twuz. I got burned once real bad by a trucker with a stolen card, so now I always write down the license number on the credit card slip."

"And you still have the imprint?"

"A course I do," Gaines said. "You wouldn't think much a me as a businessman if'n I didn't."

CHAPTER 7

And will not the bravest and wisest soul be least confused or deranged by any external influence?

—PLATO, *The Republic,* Book II

Time is a flexible concept in Rio. Unless you are talking business meetings, and serious business meetings at that, half an hour late means perfectly on time.

"I love it," Natalie whispered to herself, smiling at the description in the *VARIG* magazine.

If anyone ever needed eight days away in a city where half an hour late meant on time, it was she. Images of dancing with a mysterious stranger at an all-night salsa club and running on the spectacular black-and-white mosaic sidewalks of Copacabana had dominated her thoughts since the invitation from

Doug Berenger to replace him and present a paper at the International Transplant Congress. Now it was about to happen.

For a time, she had flipped through the *Air Shopper* and made a mental list about what she might buy for her mother and niece and a few of her friends. For her girlfriends and Hermina, it had to be jewelry made of Brazil's legendary precious and semi-precious stones; for Jenny and Terry, polished agate bookends; for Doug, perhaps a high-end replica of the Christ the Redeemer statue.

She set the guidebook aside and peered out the window of the 747, trying to catch a glimpse of the city through scattered clouds. Night had settled in, but even after fifteen hours of flying, she wasn't particularly tired. Out of daylight savings time for their winter, Rio was just two hours ahead of Boston, and thanks to the luxury of business class, she had been able to get plenty of sleep. The married heavy-equipment salesman sitting next to her, a veteran traveler, had made several ill-disguised forays into forming a connection, had been politely rebuffed each time, and finally had retreated into a Grisham novel, which it looked like he might finish before they landed.

Because of what they had been told was a problem of dense traffic, the plane had been circling Antônio Carlos Jobim Airport for most of an hour. Of all those on the flight, Natalie decided, she probably cared the least about the delay. With the help of a couple of glasses of Merlot, her type A personality had been downgraded to possibly an A minus. *Antônio Carlos Jobim.* What other city in the world had an airport named after a composer—and a jazz composer at that?

". . . the girl from Ipanema goes walking . . ."

Natalie checked to ensure that her travel documents were in order, and was debating between opening her laptop and closing her eyes when the plane banked to the right, then leveled off. She felt the landing gear grind into place and then engage. Moments later the orders for landing were given in English and Portuguese. Her ear felt tuned to the language, thanks largely to nine days of study, tapes, and as many conversations with her mother as she could handle. There were differences between Brazilian and

Cape Verdean Portuguese, some of them striking, but she had always had a knack for languages, and had made quite a bit of progress.

Eight days in Rio. She had always believed that living well was the best revenge. Maybe she should send postcards of thanks to Cliff Renfro and Dean Goldenberg.

The landing was flawless, and customs was much better organized than she had anticipated from her experience in São Paulo. Her guide to Rio had prepared her for winter temperatures in the mid to high fifties, and also suggested that she buy a cab voucher inside the airport rather than trust the meters. She pulled on a light leather jacket as she entered the main terminal, and easily found the taxi kiosk. As she was putting the change and the voucher into her wallet, she began to feel light-headed and vague. The sensation was unpleasant and disturbing, but easily explainable by the long flight and the Merlot.

Outside the terminal, the air was cool and fragrant, despite the chaotic traffic. The Jobim airport was twenty miles north of Rio. She had been looking forward to her first encounter with the magical city, but all she

could think of at that moment was getting inside a cab and getting to her hotel. Her presentation wasn't scheduled for two more
days, so there was no reason at this point to
be rested. Besides, according to the guidebook, nightlife in Rio didn't even begin until
the early morning. After a few hours of rest,
she would be ready to try some of it out.

The red dress, she decided, mentally
choosing one of three she had brought. She
had no intention of being foolish in a city
known for punishing such behavior, but she
was adventurous, and she loved dancing—
especially to Latin music. The concierge at
the hotel would direct her to a place that was
both fun and safe.

Near the taxi queue, a uniformed attendant took her bag, checked her voucher, and
led her over to a yellow cab with a blue stripe
around it. Her feeling of disconnection intensified as she slid into the backseat.

"Inter-Continental Rio Hotel," she heard
herself say.

The driver, a dark man in his thirties,
turned and smiled at her, but said nothing.
His features were indistinct, and as the cab
pulled away, Natalie tried unsuccessfully to
focus on his appearance. The ride toward

the city was also a blur. More than once, she thought she might be close to getting sick. Sooner than she had anticipated, the driver pulled off of the highway. In a short time they were driving through a poorly lit slum. Natalie felt a jet of adrenaline drive much of the uncertainty and vagueness away.

"Where are we going?" she asked in Portuguese.

"You said the Inter-Continental," came the reply. "This is the quick way."

"I don't want the quick way. I want to go back on the highway," she demanded, sensing that she had gotten a number of the words wrong.

"You are a very beautiful woman," the driver said over his shoulder in decent English.

"Take me back to the highway this minute!" she insisted.

"Very beautiful."

The man accelerated slightly. The area through which they were passing was even more dilapidated. What streetlights there were had been smashed, and most of the rickety houses and tenements were shuttered. Almost nobody was on the streets except for an occasional furtive shadow, skulking around a corner or down an alley.

Natalie glanced at the cabbie's license. In the gloom she could barely make out anything, and so what if she could? This was serious, serious trouble. She mentally inventoried the contents of her purse. Was there anything there she could use for a weapon? Thanks to airport security, the answer was almost certainly no.

"Goddamn it!" she shrieked, pounding on the thick Plexiglas that separated front seat from rear. "Take me back to the highway!"

"The customers at the House of Love will adore you. You will be very happy there. . . . Very happy there. . . ."

The words echoed eerily. Icy panic took hold. Her dizziness, never really gone, had begun to worsen. The driver's words seemed sharp and clear one instant, thick and repetitive the next. Natalie scanned the dark, uninviting slum. It seemed like they were going thirty or forty. Could she possibly escape by jumping out of the cab then rolling and scrambling to her feet and running? If she could somehow get out and get upright, provided her leg wasn't broken, she could outrun anyone. With the alternative of being made a narcotics whore in some brothel, it had to be worth taking the chance. She slipped her wallet and passport from her purse and jammed them into the pocket of her jacket.

"Money," she pleaded. "I'll give you money to let me out right here. Three thousand reais. I have three thousand reais. Just let me go!"

She inched toward the right-hand door and eased her fingers around the handle, trying to visualize what she should do with her body as she hit the pavement. Around her the scene seemed to fade, then sharpen, then fade again. She shook her head, trying to clear her thoughts.

It had to be now.

At that instant the cab screeched to a jolting stop and Natalie's door was ripped open by two men, both wearing black stocking masks. Before she could react, she was pulled out and forced onto her belly. The cab roared away. A needle was thrust into the muscle at the base of her neck, and the contents of a syringe were emptied into her. A narcotic, she thought—a disabling dose of some sort of narcotic, probably heroin.

Her situation was absolutely terrifying, but she felt oddly detached from it—detached yet at the same time determined not to give in to her attackers without a fight. They each had one of her arms now and were dragging her facedown into what seemed like a narrow, unpaved alley, fetid with refuse. She screamed for help, but sensed that in this neighborhood, such cries happened often, and would nearly always go unheeded. Still on the ground, she twisted her body and pulled her arms. Instantly, the man holding her right wrist lost his grip. Natalie spun that way, pushed herself to her knees, and slammed her fist as hard as she could into the other man's groin. His grip on her other wrist vanished and he dropped to his knees. Before either man could react, she pushed to her feet, this time punching one of them flush in the face.

In a second she was on her feet and sprinting away from the men down the alley. Ahead of her, through dim light, she could make out two rows of darkened buildings, some of them two stories high, some three. Ahead and to the right she thought she saw a light wink on.

From behind her, one of the men cried out in Portuguese, *"Tenho uma pistola. Pare já ou eu atiro!"* I have a gun. Stop right now or I will shoot! Ahead of her the alley was

completely blocked by a pile of trash barrels, boxes, and refuse, propped against
some sort of fence, and extending up well
over her head.

"Stop!" the voice from behind her cried.

Natalie had scrambled up the trash heap
and was reaching for the top of the fence
when a shot rang out from behind her. Nothing. She grabbed the coarse wood and
swung her leg over. Another shot snapped
off, then another. Both times, white-hot pain
exploded from the shoulder blade on the
right side of her back. She was slammed forward. Her arms flew off of the fence. Grunting against the pain and gasping for air, well
aware that she had been shot more than
once, she toppled backward and fell helplessly into the pile of garbage.

CHAPTER 8

"And who is best able to do good to his friends and evil to his enemies in time of sickness? The physician.
—PLATO, *The Republic,* Book I

Yaoundé was just four degrees north of the equator. Joe Anson had never handled the heat and humidity of Cameroon as well as those who were born there, but this day, with monsoon season just a couple of weeks away, was the worst he could remember. The air-conditioning units in the hospital were fighting a losing battle; the odors of illness were intensified throughout the building; flies were everywhere; and worst of all, the air was just about too heavy for him to breathe.

If there was a bright spot in the oppressive day, it was the girl, Marielle, who had responded remarkably to her clandestine treatment with Sarah-9, and was now sitting up in a chair by her bed, taking fluids and nourishment. The drug was an absolute miracle, just as he had known from the beginning it would be. Another day, perhaps, and the Whitestone Center for African Health van would bring her back to her mother, along with enough rice and other staples to improve the health and well-being of the village until the monsoons hit. After that, the cycle of malnutrition and illness would begin anew.

"Okay, dear one," Anson said, placing his stethoscope on the girl's back, "breathe in, breathe out. . . . You are doing so well. So well. Maybe tomorrow you will go home."

The child turned and threw her arms around Anson's neck.

"I love you, Dr. Joe," she said. "Love, love, love, love, love."

"And I love you, too, dear peanut."

The few words took more out of Anson than he would ever care to admit to anyone. He handed Marielle a picture book and inched away from her bedside to the small office he shared with whichever doctors were on call. What in the hell was going to happen to him? What should he do? After thirty seconds, with his air hunger mounting, he used the emergency two-way radio he always carried to summon help.

"This is Claudine, Dr. Anson," the nurse said. "Where are you?"

"Doctor's office . . . in the hospital."

"You need oxygen?"

"Yes."

"One minute."

It was half that when Claudine raced in pulling a green 650-liter tank of the precious gas, dropped into a frame on wheels. She was a tall woman nearing fifty, with a regal bearing, caring eyes, and a smooth, richly dark complexion. She had been at the hospital almost since its inception.

"You are working the day shift?" Anson managed as she set his mask in place and started the oxygen flow at maximum.

"Just breathe," she said. "I . . . um . . . one of the other nurses got sick. I am working for her."

Anson missed her deeply troubled expression. He withdrew a cortisone inhaler from the top drawer and took two deep breaths from it, followed by two puffs from a bronchodilator.

"It is good to see you," he said.

"You are feeling better?"

"The humidity makes it hard."

"The humidity is only going to get worse until the rains start."

"Then it will be worse still. A hundred percent humidity. I do not know how I will ever deal with that."

Again, a shadow crossed the nurse's face.

"You are going to be all right," she said with more than casual determination.

"Of course I am, Claudine."

"You are scheduled for your Wednesday lunch with Dr. St. Pierre. Should I cancel that?"

"No, no. I do not cancel things. You know that."

Anson, once no more reliable than the wind, had become a creature of absolute discipline and unwavering habit. On Wednesdays at noon—*every Wednesday*—he met with St. Pierre in the small hospital dining area, where he ate conch chowder and a green salad, drank a bottle of Guinness Cameroun, brewed in Yaoundé, and finished his meal off with a scoop of chocolate ice cream. It was there they informally discussed the business affairs of the hospital, clinic, and laboratory, as well as his

Sarah-9 research and, over recent years, his health.

"Excuse me for saying so, Doctor," Claudine said, "but your breathing is as labored as it has been for some time."

"It is . . . unpredictable."

"And there is no other treatment I can get for you?"

"I . . . am . . . on so much . . . medication I . . . am jittery . . . most of the . . . time."

"Please, just relax and breathe. Perhaps I should get Dr. St. Pierre, or a respirator."

Anson motioned her to stay calm and wait. The nurse backed off to one side of the room, but her dark eyes, moist with caring and concern, never left him. Unseen by Anson, she reached into the pocket of her uniform and nervously fingered the vial of clear liquid that was there.

Exactly one-point-four cc's—no more, no less.

That was the instruction.

Exactly one-point-four . . .

Lunch was scheduled for noon, but it was a quarter after before Anson had enough breath to set the oxygen aside and make his way to the dining area. The room was empty save for St. Pierre, who was seated at one of

the three small tables, eating a tuna sand-
wich, drinking a tall iced tea, and going over
some ledgers. She wore khaki shorts and a
white tee that accented her alluring breasts.
For a few moments, Anson was actually diverted from his respiratory difficulty. Over the
years, he had often felt their relationship was
about to move beyond a close friendship, but
that had yet to happen. He settled in at the
table, and moments later the cook reverently
set his meal in front of him, a reminder that
there was no one in the hospital or lab at the
center whose life had not in some way been
touched by the man.

"I'll never know," he said to St. Pierre in English, pausing once for air, "how you manage
to look so fresh in the face of this humidity."

"I suspect you would look fresher if you
were breathing at something better than an
oxygen saturation of eighty percent."

"I have managed to put in a full day's
work."

"I fear that won't last much longer."

"Who can say? Lungs adjust."

"Not with pulmonary fibrosis they don't,
Joseph, and you know that as well as I do."

Anson picked at his salad and, as was his
habit, took a lengthy pull straight from the

bottle of his Guinness Cameroun. Elizabeth was right, he was thinking. She was always right when it came to his health. Still—

"It just isn't the time for me to submit to a transplant. The monsoons are almost upon us. Our work in the lab is going so well. I simply have too much to do."

"You are risking death every day from sudden heart failure or even a stroke." She reached over and placed her hand on top of his. Her expression left no doubt that her concern for him was personal as well as professional. "You have done so much for so many, Joseph. I don't want anything more to happen to you. Your breathing is getting worse, and it is destined to get even worse still. If matters deteriorate much more, any operation will become far more risky."

"Perhaps."

"The recovery from surgery won't be nearly as lengthy as you think. The doctors with whom I have been working are some of the greatest transplant surgeons in the world. They are standing by to ensure that you get the best care possible."

Anson drained his bottle, hoping for at least a little fortitude in the battle to convince Elizabeth that the medical indications for a transplant were not overwhelming, and the timing was poor.

"I've had several good days in a row," he tried.

"I beg you to get honest with yourself. Just because you haven't stopped in the middle of the day for therapy on a respirator doesn't mean you've had a good day. Look at you now. You are an intellectual, a scholar, yet you don't say half the things that are on your mind because you don't have enough breath to get the words out." Again she took his hand in hers. "Joseph, listen to me, please. The doctors at Whitestone have learned of a donor—a twelve out of twelve donor, Joseph—a perfect tissue match for you. It's what we've been searching the world for. You will be on virtually no antirejection medication. That means no debility or side effects. You will be back here at work before you even know it."

Anson stared across at her. This was the first time a donor had actually been located, let alone one who was a virtually perfect tissue match. Elizabeth and the others with whom she had been consulting had just increased the ante in this high-stakes game.

"How long have you had people looking for someone?"

"Ever since we tissue-typed you and realized that your profile was unusual and rare."

Anson slumped back, shaking his head.

"Where is this match?" he asked.

"India. Amritsar, India. It's in Punjab State, north and west of Delhi. A man lies on machines in the hospital there. He is brain-dead from a massive cerebral hemorrhage. His hospital wants to move forward with the harvesting of his organs, but we have begged them to wait."

Anson stood and walked across the room. The short distance strained his breathing, but, he rationalized to himself, the humidity was intense.

"I can't do it," he said finally. "I just can't. There's work to do here and Sarah to notify and . . . and . . ."

"Please, Joseph," St. Pierre said firmly. "Please stop! If this is something you're not ready to do then that's the way it's going to be. Why don't you go on back to your apartment and rest for an hour until afternoon clinic. I'll cover for you here."

"O-okay," Anson said, his tone almost a baby's. "I'm glad you're not angry with me."

"I'm worried for you, Joseph, and I'm worried for our Sarah-nine project, but I am hardly angry. Let me get the security guard to accompany you to your room. Would you like a wheelchair?"

"No!" Anson snapped. As he turned away, a sudden wave of weakness and profound fatigue swept over him. "On second thought, maybe a wheelchair would be best," he capitulated.

By the time the guard entered the dining area and helped Anson into a wheelchair, his fatigue had intensified, and he was barely able to take in any air at all. He strained to breathe, but it was as if his mind had decided it could no longer be involved in such an effort. He tried to speak, to call for help, but no words emerged.

The room was whirling as the guard wheeled the chair out the doorway and onto the path to the living quarters. Just a few feet into the journey, Anson realized his breathing had stopped altogether. The scene around him dimmed, then grew black. Helpless and rapidly losing consciousness, he toppled forward out of the chair, landing face-first on the gravel.

The guard, a stocky man with massive arms, scooped Anson up as if he were a rag doll and raced back into the hospital crying for help. In seconds, the physician's limp form was supine on a stretcher in the critical care room, and Claudine had readied the well-equipped crash cart. St. Pierre, a cool head in even the most dire medical emergencies, ordered a cardiac monitor, urinary catheter, and IV, then positioned Anson's head chin up, and began inflating his lungs with a breathing bag and mask. One of the medical residents from Yaoundé offered to take over for her, but St. Pierre declined.

"No matter how proficient you are, Daniel," she said, "I will never trust your technique in situations such as this as much as I trust my own. Without this man, we are all lost. Check his femoral artery for a pulse. Claudine, prepare for me to intubate. A seven-point-five tube. Be certain to check the balloon on it before giving it to me."

There was a momentary, silent spark between the two women, unseen by anyone else in the room.

"He still has a pulse," the resident said. "Faint at one-twenty."

"Help get the monitor running and see if you can get a blood pressure."

St. Pierre continued breathing effectively for Anson, whose color had marginally improved, although his level of consciousness had not. Claudine inflated the balloon used to seal the breathing tube in place inside the trachea and found it to have no leaks. Then, still as composed as if she were selecting fruit at the market, St. Pierre crouched at the head of the stretcher, had the resident hold Anson's head steady in the chin-up position, set a lighted laryngoscope blade against her colleague's tongue, and in just seconds, slid the tube between the delicate half-moons of his vocal cords. A syringeful of air inflated the balloon and sealed the tube in place.

St. Pierre then replaced the mask on the breathing bag with an adapter that hooked to the tube, and breathed for Anson until the tube could be taped in place and attached to a mechanical respirator. With six people working so closely and intensely, the heat and humidity in the small room was staggering. Only St. Pierre showed no external signs of being affected, although once she removed her glasses and wiped them on the hem of her shirt.

For fifteen minutes a tense silence held sway. There was no change in Anson's appearance, but his vital signs steadily im-

proved. Then, with obvious effort, Joe Anson
opened his eyes.

One by one, St. Pierre thanked her assis-
tants and the nurses, and asked each to
leave the room. Then she bent over the
stretcher and positioned her face just a few
inches from his.

"Easy does it, Joseph," she said when they
were at last alone. "The heat and humidity
were too much for you. You just had a complete respiratory arrest. Do you understand?
Don't even nod if you do. Just squeeze my
hand. Good. I know that tube is uncomfortable. I'll give you some sedation in just a few
minutes. As long as the tube is in place, the
danger of disaster is greatly lessened.

"Joseph, please, please listen to me. If
this had happened in your apartment, we
never would have gotten to you in time. We
need you, Joseph. *I* need you. Sarah-nine
needs you. The world needs you. We can't
have this happen again. Please, please con-
sent to the transplant."

Minutely at first, then with greater force,
he squeezed her hand.

"Oh, Joseph," she said, kissing him on the
forehead, then on the cheek, "thank you,

thank you. We're going to move quickly. Do you understand? Whitestone has a jet to fly you to India. It's waiting in Capetown right now. I will be with you all the way. We'll keep you sedated and on the ventilator for the whole trip. Understand? Good. Please don't be frightened. This is what is needed. Soon all your troubles will be over and you will be back here making all of mankind better. I ask you one last time, do you understand? All right, Joseph, I will make the call. Soon we will be on the way to Yaoundé Airport to meet our jet."

St. Pierre mobilized the team who would be caring for Anson while she was off arranging the ambulance ride to Yaoundé Airport and the subsequent flight to Amritsar International. When Claudine moved in to take over the nursing, St. Pierre shook her head and motioned the woman outside.

"You almost killed him," St. Pierre snapped before Claudine could get out a word.

The nurse's eyes glossed over at the rebuke. Elizabeth St. Pierre was a person—a Yaoundé-born woman—whom she had respected for many years. Had she not thought so much of her, she would have

never agreed to add the mixture of tranquil-
izers and respiratory depressants to Dr. Anson's beer.

"I did nothing wrong," she said. "You told
me to add one-point-four cc's to the bottle,
and that is precisely what I did."

St. Pierre was at once fire and ice.

"Nonsense," she said. "All I wanted to do
was force him into more difficulty so he
would opt to go ahead with a transplant before it was too late, and while we had a perfect donor. I formulated that preparation
based on his body mass and oxygen levels.
If you had given the proper amount, he
would never have stopped breathing."

"But it is extremely hot and humid today
and—"

"Just imagine if that had happened five
minutes later in his quarters. If he was unable to call for help, then he would be dead
right now, and we would have lost one of the
greatest men who ever lived. Clearly you
misread the dose. Admit it."

"Dr. St. Pierre, I cannot admit to something I did not—"

"In that case, I want you packed and out
of here by two. I'll have one of the guards

drive you back to Yaoundé. If you wish a positive recommendation from me, let there be no talk of what went on here today."

Without waiting for a reply, St. Pierre whirled, stalked to her office, and placed a long-distance call. Again, the man who called himself Laertes answered.

"All right," she said in English. "Set the team in motion. If this tissue match is all you say, A should be renewed and working for us for as long as is necessary. We have accomplished so much."

"Agreed."

"Has the donor been certified brain-dead?"

"Do you care, Aspasia?"

"No," St. Pierre said without hesitation. "No, I don't."

CHAPTER 9

And from being a keeper of the law, he is converted into a breaker of it.
—PLATO, *The Republic,* Book VII

Let me get this straight, Mr. Callahan. Your source for this information about a recreational vehicle was an old man in an out-of-the-way garage, and you found him after being encouraged by a psychic not to quit your investigation."

"Um . . . I suppose you could put it that way, yes."

"You believe the old man?"

"I do. I think the RV he described is the one we're looking for."

"And the psychic with the zodiac tattooed on her head?"

"She knew my cat was missing, and I don't remember telling her that."

"But she didn't tell you where to find him."

"No, no she didn't."

"But you found him anyway?"

"He was in the bushes right in front of my building. I think he got enough mice and rats there without ever having to move."

Gustafson suppressed a grin, but not before Ben saw it.

"So," she said, "after a week of near futility in Florida, where we still don't know who the man was you were investigating, or why he had a bone marrow done, you want me to pay you to go to Cincinnati."

"It's only three hundred or so miles."

"Each way. I know that."

Ben leaned toward her conspiratorially.

"Don't tell anyone, Doc, but I'm going to Cincinnati whether you pay me or not."

Alice Gustafson leaned back across her desk and mimicked his gesture.

"Well then," she said, "in that case you'd better get a move on."

Ben made the drive from Chicago to Cincinnati in a steady, raw drizzle. For much of the trip he listened to a John Prine CD with most of the songs dealing with imprisonment—either behind bars or within the walls of one's life. When he wasn't listening, he was singing the chorus of his favorite cut on the album, which he had decided would be his theme song until something better came along.

> **Father forgive us for what we**
> **must do**
> **You forgive us, we'll forgive you**
> **We'll forgive each other till we**
> **both turn blue**
> **Then we'll whistle and go fishing**
> **in heaven.**

Using the information provided by Schyler Gaines, some software he had bought from a private detective catalogue (and could use only after paying off the overdue account with his Internet server), and a cop who owed him a favor, Ben had relatively little trouble pinpointing the location of the Winnebago Adventurer and its owner—Faulkner Associates, 4A Laurel Way, Cincinnati. There was no such business listed in the Cincinnati phone book, and none in any search engine online. Now, as he cruised around a curve on I-74 and saw the city stretched out ahead, Ben tried to make sense, any sense at all, of an RV that would scoop victims up, perform bone marrow aspirations on them against their will, and then release them. Nothing came to mind.

He knew that Alice Gustafson liked him and was going to pay him for his time no matter what, but he was relieved he hadn't yet brought up the five hundred dollars he had paid Madame Sonja for the renderings of Glenn. In fact, rather than try to explain the variation between the two sets of drawings, he had only shown her the "real" one. Altogether, adding the five hundred to the cost of reactivating his browser, paying off a few people in Florida for what proved to be useless information, and assuming that he had lost at least some work while in the Sunshine State, he had probably not come close to breaking even on this gig.

If this six-hundred-mile junket to the Queen City and back proved to be a bust, he decided, he was through, finished. He would ignore the hideous photos of Glenn, and the tabloid-worthy account of Juanita Ramirez, and he would put the mystery of Madame Sonja behind him. Organ Guard could go back to guarding organs, and he would go back to stalking and gawking.

Father forgive us for what we
must do
You forgive us and we'll forgive
you.

With its emerald necklace of parks, stunning concert hall, art galleries, universities, bohemian section, sporting venues, and zoo, Ben had always considered Cincinnati a little-known jewel among cities. After checking his MapQuest printout, he eased off the highway and toward the Ohio River. He had been driving most of eight hours, and his balky back was demanding some relief. Regardless of what happened on 4A Laurel Way, there was a motel and a hot shower in his near future.

The dense overcast, persistent rain, and Cincinnati's place on the western edge of the eastern time zone made the early evening almost midnight dark. MapQuest took him east past the downtown area, and down into the flats by the Ohio River—an area of gnarled little streets, narrow alleys, and warehouses that was just begging for some sort of urban renewal.

Unlike most of the truncated, dimly lit streets, Laurel Way had a sign. Ben parked just around the corner and then stared at his locked glove compartment, wondering if there was any sense in bringing along his Smith & Wesson .38. Except for a single session at a range a couple of years ago, he had never once fired the thing, and given his woeful aim, he hoped he would never have to. The vote was a decisive one-to-nil to leave it where it was. His soft leather bag was another story. A sale purchase at Marshall Field's, it now contained a hooded flashlight, crowbar, skeleton keys, digital videocam, digital still camera, laser listening device, rope, string, duct tape, and as many varied tools as the zipper would allow.

Traffic in the area was extremely light. Aware of the pounding in his chest, Ben slipped the drawings of Glenn into the outside pocket of his bag and pulled on his Cubs cap, brim low. Then he turned off the interior light of his aging Range Rover and silently opened the door. For one of the rare times in his years as a private investigator, he was actually investigating.

Scattered cars were parked on the street in front of a featureless mélange of auto-body and welding shops, garages, and warehouses—some concrete, some corrugated metal, and some wood. The buildings themselves were separated from the road by narrow sidewalks in ill repair, and from one another by narrow alleyways. Potholes, most of them filled with muddy rainwater, were as much a part of the roadway as the pavement was.

Staying on the sidewalk and in the shadows of the buildings, Ben turned onto Laurel Way. Having visited an RV center just south of Chicago to get a look at a thirty-nine-foot Adventurer, Ben was relieved to find that the street was wider than most of the others in the area. He was still questioning whether or not a bus-sized vehicle could swing into any of the structures, when he noticed a vacant, trash-strewn lot across from a faded, peeling, wood-framed building. The place was two stories high, maybe even three, and somewhere in its history might have been a barn. Facing the road was a massive pair of sliders on a metal track, quite large enough to admit an RV. If there was a 4A on Laurel Way, and if it housed a thirty-nine-foot mobile home, this really had to be the place. Also, he reasoned, someplace

around the building there had to be a
pedestrian door.

Ignoring the persistent drizzle, Ben cautiously made his way along the three-foot
space between the building and the one to
his left. There was a single, eye-level window
midway, but a curtain of some kind was
drawn. On the street parallel to Laurel Way,
there were no doors or windows, just a
broad, shingled façade, rising twenty-five
feet to a sharply peaked roof. He checked
the street, then started back toward Laurel
Way on the other side of the building, using
the hooded flashlight to illuminate the dark,
narrow alleyway. Halfway along that wall he
found the door he sensed had to exist. It was
solid, paneled wood, with a lock and knob
that had clearly been added recently.

Shortly after his decision to become a PI,
Ben had attended a detectives-only class on
identifying and negotiating locks of all kinds.
Included in the pricey tuition was a syllabus,
some credit card–like slabs of plastic cut in
various shapes, and a ring of twenty heavy
wires bent at odd angles and named Taggert
Wires after the man who invented them. For
a while after the course, he practiced on the
locks of his apartment, as well as those on

the doors of many of his friends and neighbors, and actually became quite proficient at selecting and manipulating the right wire. But that was it for the grand adventure. Over the ensuing years, he hadn't had cause to use the wires even once, until now.

Virtually invisible in the dark passageway, he crouched by the door and listened with his stethoscope against it for several minutes. Not a sound. Finally, he set to work with the Taggert Wires. It took tries with three different wires before he felt the tip of one catch and hold. A turn to the right and the lock gave way. Even before his eyes adapted to the near-perfect darkness, Ben knew.

The thirty-nine-foot Adventurer was there, just ten feet away, stretching nearly from one end of the building to the other. He slipped inside, silently pulled the door shut behind him, and dropped to one knee on the concrete floor, trying to will his heart to beat slower and at least a little softer. When the din had finally lessened, he once again eased the flashlight from his bag and panned the beam around.

The gleaming RV, door closed, curtained windows dark, was in sharp contrast to the cluttered, rough-hewn space in which it was garaged. Ben noted that Schyler Gaines's recollection about there being no windows in the back was accurate. The fifteen or twenty feet above the vehicle were open to the barn-board ceiling, save for several beams crossing just above its air-conditioning unit, antennae, and what looked like a satellite dish. To Ben's left was a tall set of shelves packed with brushes, rags, and a dozen or more gallon and spray cans of paint. To his right were stacks of cleaning and automotive supplies. Beyond the supplies, though, was something much more interesting—a short staircase, which led up to what looked like a small, enclosed office with two large glass windows facing inward.

He headed for the office, trying to ignore the niggling thought that the more intelligent of his fictional role models probably wouldn't have elected to be alone here in the first place. Clutching the leather case, he made his way quietly up the stairs, which felt surprisingly sturdy. Through the glass, he could see a desk and chair, two-drawer filing cabinet, fax machine, copier, and a computer. The two walls without windows were unadorned, and the office door was locked.

Ben shut off the flashlight and knelt in the

darkness on the topmost step, waiting again for his pulse to slow and the paralysis of his limbs to let up. He had always wanted to view himself as adventurous, but he knew that compared to most of his friends over the years, he had really never been that much of a risk-taker.

So what in the hell was he doing here?

The lock on the office door was no match for the Taggert Wires, and in less than a minute he was inside, using the hooded flash in short bursts and trying to convince himself that the precaution of turning it off and on was unnecessary. Finally, he gave in and kept it lit, albeit below his waist. There were a few papers on the desk, but none was any more interesting or incriminating than a fantasy baseball league score sheet and a few bills related to the RV.

The file cabinet, standard Office Max or Staples, was locked. Rather than waste time with the wires, Ben took a heavy screwdriver and popped the drawers open. The top one of them was completely empty except for several old sports page sections from the *Cincinnati Enquirer,* and a dog-eared copy of *Hustler.* The bottom drawer was something else again. It was virtually filled with guns—revolvers, pistols, and one snub-nosed submachine gun, plus a dozen or more boxes of ammunition and three hand grenades. For a full minute, Ben stared down at the cache, his sensible self screaming that he was in well over his head and needed to get out of the place and far away as quickly as possible.

Perhaps some sort of anonymous tip to the police about guns and terrorists would get a response, or maybe one of his friends on the Chicago force would have an idea of what he should do next. But neither of those actions was likely to address the still-unanswered question of whether, in fact, this RV had something to do with illicit bone marrow theft or anything else in which Alice Gustafson might be interested.

Ben flicked off the light again and stared down through the window and the darkness at the silhouette of the massive Adventurer. Assuming the door to the RV was locked, was there any percentage in trying to get inside? There had to be a security device of some sort in play. Perhaps the best move was to leave and return with someone who could handle that. Offhand he could think of two men he knew who were skilled enough to fill the bill.

Having made his decision, he turned and was about to leave the office when, as almost an afterthought, he pulled the single wide desk drawer open and shined his flash inside. There were more invoices relative to the Winnebago, and some off-color printouts from the Internet. He was flipping through the invoices when he noticed, still in the drawer, a three-by-five file card clipped to a photo—a small, three-by-three color headshot, slightly blurry, but totally distinguishable.

Ben caught his breath.

Although there was no need to confirm the identity of the man, he did so anyway. The likeness to the first of Madame Sonja's renderings was remarkable. From a mass of shattered bone and torn flesh, she had reconstructed this man's face almost perfectly. Written on the file card, in a heavy, masculine hand, was: *Lonnie Durkin, Little Farm, Pugsley Hill Road, Conda, Idaho.*

Ben's tense smile was bittersweet. After so many days and so many miles, the man he had dubbed Glenn now had a real name and an address. But for a family in Idaho, there was great sadness in store.

Ben slipped the photo and card into his pocket and quietly exited the office. At the bottom of the stairs, he hesitated, then approached the mobile home and stood in the silent darkness in front of the door, debating. He had what he had come for, his sensible self reasoned. Why push things? Even if there was a security system and he tripped the alarm, his suddenly emboldened self countered, he could race out to his car and be headed out of town before anyone responded to it.

He opened the door to the alley just a crack and set his tool bag beside it. Feeling vaguely detached from himself, he returned to the Adventurer and gently tried the handle. The door opened, but not in the way he expected. It was viciously kicked open from the inside, striking Ben square in the face and driving him back, dazed, onto his butt. Momentarily blinded by the interior light, all he could see was the silhouette, lit from behind, of a large, narrow-waisted man, whose shoulders virtually filled the doorway.

"You were right!" the man said to someone inside the RV. "There *was* someone out here!"

Laughing, the man leapt from the stairs, and in the same motion, though barefooted, kicked Ben viciously in the chest and up to his jaw, snapping his teeth together with the sound of a drummer's rim shot. Ben, who had just made it to his knees, slammed back into the shelves of paint, scattering the cans noisily across the concrete. Stunned, he rolled to one side, catching enough of a look to see a man in shorts and a black tee, with shoulder-length blond hair. Before he could take in any more, he was kicked again, this time in the side of his chest. His breath burst out as pain exploded from his ribs. From within his body, he was certain he heard the snapping of bone.

The agony in his chest was nearly disabling, and blood was cascading from his nose into his mouth and down the back of his throat. His tumbling, ill-focused thoughts searched desperately for something he could do, some weapon he could use, or some convincing story that would fit the circumstances and at least slow down the onslaught. That was the instant his hand hit against a spray can of paint. The top of the can had apparently been knocked off.

"Connie, get the fuck out here and turn the lights on!" the bull hollered, bending down, grabbing Ben's jacket, and pulling him up like a puppet.

Praying at once that there was paint in the can and that the nozzle opening was pointing in the right direction, Ben was still being hauled upright when he swung the can to within six inches of his assailant's eyes and fired. The results were all that he could have hoped for. Instantly, thick, dark paint filled both of the man's sockets. Shouting obscenities, he reeled backward, pawing at his eyes. Ben had already reached the door when the behemoth slammed onto the steps of the RV.

"Jesus, Vincent!" a woman's voice cried out, but Ben, hauling his bag along, was already in the alley, hobbling painfully toward Laurel Way.

CHAPTER 10

No human thing is of serious importance.
—PLATO, *The Republic,* Book X

The first thing Joe Anson became aware of was the steady swoosh of the respirator, gently forcing air into his disease-ravaged lungs. The second was the white-noise thrum of the jet engine. They were airborne and on their way east, more than four thousand miles from Cameroon, to a surgical team awaiting him in Amritsar, India. His years-long, worsening struggle to breathe was very nearly over.

Anson knew the endotracheal tube was in place down his throat, but it didn't bother him much. It had to be medication, he reasoned—some sort of narcotic with a little sedative and just a pinch or two of memory eraser thrown in. Psychopharmacology was becoming more and more like the military's smart bombs—able to pinpoint targets in the brain with ever-increasing accuracy. Whatever the nature of the drugs, the combination he was being given was working. He was experiencing none of the choking, strangulating sensation so many intubated patients complained about.

What he was experiencing at that moment were overriding feelings of relief, wrapped around a profound sadness—relief that the ordeal of his pulmonary fibrosis was almost over, and sadness that it required the death of a man for him to reach this point.

It was then that he realized that Elizabeth St. Pierre was sitting quietly beside the stretcher, her hand wrapped around his. He turned his head slightly to see her, and nodded that he was aware of the situation. Her expression was more peaceful than he had ever seen it, almost beatific.

"Hello, Joseph," she said softly in French. Then she continued in English, the language in which he was more comfortable. "I have tapered the sedation down just for a little while so you could wake up and know everything is all right. In fact, everything is going perfectly. We're more than halfway there. Well before we arrive, everything will be in place. The pulmonary transplant surgeons who are being brought in to perform this operation are the best in the world. Do you understand?"

Anson nodded and then made the motion of writing.

"Oh, yes, of course," St. Pierre said. "How foolish of me. I have some paper right here."

She handed him a clipboard and a pen.

Have you learned any more about the man who is soon to save my life? Anson wrote.

"No more than we already know. The man is—*was*—thirty-nine. A week or so ago, he suffered the rupture of an aneurysm in his brain. Bleeding was massive, and there wasn't anything that could be done to save him. He has been pronounced brain-dead by the physicians at the Central Hospital in Amritsar, and has been maintained on life support pending the donation of his heart, lungs, eyes, liver, kidneys, pancreas, and bone. Many will live because of this gallant man, including you."

Does he have a family?

"I know he has a wife. It is she who has given permission, indeed, who has *requested* that these transplants go ahead."

Children?

"I don't know. I will find out."

Good. I wish to do something for the family.

"All in due time, Joseph. If they will accept our gratitude in any tangible way, I will be certain they are well compensated."

I will wish to meet my savior's widow.

"If that is possible, I shall make it happen. Now please, my friend, you must rest."

Wait.

"Yes?"

Has Sarah been notified?

"Not yet."

Contact her before I go into the operating room. Tell her I love her.

"I will do my best to locate them and tell her."

I am afraid of dying before my work is done.

"That is nonsense. You *were* facing death. In fact, as you remember, your breathing stopped altogether. But now you will live and be healthy. We have a perfect match,

Joseph—a twelve-point match. That is one in a million. No, no, given your unusual protein pattern and blood type, one in ten million. You will not die."

I will not die, he wrote.

"Now rest, Joseph. Rest and dream of a life where the air is sweet and fragrant and rich with oxygen as only jungle air can be, and you can get as much of it into your body as you want."

Elizabeth took away the clipboard and kissed him tenderly on the forehead. Then Anson saw her take up his intravenous line and inject something into the rubber port. In just seconds, he felt a wave of warmth and serenity sweep over him.

Anson opened his eyes and saw the gleaming giant saucer lights of the operating room shining overhead. The scent of disinfectant was in the air. The temperature in the room was rather cool, and involuntarily, he shuddered.

"Dr. Anson," a reassuring male voice, Indian, speaking fluent, accented English, said, "I am Dr. Sanjay Khanduri. You are doing very well, and so are we. Your new lung is here and we are ready to put it in place.

We will transplant only one lung. The other will go to a person also in desperate need. In a very short time, the volume of your new lung will expand in such a way that you will be able to function as if you had two. I assure you, Dr. Anson, that I am very, very good at performing this procedure. In fact, if I were going to have this operation done, I would be sad because it wouldn't be me doing it." Khanduri's laugh was high-pitched and merry. "Okay, then, Dr. Anson," he went on, "just close your eyes and in your mind count with me backward from ten. When you awake you will be a new man. Ready? Ten . . . nine . . ."

CHAPTER 11

Some of you have the power of command, and in the composition of these God has mingled gold, . . . others he has made of silver, to be auxiliaries. . . . . others again who are to be husbandmen and crafts-men he has composed of brass and iron.
—PLATO, *The Republic,* Book III

Where are we going?"

"You said the Inter-Continental. This is the quick way."

"I don't want the quick way. I want to go back on the highway."

"You are a very beautiful woman."

"Take me back to the highway this minute!"

"Very beautiful."

The cab accelerates. The area around us deteriorates. What streetlights there are have been smashed. Most of the houses are shuttered. Almost nobody is on the street.

I am more frightened every second. I try to see the cabbie's license, but it is too dark. Something terrible is going on. Something terrible. Is there anything I can use as a weapon? Anything at all I can do?

"Goddamn it! Take me back to the highway."

"The customers at the House of Love will adore you. You will be very happy there. . . . Very happy there. . . . Very happy there. . . ."

I am more terrified than I have ever been. I have heard of women being kidnapped and then addicted to narcotics and used in whorehouses. I have heard of women vanishing, never to be heard from again. The scene around me continues to blur then comes back into focus. It is so real one moment, so surreal the next. I need to get out. No matter how fast we are going, I need to get out of this cab. I can run. If I can just get out without hurting my legs, I can run faster than this bastard . . . faster than anyone. I will not be anyone's crack whore. Not ever. I would kill myself

first. My passport. I need my passport and
my wallet. I take them out of my purse and
jam them into my jacket pocket.

"Money. I'll give you money to let me
out right here. Three thousand reais. I
have three thousand reais. Just let me
go!"

I reach for the door handle and prepare
myself to hit the pavement at forty miles
an hour. But before I can move, the cab
screeches to a halt, throwing me hard
against the back of the passenger seat.
What is happening? Again, the scene
blurs. The movement around me is indistinct. Suddenly the door is ripped open. A
large man reaches in and grabs me. I
fight, but he is very strong. A black nylon
stocking covers his face. I try tearing at
the mask, but a second man is on me. His
face is also covered. His breath smells
terribly of fish and garlic. Before I can react, a syringe appears in his hand. The
heavier man tightens his grip on me. No!
Please no! Don't!

The needle is jammed down into the
muscle at the base of my neck. I scream,
but hear no sound. Heroin. It must be
heroin. This can't be happening to me.

The cab peels away, spraying dirt and stones. I feel weak and disconnected from the two men. My mind is spinning, trying desperately to sort things out. But that effort confuses me even more. It is still too soon for any drug to take effect. Don't let this happen. Keep fighting. Kick and punch and try to bite. Don't give in. Don't let this happen.

They have my arms now and are dragging me facedown through the dirt of an alley. I can smell the garbage. I twist and kick violently, and suddenly my right arm is free. The smaller man's groin is inches away. I punch him there with all the strength I have. He cries out and falls. Now I am on my feet, gasping for breath, terrified and angry. Goddamn animals!

Get away! Get away from them before the drug kicks in. The larger man comes at me. I punch him in the face. He stumbles backward. Run! Run! Down the alley is the only way to go.

There are buildings all around—one story, two, some even three. The details are vague and indistinct, yet I clearly see a light wink on in one of the windows. Everything is blurry now. I feel detached . . . distant . . . surreal. The drug must be kicking in.

"I have a pistol. Stop right now or I will shoot!"

My legs are fueled by terror. I would rather die than live as they plan. Ignore the gun. Just run! Run, damn it!

My body responds. I'm running . . . running as hard as I can.

Oh, God, the alley's blocked. A pile of trash and garbage and barrels and cardboard boxes . . . and a fence. There's a fence! I can make it. I can make it over the trash and the fence. I've got to.

From behind me I hear a shot. No pain. I wasn't hit. I can make it. Leg up onto the top of the fence. Almost there. Another shot. Burning pain in my back on the right. Oh, God! I've been shot. No! This can't be happening. . . .

"Dr. Santoro, I think she is waking up."

Another shot. More pain. No! I don't want to die. . . .

"She is waking up!"

The woman's words, spoken in Portuguese, forced themselves into Natalie's consciousness, dispelling the terrible images from the alley.

This has to be real. . . . I must be alive.

"Miss, wake up. Wake up and meet us. Just nod your head if you hear me. Good, good. Don't try and open your eyes yet. We have them covered."

Natalie could understand enough of the woman's Portuguese to interpret it. Still, she felt unable to speak.

"Dr. Santoro, she hears us."

"Well, well. Our dove begins to spread her wings." A man's voice—deep and calming. "Perhaps soon the great mystery will be over. Turn off the lights and we shall uncover her eyes. Miss, can you hear me? Please squeeze my hand if you can hear me."

"I . . . am . . . American," Natalie heard her strained, hoarse voice say in somewhat awkward Portuguese. "I . . . do not . . . speak . . . Portuguese . . . very well."

She felt extremely vague and hungover, but one at a time, her senses were checking in. There was a pounding in her temples and behind her eyes that was extremely unpleasant, but bearable. The smell of isopropyl alcohol and disinfectant was distinctively hospital. The institutional texture of the sheets supported that conclusion. Then she became aware of the oxygen prongs in her nose. The message from her senses blended with the all-too-clear memories of being assaulted, nearly escaping, and then being shot in the back.

"Actually, it sounds as if your Portuguese is quite good," the man said in accented English, "but I will try and accommodate you. I am Dr. Xavier Santoro. You are a patient in the Santa Teresa Hospital in Rio de Janeiro. You have been a patient here for a number of days. The lights have now been turned off. I will take the pads from your eyes, but I will have to replace them soon. Your corneas were quite scratched, the right more than the left. They have responded nicely to treatment, but they are not all better. After I remove the pads, please open your eyes intermittently to allow them some time to adjust. If you have any significant discomfort, we will immediately replace the patches."

The tape, holding pads over Natalie's eyes, was gently pulled away. She kept her lids closed for a minute as she tested her hands and feet, then her arms and legs. Her joints were piteously stiff, but they all seemed to be working. *No paralysis.* Her hand brushed across a urinary catheter, which suggested she had been in Santa Teresa's for some time. Cautiously, she opened her eyes. The room was dimly lit from fluorescent light flowing in from the corridor outside her door. The glare was unpleasant, but objects quickly came into focus. An IV was draining into her left forearm. There was an ornate crucifix over the doorway. There were no windows on the three walls she could see.

Dr. Xavier Santoro, wearing scrubs and a surgical coat, gazed down at her benignly. His face was scholarly, long and narrow with a prominent nose and wire-rimmed glasses, and from where she lay, he seemed quite tall.

"I . . . I was shot," she said. "Am I all right?"

"Here, let me help you up in bed a bit."

Santoro pulled her up toward the head of the bed, then raised it forty-five degrees.

"I'm a medical student . . . a senior medical student in Boston. . . . My name is Natalie Reyes. . . . A taxi driver took me from the airport to an alley and . . . am I all right?"

Santoro inhaled deeply and exhaled slowly.

"You were found in an alley with only your panties on, Miss Reyes. No bra. As you said, you had been shot twice—twice in the back on the right. We estimate you were there, lying unconscious beneath a pile of trash in the alley, for two days. You lost a good deal of blood. This is midwinter here in Brazil. The temperature at night has been less than ten degrees Celsius—not freezing, but cold enough."

"What day was I brought in here?"

Santoro consulted her bedside chart.

"The eighteenth."

"I flew in on the fifteenth . . . and was attacked on the way from the airport, so it was three days. . . . What day is it now?"

"It is the twenty-seventh, a Wednesday. You have been in a coma since your arrival—probably from the prolonged exposure, shock, and infection. We had no idea who you were."

"Nobody called the police . . . looking for me?"

"Not as far as we know. The police have been here, though. They will want to come back and get a statement from you."

"I feel short of breath."

Santoro took her hand.

"That is understandable," he said, "but I promise you that symptom will improve with time."

"With time?"

Santoro hesitated.

"You were quite ill when you were brought in," he said finally, "badly dehydrated and in shock. Your right lung had collapsed completely from the gunshots and the bleeding into your chest. There was life-threatening infection. . . . I'm sorry to have to tell you this, but with the bullet wounds and infection we could not reinflate the lung and your vital signs were slipping. The decision was made that to save your life, the lung had to be removed."

"Removed?"

Natalie felt a sudden wave of nausea sweep over her. She began to hyperventilate. Bile swept up into her throat. *My lung.*

"We had no choice," Santoro was saying.

"No, this can't be."

"But on the positive side, you have made a remarkable recovery to date."

"I was an athlete," she managed to say. "A . . . a runner."

Please . . . please let this be a dream.

Images of herself dragging ahead using a walker swirled through her brain. *My lung!* She would be a pulmonary cripple forever, never to run again, always short of breath. She tried chastising herself for not responding to the fact that these people had saved her life, but all she could focus on was that life as she had known it was over.

"An athlete," Santoro said. "Well, that explains your response to the surgery. I am sure this is a terrible shock to you, but take it from a chest surgeon, Miss Reyes, having this operation does not mean you will no longer be able to run. With time your left lung will compensate and your breathing capacity will increase to the point where it could come close to equaling what you could do with both lungs."

"Oh, God. I can't believe this."

"Perhaps you would like us to contact someone back home?"

"Oh, yes, yes. I have family who must be frantic with worry. Dr. Santoro, I'm sorry for not sounding more appreciative to you and everyone for saving my life. I just can't believe what's happened."

"It is normal in situations like this. Believe me. But your life will not be altered nearly as drastically as you think."

"I . . . hope so. Thank you."

"When you are able, we have some hospital business to attend to. You were in the intensive care unit for several days, but because the hospital has been filled to over-flowing, you have been moved to the building we call the annex. It is not connected to the actual hospital. Estella will be in to take some information for billing and for our records."

"I have insurance that will cover every-thing. . . . I can get the policy number when I call home."

"We do a great deal of charity work here at Santa Teresa's, but we certainly appreci-ate it when we can get paid. We have a small rehabilitation room here in the annex, and we would like to get you up on the treadmill or the bicycle as soon as possible."

Natalie recalled the countless hours she spent in physical therapy rehabbing her torn Achilles. Would this rehabilitation be as bad? It was probably normal after a trauma like this, but she wasn't able even to consider the prospect of recovery. First the suspension from school, now this. *How could this have happened?*

"A phone?" she asked.

"Of course. I'll have Estella take care of that also."

"I wonder if you could stay around. . . . I'm going to call my professor, Dr. Douglas

Berenger. . . . Maybe you could speak with him."

"The cardiac surgeon in Boston?"

"Yes, you know him?"

"I know *of* him. He is regarded as one of the very best in his field."

"I work in his lab."

Natalie had neither the desire nor the wind to go into the reason for her ill-fated trip to Brazil. All she really wanted, in fact, was to get home as soon as possible.

"You must be a very brilliant student," Santoro said. "Wait here, we'll get the phone. Also, the police have asked to be notified if—when—you woke up. They would like to take a statement from you as soon as you are strong enough to give one. And I must replace those eye patches."

"I don't feel any pain."

"We have used numbing drops."

"I will tell the police what I know . . . but it isn't much."

"Contrary to what we Brazilians often hear when we travel, our Military Police are quite efficient and effective."

"Even so," Natalie replied, "I doubt they'll have much success with this case."

* * *

. . . I reach for the door handle and prepare myself to hit the pavement at forty miles an hour. But before I can move, the cab screeches to a halt, throwing me hard against the back of the passenger seat. What is happening? Again, the scene blurs. The movement around me is indistinct. Suddenly the door is ripped open. A large man reaches in and grabs me. I fight, but he is very strong. A black nylon mask covers his face. I try tearing at the mask, but a second man is on me. His face is also covered. Before I can react a syringe appears in his hand. No! Please no! Don't!

As in the past, Natalie was at once both a participant and an observer in the events that were so radically altering her life. She was a prisoner of her memory, watching and feeling, terrifyingly involved yet strangely detached, and above all powerless to escape the scenario or to alter the outcome. As always, the cab driver's voice was as distinct as his appearance was blurred. He might be sitting next to her and she wouldn't have recognized him, but if he said just one word, she would know.

. . . The alley's blocked with trash and

garbage and cardboard boxes . . . and a fence. . . .

An unwilling captive, Natalie, as always, ran from her masked pursuers and clambered over the boxes and trash, and heard the shots and felt the pain, and collapsed into blackness. Then, as had often happened, a voice wedged itself into the hideous experience. This time, the voice was a familiar one.

"Nat, it's me, Doug. Can you hear me?"

"Oh, thank God. Thank God you're here."

"You're at the airport, Nat, ready to fly home. They gave you something to knock you out for the transfer and the ambulance ride out here. It should wear off in just a few minutes."

"How . . . long since I called you?"

"It's less than twenty-four hours since we spoke. I came down on a medevac flight to get you. The school has consented to pay for whatever your insurance doesn't."

"Thank you. . . . Oh, thank you. This is terrible."

"I know, Nat. I know it is. But you're alive, and your brain is intact, and take it from me, your body will improve more than you can imagine. Emily Trotter from Anesthesia is here with me just in case. She's waiting in the plane. Terry's here, too."

"Nothing could keep me from coming, Nat," Millwood's comforting voice said. "We have to get you home so we can go running again. I've told everyone who would listen about how you ran away from those arrogant high-school track stars. Now I need some more stories."

He stroked her forehead and then squeezed her hand.

"Nat, we're all so sorry for what's happened," Berenger said. "We've been worried sick."

"The policeman who came to interview me . . . said that no one had called."

"That's nonsense. I even had one of the Boston police who's originally from Brazil call them."

"The one who interviewed me . . . couldn't get away fast enough. . . . It was like he just didn't care."

"Well, we certainly called and called."

"Thank you."

"Dr. Santoro says you're strong and your recovery has been astonishing—a miracle, he calls it. He says your left lung is doing incredibly well, and your body is compensating beautifully for the loss of the other one."

"My eyes . . ."

"I spoke to the ophthalmologist. They're covered because you've had some temporary damage to your corneas from exposure in that alley. He said that if your discomfort isn't too bad, we could remove the patches for good when we have you settled on board. We'll have someone from the eye service go over you as soon as we get home."

Natalie felt the stretcher begin to roll across the tarmac. In just a few minutes, she had been transferred to one inside the plane. Moments later, her eye pads were removed. Berenger, stethoscope in place, was listening to her chest.

"Doing great," he said.

Natalie reached up and touched his face.

"I never got to present our paper."

"That's okay. You can do it next year."

"That depends. Where's the meeting?"

Berenger grinned.

"Paris," he said. "Now get some rest. Everything's going to be all right."

* * *

As always, the conference call of the Guardian council took place on Tuesday at precisely noon, Greenwich mean time.

"This is Laertes."

"Simonides, here."

"Themistocles. Greetings from Australia."

"Glaucon."

"Polemarchus."

"The meeting is called to order," Laertes said. "I have heard from Aspasia. The operation on A has been a complete success. The match was twelve out of twelve, so only minimal drugs will be required, if any at all. Aspasia expects A to be back at work within two weeks. His prognosis is for a full recovery and unimpaired life span."

"Well done."

"Marvelous."

"Other cases?"

"Polemarchus here. We might as well start with me. This coming week we have two kidneys, one liver, and one heart scheduled. The recipients have each already been certified as worthy of our services, and all necessary arrangements—logistical and financial—have been taken care of. In the case of kidneys, the procedure would usually result in the transplantation of both kidneys into our recipient. The liver would result in transplantation of the largest organ segment anatomically possible. Let's consider the kidneys first. Twenty-seven-year-old male laborer, Mississippi, United States."

"Approved," all five called out in unison.

"Forty-year-old female restaurant owner, Toronto, Canada."

"What sort of restaurant?"

"Chinese."

"Approved," they all said as one, and laughed.

"The liver, a thirty-five-year-old male teacher from Wales."

"Glaucon, here. I thought we agreed no teachers. Have we any options?"

"None that I know of," Polemarchus said, "although I can check again. This is a perfect twelve-point match for L, number thirty-one on your lists. As you probably know, he is one of the wealthiest men in Great Britain. I do not know what he has agreed to pay for this procedure, but knowing the way Xerxes negotiates, I would guess it was substantial."

"In that case," Glaucon said, "approved, but let us not make this a precedent."

"Approved," the others echoed.

CHAPTER 12

A State . . . arises . . . out of the needs of mankind.

—PLATO, *The Republic,* Book II

Althea Satterfield bustled around Ben's small kitchen to the extent that her years allowed.

"Would you like lemon with your tea, Mr. Callahan? You don't have any in your refrigerator, but I do in mine."

Ben was impressed that his neighbor chose not to remark on those other food items that he also did not have in his refrigerator—virtually all, in fact. It had been three days since his return from Cincinnati, and the octogenarian had interpreted his two blackened eyes as a call to action, along with his swollen nose—"Just a crack at the tip," Dr. Banks had said. "Nothing to do for it but don't get hit there again"—and unremitting pain in his chest—"Just a crack in one of your ribs. Nothing to do for it but don't get hit there again." The truth was that as frustrating as the woman could be sometimes, Ben was grateful for the help. The headaches he was experiencing, which Banks was attributing to a concussion—"Nothing to do for it but don't get hit there again"—had diminished from an eight to somewhere around a four, and from present all the time to present only when he moved. He had never been very macho when it came to dealing with any sort of pain, and at the moment he was exhausted from coping with his various discomforts, and more than a little annoyed at being inactive. There were things he needed and wanted to do.

"I'll take the tea straight up, Mrs. Satterfield. I really appreciate your help. I only wish I could find a way to repay you."

"Nonsense, dear. Just wait until you're my age. You'll be desperate to matter to somebody."

Don't bank on it, Ben thought.

The quixotic dedication of Alice Gustafson, the draining week in Florida, the remarkable encounter with Madame Sonja, the surprisingly lucid Schyler Gaines, the close call on Laurel Way, and finally the identification of Lonnie Durkin—granted each had made a dent in his armor of detachment and ennui, but he saw those dents as insignificant. He had done what he had been hired to do, and mostly he still planned to crawl back into his cocoon until the next call came along. Before he did that, however, there was one final loose end he wanted to tie up—this one involving a family in Conda, Idaho.

"Well, Mrs. Satterfield," he said, "if you really mean that, I could use another favor."

"Just name it, dear."

"I have to go away again. I need you to feed Pincus and water my—what I mean is I need you to feed and water Pincus."

"Pardon me for saying so, Mr. Callahan, but you're in no condition to travel."

"Probably not, but travel I must anyway."

The continuous, stabbing pain in his side, made worse by even minor movement, he could handle. But until today, the headaches had made a trip to Idaho impossible. After his return from six hours with Dr. Banks and the radiologists, a concerned Alice Gustafson, bearing a vase of wildflowers, had visited

him at his apartment. Over tea and Danish,
courtesy of Althea, he recounted in minute
detail the findings and subsequent assault in
the garage on Laurel Way.

"I knew it!" she exclaimed when he had
finished. "I knew that woman in Maine was
telling me the truth. You can tell these
things." Her grim expression held an odd
mix of vindication and toughness. "The guns
worry me greatly," she went on, "but they do
not surprise me. Where there is illegal organ trade of any kind, there is very big business, with very high price tags. Many of
those involved in the trade are little more
than gangsters."

"Most of the gangsters I know would be
envious of the weapons in that garage."

"There is really no estimating the money
involved. In certain countries, those who go
abroad to receive illegal kidneys are reimbursed up to one hundred thousand dollars
by their health ministries. They ultimately
save the system much more than that in
dialysis fees and other medical costs, and
also make the transplant waiting list for kidneys that much shorter, thereby lowering the
dialysis expenses even more."

"I would imagine those needing a bone

marrow transplant would be in even more desperate medical straits."

"Exactly. It's always under the sword of life and death that the procedure is done. And of all the organs, the one demanding the closest tissue match between donor and recipient is bone marrow. I can't help but wonder if these people are dealing with other organs as well."

"I wouldn't be surprised. Whatever they *are* into, those guns I saw say they're deadly serious about it. Speaking of deadly, why do you think the RV people didn't just kill Lonnie and the woman from Maine?"

Gustafson shrugged.

"Maybe they draw the line at murder," she said. "Or maybe they keep these people alive in case they have to repeat the procedure. Remember, the woman said she was blindfolded or drugged most of the time. She recalled few details of what happened to her, so maybe there was just no need to kill her."

"Or maybe they purposely choose people whom the authorities aren't likely to believe."

"That's a theory, except that if these RV people know what they're doing, the completeness of the tissue match is all that matters."

"How many perfect matches does each person have?"

"Perfect, not very many—especially if the recipient has type O blood and an unusually rare protein or two on their white blood cells."

Initially, Gustafson wanted to call Lonnie Durkin's family on the spot, but Ben insisted he be allowed to go there in person.

"I feel like I need to do this," was all he could say.

"You're not fit to go anyplace."

"I will be. Give me three or four days."

"Why the sudden zeal, Mr. Callahan? I really don't have much left to pay you with."

"It's not about money, Professor. It's, I don't really know . . . maybe it's about closure."

"I see. . . . Well, please don't be embarrassed by those feelings, Mr. Callahan. Many of our supporters find that the more they understand of what is going on in the world, the more their fog of skepticism burns off." She handed him an envelope. "You've done an excellent job. Someday maybe we'll be in a position to keep you on a retainer. Now, what do you want to do about the Winnebago?"

"I don't think the guy in the van who did all this to me could be certain whether I was a detective of some sort or just a run-of-the-mill burglar," Ben said. "In fact, I don't think he even got a good look at my face before I blacked out his eyes. It was quite dark in that garage. If cops show up there now, that's it. The people who own that Winnebago will be alerted that I wasn't just a petty thief."

"But Lonnie Durkin is dead because of them. If we chose to do nothing and someone else got hurt, or . . . or worse, I for one would be terribly upset."

"Okay, okay. Point made." Ben thought for a time, then offered, "How about if I go online and also make some calls to people I know, and see if I can locate a PI in Cincinnati who has some connections on the force? He can make sure the RV is still there, and then bring the cops in with a warrant to search for weapons or some such."

"I'm afraid we don't have any money left to pay him," Gustafson said.

Ben held up the Organ Guard check.

"I do."

It took a painful trip to the office and more than twenty-four hours for Ben to connect with a PI in Cincinnati who was willing to do what they needed for what he could afford. The man's name was Arnie Dolan, and it didn't take long for him to complete his investigation.

"It's gone," he said, calling back after just a couple of hours.

"The van?"

"That, too, but I mean the garage. Burned to the ground yesterday. The charred remains are still smoldering. Took another building down with it. Three alarms."

"Do the police know it's arson?"

"Clumsy arson, they're calling it. Apparently they found a gas can."

"That *would* be just a bit suspicious," Ben said, wondering if the response meant the people in and around the van knew he wasn't just a burglar, or if they were merely taking stringent precautions. Either way, when he found the photo of Lonnie Durkin, he knew he simply should have tiptoed out of the garage and driven off.

Even in the stable cocoon of his Range Rover, there wouldn't have been enough Tylenol and Motrin in the state to enable Ben to drive the sixteen hundred miles from Chicago to Conda, Idaho. The town was just north of Soda Springs, which was fifty-seven miles south and east of Pocatello, which was in the southeast corner of the state, not a hundred miles from both Wyoming and Utah. Instead, he flew into Pocatello via Minneapolis and rented a Blazer.

The money from Organ Guard had already melted like spring snow, and his bills remained virtually unchanged—at least until the mailman's next delivery. Perhaps when he got back to Chicago, he would put some sort of ad in one of the local papers. For the moment, though, he was where he should be, doing something that, in truth, he wanted to do.

Throughout the trip, he continued to wonder why the inventor of the elastic rib belt had never been awarded a Nobel prize. His headache had become manageable, and his nostrils had actually begun to admit some air. But the rib fracture was something else again. Dr. Banks had assured him that only one rib was cracked, and that there was no displacement of either of the two pieces, but after almost six days, Ben still refused to believe it. Even with the miraculous rib belt strapped on, most movements were still broadcast to his pain center in Dolby Surround Sound, but without the elastic splint, even shallow breaths were a challenge.

No matter what the pain, though, it did not measure up to the emotional ache at the prospect of having to sit with a mother and father and tell them that their son was dead. Not wanting to upset Lonnie Durkin's family for too long, but also unwilling simply to show up unannounced at Little Farm, Ben called from the airport in Pocatello. Lonnie's mother, Karen, did not press him to say over the phone that her son was dead, but it was clear to Ben that in her heart, she knew. They set a time when he would meet with her and her husband, and she gave him directions to their farm. Then, after a brief stop in Soda Springs to compose himself, take a few Motrin, register at the Hooper Springs bed-and-breakfast, and pass some time joylessly viewing the impressive geyser at Hooper Springs Park, Ben turned onto Route 34 and drove north to the hamlet of Conda.

Sleepy, peaceful, and very small, Conda reminded him eerily of Curtisville, Florida, home of Schyler Gaines and his gas station. He tried to imagine the massive Adventurer, with Vincent at the wheel and Connie perched on the thronelike passenger seat, gliding through the town like a hungry great white on a reef, searching for Pugsley Hill Road and the man whose cells, they somehow knew, were a near-perfect match for those of a person twenty-five hundred miles away.

Karen Durkin's directions brought Ben onto a long, dry dirt road that knifed through a vast tableland of grain fields. He wondered where, in the flatness, Pugsley Hill could possibly be. After nearly two miles, the fields gave way to corrals, stables, and some horses. Beyond the corrals was a large, rust-red barn, and across from that a prim, white two-story home, perched on a modest rise. A wooden sign arching over the drive announced it to be Little Farm.

Karen Durkin and her husband, Ray, were waiting anxiously on their narrow front porch. Both were in their fifties, but might have been a decade older. Their faces were weathered and honest, and spoke of years of hard work in an often harsh and unpredictable profession. Ray's handshake was firm and his hands callused, but the soft sadness in his eyes was inestimable.

"Lonnie's dead?" he asked before they had even entered the house.

Ben nodded.

"I'm truly sorry," he managed.

Karen led them into a bright, homey kitchen, with print curtains and a worn, round oak table that was almost certainly handmade. He paused by the door to scratch the family dog behind the ear.

"That's Joshua," Karen said.

"A black-and-white pit bull," Ben replied. "He's just beautiful."

"Thanks. He's our second one. Just turned four. Woody, our first one, lived to be sixteen. Lonnie named them both. Totally gentle and totally loyal. Maybe if Joshua had been with Lonnie that day—"

She stopped speaking and dabbed at her tears with a tissue.

Off to one corner of the kitchen was a built-in desk, and on it were several framed photos of a young boy, and one of a young man. All of them, Ben felt fairly certain, were of Lonnie.

"He was always a very good boy," Karen said, after she had placed mugs of coffee and a platter of brownies on the table. "They said the cord was around his neck in the womb, and he didn't get enough oxygen to his brain, so he wasn't much in school. But he loved animals and all the people who work on the farm loved him."

Ben flashed on Madame Sonja's explanation for making two sets of drawings. One was clearly the Lonnie depicted in his photographs. Was the other the man he might have become? He wondered that as he went through the details of Lonnie's death. There seemed no need to expose them to the coroner's photos and Madame Sonja's renderings unless, of course, they asked to see them.

"Here are the numbers of the police in Fort Pierce and Dr. Woyczek, the medical examiner. They'll tell you whether or not you will have to identify him in person, or whether you can send down something with his fingerprints on it and possibly some dental records. The state police here should be able to help you deal with them, and whatever mortician you choose should be able to help you out, too—especially in making arrangements to bring Lonnie's body back."

"I told you, Karen," Ray said stonily. "I told you he was dead."

"I'm just glad he didn't suffer none," his wife replied. "Mr. Callahan, I think we both want to know everything you can tell us about how our son ended up in Florida, and who might have done this to him."

"I think I know *why,* in a general sense, and even *how,* but as for *who*, and why specifically Lonnie, well, believe it or not, you might help me answer that question."

Over the next hour, with very little interruption from the Durkins, Ben recounted his involvement from the first meeting with Alice Gustafson through his decision to visit Conda and personally deliver the sad news of Lonnie's death.

"So that's how you got them black eyes," Ray, clearly impressed, said when he had finished.

"It was kind of you not to ask before. Believe it or not, I still think I got the best of him."

"You haven't told us why these people chose our Lonnie," Karen said.

"That's because I don't know. I can tell you this much—it makes no sense that they would have come all the way up here for Lonnie unless they already knew his tissue type."

"But how would they get that?"

"There's only one way—through a blood test."

"Except he never had that sort of test."

"Has he had any blood test at all?"

The Durkins exchanged inquiring looks.

"Two years ago," Karen said suddenly.

"When he had those dizzy spells," Ray added. "Dr. Christiansen ordered them."

"Do you think he would speak with me?" Ben asked.

"She," Karen said. "Dr. Christiansen is a lady doctor. I would think so—especially if I come into Soda Springs with you."

"Can we call her today?"

"I don't see why not. She's a very nice doctor."

"Even *I* go to her," Ray said proudly.

"Hopefully, after I speak with her, she'll agree to see you without us. I don't mind driving down to Soda Springs if I have to, but with what you've told us today, we have quite a bit to do."

"Oh, yes. I'm sorry for being so inconsiderate."

"Nonsense. You're a fine man. There's nothing you can do about what's happened except to get to the bottom of things, and that's what you're doing."

Ben sat quietly for a time, looking at the woman and her husband—trying to comprehend their inestimable emptiness. Could there possibly be anything worse than the loss of one's child? In that moment, studying their strained, worn faces, he sensed something else as well—something that he now acknowledged had been percolating within him over the weeks since he first met Alice Gustafson. He cared. He cared about this couple, now without their son for the rest of their lives. He cared about a frightened, confused, ridiculed motel housekeeper in Maine, whom he had never met. He cared about bringing some sort of justice to a remorseless killer, who was responsible, at least partly, for so much pain and suffering.

"So, is there a hospital in Soda Springs?" he asked finally.

"Caribou Memorial Hospital. It isn't very big, but folks say it's a terrific place. Thankfully, we haven't any need for it. What I mean is—"

In spite of herself, Karen Durkin began to cry.

Ben sat quietly, sipping absently at his coffee, swallowing against the fullness in his throat. He had always thought he'd be a father—two or three times over, in fact. Since the breakup of his marriage, and his gradual descent into ennui and detachment, he hadn't cared much about the time that was slipping past. Now, despite the anguish of his hosts, he found himself wondering what it might be like to have kids.

"I'm staying at a bed-and-breakfast in Soda Springs," he said. "Why don't I go there now and we can talk about things tomorrow."

"No, no," Karen said, regaining her composure. "I'm okay. Let's call Dr. Christiansen now."

"If you're sure you're up to it. Caribou Memorial, is that where Lonnie's blood test was done?"

"I suppose so," she said.

"No twasn't," Ray cut in. "That new lab had just opened right by the pharmacy. I took him there myself."

"New lab?"

"That's right. Brand-new building. It opened maybe six months, maybe a year before we went there. I can't remember its name."

"I don't think I ever knew it," Karen said. "Let me call Dr. Christiansen to see if she'll meet with you, Ben. She's gonna be very sad about Lonnie. Even though he never had to see her all that much, he was one of her favorites."

She made the call from a phone on the

built-in desk while Ray and Ben sat in silence, both staring down at their coffee.

"No problem, Ben," Karen announced
when she had finished. "The doctor will see
you in her office at ten tomorrow morning.
That'll give you time for a good breakfast,
and maybe to see the geyser in Hooper
Springs Park."

"I'll do that," Ben said, rising and shaking
their hands.

He turned, patted Joshua, and was
reaching for the door when Karen said, "Oh,
by the way, it's the Whitestone Laboratory."

"Pardon?"

"The lab where Lonnie had his blood
drawn, it's called the Whitestone Laboratory.
I think it may be part of a chain."

"Only the largest chain in the world," Ben
said.

CHAPTER 13

Can you see, except with the eye?
         —PLATO, *The Republic,* Book I

There was blood everywhere—splattered across a roadway, exploding from the ground, flowing down his own face. Ben seldom remembered dreams, but he awoke at four thirty in the morning knowing that his fitful night of sleep at the Hooper Springs bed-and-breakfast had been full of very violent ones—a string of macabre scenarios held together by a blood-drenched Winnebago. Sometimes, he was driving, other times it was Vincent, the wrestler-sized denizen of the now-extinct Laurel Way garage. Twice during the night Ben woke up in a panic from something in his nightmare, then quickly forgot what it was. Both times, he used the small bathroom and returned to bed, only to immediately become immersed once more in the dream and the blood and the terror.

Finally, he willed the images to be over, turned on the bedside lamp, and propped an old Travis McGee paperback on his chest, trying to make some sense of the lurid dream. When he felt himself drifting off again, he took a long shower and left the bed-and-breakfast for a walk around the still-sleeping town.

How big? he wondered, as he wandered past the sleeping shops and paused briefly by the Soda Springs Apothecary. Assuming that the Winnebago Adventurer was the means by which unwilling donors were brought to anxiously awaiting recipients, how big was the scope of the business?

Just a few more steps brought him to the front of the modest redbrick building that housed the Whitestone Laboratory. In Chicago, it seemed that there was a Whitestone lab on almost every corner. Some of them, like the one he had gone to a few years ago, were no more than phlebotomy centers—blood-drawing offices. The vials of blood were then brought by courier to an area lab where most of the tests were run. The Whitestone lab in Chicago, where he had had his blood taken, was a storefront not five blocks from his office. He remembered Dr. Banks remarking on the speed, efficiency, and dependability of the lab, and also the militarylike precision with which they had transitioned from a small, little-known operation to, perhaps, the number one clinical laboratory in the world.

Soda Springs, according to the sign west of town, had a population of just more than thirty-three hundred. Apparently that was more than enough for Whitestone. At the moment, the room beyond the plate-glass street-side window was dark, but peering inside, Ben could make out a warm waiting area with several large plants. A police cruiser rolled up the street and slowed enough for the lone occupant to check him over, then smile and wave, before driving on. Ben wondered if someone might have called in about the odd-looking stranger making his way up Main Street through the gloom, in no particular hurry. Welcome to small-town America.

With several hours still to kill before his appointment, he wandered back to his bed-

and-breakfast, had a better-than-average breakfast of poached eggs and homemade corned beef hash, and then checked in with his office answering machine.

"Mr. Callahan," a man's deep voice said. "I have been referred to you by Judge Caleb Johnson, who says you're the best detective in the city. . . ."

If Johnson knows who I am, Ben thought, *then he's a far better detective than I am.*

The voice went on to say that his was a case of possible spousal infidelity, and that there would be millions of dollars hinging on the results of Ben's discreet investigation. Whatever Ben's usual rate, he would triple it in exchange for having this matter be made his top priority.

Triple. Ben did some quick mental math and realized that even if the stalk-and-gawk case resolved quicker than usual, and he suspected that it might not, he would be able to make up several times over for the Organ Guard check he had already nearly spent, or the money he had turned down in the Katherine de Souci case. Triple. The rich bass voice was a ladder out of the deep red hole he was in. Ben hummed a chorus of Prine's "Fish and Whistle."

**Father forgive us for what we
must do . . .**

For the immediate future, there would be
no wolf at his door.

What goes around comes around, he
thought, smiling. *Bad or good, what goes
around comes around.*

Dr. Marilyn Christiansen, an osteopathic
general practitioner, was a kindly woman in
her midforties, practicing out of an old Victo-
rian house on the east edge of the town. The
antithesis of the always rushed and harried
Dr. Banks, she was bereft at learning of the
death of Lonnie Durkin, and stunned at the
notion of his being used as an unwilling
bone marrow donor.

"This is very sad," she said. "He was the
Durkins' only child. Is there any other possible explanation for what happened to him?"
she asked.

"Not according to the medical examiner in
Florida. The holes of a bone marrow aspira-
tion were present in the bone in each hip."

"How bizarre. Well, I didn't see Lonnie in
the office very much. He was seldom sick.
But I certainly knew him. Most everyone in

the town did. Very sweet boy. I say boy even though he was in his twenties because, as you probably know—"

"I *do* know," Ben said, sparing her the explanation. "His parents told me you saw him for dizziness."

"Two years ago. Even though I never suspected anything serious, I ordered a routine laboratory panel. The results all came back normal, and his dizziness simply went away. Some sort of virus, I guess."

"The tests were done at Whitestone?"

"Yes. I could have used the hospital lab, but I've found that Whitestone is just a bit, well, more efficient."

"Do you know the director of the lab?"

"Shirley Murphy. I don't know her well. Single woman with a teenage child—a girl."

"Do you feel comfortable calling her to see if she could meet with me today?"

"Of course, but I suspect you won't have any problem getting in to see her."

"How do you know?"

Christiansen hesitated, smiling enigmatically.

"I see that you don't wear a wedding ring," she said finally.

"Divorced."

"Well, as I said, Shirley is single, and she's educated, and Soda Springs is, well, pretty much of a small, family-oriented town."

Ben had never been very intuitive or aware when it came to women, but even he could tell that Shirley Murphy was coming on to him. She was an attractive enough woman, about his age, with streaked hair, large breasts, and full hips. However, whether it was the introductory phone call that Marilyn Christiansen made to her, or the way she actually came to work every day, Shirley was wearing some sort of highly aromatic perfume in addition to a great deal of makeup, neither of which he ever found pleasing in any way. Still, as long as she might be of help to him, there was no way he was going to rain on her fantasies.

The real question was how much information to share with her. If she knew anything about what had happened to Lonnie Durkin, or mentioned Ben's visit to someone who did, he would have made a mistake as grave as trying to open the RV door. It was time for some creative flirting, and some creative lying, neither of which he was particularly skilled at. Gratefully, Dr. Christiansen had agreed not to mention his real profession.

"I don't think we needed to concoct too elaborate a story around who you are, Mr. Callahan," she had said when she finished her call to the lab. "It didn't seem like Shirley heard too much beyond the words 'single' and 'good-looking.' I told her that you came in because of some blurred vision after your auto accident, and mentioned you were interested in the Whitestone lab. How'd I do?"

Murphy's office was tidy and businesslike, with framed French Impressionist prints on the wall, along with some diplomas and two awards for being a Whitestone Laboratories Regional Employee of the Month. The volumes filling the small bookcase didn't look as if they had seen much use.

As the doctor had predicted, Shirley was much more interested in the teller than in the tale.

"I own a small company that does HLA— you know, human leukocyte antigen—typing for transplants," Ben had said, watching her closely for any reaction. "Whitestone is on the verge of buying us out, but keeping me on as director. They want to move our headquarters from Chicago, and one of the places they're considering is Pocatello. Another, from what they told me, is Soda Springs. Something about a smaller town having more employee loyalty and longevity."

"That's certainly a fact. Most of our people have been here since we opened, three years ago. Funny, I haven't heard anything at all about this."

"It's only now being made public. I'm sure that after they narrow their choices down to this area, you'll be brought in."

"I suspect you're right," she had said, and that was that.

"So, Ben," she said now, clearly taking pains to hold her shoulders back, her eyes locked tightly on his, and her head at just the right angle, "tell me about Chicago."

"Oh, it's a great city," he replied, wanting to bring the subject back to HLA typing, but not wanting to appear to ignore her. "Vibrant and very alive. Museums, symphony, great music, and of course, Lake Michigan."

"Sounds exciting."

"And romantic. I think you would love it."

"Oh, I definitely think I would, especially with the right guide."

"Perhaps that can be arranged."

"Well . . . perhaps you'd like a tour of beautiful downtown Soda Springs first. My daughter has cheerleading practice after school and won't be home until six. I think I can get off early. Wait, what am I saying? I'm the boss. I *know* I can get off early."

"After I finish here I have some calls to make, so I can only say that I'd like a . . . um . . . *tour* very much, but we'll have to see."

The implied promise brought her shoulders back another half inch.

"So, Ben, tell me what I can do to help you learn about our operation. We're doing half again as many tests as the hospital lab and as I said, we've only been open for about three years."

"Only three years. Impressive, very impressive. What do you do with your HLA typing now?"

"To tell you the truth, we don't get much call for it. Transplant candidates from here usually have been worked up in one of the university medical centers. What little we do get, we send out to Pocatello."

"Do you keep a record of those you tissue-type?"

"Not specifically. We do have the capability in our quality control program to pull up a list of those who had a specific test drawn, including tissue-typing, but I'd have to think a bit about sharing our patients' names. Oh, heck, I suppose if it's really important to you, Ben, I could make an exception. I mean, you are about to become one of the Whitestone family, so to speak."

She favored him with intense eye contact and an expression that spoke of many long, lonely Idaho nights. He knew that given his imminent position with Whitestone, her willingness to share patient data with him wasn't all that unprofessional, just desperate. She was asking him to take advantage of her. There was strong reason for his wanting to get a printout of those whose blood had been drawn for tissue-typing. Finding Lonnie Durkin on that list would mean that Marilyn Christiansen, for all of her kindly, concerned ways, would have some serious explaining to do. Still . . .

"Listen, Shirley," he heard his voice saying, "that's really kind of you to offer, but I'll be okay just taking a look around the lab. And about getting together later, I'd love to take you out for dinner and some conversation, but I need to tell you that I've just gotten into a relationship with someone back home that's starting to get pretty serious, so conversation is all I can do."

All right, that's it! If you're going to succeed in this private detective business, no more Rockford *reruns or Travis McGee books for you.*

Shirley Murphy's expression reflected something other than disappointment. Oddly enough, Ben thought it might be relief.

"Thank you, Ben," she said. "Thank you for being honest with me. Come, let me show you the lab."

As he followed the director around the busy operation, a surprisingly vivid scenario began running through his mind. He was in an ornate courtroom of some sort, pacing back and forth as he cross-examined a fidgeting woman his mind's eye could not see clearly. He felt certain, though, that the woman was Shirley.

Let's assume, he was saying, *that Lonnie Durkin would never have been used as the donor in a bone marrow transplant unless his blood had been tissue-typed. And yet . . . and yet, we must start with the reality that such a transplant did, in fact, take place.*

Could blood have been drawn on Mr. Durkin without his understanding that it was being done? After all, the man has been acknowledged by his parents and his physician to have been somewhat slow. Perhaps someone drew his blood, then threatened to harm him or his parents if he told anyone it had been done. Does that make sense to you? It sure doesn't to me. Why would they have chosen him in the first place? No, ma'am, it really couldn't have happened that way. The only place it could have happened was right here in—

Ben's imagined rhetoric was cut off abruptly. He was standing behind Shirley as she was extolling the virtues of a new machine, whose name and function he had missed completely. Over her shoulder, he could see a young technician, slightly built, with a strawberry blond ponytail. She was removing a large number of tubes of blood from a freezer and gingerly placing them into racks in several Styrofoam shipping coolers filled with dry ice.

"That's a wonderful machine, Shirley," he said, hoping she wouldn't ask even the most elementary question about it. "Tell me, what percent of the tests that are ordered do you actually do here, and how much do you end up sending out?"

"Good question. Actually, the equipment has gotten so sophisticated, accurate, and efficient that just a couple of techs can run virtually all the chemistries and hematology we get. We still send the more obscure and difficult-to-run tests out to the larger, more regional Whitestone labs, and also to specialty labs like yours. But on the whole, what we get in, we run here."

"Excellent. Those tubes that are being handled over there. Are they being sent out for a specific test?"

Murphy laughed.

"When I told you we send some things out, I wasn't talking about that sort of volume."

She took him gently by the arm and guided him over to the tech.

"Sissy, this is Mr. Ben Callahan from Chicago. He owns a lab that does tissue-typing for transplants."

"Hazardous duty," Sissy said, motioning to the bruises still enveloping his eyes.

"Hey," Ben replied with candor he hadn't planned, "you should see the other guy."

"Sissy," Shirley went on, "Mr. Callahan is interested in these vials you're packing up."

"These? They're backups."

"Backups?"

"In case a sample gets contaminated or the results get questioned. Or in case we need to do a retest for any legal reason."

"As far as we know," Murphy added proudly, "Whitestone is the only lab that takes such precautions. Perhaps that's why we're number one by such a wide margin. I'm sure it adds some to the expense of the tests, but from what I've been told, Whitestone covers that and doesn't pass it on to the consumer or their insurance company."

Ben's mind was whirling.

"So every patient you draw has extra tubes of blood frozen and put in storage?"

"Just a green top," Murphy said. "We've been told that thanks to new technology, that's all they need. We draw an average of four vials of blood on each of our clients— red tops, gray tops, purple tops, black tops. The colors of the rubber stoppers refer to the chemicals that are inside the vials. We refer to the green top as the fifth vial, even if we only draw two on a given patient."

"But you have to ship those green tops out?"

"Oh, yes," Sissy said. "We'd run out of

room in no time if we didn't. They're flown to a storage facility in Texas."

"And kept there for a year," Shirley added.

"Amazing," Ben muttered, wondering if it was even legal to draw such a tube without the patient's knowledge, and deciding in the same moment that it probably was—so long as the blood was only used for quality control.

Casually, he glanced down at the FedEx shipping label. Whitestone Laboratory, John Hamman Highway, Fadiman, Texas 79249. It was so simple, yet it fit the facts of the case so powerfully. At a lab, possibly in a place called Fadiman, Texas, Lonnie Durkin's tissue type had been run and undoubtedly recorded. Ben wondered if a tube containing his own blood had also made the trip to Fadiman. If so, it seemed quite possible that his and Lonnie Durkin's tissue types were two items in the same database—a very massive database at that.

It took a while, and the promise of dinner on his next visit, for Ben to extricate himself from Shirley Murphy, but when he finally had, he hurried to a phone and called Alice Gustafson with a summary of the news from Soda Springs, and a single question.

"What kind of vial is drawn to do a tissue-typing on someone?"

Her reply, though made in a second, seemed to him to take an hour. "That would be a green top," she said.

CHAPTER 14

No physician, in so far as he is a physician, considers his own good in what he prescribes, but the good of his patient.
—PLATO, *The Republic,* Book I

Unbelievable!"

The physical therapist and pulmonary therapist stood back from the treadmill and watched in absolute amazement as Natalie passed thirty minutes of brisk uphill walking—4.5 miles per hour with an elevation of four.

Gradually, Natalie had felt her breathing becoming more strained, and a burning beneath her sternum, but she was determined to hang on for another few minutes. It was little more than two weeks since her medevac return from Brazil, and little more than three since her right lung had been removed at

Santa Teresa Hospital in Rio. She had spent the first three days out of the hospital at her mother's, and might have stayed longer were it not for the pervasive odor of cigarettes—present even though, out of respect for her daughter, Hermina was limiting her smoking to the porch and bathroom.

Jenny delighted in having her aunt around, and especially in having the chance to be the caregiver for a change. The two of them spent hours talking about life and standing tall against adversity, as well as about books (Jenny had reluctantly tried the first Harry Potter, and was now devouring the series), movie stars, opportunities in medicine, and even boys.

"Aren't you a little young to be interested in boys?"

"Don't worry, Auntie Nat, the boys are young, too."

Natalie's progress and her attitude had astounded her physicians and rehab specialists. The scimitar scar on her right side was still sensitive, but there were no other outward signs of the massive operation she had undergone. And with each passing day—each passing *hour*—her left lung was accepting more and more of the responsibilities for gas exchange that once two lungs had shared.

"Hey, Millwood," she said, "I think tomorrow we should hit the track."

The surgeon, trotting briskly on the adjacent treadmill, looked over at her incredulously.

"Just don't hurt yourself," he said. "You know, time is nature's way of keeping everything from happening at once. You don't have to totally rehabilitate in a single session."

"Before this is all over, I'm going to run a triathlon. That's going to be my new sport."

"I think you should stop now, Nat," the physical therapist said. "I promise we'll add something tomorrow."

As Natalie started a cooldown, Millwood turned off his treadmill and hopped off.

"Thank you, ladies, for allowing me to take up your machine like this, but I had to see for myself if the rumors about superwoman, here, were true."

"Are you a believer?" Natalie asked.

"Believer, hell, I'm a disciple."

"In that case you can disciple me over to Friendly's for a hot fudge sundae. If you can stand my grubbiness, I'll wait and shower after I get home. I have to do a little grocery shopping for my mom anyhow, and Friendly's is sort of on the way. We can meet there."

Natalie finished the short cooldown and performed a set of pulmonary function studies under the guidance of her pulmonary therapist.

"The numbers are okay," the woman said, "but your actual performance is much, much better. I honestly have never heard of anyone making this sort of progress after a total pneumonectomy."

"You just watch. If it can be done, I'm going to do it."

Natalie toweled off and changed into a floppy sweatshirt. Macabre and disastrous as losing an entire lung sounded, the recovery, at least to this point, had been nothing like the agonizing ordeal of rehabilitating her surgically repaired Achilles. She had bounced back from that ordeal, and she was determined to make it through this one.

Her phenomenal recovery so far had been marred only by recurrent flashbacks to her attack, which were disrupting her sleep and sometimes even occurring during the day. They were almost identical to the ones she experienced at Santa Teresa's—

distorted, indistinct, and emotionally detached in some ways, utterly detailed and
viscerally terrifying in others. One minute
she was a frightened participant in the hor-
rific cab ride from the airport, the next she
was little more than an observer to her assault and subsequent shooting. She had discussed the phenomenon with her therapist,
Dr. Fierstein, who spoke to her of the many
faces of post-traumatic stress disorder.

"Your mind chooses to remember what it
can handle," she had said. "Much of the rest
is dummied down, if you will—put in a form
that your emotions can deal with. It's a matter of preservation and sanity, and when
those defenses begin to break down, the
true emotions connected with the precipitat-
ing event can be quite overwhelming. We
would both do well to watch out for that."

For the time being, it was decided not to
treat Natalie's PTSD with any medications unless and until the symptoms began to interfere
with her life. But except for some lost sleep, to
this moment, at least, that was hardly the
case. Fierstein's belief was that Natalie was
meeting the challenge of her rehabilitation so
successfully because she functioned best
when she had something to push against.

Millwood met her in the parking lot of Friendly's, a seventy-year-old chain throughout the Northeast that had survived inconsistent food and service largely because of their matchless ice cream.

"I can't totally explain what's happened to me since I woke up from the operation," she said to Millwood after they had settled into a booth and begun quickly replacing the calories they had burned off on the treadmill with hot fudge sundaes, "but something inside me has changed." She grinned, pointed to her thoracotomy scar, and added, "I mean something besides the obvious."

"I've seen the changes in you," Millwood said. "So has Doug. We expected to bring home a morose, self-pitying, bitter woman. And to tell you the truth, that wouldn't have surprised us in the least. I suspect that if I were in your situation, that's the way I would have responded."

"I did feel that way for a while, but then something started happening to me. It began after I moved back to my own place from my mom's. I found myself thinking about how this whole business would never have happened if I hadn't gotten suspended from school, and I would never have gotten suspended if I hadn't decided that I needed to show Cliff Renfro what being a good, compassionate doctor was all about."

"You had a near-death experience," Millwood said. "Different people react to that sort of trauma in different ways. Some enter a life of fear and hesitation. Others are absolutely liberated."

"Dr. Fierstein thinks I might just be in denial, but I don't. It's like what happened in Rio has begun opening my eyes about myself—my own intensity and the effect it has on people around me. You know, sometimes it's possible to care too much about some things. Over the years, I've sort of been caring too much about *everything.* Passion is wonderful when it's focused, but applied without any filter, it can be crazy-making for all concerned."

Millwood reached across the table and put his hand on hers.

"I can't believe I'm hearing this," he said.

Natalie made no attempt to wipe aside the tear that had broken free on a course down her cheek.

"I've always taken such pride in being as tough as I was smart—especially in my belief that whomever I might be dealing with was lacking because they didn't care with as much energy and commitment as I did. It's always been, like, this is who I am. Take me or leave me, but don't expect that I'm going to change. Now, at thirty-five, with one lung and every reason to pack it in, I don't care anymore if I'm tough or not."

"Believe me, Nat, even at your most difficult, you still bring more to the table than almost anyone I know. Your friends love and respect your passion for things, although I'll admit that sometimes we're a little scared of you going off like a Roman candle."

"Well, I'm going to try like hell to be a little gentler on people. And if you catch me going off on anybody, you can rub the bridge of your nose or something to tell me to back off. Got that?"

"Got it."

Millwood practiced the maneuver.

"Perfect, thanks. Until I really get it down, you can be my Jiminy Cricket."

"Count on it."

"Speaking of consciences, Terry, you'll never guess what I did the other day. I wrote letters of apology to Dean Goldenberg and also to Cliff Renfro. There was nothing in it for me, but I really wanted to do it—to go on the record that I finally know what I did wrong and why it was wrong. I also wanted to thank the dean for not kicking my butt out of school for good."

Millwood's expression was enigmatic, but there was a spark in his eyes.

"You said there was nothing in it for you to write those letters, but you did it anyway?"

"That's what I said, yes. . . . . Why?"

He leaned back in the booth, arms folded, his gaze fixed on her.

"Because you're wrong," he said simply. "There was everything in it for you— especially since you didn't think there was. I read the letters, Nat, both of them. Dean Goldenberg asked for my opinion about them—Doug's, too. They were powerfully written and undeniably from your heart. You can say all day and all night that you're changing, but those letters say it better." He paused a moment for emphasis. "Nat, the dean's going to recommend that the committee on discipline allow him to terminate your suspension."

Natalie stared at him, wide-eyed.

"You're not messing with me?"

"I'm cruel," Millwood said, "but I'm not *that* cruel. He's also going to have a talk with Dr.

Schmidt about the possibility of reconsidering your residency. No guarantees, but he sounded somewhat optimistic. I really wanted to be the bearer of the news, so Sam gave me permission to tell you. Welcome back, pal."

"Oh, man, this is just—I . . . I don't know what to say."

"You don't have to say anything that you didn't already say in those letters. On the track that day you raced the St. Clement's kids, we talked about how *who* you are should always be more important than *what* you are. But there is a balance we all need to find, and it appears you're in the process of finding it. So"—he reached across and shook her hand—"congratulations."

"Hey, thanks, Terry. Thanks for hanging in there with me."

"Anything else?"

"Yeah, just one. Are you going to finish the rest of that sundae?"

Nearly airborne with excitement, Natalie managed to make it through the Whole Foods Market. When it happened, she had chosen not to tell her mother that she had been suspended from school. Sooner or later, though, especially as graduation time approached, she knew she was going to have to say something. Now, thanks to the dean, and Doug, and Terry, and whoever else had stepped in to speak on her behalf, that wouldn't be the case.

Best of all was that what she had told Terry was the absolute truth. She had written the letters taking complete ownership of her actions without any consideration that things would change for her externally. During their second-year course on addiction medicine, her class had been required to attend at least two AA meetings and to read in detail about the famous twelve steps—the tools for changing the person in various programs who found it necessary to drink, or drug, or overeat, or gamble, or sleep around. The eighth of those steps had to do with making a list of those the addict had harmed by word or deed. The ninth required making amends to those people without any adherent agenda or expectation of forgiveness. Perhaps, she was thinking now, it might be time for her to expand her list—beginning with her mother.

A detour and subsequent four-block tie-up made the drive to Dorchester twice as long

as usual. Natalie noted proudly that her pro-
fanities, traditionally X-rated in all traffic situations, would barely have made PG.

**Who is this woman, and what have you
done with the real Natalie Reyes?**

Humming softly, she pulled up in front of
Hermina's house and looped two plastic bags
of groceries around each wrist, then set them
down and retrieved the key from beneath the
planter on the front porch. She turned to the
front door, and at that moment smelled
smoke and noticed that gray-black wisps
were floating out from beneath the door.

"Oh, Jesus," she muttered, plunging the
key into the lock and grasping the ornate
doorknob, which was hot to the touch.

"Fire!" she screamed to everyone and no
one in particular. "Fire! Call 911!"

She slipped her hand under her sweatshirt to hold the knob, and turned the key.
Then she lowered her shoulder and
slammed it against the heavy door with all
her might.

CHAPTER 15

The people have always some champion whom they set over themselves and nurse into greatness.
—PLATO, *The Republic,* Book VIII

The front door flew inward, and Natalie plunged ahead into a wall of black smoke and heat. The thought flashed through her mind that somewhere she had heard that it wasn't wise to open the door to a fire because the conflagration would be worsened, but she really had no choice. Her mother and her niece were inside.

The heat was bearable, but the smoke grew more intense with every step, stinging her eyes, nose, and lung. Halfway down the hallway to the kitchen, sputtering and coughing, she was forced to pull her sweatshirt over her mouth and nose and drop to her hands and knees. To her left, the living room was filling with smoke, and the flowered paper on the wall by the kitchen was smoldering, but there was no sign that the fire had started there. The real trouble was ahead of her.

"Mom!" she screamed as she reached the kitchen. "Mom, can you hear me?"

The curtains on the windows were ablaze, as was the wall behind them, the wall adjacent to the living room, the oak table, and parts of the floor. Acrid smoke, lit eerily by the flames, was swirling through the room. Tongues of fire seemed to be shooting across the ceiling, and flickering up from an area of floor by the table.

"Mom? . . . Jenny?"

Natalie inched her way toward the bedrooms. The fire had to have started here, she was thinking, her mind forming a vivid image of Hermina, nodding off at the table, hunched over the *Times* crossword puzzle, a pencil in one hand, a glowing Winston in the other. But where was she? The heat was intense now, and Natalie began worrying about the gas stove. There were pilots going all the time without flame finding its way backward into the pipes, and she had never heard of a massive explosion from a stove unless unlit gas was actually leaking into the room. The pipes to the stove must offer some protection, she decided. It really didn't matter. She wasn't leaving until she found her mother and Jenny.

The heat and swirling smoke were building. Natalie dropped to her elbows to get more relief from both. Now, in addition, there was noise—a crescendo of snapping wood, falling plaster, and hissing flame. She was squinting ahead, peering through nearly closed eyes, when she spotted her mother lying facedown, no more than five feet away. She was wearing a housecoat and no shoes, and was lying motionless in the doorway that led to the bedrooms. *Jenny!* Unless Hermina had become disoriented, she had to have been trying to get to her granddaughter.

Operating off a surge of adrenaline, Natalie grabbed her mother by the ankles, stood up as high as she could tolerate, and began hauling her, six inches at a time, back into the kitchen. The air was significantly hotter than it had been just a minute or so before. Breathing it was like standing in front of an open furnace. There was no movement from her mother—no reaction to being dragged, facedown, across the floor. Natalie fought the urge to check for signs of life. Maybe a heart attack had precipitated all of this. Instead, she pushed backward some more. She had to get Hermina out of the house, then get back inside for Jenny.

The back door, just beyond the blazing table, was engulfed in a sheet of fire. There was absolutely no way out except back down the hallway to the front door. Had anyone called the fire department? Smoke must be billowing out of that door by now. Would anyone be out there waiting to help?

Twice Natalie's hands slipped and she fell backward, gagging and coughing, trying to clear her throat and chest. Each time, she regained her composure and her grip and dragged her mother another few feet. She was nearing the open front door, when Ramon Santiago, the seventy-year-old upstairs tenant, appeared at her elbow, trying to help as much as he was able.

"Be careful . . . Ramon," Natalie sputtered, knowing that the man had arthritis and some sort of heart problem as well. "I don't . . . want you . . . getting hurt."

"Is she alive?"

"I . . . don't know."

If anything, Ramon was slowing down her progress to the door. Finally, he let go.

"I think people have called the fire department."

"Go be . . . sure!"

"It was her cigarettes, wasn't it."

"Ramon, go . . . get the . . . fire department!"

"Okay, okay."

He turned and ran off just as Natalie reached the porch. She was coughing nonstop now and gasping for breath. The burning in her chest was intense. There were several neighbors on the front walk. Only one of them, a fifty-year-old man, who she knew wasn't working because of some sort of illness or injury, was young enough to be of much assistance.

"Help me!" she cried, now wondering what she would do if, in fact, her mother wasn't breathing—trust a neighbor to do effective CPR and go back in after Jenny, or pray the girl was at school, and tend to things with Hermina?

Together, she and the neighbor rolled her mother to her back and half-dragged, half-carried her down the stairs to the front walk. She was covered with soot and grime, and her long, raven-black hair was badly singed. Quickly, Natalie knelt beside her and checked for a carotid artery pulse. At the moment she felt one, the woman took a rasping, minimally effective breath.

Thank God!

Natalie pinched her mother's nose shut with the thumb and forefinger of one hand, slipped her other hand under her neck to tilt her head back, and gave her three rapid mouth-to-mouth breaths. After the third, Hermina inhaled again—this time more deeply.

"Ma, can you hear me? Is Jenny in there?"

Hermina's head lolled, but she made no response. Natalie scrambled to her feet, working for every breath. "Keep an eye on her!" she yelled to everyone and no one in particular.

"Don't go back in there," the man cried out as she raced back up the stairs and into the smoke.

From somewhere behind her, she thought she heard a siren, but there was no way she was going to turn back and wait unless she absolutely couldn't move ahead. Her niece had gotten an incredibly raw deal in life as it was. She couldn't be left to die this way.

The smoke, heat, and noise were magnitudes greater now, but close to the floor, there was still breathable air. With her eyes nearly closed and her nose and mouth covered, Natalie drove ahead toward the kitchen. The small, neat living room was ablaze now. Flames had opened a rent in the wall by the kitchen, and embers had set the couch and carpet ablaze. Holding her breath as much as possible, Natalie risked standing. The kitchen was a conflagration, the heat almost unbearable, the noise hideous.

She tried to gauge whether she was in more immediate danger from the ceiling collapsing or the floor giving way. Halfway across the kitchen, her legs buckled and she pitched forward onto the linoleum. She could no longer see and couldn't seem to inhale enough of the hyperheated air. It was at that instant, prone on the floor, that she heard Jenny's voice.

"Help me! Oh, please help me! Grandma! Aunty Nat! Someone please help me."

Driven by the girl's cries, Natalie pushed to her hands and knees and willed herself forward. She was on the last hundred meters of a fifteen-hundred-meter race, elbow to elbow with another fierce competitor. Her lung was on fire, and her legs were screaming that they could give no more than they were, but the finish line was closing, and she knew she wasn't going to lose. No matter how much the runner beside her had left, she was going to have more.

Blinded and smothering, she hurled herself through the doorway to Jenny's room, and struck heads with the girl, who was lying next to her toppled wheelchair, and whose unbridled hysteria kept her from even registering what was happening.

"Hi, baby. . . . It's okay now. . . . It's . . . Aunty . . . Nat."

Jenny's only response was a whimper of Nat's name.

Compared to Hermina, the ten-year-old was a feather, but she was also virtually deadweight, and Natalie was spent. She pulled Jenny's tee up to cover her mouth and nose, hooked her hands under the girl's arms, and pushed back just as she had done with her mother—six agonizing inches at a time. But before she had crossed a third of the kitchen, her legs and her lung would respond no more.

With flaming embers raining down, she

pulled her sobbing niece close to her and shielded the girl with her body. Then she closed her eyes tightly, and prayed that the inevitable wouldn't be too painful.

CHAPTER 16

If you could imagine anyone obtaining this power of becoming invisible, and never doing any wrong or touching what was another's, he would be thought by the lookers-on to be a most wretched idiot.
—PLATO, *The Republic,* Book II

Socrates, welcome back to the council."

"Thank you, Laertes. My next term actually doesn't begin for another two months, but I assure you I am looking forward to it. Is everyone on?"

"They are."

The four members of the council, speaking at the same time from three continents, greeted one of the founders of their organization.

"So?" Socrates asked.

"So," Laertes said, "we are calling you about H, client number fourteen on your list.

With little warning, his health has begun a fairly rapid deterioration. He needs his procedure done within ten days, his physicians estimate—sooner if at all possible. As you can no doubt extrapolate from his name, there is a great deal at stake politically and financially. We know you have been very busy on our behalf, but we need to know if you can take this case."

"I will make it my business to be available. Donor?"

"We have three possibles. Forty-year-old male baker from Paris, eleven-point match."

"Information on him?"

"Some. He's a pretty typical Producer. Doesn't own the bakery, never will. Two children. People in his neighborhood say he makes excellent bread."

"Themistocles here. It seems to me that to remove even one good baker from the world would be a sin. I vote we look elsewhere."

"The next two are from the United States. First is an actor from Los Angeles—thirty-seven years old. Eleven-point match."

"What has he been in?"

"Grade B horror films, mostly. He's already been married at least four times, has a gambling problem, and is loaded with debt.

Credit rating is poor, doesn't seem to have much respect in the industry."

"No matter," Glaucon said. "However untalented, he is still an actor, and that makes him an Auxiliary. And furthermore, he's an eleven. I vote last resort only."

"I agree," Polemarchus chimed in. "Producers before Auxiliaries. That is our policy. Besides, I'm sure Socrates would be first in line for a twelve if we can get him one."

"That is true," Socrates said, "even though our work has shown that the difference in outcome between an eleven and a twelve is minimal. Still, all else being equal, I would certainly prefer a perfect match. An adult Producer, negative health history, the younger the better."

"I am pleased that we have such a match," Laertes said. "Thirty-six-year-old female. Lower-level Producer. Works waiting tables in some sort of restaurant. Divorced. One child. Doesn't do much of anything outside of her work. Our investigator reports that some of the married women in her town do not trust her."

"And she's a twelve?"

"She is."

"What state is she from?" Socrates asked.

"Let me see. I think it's ... yes, Tennessee. She is from the state of Tennessee."

"Probably listens to that ghastly country music all day," Polemarchus muttered.

"We will do her the honor of selection. Objections?"

"None."

"None."

"Good choice."

"Okay, then, Socrates. As of now, you are on standby. Good day, gentlemen."

CHAPTER 17

You remember what people say when they are sick? What do they say? That after all, nothing is pleasanter than health. But then they never knew this to be the greatest of pleasures until they were ill.

—PLATO, *The Republic,* Book IX

All right, Nat, it's time. Your blood gasses are back and they're pretty good. Your oxygen saturation is ninety-eight. I see no reason we can't pull that tube out. You ready?"

Natalie nodded vigorously to her doctor, Rachel French, the head of pulmonary medicine at White Memorial. For many hours she had been on a ventilator in the intensive care unit, drifting back and forth across the line separating awareness from the beyond, and often, when she awoke, French's kind, intelligent face was looking down at her.

It was probably whatever medication they

had her on, but the endotracheal breathing tube wasn't nearly as bad as she had often feared it would be. She had no memory at all of the one that had kept her alive in Santa Teresa's, and doubted she would remember much of this ordeal, either. *God bless the pharmacologists.* After blacking out on the kitchen floor, her first indication that she wasn't dead was the siren of the ambulance that was speeding her up the Southeast Expressway to White Memorial. Apparently her oxygen levels were bad, because, according to Rachel, the tube was immediately inserted by somebody in the emergency ward. But of that turmoil, she had no recollection whatsoever.

According to the clock on the wall across from her bed, it had been about twelve hours since the sedation and painkillers had been cut back to where she could hold on to a thought for more than a few minutes. Altogether, nearly forty-eight hours had passed since the fire.

She had to be told several times before she had finally retained the news that both her mother and Jenny were alive and doing well in another hospital, and that she was being given full credit by the fire department and in the press for having saved their lives. Word was that only minutes after the fire-fighters pulled her and Jenny from the kitchen, the ceiling in Jenny's room collapsed, and the house went up completely— a total loss. The main unanswered question now in her mind was what, if any, damage had been done to her. It was one of those situations common to medical students and physicians, where she simply had too much knowledge of the possibilities.

French, the mother of twins as well as one of the youngest department heads in the hospital, was the sort of dedicated, widely regarded female physician that Natalie, herself, had hoped one day to become— assertive and effective without ever compromising her femininity and compassion. During Natalie's brief hospitalization following her return from Brazil, French had become her physician, and the two of them had spent hours sharing philosophy, life stories, and thoughts about the future.

"A few crackles at the base," French said after a prolonged examination with her stethoscope, "but that's not a surprise. Dr. Hadawi is here from Anesthesia. Just do what he says, and that tube should be out in a few seconds. You understand that if things aren't perfect, we're not going to wait too long before we put it back, yes?"

Natalie nodded. Her deep trachea was suctioned out, a totally unpleasant sensation for her. Then, as instructed by the anesthesiologist, she coughed, and just like that, the tube was out. For several minutes, all she could do was lie still, a mask in place, taking in humidified oxygen in slow, deep, grateful gulps. A pervasive, quiet tension held as she adjusted to the change, waiting fearfully for signs that her breathing was deteriorating and a new tube needed to be inserted. French examined her several times, and then finally thanked the anesthesiologist and sent him away. Natalie continued almost motionless, gauging her degree of discomfort, anxiety, and air hunger.

Something wasn't right.

Even after two days, the odor of smoke was still present, probably coming from within her nose and sinuses. Although her vision was unclouded, her eyes still felt gritty and uncomfortable, despite an ointment that was being layered under her lower lid every few hours. But the real trouble, she sensed, was in her lung. Thanks to her intense workouts during therapy, her breathing had come to feel essentially normal. Now, despite being able to inhale deeply, it felt as if not quite enough air was getting in with each breath—not enough to be called air hunger, or even to cause panic, but she knew her body as only an athlete could, and something wasn't right. A look at Rachel's expression and Natalie could tell the pulmonologist knew as well.

"You okay?" French asked.

"I don't know, am I?"

"You're doing fine."

Natalie could see the concern shadowing her doctor's face.

"You're doing fine. Isn't that what they told Marie Antoinette . . . right before they dropped the blade?"

The midsentence pause she took to breathe wasn't natural.

"Believe me, your outlook is significantly rosier than hers was," French replied, smiling at the image, "but even though I thought you were well enough to have the tube removed, your oxygen saturation is still a little low, and you still have some edema fluid in parts of your lung. I think that's what you're feeling right now."

"You expect that to go away?"

"Much of it has already."

"But were the alveoli in my lung burned? . . . Is that why I have the edema and the low oxygen?"

"Nat, you did inhale a lot of smoke and hyperheated air."

Natalie felt a knot of fear materialize in her chest.

"And?"

French raised the head of the bed past forty-five degrees, then sat on the edge.

"The lining of your trachea, bronchial tubes, and alveoli were damaged. There can be no question of that."

"I see. Damaged. That edema fluid is not just a reaction to . . . my lung having been irritated by the smoke?"

"Some, I'm sure, but a lot of what's happened is from the heat. You know how someone in a fire might have first-, second-, and third-degree burns on his skin? Well, that's what your injuries are—first-, second-, and third-degree burns to the tissue in your lung."

"First and second degree tend to heal completely," Natalie said.

"Exactly. But third-degree burns are full-thickness—through the epidermis, the dermis, and the subcutaneous tissue. Rather than heal as it was, tissue burned to the third degree generally heals by scarring. Scar tissue offers some physical protection, but little in the way of natural function—in your case, gas exchange."

"So the question here is how much . . . of my lung has third-degree burn."

"And at the moment, we don't know. That was an amazingly heroic thing you did, Nat. I've been praying since they brought you in that the damage isn't too extensive."

"But you don't know," Natalie murmured, as much to herself as to French.

"I don't know. Nat, with what happened to you in Brazil, and now this, you've had a real raw deal. I don't want it to get any worse."

"But it might."

French seemed to be searching for an answer that would skirt the statement.

"We don't know how much damage has been done, or how much of what may be second-degree burn turns out functionally to be third."

"Jesus. Is there anything I can do?"

"Wait a week or so and then we'll get some pulmonary function studies and also get you back into the therapy room."

"I . . . I don't know if I can."

"The woman who crawled back into that burning house to save a ten-year-old girl can do it."

"I don't know," Natalie said again, trying a deep breath that seemed only marginally to fill her lung. "What if it's bad? What if there's too much damage for me ever to breathe normally?"

French looked at her evenly.

"Nat, you mustn't project like this. You'll end up getting so wrapped up in what might happen that you'll paralyze yourself."

"Wouldn't you want to know? . . . Wouldn't you want to know if you were ever going to be able to run again? . . . Or even walk without having to gasp for air? . . . Isn't there anything I can do?"

"Easy does it, Nat, please."

"There must be something."

"Okay, there is," French said reluctantly. "I've taken the liberty of having your blood sent off for tissue-typing."

"A transplant?"

"I'm not saying you're going to need one, but as you probably know, the process can be a complicated and drawn-out one."

"Get on the list."

"There is a regional list, yes, but for the past year or so it's not like the kidney list, which is sort of a first-come, first-served deal. The lung waiting list involves a pretty complicated mathematical evaluation called the lung allocation score. But listen, this is probably not the time to talk about all this. I only started the process because it's so time-consuming. You are a long way from needing a transplant."

"If I can't be normal or close to normal," Natalie said, "I don't think I want to live."

French sighed.

"Nat, I really should have waited to bring all this up. I'm sorry."

"I'm blood type O, you know. That's the most difficult blood type to match for a transplant."

"Nat, please."

"No way I'm going to take immunosuppressant drugs . . . every day for the rest of my life. . . . They cause a list of side effects as long as my arm. . . . Infection, osteoporosis, diabetes, renal failure."

"Honey, please, take a deep breath and get ahold of yourself. You're running way ahead with this thing. I don't even know if you're ever even going to—"

"I'm never going to be right, am I? . . . No matter what I'm never going to run again. . . . And a surgical residency takes stamina—so does standing in the OR for hours at a time. . . . There's no chance I'm going to make it as a surgeon . . . when I can't even walk to the damn corner grocery without getting winded. How much can a person take?"

Instead of recoiling from Natalie's projections and verbal onslaught, Rachel French did what came naturally to her as a physician, moving forward and putting her arms around her patient.

"Easy," she whispered. "Easy does it, Nat."

Natalie momentarily felt herself about to break down. Instead, she stiffened and stared stonily at the opposite wall, her tears unshed.

The next twenty-four hours did not pass pleasantly, even though Natalie sensed some small improvement in her breathing. She certainly felt grateful at having been able to save her mother and niece, but still the depression that accompanied news of her lung damage continued to deepen. Her psychotherapist stopped by several times, and finally succeeded in getting her to try a mild antidepressant. Rather than give the medication a chance, Natalie convinced a friend to bring in her laptop, and spent much of her time awake and online, reading about lung transplantation, tissue-typing, histo-compatibility, and the newly adopted formula for deciding who would receive one of the very limited supply of lungs—the lung allocation score.

Heavily weighted in determining the score was the survival probability for the upcoming year. Very little emphasis in the complex mathematical equations was given to the extent of disability—only to the likelihood of death. Natalie's already deflated mood became even more somber as she realized that the rather remote possibility she would die in the near future actually mitigated against her even being considered for a transplant. She could drag herself around indefinitely, working for every breath, but that didn't count. Quality of life mattered little when measured against quantity.

But what difference did it make? She didn't want a transplant anyway. She didn't want the preparation and the waiting, and she didn't want the surgery, and she didn't want the damn antirejection drugs and their hideous side effects, and she didn't want to spend her life under the Damocles' sword of organ rejection and emergency rehospital- ization. Live with all the energy of a veg- etable, or live on toxic medications designed to make someone else's lung keep her alive. *Great choice.*

To make matters even worse, the vivid re- current visions of her horrible experience in Rio continued without warning, seizing her thoughts, usually at night, but sometimes in the day as well. The scenes were not memories—they never had been. They were powerful and terrifying at the most primal, visceral level. Having them continue with this intensity a month after the actual incident was something that Dr. Fierstein could not explain other than to invoke the old PTSD catchall.

Natalie was hanging from the fence in the squalid alley when movement and shuffling pulled her from the ghastly, terrifying situa- tion. She opened her eyes slowly, half ex- pecting to see another reporter, even though she had expressly requested that security and the nurses keep them away. What she saw instead was her mother, holding open the huge two-page article in the *Herald* about the daring rescue. Behind her were Doug Berenger and, holding some sort of a small plastic bin, Terry Millwood, both of them frequent visitors to her room.

"Hey, Mom, you're out," Natalie said flatly. "Jenny, too?"

"They discharged us both last night. We're staying at your place until we figure out what to do. My friend Suki is with Jen until I get back."

"That's fine. I think I'm getting sprung tomorrow. . . . There's room for the three of us, at least for a while."

"I've been so worried. You're doing good?"

"Fine, Mom. I'm doing fine. You remember Dr. Berenger . . . and Terry?"

"Of course, we were all just talking in the hall."

Natalie tried to keep her anger at Hermina in check, but the news about her lungs and the possibility of a transplant was just too raw.

"Well, they're both chest surgeons, Mom," she said, "and I hope they read you the riot act. . . . The house is gone, everything you owned is up in flames. . . . And you and Jenny nearly died. For what? So you can suck in just one more Winston. . . . I know what the courts have determined about the cigarette companies, and I know how horrible it was to lose Elena the way we did, but I also know how little effort you have put into trying to stop. . . . Here you do everything you can to make Jenny's life as good as it can be, then you nearly kill the poor kid."

Natalie was breathless from the effort of her verbal onslaught.

Hermina recoiled from the force of the attack.

"I . . . I'm sorry, Nat. Really I am."

Natalie refused to let up.

"Sorry's not enough, Mom."

Hermina held her right hand out and rotated it back to front.

"For what it's worth," she said sheepishly, "I've been clean for three days now. No nicotine stains, see?"

Berenger and Millwood muttered words of approval, but Natalie was stony.

"No more, Mom. Not one more butt!" she snapped.

"I promise. I'll try my best."

"No more," Natalie said again, visualizing the damaged alveoli in her one remaining lung. Finally, she sighed and added, "Well, you and Jen are alive and unharmed, and that's what matters."

Doug Berenger, looking totally professorial in his knee-length clinic coat, stepped forward, kissed Natalie on the forehead, and handed her a box of Godiva chocolates. Then he turned to her mother.

"Mrs. Reyes—Hermina—I wonder if Terry and I could speak alone with Natalie for just a few minutes."

Hermina, bewildered, and trying not to pout, muttered, "Of course," and left.

"You are certainly the buzz around this place," Berenger said. "I heard the mayor and Sam Goldenberg have already been talking about some sort of award ceremony."

"Do what you can to get me out of that one," Natalie said.

"I never did get the chance to congratulate you on getting reinstated at school."

"Thanks. I always celebrate good news by getting myself put on a ventilator. It's a tradition."

Millwood set the plastic bin down beside her.

"Get well cards," he said. "Everyone loves a good old-fashioned heroine, including us. These are from all over, not just Boston."

Although their eyes met only momentarily, Natalie had no doubt her friend sensed her deep melancholy.

"Just set them in the corner," she said. "I'll open them all when I get home."

"Natalie," Berenger said, "I have an idea I'd like to discuss with you. Some friends and I have a small business rehabilitating apartment buildings and turning them into condominiums, which we then sell at an obscene profit. Well, it just so happens that at the moment we have a new building in East Boston that we've just finished, and all the units are sold except for the demo, which is a nicely furnished two-bedroom. I'd be honored to have your mother and your niece live there until they can settle up with their insurance company and work out something more permanent. It's on the first floor and totally wheelchair accessible."

Natalie suppressed the knee-jerk impulse to say they would be fine in her place.

"That's very kind of you," she said instead. "It's a wonderful gesture. Just one thing if you do it. If my mother smokes . . . she's out. No second chances. She can go and rent a room or an apartment, and I'll take Jenny. I should have put my foot down more firmly years ago."

"If she smokes, she's out," Berenger said. "Hopefully this will be the event that does it for her, and if you say that's the rule, that's the rule. But nicotine addiction is a powerful monkey. Just think about Carl Culver, that patient of mine whose head your pal Tonya Levitskaya almost bit off. Getting a new heart put into his chest wasn't enough to keep him from smoking again. You'd be amazed at how many liver transplant recipients drink alcohol—some quite heavily, even though it's been proven that as little as a couple of ounces causes fatty changes in the liver."

Natalie wouldn't be moved.

"We've got to keep the pressure on," she said.

Berenger tented his fingertips and bowed.

"So it is written, so it shall be done," he said. "I shall see if your mother wishes to make the deal."

"That's terrific. I've always suspected that

my mother has mystical powers. . . . Don't let her persuade you to back down about the cigarettes."

"I will do my best," Berenger said, backing from the room.

"I'm not kidding, Doug. I love her very much, but the highway in her rearview mirror is littered with people who thought they could get the better of her."

"Mostly men, I'll bet," Millwood said after Berenger had left.

"You got it."

"Pardon me for saying it, but for a heroine you don't seem too bubbly."

"I'm not. Rachel French says my lung's been damaged. At this point there's no way to tell how badly. She said that just in case, she's turned my name in and started me on the road to a transplant."

"I know," Millwood said. "I just spoke with her. Nat, the transplant thing is just a precaution because the whole evaluation and lung allocation formula is so cumbersome and time-consuming."

"I can't do it, Terry."

"I know it's hard, but you've got to try and stay in the moment. No projecting until you know what you're up against."

"Easy for you to say. You're not the one whose lung is rotting away."

"I'm just saying don't get down about what you don't know about. You've come too far to give in to this."

"I'll see what I can do," she said acidly.

Millwood stood.

"Nat, I'm sorry. I really am. If you need anything, anything at all, I'm your man. Our friendship means everything to me."

"Good enough," Natalie said with little enthusiasm.

Millwood seemed for a moment as if he were going to say something else. Then he merely shook his head in frustration and sadness, and left. Once in the hallway, he turned to the right, away from the elevators, and went to the nurses' station. Rachel French, working on some notes, was waiting for him.

"Well?" she asked.

Millwood sighed.

"She's as close to beaten as I've ever known her to be. Just a few days ago she was high as a cloud over the news that she had been reinstated at school. Now this."

"I'm afraid I haven't handled things too

well. I should have waited until after she was discharged before even bringing up the word 'transplant.' The whole business has her believing that her lung is done for even though I keep telling her that we have no way of knowing at this point."

"She's very smart and very intuitive."

"Good thing she doesn't have all the facts yet."

"What facts?"

"I have some friends in the tissue-typing lab, so I decided to call in a favor or two and have them do a rush job on her."

"And?"

"She's O-positive, which as you know already puts her in a reduced recipient pool. But there's more. I just got the preliminary analysis of her twelve histocompatibility antigens. Many of them are rare—some very rare. The odds on finding a donor are long, and even if we are willing to cut some pretty big corners in terms of donor-recipient matching, she would require a lifetime of fairly high doses of antirejection drugs. We haven't addressed the fact yet that in her mind, she's blown the toxicity of the medications out of proportion, but her fears aren't groundless either."

Millwood grimaced.

"So where does that leave her?"

"It leaves her," French said, "squarely between a rock and an extremely hard place."

CHAPTER 18

We mean our guardians to be true saviors.
—PLATO, *The Republic,* Book IV

It would do something of a disservice to the jungle surrounding the Whitestone Center for African Health to say that it was ever quiet, but over the years, Joe Anson had noticed a strange, predictable lull in the white noise between three and three thirty in the morning. Over that specific span—not much more than thirty minutes, and not much less—the peepers, Popillia and stag beetles, chimpanzees and other monkeys, bees and cicadas all seemed to quiet in unison. None of the Cameroon natives was willing to substantiate his observation, but Anson knew what he knew.

On this particular early morning, he leaned against the bamboo railing outside his main lab, and listened as the cacophony from the blackness all about him began to fade. The air was rich with the scents of hundreds of different species of flowering plants, as well as curry, licorice, mint, and a myriad of other spices. Anson inhaled deeply, treasuring the act.

Life following his transplant was as Elizabeth had optimistically predicted it would be. The surgery itself was hell, but he was heavily medicated for the two or three days afterward, so even those memories were vague. The only real problem his doctors encountered occurred in the immediate postoperative period. An epidemic of inhospital infection with an often deadly bacterium caused them to transfer him precipitously out of Amritsar, and in fact, out of India altogether. He was flown, anesthetized and on a respirator, to a renowned hospital in his native Capetown, where the rest of his recovery was uneventful. Thanks to a virtually perfect tissue match with the donor of his lung, the amount of antirejection medication he was given initially and was still taking could be kept to an absolute minimum, thus greatly reducing the chance of infection from opportunistic organisms.

If he knew how effective the procedure was going to be in restoring his breathing to normal, Anson admitted to anyone who would listen, he would have sought the transplant several years ago.

"This is your favorite time here, isn't it."

Elizabeth had materialized beside him, and now stood with her hands on the railing and her arm just barely touching his. Following the surgery, their relationship had more or less settled back to what it always had been—a deep friendship built on mutual respect, and constantly on the verge of burgeoning into a romance. It was a comfortable, secure place to be, and with Anson's critical research so close to clinical acceptance, neither of them seemed anxious to cross the line.

Anson reminded her about his belief surrounding the white noise of the jungle, and then pointed to his watch. For a time, the two of them stood there without speaking.

"Listen, now," he said finally. "Listen to how the sound begins to build. There, there, did you hear that? DeBrazza's monkeys. They haven't made a peep for half an hour, now here they go again. It's like they are re-newed from a brief siesta."

"I believe you, Joseph. You should docu-ment your observations and we will submit them to a zoological journal. Of course, there is the small matter of the research you must complete *before* you can do that."

He laughed.

"I understand."

"The British and French drug agencies are poised to approve extensive clinical tri-als of Sarah-nine."

"Yes, that's wonderful."

"The FDA in America is not far behind. You are on the verge of changing the world, Joseph."

"I don't often allow myself the luxury of thinking of our work that way," he said, "but I am pleased with what is happening here and at the Whitestone facility in Europe. Of that you can be certain."

"Have you been sleeping at all?"

"No need. My energy is boundless. You and your surgeons, and of course, my mag-nificent donor, have given me a new life. Every breath had become such an effort. Now it is as if I am running without weights on my ankles."

"Well, please be careful, Joseph. Just because you have a new lung doesn't mean you are immune to the ill-effects of exhaustion."

"Just think of it, though. We have documented cures from forms of cancer that were thought to be incurable."

"I think of it all the time," St. Pierre said.

"And heart disease."

His ebullience was childlike.

"As I said, my dear friend, your work is about to change the world. Pardon me for asking, but how much investigation do you think you have left to do before you turn your notes over to Whitestone?"

Anson stared off into the darkness, a smile in his eyes, though not yet on his lips. Over the last two or three weeks he had been battling his eccentricities—possessiveness, perfectionism, and mistrust. It *was* time, he kept thinking—time to thank Whitestone and Elizabeth for setting him up with everything he needed to complete his work; time to thank them for the hospital and the many whose lives had been saved there; time to sit down with their scientists and turn over all the remaining secrets of Sarah-9, time to decide upon a new direction for his life.

"You and your organization have been

very patient with me," he said, somewhat
wistfully.

"Then we can arrange a meeting with our
scientists?"

Anson did not answer right away. Instead,
he looked up past the panoply at the sky,
which had, in just a few minutes, gone from
black to a rosy gray. Dawn was so beautiful
in the jungle. It was time to cooperate with
Whitestone, he acknowledged to himself.
But he had another agenda that he wanted
attended to first—an agenda that had everything to do with his being able to appreciate
sunrise in the jungle.

"Actually," he said, "there is something I
need from you first."

"Something we haven't already provided
for you?"

"I know that may be hard to believe, but
yes, there is one thing. I want to meet the
family of the man who gave me back my life,
and to help them financially in any way that
I can."

St. Pierre did not respond right away.
When she did, she spoke firmly.

"Joseph, I hope you really do know and
appreciate how tolerant and patient Whitestone has been with you."

"I do."

"We own world rights to Sarah-nine and anything else that comes out of this laboratory, yet we have allowed you to keep to yourself the methods and cell lines that you use. We know that most of the vats of yeast in your lab are not used in the production of the drug."

"And I am grateful for th—"

"Joseph, please. Listen to me. The patience of the development people and board of directors at Whitestone is running very thin. Our protocols have been limited by the fact that all of the Sarah-nine we get for our research here and in Europe comes from you. You can say that you are supplying the drug fast enough, but that is simply not so. Every day of delay in getting this wonderful treatment onto the world market translates into millions of dollars lost. I know that you don't care a bit about money, but think of the lives that are lost as well. We need to complete the circle, Joseph. We need the microbes and the source of the recombitant DNA, and we need your notes so that we can finish our clinical testing and begin mass production. We promise that you will get full credit for having created Sarah-nine."

"You know that doesn't matter to me."

"Joseph, I don't really know what matters to you anymore. If what matters to you is getting the drug onto the market where it can help the many, many people who need it, then you need to take some action. It boils down to this. You want something more from Whitestone, and we wish something more from you."

"Be specific, please."

"Okay. Provided the widow of the donor of your lung approves, we will arrange for you to fly to Amritsar to visit her, and possibly her two children as well."

"And me?"

"Upon our return from India, we shall fly a research team down here from England along with the equipment to bring your cell line back to our facility there. While they are here, you must go through your notebooks with them—not the dummy ones I know you have so meticulously created, just the real ones. We have paid and paid handsomely for this research, and it is time that we became the proprietors of it."

"You may disagree, Elizabeth, but I believe strongly that the secrecy I have maintained around my work is both justified and in everyone's best interest. Since I have been solely in charge, things have been done my way, without the confusion of multiple captains, and also without the danger of espionage from the pharmaceutical industry. But I agree with you that it is time for the secrecy to end."

"So we have a deal, then?"

"We have a deal."

"Thank you, dear Joseph. On behalf of the world, thank you."

St. Pierre embraced him, then brought his lips to hers and kissed him briefly but tenderly.

"We have been through a lot together," he said.

"The end to this phase of our work is near. You should be very proud of what you have accomplished. I know that I am. Now it's time for me to get a little rest. I am on the schedule at the clinic today. And so, as a matter of fact, are you."

"I'll be ready," Anson said, taking a deep, delicious breath.

St. Pierre returned to her quarters, a single room and shower down the covered corridor from Anson's suite. She was tiring of the small space and the mold that continually reappeared on the bathroom tile, and she stayed there as little as possible, preferring her elegant house, high on a verdant hill overlooking Yaoundé. Whether she stayed in Cameroon or not after the Guardians' use for Anson was done was still uncertain. Either way, she was due a bonus that would make her a wealthy woman, and stock options in the new Whitestone pharmaceutical company that would make her positively rich. Not bad for a few years' work baby-sitting an eccentric, mistrusting genius.

Using a private line, she called a number in London.

"The deal's been made," she told an answering machine. "We bring him to India to visit the family, and he sits down with our people for the final transfer of his notebooks and cell cultures. I believe him. He's always kept to his word, and there's nothing in it for him financially that would cause him to hold back on us. Not that he cares about money, but the stock options he'll get in Whitestone Pharmaceuticals should be enough to keep this place functioning indefinitely.

"It has been a very long haul, but it is almost over. My biggest error when I started here was that I just never anticipated the depth of the man's paranoia or the extent to which he would go to protect his work from the very people who were funding it. It is good that I have found ways to work around his madness and to encourage his genius. Try to push my darling Joseph, and he is just as likely as anything to push right back."

CHAPTER 19

The mind more often faints from the severity of study than from the severity of gymnastics.

—PLATO, *The Republic,* Book VII

Natalie wasn't going to make it through the session and she knew it. It was stupid to have agreed to get back into physical and pulmonary therapy so soon after the ordeal of the fire. She checked the elapsed time on the treadmill clock and then glanced up at the one on the wall just in case the electronics had failed. Seventeen minutes at zero incline. *This is bullshit,* she thought. There was no sense in prolonging the charade. Her lung wasn't working well. It was as simple as that. Rachel French could talk all she wanted to about healing burns and recovery of function, but it just wasn't going to happen.

Oh sure, Lefty, you're going to be pitching real good again before you know it—just as soon as that ol' missing arm of yours regenerates.

"Come on, Nat," her therapist urged. "Five more minutes. You're doing great."

"I'm doing sucky, and you know it."

"You're wrong. The pulmonary people tell me that your function tests have largely stabilized, and that there should be steady improvement in them for some time to come."

"Nobody in medicine ever predicts improvement," Natalie snapped, pausing to get an extra breath. "In fact they usually go . . . out of their way to predict *no* improvement. That way they'll either look smart and tuned in . . . or they'll look like heroes when things *do* get better."

"You know, you're not going to help yourself very much thinking negatively all the time."

"Correction," Natalie said, flicking off the power. "I'm not going to help myself at all. . . . Thanks for your time. . . . I'll call when I feel ready to come back."

She snatched up her warm-up towel and stormed from the unit, sensing the woman might actually be coming after her. She knew she was acting like a jerk, but in truth, she really didn't care. She had accepted the tragic loss of her lung with grace and spirit, and a positive philosophy. But at the moment, even though her mother and niece were alive because of her, and cards were continuing to flood in, and testimonials were being planned, there simply didn't seem to be enough grace or spirit remaining to undo what had been done.

She sped home, half hoping that a cop would have the temerity and bad fortune to try to ticket her. Perhaps with time, her feelings of despair and self-pity would yield to a renewed sense of purpose and perspective. Meanwhile, somewhere, some mathematician who probably couldn't get a job teaching in junior high was preparing to pull out his calculator to determine her lung allocation score.

Let's see, plus twenty-two and she limps along indefinitely, stopping every few feet to catch her breath. Plus twenty-eight and she gets to wait on tenterhooks for the privilege of taking poison that will blot out her immune system, and make riding in a public elevator a potentially lethal affair. . . .

Hermina, with two plastic bags of cleaning supplies at her feet, was writing a note to her at the dining table.

"Hi, baby," she said. "I didn't expect you home so soon."

"Jenny here?"

"She's in the car. I was just getting set to drive her over to the new digs. I think we might sleep there tonight."

"That's great, Mom."

"Honey, I'm really sorry for all this. I know you're furious with me, and you have every right to be."

"Things happen. I'm just grateful you and Jenny are okay. If you're feeling bad about what happened to me, you know what to do about it."

"I know, and so far I'm doing it."

"I hope so."

"You want to come over?"

"Maybe tomorrow."

"The rehab therapy go all right?"

"Terrific."

"Pardon me for saying it, but you don't sound so terrific."

"I'm fine."

"Believe me, if I could turn back the clock and either stop smoking a year ago or just crawl into a closet during that fire and get burned up, I would."

"That's nonsense. You've stopped smoking. That's what matters. And now, I want you to stop saying you wish you had burned up. That doesn't help anything."

"Nat, please, come help me fix up the new place."

"Mom, I'm fine. Really."

"Did they say you're getting better?"

"Yes, they did. Steady improvement, that's what they said."

Clearly sensing the truth, Hermina put her arms around her daughter, and Natalie made some pretext of responding.

"Baby, I'm sorry. I really am."

"I know you are, Mom."

"You sure there's not anything—?"

"I'm positive. I need to get some rest, that's all."

"Well . . . I don't want to leave Jenny sitting in the car too long. Do you think maybe you could come over later for dinner?"

"No, no. I have some studying to catch up on after I nap."

"Thanks for the loan you gave us to get set up in the apartment. I'll pay you back as soon as the insurance comes through."

"That's okay."

"No, I really want to."

"Okay, Mom. Pay me back whenever you want."

Natalie stood for a time in the dining area even after the front door had closed. At some point she would surely end up in the shower, but she really hadn't even broken a sweat in rehab. Finally, she pulled off her tee, threw it onto the floor, thought about putting on some music, then just sank heavily into the deep recliner in her living room. Across from her, just above the ornate marble mantel of her small gas fireplace, was a large, framed color photograph, remarkable for its composition, clarity, and detail. It had been taken by a professional at the Pan Am Games in Mexico City seven years ago, just as Natalie was breaking the tape at the finish of the 1,500 finals. Her arms, fists clenched, were extended skyward, and a true description of the sublime exhilaration on her face would have defied words.

Never again. Not on the track. Not in the operating room. Probably not even in the bedroom, for chrissakes. . . . Never again.

She reached across with her left hand and massaged the still-sensitive scar on the side of her chest. What did that song from *M*A*S*H* say? Suicide is simple? Suicide is painless? Maybe it was suicide is easy. Simple . . . painless . . . easy. Hardly words anyone would ever apply to pulmonary rehabilitation after burning up your only lung.

If she could just get up the nerve, how would she do it?

This wasn't the first time she had actually considered the possibility of ending her own life, but it had been many years. Living as a pulmonary cripple simply would not compute. Nor would the debility of immunosuppressive therapy following a lung transplant. And worst of all would probably be waiting around, watching her lung allocation score rise and fall like the Dow-Jones average.

It was hard to believe that a life with such promise had come to this.

The walls were closing in on her, and there seemed to be no way, no way at all, to stop them.

Pills, probably, she decided. It had to be pills. She remembered hearing someplace that the Hemlock Society recommended enough sedatives and painkillers to go into a coma, in conjunction with a plastic bag over the head just before consciousness vanished altogether. That didn't sound all that pleasant, or even all that possible. Perhaps it was worth going online. If one could learn to make a thermonuclear device there, one could certainly learn the most efficient, pain-free way to commit suicide.

Staring across at the Pan Am Games photo, and almost in spite of herself, Natalie began mentally ticking through how she would go about obtaining enough OxyContin or Valium to induce coma. The phone on the end table beside her had rung several times before she became aware of it. Caller ID listed only the words "New Jersey" and a number.

Probably a telemarketer, she thought, smiling tightly at the notion of something so trivial interrupting something so profound. Bemused at the irony, she answered the call.

"Hello?"

"This is June Harvey of Northeast Colonial Health calling for Miss Natalie Reyes."

Northeast Colonial—her medical insurance carrier. *What now?*

"This is Natalie Reyes."

"Miss Reyes, I've been assigned the claim for all charges connected with your recent operation in Rio de Janeiro, Brazil, and your medevac flight back to the United States."

"Yes?"

"First of all, I hope you are doing well."

"Thank you for asking. I don't think I've ever had someone from my health insurance company actually inquire about my health. The truth is, I've had some recent setbacks."

"I'm sorry to hear that. Well, I'm calling with the good news that Northeast Colonial has reviewed your case and has committed itself to reimbursing you in full for your flight back to Boston."

Reimbursing. Until this moment, Natalie hadn't considered at all how her flight back had been paid for. Now, she realized, Doug Berenger had taken care of it. Not that he would have gone under financially without being reimbursed, but such a flight had to have been a good-sized nut. Typical of the man, he had never mentioned that he had paid for it out-of-pocket.

"Well, thank you," she said. "Thank you very much."

"There's just one thing."

"Yes?"

"Our records state that you had a lung removal performed at the Santa Teresa Hospital in Rio de Janeiro."

"That's right."

"Well, we have received no medical records from the hospital validating that fact, and in fact, although you are fully covered, no claim has been filed for your surgical procedure or hospitalization."

"Well, I was unconscious for a while, but after I woke up I called home and got my insurance number and gave it to the people at the hospital. I don't remember a lot of things from that hospitalization, but I do remember very clearly doing that."

"Well," June Harvey said, "perhaps you could write or call Santa Teresa Hospital. We need copies of your medical records, plus a claim. If you wish, I'll send you the appropriate forms."

"Yes, yes. Do that, please."

June Harvey wished her well with her setback, confirmed her mailing address, and then ended the conversation. Natalie remained in the recliner for a few more minutes, aware that, for whatever reason, the call had defused some of the urgency of her self-destructive impulses. *There will still be time,* she thought now, *plenty of time.*

She pushed herself up, boiled some water, and brewed a cup of Constant Comment tea, which she then took into the tiny study off her bedroom. Instead of doing a Google search for the Hemlock Society, she did one for Santa Teresa Hospital. There were 10,504 entries, the vast majority of them in Portuguese. The search engine found them all in 0.07 seconds.

Who would want to leave a world where this is possible? she asked herself. A backpack-sized mechanical lung might be just around the corner.

It took half an hour, but finally Natalie had an address for the hospital in the Botafogo section of Rio, and a phone number.

After considering, then rejecting, the notion of enlisting her mother's help in making the calls, Natalie looked up the country code for Brazil and the city code for Rio, and began dialing. Initially, her conversations were limited by lost connections while being transferred, as well as by her awkward Cape Verdean Portuguese. Little by little, though, her navigational skills improved. She made it to patient information, then to billing, to records, and even to security. An hour and fifteen minutes after she set the receiver down from her conversation with June Harvey, she finished an animated discussion with the director of the Santa Teresa record room, a woman named DaSoto, who actually spoke English—probably about as well as Natalie did Portuguese.

"I am sorry, Miss Reyes," she said, "but Santa Teresa is one of the fine hospital in all Brazil. Our electronic record system is be very good. You were not admit to our hospital on July eighteenth. You never did received an operation on in any of our operating rooms. And you were not certainly a patient in here for twelve days, or even one day. You ask if I am positive of which I say. I tell you that I would hang my career on it. No, I would hang my life."

"Thank you, Senhora DaSoto," Natalie said, aware of her heart beginning to beat heavily, but still unwilling to fully believe that the woman, however certain she was, hadn't overlooked something. "I know it was a hard decision for you to talk with me about this without proof of who I am."

"You are welcome."

"I have one last request."

"Yes?"

"Could you give me the number of the police station that would have been most likely involved with my shooting?"

CHAPTER 20

His life is manifold and motley and an epitome of the lives of many.
—PLATO, *The Republic,* Book VIII

Big Bend Diner. Sandy Macfarlane flicked off the red-and-green neon sign even though, technically, the place was still open for another ten minutes. What the heck, the Corlisses wouldn't mind. In six years of working for them she had hardly missed one day. She was a pretty woman with orange-red hair, and a sensual, desirable figure that she often boasted about by bemoaning the weight she had to lose.

"Closin' early, Sandy?" Kenny Hooper asked.

Hooper, a widower in his late sixties, still held down a regular job working for Ten-

nessee Stone and Gravel. There was nothing for him to go home to except his old
hound dog, so every evening after his shift
was over he stopped by the Big Bend for a
late dinner.

"Got some errands that need doin',
Kenny," Sandy said. "Besides, there ain't no
one comin' in between now and closin' anyhow. I got me a sixth sense about such
things."

Sandy didn't like lying, even about something as insignificant as her plans for the
evening, but if Twin Rivers, Tennessee, was
the world's best at anything, it was gossip-
ing, and Kenny Hooper was as good at that
as anyone. If he learned that she was dating
one of the customers from the diner, the
whole town would be talking about it in no
time, and every Jack Snap in the valley, married or not, would be considering making a
run at her. A single woman with an eight-
year-old kid and a decent body was fair
enough game as it was, without people
thinking she was desperate.

But Rudy Brooks seemed like he was
worth the risk.

"Any possibility a gittin' one last cup a joe
before you dump the pot?" Kenny asked.

Sandy was about to say that the coffee had already been emptied and the grounds cleaned out when she saw the man staring right at the pot behind the counter.

"All right, all right," she said, filling a mug and adding two creams and two sugars without having to be asked. "But make it quick."

Hooper watched her fix her hair and apply a swatch of lipstick at the mirror behind the bar.

"You sure you just got errands?" he asked with a glint.

"Just drink your coffee, Kenny Hooper. Here. Here's the last piece of blueberry pie. I was gonna throw it out anyway."

Rudy was a Texan, rugged-looking and smart, with jeans and a sports shirt that didn't come off the racks in any Army-Navy store. He was narrow in the waist and real broad across the shoulders—just the way she liked her men. But what got to her most was his smile. It was sexy and sly, like that of a gunslinger who knew that no matter how fast you were, he was quicker. Of course, in Twin Rivers, when it came to available men, there wasn't a heck of a selection—certainly few or none that looked like this one.

Sandy finished wiping down and made a

last check of the kitchen. Rudy might be married, she acknowledged. Men were always lying about that. But tonight they were just going to meet at the Green Lantern for a couple of drinks. No fancy stuff. If, as he said, his company was going to build the first shopping mall in Twin Rivers, and if, as he said, he was going to be a regular visitor to the site just west of town, he would get his chance to be amorous. Maybe plenty of them.

"So, where's little Teddy tonight, Sandy? Nick got 'im?"

"Nick has Teddy every Wednesday."

"I heard your ex put on quite a show at Miller's t'other night. Took four men to throw him out. Man has a problem, I'd say."

"And I'd say keep your notions to yourself unless you have proof and it involves Teddy."

Sandy felt her heart tighten at the notion of Nick hitting the bottle again. Although as far as she knew, he had never hit their son, he had hit her plenty over their five years of marriage—always when he was drinking. She had told the judge about his temper and his alcohol problem, and had even provided witnesses to support her request that there be no overnights at all until Nick could document he had been going to AA or therapy or something. But the judge had strong ideas about a child's need for two involved parents, and turned her down. So every Wednesday and every other Saturday, there wasn't a damn thing she could do except to pray that Nick could keep it together, and that his girlfriend Brenda could keep her drinking together, too, and then the next day ask Teddy indirectly if there had been any problems.

Even though there hadn't been any alcohol-related incidents, at least until now, the truth was that Sandy ached every time the boy was away from her—even when it was for an overnight play date with one of his friends. He was the sort of kid who made even long hours of waiting tables seem worthwhile. People met him, and after just a few minutes, they loved him. He just had that way. Maybe it was his smile, maybe his freckles, or maybe just the fact that he had never done or said an unkind thing to anyone in his life. Whatever the reason, Sandy knew, as did almost everyone in town, that Teddy Macfarlane was going to amount to something special.

Finally, after what seemed an eternity, Kenny Hooper pushed himself back from the table, left enough money for the tab plus his usual five-dollar tip, then shambled out the door. Anxiously checking the time, Sandy wiped down Hooper's table and shut out the lights. Then she hurried to her fire-engine red Mustang convertible, decided in the interest of her hair to leave the top up, and skidded out of the parking lot onto the Brazelton Highway. Brazelton, about the size of Twin Rivers, was much more interesting, with more bars and clubs, it seemed, than there were people in the town. She was two miles down the highway when she picked up her cell phone and called Nick.

It was not usual for her to interrupt Teddy's time with his father, and Nick really didn't like her doing it, but even through the anticipation of meeting up with Rudy Brooks, she felt a powerful ache to connect with her son— and, she admitted, to check up on his father.

"'Lo?"

"Hi, it's me."

"Yeah?"

"I was just calling to see how you guys were doing?"

"We're doin' fine. Jes fine."

That was already plenty of words for her to tell that Nick had a couple under his belt, although he wasn't in the bag. His speech was always the first to go. Asking for confirmation that he was drinking, though, was the same as asking him to hang up on her.

"Think I could just say good night to Teddy?"

"He's watching cartoons with Bren. I don't want to bother him unless you have somethin' important to say."

"No, not really. I . . . I just wanted to say good night."

"I'll tell him you called."

"Do that, Nick, okay?"

"See you tomorrow."

"Yeah . . . thanks."

Helpless, Sandy set her cell phone down. Almost instantly, it began ringing.

"Sandy, hi, it's Rudy."

Damn, she thought, *first Nick won't let me talk to my boy, and now I'm about to get blown off.*

"Well, hi, yourself," she said. "I just got out of work. Are we still on?"

"Been looking forward to seeing you all day."

At least something was going right.

"That's sweet of you to say. Well, I been

lookin' forward to seein' you, too, Rudy Brooks."

"Just one little change. I'm still here at the mall site with one of the contractors—Greg Lumpert. I think you know him."

"I know who he is, but we're not really personally acquainted."

"Well, me an' Lumpert got some more business we need to finish. Any chance you could stop by here for a few minutes? We could actually use your opinion about some things. The site's right on the way to the Green Lantern, and just a couple a hunnert yards off the Brazelton Highway."

"I . . . guess so, sure," Sandy said, deciding that Greg Lumpert had no reason to start rumors about her, and grateful that her date with Rudy was still on.

Rudy described the turnoff in some detail, although he needn't have bothered. Sandy knew almost exactly where it was.

"I'll be there in less than ten minutes," she said.

"Terrific. See you soon by the light of the moon."

The turnoff to the mall site was not more than a mile from the Brazelton line in a

wooded area that was still largely undevel-
oped, but had been the subject of much
speculation over the past few years. Sandy
found it exciting—even titillating—to be in on
the ground floor of a project that was going
to change the physical and economic landscape of the town she knew so well.

She turned off the highway onto a stony
dirt road and slowed way down to keep from
bottoming out or sending a stone up
through the muffler. Her high beams
jounced up and down off the forest ahead.
Just as she began to think she was too far
off the highway and might have actually
taken the wrong turn, the woods fell away
into a good-sized clearing that looked as if
some sand and gravel operation might have
done some excavating there. Parked off to
one side was a Ford Bronco, with Rudy
standing there alone, leaning against the
hood. Just beyond the Bronco, close to the
trees, stood a massive mobile home. Lights
from inside the RV shone through the huge
front windows.

Rudy waved her over. He was wearing
tight-fitting jeans, tooled cowboy boots, and
a colorful long-sleeved sport shirt. *Just a
fine-looking man,* Sandy thought.

"Hi," she said.

"You look great."

"Thanks, where's Greg Lumpert?"

"Oh, his wife called. Some sort of problem at home. We were just about done, anyhow, so I told him to go ahead."

"You sure it was his wife? I was pretty certain I heard she died a few years ago."

"I thought that's what he said," Rudy replied, "but I coulda misheard. I had other things on my mind."

He nudged Sandy's arm for emphasis, and gave her a gunslinger smile. From his two visits to the Big Bend, she knew he was well built, but tonight he seemed even bigger and stronger than she had pictured.

"So, what's with the bus?"

"Callin' that just a bus is a little like callin' Jessica Simpson just a girl."

Sandy decided against mentioning that she couldn't stand Jessica Simpson.

"Does it belong to your company?" she asked instead.

"It's like my home away from home when we're doin' site work. Wanna peek inside?"

Suddenly, inexplicably, Sandy felt uneasy.

"Some other time, maybe. It's like, I don't know, it's like that's your hotel room."

"I don't see it that way," Rudy said, "but suit yourself."

Sandy looked around at the absolute blackness of the forest. The traffic noises from the highway were barely audible.

"Maybe we should get going to the club," she said nervously. "I hear the band they have playing there is great."

"What's the rush?" Rudy asked, not moving from his spot by the truck.

"Rudy, please, let's go. This is starting to creep me out."

"Trust me, darlin', there's nothing to be creeped out about."

She stood just a few feet away and watched in confusion and mounting fear as he took a handkerchief from his pocket, folded it neatly on the hood of the Bronco, then doused it thoroughly with something poured from a metal flask.

Sandy gauged the distance to the Mustang. It wasn't a good bet that she could make it. Then the sickly sweet odor of chloroform reached her. At that exact moment, the door to the massive RV opened, and a young woman, thin, shapely, and blond, stepped out.

"Hey, Sandy," she called out cheerily, "come on over and let us give you a tour of this thing."

Reflexively, Sandy swung around toward the voice. In that single second, any chance she had to resist vanished. Rudy closed the distance between them with two quick steps and clamped the chloroform-soaked rag across her mouth and nose so tightly that she could not even struggle. In just moments, the scene around her began to swirl, then dim. Terror exploded through her mind, but was immediately replaced by a single image, a single word. *Teddy.* The vision of her boy was the last thing Sandy saw before darkness engulfed her.

Fifteen minutes later, the magnificent Winnebago Adventurer swung left onto the Brazelton Highway. It was followed not too closely by a bright red Mustang convertible. Eighteen miles down the highway, the RV pulled into a rest area while the Mustang bounced down a two-mile-long dirt road that ended at Redstone Quarry—a small lake that was reputed by the locals to be bottomless. The drop from the cliff's edge to the water was fifteen feet. The empty Mustang had vanished into the blackness before it hit the surface.

No one, except the man who had called himself Rudy Brooks, heard the splash.

CHAPTER 21

Would not he who is fitted to be a guardian, besides the spirited nature, need to have the qualities of a philosopher?
—PLATO, *The Republic,* Book II

Natalie, you're supposed to be starting back on your surgical rotation next week."

Dean Goldenberg held up the stack of paperwork that had been generated in order to get her back on track at school.

"I know."

"And you say that physically you think you can handle such a trip?"

"From the moment I finished making all those calls to Brazil, I've been spending three hours a day or more in rehab. My pulmonary function studies have improved nearly twenty-five percent since the first time they were measured after the fire. I'm even able to jog."

"But now you want to take more time off."

"I feel that I have to."

Goldenberg's office looked the same as when Natalie had been suspended from school, except that everything had changed. The people there this time, in addition to Natalie and the dean, were Doug Berenger and Terry Millwood. Veronica had offered to come along for moral support, but Natalie saw no reason for her to take time from her obstetrics rotation.

After her initial flurry of calls to various departments at Santa Teresa Hospital, Natalie had spoken to several police stations around the city of Rio. To the best that she could tell, there was a law requiring hospitals to report all gunshot wounds, and no such report had been filed on her, nor did the police themselves have a record of responding to her being shot.

First thing the next morning, she had brought her mother over for another try. The results were all the same, with one additional failure—the failure to find any Dr. Xavier Santoro on the staff of Santa Teresa's or, in fact, in the entire city. Within an hour of

her mother's last call—this one to the Rio de
Janeiro State Medical Board, where there
was no record of any Dr. Xavier Santoro—
Natalie was at the gym, dragging herself
through a series of aerobic and anaerobic
exercises. The next morning she called her
pulmonary therapist with an apology and a
request for more time—much more time.

"Terry, you have a note from Natalie's pulmonologist?" Goldenberg asked.

"I do. Rachel French dropped it off with me
because she couldn't make it this morning."

Millwood passed the sheet over, and the
dean scanned it, nodding that the conclusions were clear.

"Natalie, you are behind on your schedule
if you wish to graduate with your class," he
said. "And you, yourself, said that this whole
business in Brazil is probably a misunderstanding due to language barriers and the
difficulty in negotiating through a hospital
system that is half a world away."

"If I get there and discover that the hospital and the police do have records of me, I'll
be home on the next available flight. I won't
even try and find out who and where Dr.
Santoro is."

"Doug, you spoke with this Dr. Santoro?"

"Once," Berenger replied. "According to Nat, the man said he knew who I was, although I had never heard of him. Mostly I spoke with a surgical nurse, whose name I just don't remember."

Goldenberg looked nonplussed.

"Natalie," he said, "as you know, with your permission, I spoke to Dr. Fierstein, your therapist. She does not think it is in your best interest for you to go. Apparently you have been having some sort of serious flashbacks surrounding the evening you were shot."

"I started having them when I was still in the hospital in Rio. Dr. Fierstein is calling them a manifestation of PTSD."

"I know. She is worried that your return to the scene of your trauma might have disastrous consequences."

"Dr. Goldenberg," Natalie said, "Terry knows about what I am going to tell you, but aside from him, no one else does, not even my therapist. At the time of the call from my health insurance company, I was seriously contemplating killing myself. I felt my situation was hopeless and that I would live my life either crippled from my pulmonary condition, or debilitated from the antirejection drugs necessary for a transplant. I'm still frightened of both of those possibilities, but from the moment I finished with the first round of calls to Brazil, I have been consumed with the need to find answers to the questions of why there is no record of the crime that changed my life so radically. If I have to give up my scholarship and a year of medical school, then that's what I'm going to do."

The three physicians exchanged looks.

"Okay then," Goldenberg said finally, "here is the best I can do. I'll give you two weeks and take it off one of your electives. Half of the students don't do any work on their electives anyway. OB in San Francisco, dermatology in London. You all think we don't know, but the truth is that when we were students we all did the same thing."

The three others smiled.

"So Nat," Millwood asked, "when are you going?"

"As soon as I can get a ticket."

"Sam, thank you," Berenger said, standing and shaking the dean's hand. "For what it's worth, I think you're doing the right and fair thing."

He guided Natalie out of the office into the

reception area, and then waited until Mill-wood had gone before extracting an envelope from his jacket pocket.

"Nat, the moment you told me what was going on, I knew you were headed back to Brazil. I knew because I know you. Since I sent you there in the first place, I thought that helping you get back to Rio to straighten matters out would be the least I can do."

"Tickets!" Natalie exclaimed without even opening the envelope.

"*First-class* tickets," Berenger corrected.

Natalie hugged him unabashedly as Goldenberg's secretary looked on, amused.

"When are they for?" Natalie asked, fumbling open the envelope.

"When do you think? Remember, I have no more patience than you do. Besides, as I'm sure you recall, my wife owns a travel agency."

Natalie took a minute to find the departure date on the ticket.

"Tomorrow!"

"Now it's your turn," Berenger said. "I hope this circle gets closed quickly."

"Me, too."

"And I hope one other thing as well."

"What's that?"

"I hope you take a bus into the city instead of a cab."

The physician known among the Guardians as Laertes paced across the study of his sea-coast estate, overlooking the mouth of the Thames. He was a professor of surgery at St. George's in London, and a world-renowned lecturer on his specialty, cardiac transplantation. He was also one of the original members of the Guardians. For the past six months he had been serving his rotation as the PK, the Philosopher King of the society—providing day-to-day leadership and, in rare instances, the final word on any controversial decisions.

"Glaucon, tell us again," he said, addressing the speakerphone on his Louis Quatorze desk.

"The patient is W, number eighty-one on your list," replied Glaucon, a brilliant young renal transplant urologist from Sydney. "As you can see, he is an industrialist, and one of the most economically and politically powerful men in Australia—fifty-eight years old, and conservatively worth four billion dollars, a significant portion of which he is ready to transfer to us in exchange for our services. His cardiac situation has gone from stable to critical, and he will die within the next few weeks without a transplant."

"It says here that he is a heavy smoker."

"Yes, but he has promised he will stop."

"But there is a problem."

"Yes. His antibody pattern is quite unusual."

"The best our database has been able to do?"

"An eight out of twelve, which would require him to be treated aggressively with immunosuppressive drugs, and would, of course, greatly increase the possibility of organ rejection."

"However," Laertes said, "we have located a perfect twelve-point match for him in the state of Mississippi."

"So what's the problem?" Thermistocles asked.

"The donor is eleven years old."

"I see. Weight?"

"That's the good part. He's chunky. Our man estimates he weighs one hundred and twenty pounds. That's fifty-four kilos."

"And the recipient?"

"One hundred seventy pounds. Seventy-seven kilos."

"That's a thirty percent difference. Is that going to work?"

"Twenty percent difference or less would be ideal, but W has an excellent cardiologist. With enforced rest and medication, the transplant might serve for a while, giving us time to search for something more compatible."

"How long?"

"Maybe a month, maybe less, maybe somewhat longer."

"Profile of the donor?"

"Nothing significant. One of four children. Father drinks too much, mother works in a clothes cleaners."

"Our facility in New Guinea is ready, and I am willing to make the flight as soon as the donor has been procured and transferred there."

"So, I ask you again," Themistocles said, "what's the problem?"

CHAPTER 22

The wise man speaks with authority when he approves of his own life.

— PLATO, *The Republic,* Book IX

From: Benjamin M. Callahan
To: Congressman Martin Shapiro
Re: Investigation of Mrs. Valerie Shapiro

Enclosed are the discs and still photographs associated with my three-week investigation of your wife. It is my conclusion, with a high degree of certainty, that Mrs. Shapiro is not involved in any sort of affair in the commonly understood definition of the term. During the course of my investigation, on four occasions, Mrs. Shapiro visited the home (see photo) of

Alejandro Garcia, a mechanic at the Goodyear Automotive store on 13384 Veteran's Parkway in Cicero, and his wife, Jessica (see photos). Twice she stayed for over an hour, and twice she emerged with a girl about age twelve (photos). Each time they went shopping, mostly for clothes. Their relationship was a warm and loving one, and twice I heard the girl refer to her as Aunty Val. Enclosed are documents validating that Mrs. Garcia's maiden name is, in fact, Nussbaum—the same as your wife's. They have no other children. There is a great deal more investigation that could be done, but as of this report, I can say that I believe Julie Garcia is, in fact, your wife's daughter, born when your wife was sixteen and turned over for adoption to her older (by thirteen years) sister. I have been told that Attorney Clement Goring (see enclosed detail sheet) either brokered this adoption or knows who might have done so.

Clearly, there has been deception on the part of your wife, but it is not the sort you believed.

As I told you when I agreed to this investigation, I could give you one month, but no more—at least not until I return from attending to other business.

Best of luck in sorting this situation out. I hope you agree with my conclusions and that I have been of service to you.

Ben packaged the summary along with a thick envelope of photos, documents, DVDs, and a final bill, payment of which would take care of his financial problems for some time to come. Of all his recent cases, this one had the chance to be the most rewarding. An up-and-coming congressman, Martin Shapiro was married to a woman nearly half his age—bright, beautiful, educated, and very much of a political asset provided they could work out their issues. One of those issues concerned his wife at age sixteen, unwilling to terminate her pregnancy, but unable to care for a child.

Both of the Shapiros seemed like decent people, and Ben was pulling for them. Now it was time to complete his work on Lonnie Durkin. It was surprising to sense such commitment in himself after not really caring about much of anything for so long. But since his trip to Idaho, he had been unable to shuck from his mind the images of the inestimable sadness and sorrow on the faces of Karen and Ray Durkin.

He was convinced that Whitestone laboratory technicians all over the country, and in all probability the world, were unwitting accomplices in what might prove to be a consummate evil, and he both wanted and needed to know what was going on.

With Althea Satterfield fluttering about his apartment, Ben packed some warm-weather clothes and set out enough cat supplies for a couple of weeks. Then, after a hug for his elderly neighbor and a final scratch for Pincus, he hurried down the stairs and into his five-year-old black Range Rover. The car was battered with half a dozen dents that were too close to his deductible to bother fixing, but despite more than a little neglect, the engine was still sound. In fact, just yesterday, the mechanic at Quickee Oil Change had pronounced the car good to go for the thousand-mile drive to Fadiman, Texas.

In addition to his suitcase and a pair of twenty-five-pound dumbbells, Ben set his Moroccan leather valise in back, packed with some new equipment, including several listening devices, a used but serviceable monocular nightscope, a hundred feet of clothesline, and a new Swiss Army knife. Finally, he transferred his Smith & Wesson .38 Special, freshly oiled, from its velvet pouch to a shoulder holster, and set the holster under some papers in the glove compartment.

Initially, Gustafson, who had finally stopped calling him Mr. Callahan, had been as excited and enthusiastic as he was about the findings in Cincinnati and at the Whitestone lab in Soda Springs, but over the intervening weeks, she had become considerably more cautious.

"Ben, I think we should call in the FBI," she had said during their last meeting together.

"And tell them what? We have no hard proof of anything. Chances are these Whitestone people could easily parry any thrust as feeble as ours. Then they just retool, or relocate, and restart."

"I have some friends researching this company," Gustafson had said, "and what they've found really concerns me. Whitestone is based out of London, and financially spearheaded by their laboratories and a pharmaceutical business, they may be one of the fastest-growing privately held companies in the world."

"Pharmaceuticals?"

"Mostly generics and medications that are legal in Europe and Africa, but not here—at least not yet. Ben, I think we're in over our heads."

"So?"

"So, I don't want you to get hurt."

"Believe me, I'm no hero, but folks are already getting hurt, maybe lots of them. And there'll be more and more until these people are stopped. A doctor orders a blood sugar and his patient unknowingly gets tissue-typed. It's like they're walking around with time bombs in their pockets. How many of those vials of blood—those so-called quality control tubes—are getting sent off to Fadiman, Texas, every day? How many profiles do you think are added to the database?"

Gustafson shook her head grimly.

"I'm worried, that's all," she said. "All those blood-drawing labs, that huge van, those weapons, that thug who almost killed you— these are not petty thieves."

"Hey," Ben replied, "is this the woman who

put on a nurse's uniform and marched into the operating room of a hospital in Moldavia to document the illicit trade of a kidney in exchange for a job? As I recall, from the article you wrote, it was a lousy, menial job at that and, I might add, a lousy, menial job that never even materialized. I think you succeeded in getting some arrests in that one."

"One of the first cases where we actually put an organ broker and a surgeon out of business," she said somewhat wistfully, "at least for the moment."

"Professor, Google and Yahoo have more than a hundred thousand entries about you, running around in disguises, making power brokers back down from hundreds of thousands in profits, putting yourself in harm's way for people that were staring up from the bottom of the barrel. It doesn't sound as if you've ever backed down from anyone."

"I think most of the time I was too young to know any better."

"Well, you are a great power of example, and for what I'm getting paid by Organ Guard, I would brave any danger."

"Very funny. Okay, Ben, do what you have to do, but please, please be careful."

"I will."

"And speaking of getting paid."

"Yes?"

"Here's my Sunoco gas card."

Another night on the road playing detective, another budget motel—this one the Starlight in Hollis, Oklahoma. At three thirty Ben was still awake, staring into the blackness of room 118. By four thirty, he had showered, packed up, grabbed a cup of coffee from the desk clerk, and hit the road. He had always found the starkness and palette of the desert to be awesome, but never more so than this morning, with sand and sage washed by the pastels of early dawn, stretching out infinitely on either side of the highway.

He left the CD player off and the windows open, and thought of what might be awaiting him in Fadiman. Soon, he found himself reflecting on "Fred and Ed," a cartoon he had read religiously in his weekly college newspaper. In his favorite installment of the strip, slow, gangly Fred with a huge net and length of rope announces to his much smaller, sharper friend that he is going alligator hunting.

"If you catch one, what are you going to do with it?" Ed asks.

"I hadn't thought that far ahead," Fred replies.

Totally silly, totally profound.

Ben reached Fadiman just after noon. The sleepy town looked as if it might have been used as the set for Bogdanovich's classic *The Last Picture Show.* It was definitely more substantial than Curtisville, Florida, home of Schyler Gaines's gas station and mini-mart, but the gestalt of the two places was not dissimilar. The wooden sign on the edge of town, peeling and punctuated with more than a few bullet holes, announced that Fadiman was firmly rooted in yesterday, with hands reaching out to tomorrow. From what Ben could discern from the ride into the center of town, the main industries bridging yesterday and tomorrow were mobile-home and RV sales, and self-storage facilities. There were three of each on this side of town alone.

With a growing need for food and a bathroom, but otherwise no more of a plan than the cartoon character hunting for alligators, Ben rolled slowly down Main Street—four or five traffic lights long, and wide in the way only midwestern Main Streets were wide. He counted five taverns, all of which served food, but none of which looked as if it would be sanctioned by any health authority to do so. He wasn't really that picky about ambiance, and he certainly was no gourmet, but he had only recently gotten off Zantac and Maalox, and was enjoying an uneasy truce with his stomach. On another pass up the street he spotted a couple of restaurants he had missed—Mother Molly's and the Hungry Coyote. The choice was easy.

Molly's, done in a motif of genuine cowboy and ranch regalia, was actually larger and quainter than Ben had anticipated. Booths with red leather and dark wood were arranged around the outside, tables with red-checked paper place mats in the center. About a third of the seats were occupied. Ben was beginning to feel the fatigue of his early wake-up and the long drive. Still, he debated ordering a Coors with his mushroom and cheddar steerburger before opting instead for the caffeine boost of a Coke. The beer could wait. There was work to be done.

MapQuest had taken him to Fadiman easily enough, but had failed to come up with anything like a John Hamman Highway. In the Whitestone lab in Soda Springs he felt certain he had read the name correctly. Now, he wasn't so confident. As he worked on his lunch, he imagined himself with a rope and net, watching an endless line of alligators marching past.

What now?

First things first, he decided finally, and motioned his waitress over. She was a husky, grandmotherly woman with close-cut silver hair and a calm competent demeanor that suggested things seldom got her down. Her name tag read CORA.

"Excuse me, Cora, I'm looking for John Hamman Highway. Can you help me out?"

She looked at him quizzically and then shook her head. At that moment, the other waitress working the lunch shift passed by.

"Hey, Micki," Cora said, softly enough not to disturb the customers, "John Hamman Highway. You ever heard of that?"

"I'm looking for the Whitestone Laboratory," Ben added.

"Never heard of that either," Cora said.

"Isn't John Hamman Highway the same as Lawtonville Road?" Micki asked. "They changed the name a year or so ago,'member?"

"An' named it after that Lawtonville boy

who got that medal for gettin' killed in Iraq. I remember."

"Exactly. Just follow Main Street west an' when it forks, take the right one. Don't know of any Whitestone Laboratory, though."

"Well, thanks," Ben said, relieved that the road existed at all. "I'll find it."

"In fact you will."

The affirmation had come from the man seated alone in the next booth. He was in his mid to late thirties, with a square jaw, widely spaced eyes, and a dense mat of curly brown hair.

"You know Whitestone Laboratory?" Ben asked, sensing from the lack of interaction between him and the waitresses that he wasn't local.

"I'm going to work there tomorrow."

"You a chemist of some sort?"

"Me?" The man laughed at the notion. "Heck no. I'm a flight attendant. Friend of mine, works with me at Southwest, makes extra money doing a private gig for Whitestone, only he can't make it this time and turned it over to me. Seth Stepanski."

Ben shook the man's hand and rated his grip at least a seven out of ten.

"Ben," he said, sensing that, unlike his fictional heroes, he would fumble if he tried to make up a name on the spot, "Ben Callahan."

Without waiting to be asked, Stepanski put a bill on his table and swung around to take the seat opposite Ben.

"You expected at Whitestone?" he asked.

"Nope," Ben said, now thinking faster, and ready to ad-lib in any way he could to keep Seth Stepanski engaged, although clearly the man was grateful for company. "I sell lab equipment, and the lab director at Whitestone contacted us about an upgrade."

"Well, I'm not sure they're open for business today," Stepanski said. "I'm from Corsicana, south of Dallas. The drive here took a lot less than I had planned for, and I ended up getting in here last night, so I drove out there this morning to see if maybe they needed some help with the plane."

"And?"

"I never even made it close to the buildings. High fencing all the way around, barbed wire on top. Looks like a maximum-security prison without the guard towers. It's way out there in the middle of the desert. Nothing, and I mean *nothing* around. I could make out a bunch of buildings in the distance, but when I rang the bell at the gate and told them who I was, this woman told me I wasn't expected until tomorrow afternoon and there was no one around to take care of me today."

Ben was totally intrigued.

"So you're flying out late tomorrow?"

"No, no, Thursday morning. Apparently they have a place for me to stay tomorrow night."

"But not tonight."

"Not tonight," Stepanski echoed.

"Sounds like I may end up waiting until tomorrow, too."

"It's about a ten-mile drive each way. Maybe you should call. Not doing that was my mistake."

"I'll do it."

"If you need a motel, the Quality Inn where I'm staying is as good as any."

"Thanks," Ben said, searching for ways to expand their conversation. "Hey listen, why don't I call and see if my contact at Whitestone is there. If she's not, maybe we can go find some cowboy bar, have us a couple of beers, an' maybe play some darts."

Did I just start speaking with a twang? Ben wondered as he put a twenty on the table and headed out to the Rover, allegedly to get his cell phone and the Whitestone number. He reminded himself that while his paperback heroes might know precisely how to handle this situation, for him, every move was a swim through uncharted waters.

Seth Stepanski was anything but interesting. His hobby seemed to be watching TV and breasts in clubs, and his main goal in life seemed to be finding a replacement for a woman named Sherry, who had dropped him when he didn't come through with a pro-posal in a timely fashion.

They were drinking beer in a booth in a dimly lit bar named, simply, Charlie's, and were working their way into their second hour and third beer together.

"Women like to date flight attendants be-cause they get to fly almost anywhere cheap," he said, his speech just a bit thickened.

"I can see where that might be a plus," Ben said, having realized that he needn't worry about keeping their conversation go-ing, merely directed.

Sadly, after the initial spurt of promising information at Mother Molly's, Stepanski had dried up. He wasn't sure of the destination of his flight, and had absolutely no idea who would be aboard. He did know that wherever they were headed, he would need his passport, and that they wouldn't be staying wherever it was for more than two or three days. He also added that what he was about to be paid was equivalent to a month's salary at Southwest.

Given what Alice Gustafson had learned about Whitestone, Ben wondered if some executives might be flying back to England. He was trying to think of anything else he might ask when Stepanski's eyes widened and he gestured out the window.

"Holy shit! Look at that rig."

Ben swung around and suspected that his eyes had widened, too. Rolling slowly up the street, like a sleek, invading spaceship, was a metallic gray Winnebago Adventurer—*the* Winnebago Adventurer, he felt certain, as he strained to see if Vincent was at the wheel.

"Goodness," he murmured.

"Two hundred thousand, I'll bet," Stepanski exclaimed, whistling for emphasis. "Maybe more. A rolling hotel."

Right idea, Ben thought. *Wrong H word.*

They watched in awed silence as the impressive RV eased down Main Street headed west. Ben knew the alligator had just jumped into his net. The next move was up to him.

It took most of the afternoon and several hours away from Seth Stepanski for Ben to formulate a plan, convince himself that it was a good idea, and finally put the pieces together. He felt focused and keen, but also more than a little apprehensive. There were a thousand possibilities that could go wrong, some of which might merely mess things up, some of which might kill him.

The story he used to get free of Stepanski was a stretch, even more so when Alice Gustafson didn't answer her office phone. His alternative plan required a call to his cell phone from Althea Satterfield.

"Whatever I say, Mrs. Satterfield, you just listen," he told her slowly, having gone to the Rover on the pretext of getting a map. "Don't say a word. Not a word."

"I listen," she repeated. "I'm a very good listener, dear."

"I know you are. Okay, five minutes and you call me on the cell phone number."

"The number I have right here."

"Exactly. How's Pincus?"

"Oh, he's just fine, dear. Why just a few hours ago he—"

"Okay, Mrs. Satterfield, call me in exactly five minutes from . . . now."

His performance, while Althea listened in Chicago and Stepanski listened across the booth, was worthy of an Oscar. In the end, the flight attendant believed that Ben's boss had contacted their Whitestone Laboratory client and arranged a business meeting for the two of them at the woman's home in Pullman Hills, ten miles to the east of Fadiman. The trick from then until Ben was ready would be to keep from being spotted by Stepanski driving around town.

"I'll register at the Quality Inn when I get back," Ben said as they split up on the street outside of Charlie's. "Save your appetite and we'll have dinner together if you'd like."

It was nearly eight when Ben stopped by the motel and picked up his new friend. Everything was in place but Ben's resolve, which seemed to be wavering from minute to minute. At a quarter of ten, with the town drifting off to sleep, they finished their Texas-sized steaks at a place called the Rodeo Grille, and headed back to the Rover through a largely empty parking lot.

"Before we call it a night," Ben said, having pumped the man for as much personal information as possible, "I have something I want to show you."

They drove north for almost twenty minutes. There was some evidence along the way that Fadiman was expanding in that direction, but it would be years, maybe decades before civilization filled in the spaces. If Stepanski was curious about their destination, five beers and a huge meal kept him from voicing it.

Finally, Ben pulled into the driveway of Budget Self-Storage, the first of such businesses he had passed on his way in from Oklahoma. The neon sign was off, the small office dark.

"What's out here?" Stepanski asked, clearly unconcerned about the man with whom he had spent much of the day.

They passed the row of corrugated steel units in the front, and went to the far end of the second row. That was where Ben pulled over.

"So, Seth," he said, "we need to talk."

"What in the hell is—?"

The flight attendant stopped short when he realized that Ben was almost casually pointing a pistol at a spot between his eyes.

CHAPTER 23

But then, if I am right, certain professors of education must be wrong when they say that they can put knowledge into the soul which was not there before, like sight into blind eyes.

—PLATO, *The Republic,* Book VII

Despite her seat in first class, Natalie's flight back to Rio was not pleasant. Three times, maybe four, the powerful images of the cab ride from the airport to the slums—*favelas,* her mother said they were called—and the assault against her intruded into her thoughts. It didn't seem to matter whether she was awake or asleep. The reenactment, "reexperience" would be a more appropriate word, continued to be jagged—totally vivid and absorbing one moment, vague and ill-defined the next, more like a bad trip than a bad memory.

Once she woke up gasping and hyper-ventilating, with a sheen of perspiration across her forehead and lip.

"Are you all right?" the elderly Brazilian man next to her asked.

He was a jovial widower returning home after visiting his children and grandchildren in the States, and as a retired teacher, spoke English quite well.

"I'm fine, fine," she replied. "Just getting over a virus is all."

"Here," said the man, handing her a sheet that was clearly an e-mail printout. "My son in Worcester gave this to me. You may know that we who are from Rio de Janeiro are called Cariocas. Well, this humorous piece, 'Places to Visit in Rio,' was written by a Carioca reporter for this wonderful publication: *A Gringo's Guide to Brazil.*"

The tongue-in-cheek list, though it would have been quite funny if read in the right circumstances, was hardly the cure for Natalie's "virus." There were fourteen items altogether, including,

Downtown the street vendor riots are spectacular, comparable, perhaps, to the salmon runs in the Yukon.

Mangueria Hill by night is for those brave souls who love fireworks displays. Not the kind from Roman candles, but the kind from .38 Specials.

Like to watch violent and shocking movies? None of them can compare to any police station in Rio. As the cops like to say, "This is where a child cries and not even his mother hears."

Sick of your hometown bums and jerks? Try ours. They can be found legislating in the halls of our State Assembly.

The Central Station rest rooms. After 10 p.m. they are no-man's-land— the world's biggest bordello. Just pick a sex.

Natalie smiled palely and passed the sheet back.

"I feel better already," she said.

Before leaving her apartment for Boston's Logan, Natalie had considered and quickly rejected the notion of taking a cab or a bus from the airport in Rio to her hotel. Instead, she went online and reserved a hard-top Jeep. Now, as she pulled out of the Jobim airport and cruised south on the expressway into the city, she tried to keep her breathing even and her pulse in check. Thanks largely to the unremitting flashbacks to her shooting, the two months that had passed since her ill-fated ride into the city might as easily have been six hours.

The customers at the House of Love will adore you. You will be very happy there. . . .

It was mid-morning—cloudless and already warm. From time to time, as she drove, Natalie glanced off to her right, the direction she was fairly certain the cab had taken that night. There were shantytowns packed at the bottom of barren hillsides. Much farther up above them were lawns and palms and, with what must have been spectacular views toward the ocean, mansions. Somewhere, in one of those squalid, overcrowded *favelas,* she had been pulled from her cab and soon after, shot.

The hotel she had chosen, the Rui Mi-

rador, was given two stars by one of the online travel services, but was presented as
quaint, clean, and safe—all words that resonated for her. It was in the Botafogo section
of the city, described by the same service as
both traditional and exciting. What Natalie
cared about was that Botafogo was also
where Santa Teresa Hospital was located.

Traffic on the expressway was heavy, and
the drivers somewhat less than courteous,
but it didn't take long for her to appreciate
that thanks to years of driving in Boston, she
was well prepared. In spite of her persistent
edginess, Natalie felt herself drawn to the
steep hills, lush vegetation, and spectacular
architecture of the area. Botafogo was a
fairly narrow corridor between Centro—the
downtown—and the beaches of Copacabana and Ipanema. With the help of an excellent map, she found her way through the
sometimes narrow streets to the Pasmado
Overlook—the one tourist attraction she had
promised herself, in addition, possibly, to the
magnificent white-sand beaches. After the
stop at Pasmado, it would be strictly business. She had no desire to linger in Rio, and
planned to fly home as soon as the mystery

of exactly who had cared for her and where was settled. The rest of the city, however spectacular and exciting, would forever remain unknown to her.

Suddenly weary from the long flight, Natalie sank onto a bench at the overlook and gazed out across Guanabara Bay and up to the statue of Christ the Redeemer. *Beautiful,* she thought, realizing at the same time that she wasn't experiencing the incredible sight in any emotional part of her being.

"So, what do you think of our little statue?"

Startled, Natalie turned to the heavily accented voice. A uniformed policeman stood close by, right hand resting on his short, black rubber nightstick. He was swarthy, well built, and handsome in a matinee idol sort of way, with narrow features and a hawk's dark eyes. The name tag pinned over his breast pocket read VARGAS.

"It's very beautiful, very moving," she said. "How did you know I was American?"

"You look Brazilian, but next to you is a dead giveaway that you are a tourist." The officer gestured to the map on the bench beside her. "A guess that any tourist is American would be right more often than wrong."

Natalie managed a smile.

"My family is from Cape Verde. Are you local police?"

"Military, actually."

"Where did you learn to speak English so well?"

"I am flattered that you would even think so. I spent a year in Missouri when I was in school. Have you been in Rio long?"

Natalie shook her head.

"I haven't even checked into my hotel yet."

"Oh, and where is that?"

Perhaps it was the nightmare with the cab driver, perhaps an eagerness—perceived or actual—in the man's tone, but suddenly Natalie found herself wary. The last thing she needed at the moment was an amorous advance from a cop.

"The Inter-Continental," she lied, standing quickly. "Well, I'd better get there and register. Have a good day."

"Do you know the way? Perhaps I could—"

"No, no. Thank you, though. This map and I are becoming the best of friends."

She refused to look the man in the eye for fear of seeing hurt, or worse, anger.

"Very well, then," he said. "May I wish that you have a wonderful time in Rio."

*   *   *

The Rui Mirador, a four-story brownstone, was as described on the travel site, quaint and clean. As for safety, the clerk at the small desk by the entrance assured Natalie that his post was manned 24/7.

"We are each proficient in the use of this," he said in Portuguese, proudly brandishing an ugly, long-barreled pistol, which he produced from a drawer beneath the counter.

Not as confident in the hotel's security system as she might have liked, Natalie registered nevertheless and toted her bag up three flights to a small room that featured little else save for a pair of twin platform beds. *Two stars is two stars,* she reminded herself, but she also knew sleep was going to be a problem. Unwilling to be placed at the mercy of the city by staying out late, she decided her most prudent move would, at some point, be the purchase of a bottle of fine Brazilian whiskey along with, perhaps, a visit to the pharmacy.

It was just after noon by the time she had showered and changed into a beige linen suit and short-sleeved turquoise blouse. There was a microsized air conditioner in one of the two windows of her room, but at that point, neither the heat nor the humidity demanded its use. The Jeep was parked in a lot a block from the hotel, but her targets for this day, a police station or two and the hospital, could be reached by foot. Dense traffic—pedestrian and cars—also mitigated against driving, but then there was the matter of negotiating the hills. As it had been since the fire, her breathing was seldom natural and unintrusive. Satisfying, deep breaths were incredibly welcome when they occurred, but they were few and far between. She could have used two or three more weeks of pulmonary rehab, but her doctor and therapists had made it clear that even then, nothing at all would have been guaranteed except, perhaps, for a drop in her lung allocation score.

The desk clerk was clearly curious about why she wanted to visit two or three police stations—especially since she seemed to have little idea that there were three completely different police forces—municipal, tourist, and military. With the help of the phone book, he marked one station of each on her map and pointed her in the right direction. In fact, the man's conclusions were incorrect. Following her return home, Natalie had learned as much about the various police forces in Brazil as repeated Internet searches could teach her. What she gleaned did not make her that comfortable in relying on any of them, or in believing that her near-kidnapping in one of the *favelas* north and west of the downtown area would ever be investigated.

Anxious not to run into the officer from the Pasmado Overlook, and reasoning that he might still be out on patrol, perhaps searching out other female tourists to welcome, she chose to start at the station of the Military Police. It was a modern, single-story brick and glass structure on Rua São Clemente, about half the size of an average McDonald's back in Boston, and just as crowded. The officer at the front desk, after she asked him to please speak a little slower, referred her back to a Detective Perreira, short and at least forty pounds overweight, with a pencil-thin mustache and a cold smile. His English was serviceable, though broken and heavily accented, but Natalie decided against telling him that her Portuguese was probably better.

"So, I see that was quite a difficult welcoming to our city," he said after she had told

him her story and presented him with one of
the hundred copies of a flyer she had made
on her computer. The single sheet included
a photo of her, and a summary, in her
mother's Portuguese, of the events of her attack as she remembered them, or could
piece them together.

"I can't fully describe to you how terrible
an experience it was to be attacked in such
a way," she said. "The taxi driver said he was
going to take me to a place called the House
of Love."

Perreira reacted not at all, but instead began typing on his computer keyboard while
Natalie waited, trying not to stare at the
massive pseudo-chin rolling out from beneath his real one.

"And you say that this crime which occurred on you was reported to the police?"
he asked finally.

"I was in a deep coma when I was found,
but I was told the police had called the ambulance that brought me to the hospital."

"Santa Teresa Hospital."

"Yes."

"But you telephoned to them and they
mentioned that they have no record of you
as being a patient there."

"I am going to Santa Teresa's when I leave here to see if I can straighten that confusion out."

"And certain you are the dates you have given to me are correct?"

"I am."

Perreira sighed audibly and tapped his stubby fingertips together.

"Senhorita Reyes," he said, "we Military Police pay very close attention to people who get shot in our cities—especially tourists. We have to uphold to a reputation."

In her more cynical days, Natalie most certainly would have asked for clarification of precisely what reputation he was talking about. Her research had revealed much about the role of the Military Police in the death squads that were believed to be responsible for the murders of hundreds, if not thousands, of street urchins over the years, including the notorious massacre in 1993 when fifty street children were shot and eight killed in front of the Candelaria church.

"So, what have you learned about my shooting?" she asked, motioning toward the computer.

"The databases of the Military Police I

have searched, and also the, how do you say, civil or municipal police, and then also the tourist police."

"Yes?"

"There are in none of them records of anyone of your name to have been shot on the dates you have written here."

"But what about—"

"I have checked also for unknown females shot on those dates. Also none."

"That makes no sense."

"Perhaps it does and perhaps it does not. Senhorita Reyes, you say you are student."

"A medical student, yes."

"In our country, students are very often poor. Do you own much money?"

Natalie sensed where the man was headed and began to burn.

"I am older than most students," she said coolly. "I have enough money to take care of myself. Detective Perreira, please get to the point."

"The point. . . . Let me see. . . . I am sure that being as a medical student, you know that in countries such as this, 'Third World countries' I have heard you Americans call us, some people in desperate need for money sell on the black market a kidney or part of a liver or even a lung. The payments to them, I have heard, often are quite high."

"So even if I sold my lung on the black market, which I most certainly did not, why would I be here?"

Perreira's mirthless smile was triumphant.

"Guilt," he replied. "Guilt over what have you done, joined with denial that you did actually do it. Pardon me for saying this fact, senhorita, but in a lifetime of working on this job, I have seen stranger things—much stranger."

Natalie had heard enough. She knew there was nothing to be gained by losing her temper at the policeman, and potentially much to lose. The police in Brazil were answerable to few besides themselves, and the Military Police were, from what she could tell, the most dangerously autonomous of all.

"Believe me, Detective Perreira," she said, standing and gathering her things, "I would look a dozen times for a deficiency in your computer system before looking for one in me. If something comes up, I am staying at the Hotel Rui Mirador."

She whirled and marched through the

crowd and out of the little station. It wasn't until she was on the street that she realized her brief outburst had left her considerably short of breath.

The next four hours were an exhausting blur. On paper—specifically her map—Santa Teresa's looked to be no more than six or seven blocks from the Military Police station. Had the map been topographical, Natalie might have hailed a cab. The hills were steep and unavoidable, and the walk across Botafogo, however picturesque, was slow going in the mounting afternoon heat. By the time she passed through the main entrance to the hospital, she could feel the perspiration beneath her clothes.

The main structure of the sprawling hospital, four monolithic stories of stone, a block in every direction, looked like it might have been built by Brazilian discoverer Pedro Cabral in the early sixteenth century. To that central core, now modernized inside, wings and towers had been added in a dozen different architectural styles. Natalie chose to visit the administrative offices first, and hit pay dirt immediately—at least in a manner of speaking.

A vice president by the name of Gloria Duarte seemed quite interested in her as an accomplished, intelligent woman, and was sincerely sympathetic with her plight. They conversed in Portuguese, although from a glance at the woman's extensive library, Natalie sensed Duarte, warm, urbane, quick-witted, and insightful, could have communicated in any number of languages, including English.

"What disturbs me most of your story," Duarte said, "is how sure you are, backed by your mentor, Doctor—"

"Berenger. Douglas Berenger."

"Dr. Berenger, that the physician who did the surgery on you was someone named Xavier Santoro. We have no such physician on this staff, and I know of none in the city, although perhaps you should contact the state medical association."

"I did. You are right. There is no physician by that name."

"I see. . . . Well, one step at a time, I suppose."

"One step at a time," Natalie repeated, chagrined that Duarte's enthusiasm might have cooled.

"I would like to say that patients never fall

through the cracks of our hospital," the woman went on, "but that is simply not the case. We have all together more than two thousand beds, and they are full much of the time. A simple clerical error and all of your records might exist under a name one letter different from your own. So take heart. I suspect this part of your mystery will be solved quickly, and that the solution will prove to be trivial and mundane."

With that, she sent Natalie to the security office for a visitor's identification badge that would allow her access to any area of the hospital, including the record room and all of the medical and surgical wards. She also had copies of Natalie's flyer made and instructed her secretary to distribute them to all hospital departments with an addendum to notify Duarte herself of any information, however remote the connection might seem.

A quick espresso in a courtyard café outside the administrative wing, and Natalie headed for the record room. *Reyes, Reyez, Rayes.* Seated at a terminal in a carrel with one of the record-room clerks, she tried every permutation she could think of without success, and went through records on unknown females as well. Next she headed to the medical, then the surgical intensive care units. She had some recollection of two of her nurses' faces, and also of Santoro's, and wistfully hoped she might simply run into one of them.

Even in a city like New York or Rio, an unknown woman found shot and almost naked in an alley, and subsequently losing her lung, would have been a top cluster on the hospital grapevine. Sooner, rather than later, everyone would have heard about it. In fact, none of the nurses in either of the units had.

At five, bewildered and at an absolute loss for explanations, but physically unable to go on this day, Natalie shuffled from the hospital. Six weeks ago she had flown to Brazil, she had been attacked and shot in an alley, and she had lost her lung. Those were the givens. Somehow, someplace, there was an explanation that would tie these truths together. She checked her map, and chose a route back to her hotel that involved the largest and, she assumed, the flattest streets. The late-afternoon sun was somewhat subdued by haze, and the temperature was bearable.

She had flown to Brazil. She had been attacked. She had lost her lung.

The thought, roiling through her brain, kept her from appreciating the incredible beauty of the city, or any of the burgeoning, vibrant, rush-hour pedestrians, most probably making their way home. Despite all the guidebooks' descriptions of laid-back Cariocas, the street corners were much like New York—masses of people, shoulder to shoulder, often eight or ten deep, jockeying for position to cross while cars and taxis tried to wring every single moment out of each green light.

Natalie was at a particularly busy intersection, sardined in, perhaps the third or fourth row of bodies, when she heard a woman's voice speaking in Portuguese not far from her ear.

"Please do not turn around, Dr. Reyes. Please do not look at me. Just listen. Dom Angelo has the answers that you seek. Dom Angelo."

At that instant, the light changed and the phalanx moved forward across the street, sweeping Natalie helplessly along. She was on the curb at the far side before she turned, scanning the faces around her, and peering through the crowd toward the corner they had just left. No one seemed the least bit interested in her. She was about to give up and focus on the strange message when she caught sight of a heavyset woman wearing a brightly flowered housedress, walking urgently away from her, moving with a fairly pronounced lurch as if one of her hips were bad. A man's voice, demanding that she move out of the way, diverted Natalie's attention for just a moment. When she turned back, the woman was gone.

Natalie was stuck again toward the center of the pedestrian centipede, and with autos speeding past to clear the intersection, there was no way she could head back until the light changed. When she finally reached the previous block, the woman in the brightly colored dress was nowhere on the street. She hurried up to the next intersection and scanned both ways. Nothing.

Slightly winded by her efforts, Natalie leaned against the façade of a clothing boutique. There was no doubt in her mind that the voice that had spoken to her belonged to the woman with the limp—no doubt because she felt certain the two of them had met earlier in the afternoon, albeit only in passing, in the surgical ICU at Santa Teresa Hospital.

CHAPTER 24

Necessity . . . is the mother of invention.
—PLATO, *The Republic,* Book II

It's Stepanski. Seth Stepanski, the flight attendant."

"Welcome to Whitestone, Mr. Stepanski. After the gate opens, please drive directly to Building Six in the Oasis and come in to register. You have your own uniform?"

"Yes. Yes I do."

"Excellent. We'll see you here in just a minute."

The gate, ten-foot-high heavy chain-link topped with razor wire, glided soundlessly to Ben's right, opening onto a ruler-straight road that looked to be at least a quarter of a

mile long. Driving Stepanski's Sebring convertible, he approached the compound
slowly. In the wheel well, where the spare
had been, was his detective's valise, and
tucked beneath that was his .38.

The conglomeration of eight or nine pink-
washed adobe structures glowed in the late-
afternoon sun. Two dozen good-sized trees,
the only significant vegetation and shade for
miles, greatly reduced the starkness of the
place, which he assumed was what the in-
tercom voice had referred to as the Oasis.

One of the buildings, Ben knew, probably
the largest, housed a laboratory. The technicians working there were probably unaware
of the evil in which they were accomplices as
they tissue-typed and electronically catalogued millions of green-topped vials from
unsuspecting clients all over the country—
probably even the world.

The notion sickened him.

Beside the engine of the Sebring, the
thrum of massive rooftop air-conditioning
units was the only sound penetrating the
hot, still Texas air. As he approached a pair
of trees, flanking the roadway like sentinels,
Ben caught sight of the Adventurer, parked
toward the right rear of the Oasis. He

couldn't shake the painful suspicion that some version of Lonnie Durkin was imprisoned inside, frightened beyond imagination as he or she waited to be told why they were there.

Ben had darkened his hair and bought a pair of heavy-rimmed glasses, but made no other attempt to change his appearance. The picture in Stepanski's passport was slightly blurred, well-worn, and seven years old. He was five years Ben's junior, but had similar enough coloring and facial shape to make Ben's passing for him not too much of a stretch. Best of all, the flight attendant, now a resident of Unit 89 of the Budget Self-Storage Company, had made it clear that no one at Whitestone knew what he looked like.

Unfortunately, Ben was unable, with any comfort, to make the same claim about himself. As he approached Building 6, he played over and over again his brief, violent encounter in the dilapidated garage on Laurel Way in Cincinnati. The whole fight with the man named Vincent couldn't have lasted much more than half a minute. The lighting was minimal, and only once, a moment before the jet of black spray paint ended the struggle, did the killer get a straight-on look at his face. Was the man permanently blinded? *Doubtful.* Was he behind the wheel of the Adventurer as it rolled through Fadiman? If so, was he slated to be on board the upcoming flight? At that moment, the questions far outnumbered their answers.

Building 6 was a fairly small office decorated with framed, artfully done posters of monuments from around the world. Standing behind a counter, following him with her eyes from the moment he entered, was a slender, middle-aged brunette with the bearing of a Marine. Her navy suit had the single word WHITESTONE embroidered in script just above the left breast pocket.

Ben was trying to look and act nonchalant, but he was on absolute red alert, his pulse hammering. He wanted desperately to go back outside and try another, more composed entrance. Instead, he introduced himself.

"Welcome, Mr. Stepanski," the woman said, her eyes unwavering. "I'm Janet, the office manager. You have your passport and the letter we sent you?"

Ben set both items, retrieved from Stepanski's motel room, on the counter. Janet gave them each a cursory examination, perhaps hesitating for a moment on the passport photo. Then she slid them both to one side. Ben pressed his hands against the counter to keep them from shaking.

Do you know, Janet? Do you know what goes on here?

"I stopped by yesterday to see if I could help get the flight ready," he said for no particular reason other than to loosen up and get a little deeper into character.

"I know," she said. "That was me you spoke to. Our policy is to make plans and stick closely to them."

"I understand."

No real explanation, no apology for not being able to oblige him. Janet the office manager was all business. For him, maintaining eye contact was a must. From here on he was in enemy territory. If he were caught, it seemed doubtful he would be allowed to live.

"Okay, Mr. Stepanski, weather permitting, you will be leaving at nine in the morning. You should be in uniform at this office at seven with enough clothes for a four-day trip. It is possible, as we wrote you, that several more days will be added. You will be tending to the needs of six passengers and a crew of three. The flight will be transporting a patient to South America for an operation that cannot be performed in this country. The patient will be with her doctors at the rear of the aircraft. You are forbidden from going back there unless specifically asked. If our passengers wish to engage in conversation with you, they will do so. Otherwise, their privacy is to be respected. Questions?"

"None."

"Good. Here's the key to room seven. It is in Building Two, just down this road and to your right. You are not permitted in any part of the Oasis except on the patio by your room and in the canteen located in Building Three, which is right behind Building Two."

"I understand."

He took the key and turned to go.

"Mr. Stepanski?"

Ben stiffened, then turned slowly back to her, his pulse in crescendo again.

"Yes?"

She handed him his passport.

"It's probably time for a new photo."

Ben decided to leave his .38 in the wheel well. There was no way he was going to be in any situation he could ever shoot his way out of, especially given that he had never fired a gun at anything other than a shooting range target, and on those rare occasions, with no great skill. If he had somehow given himself away to Janet, he would know soon enough, and there probably wouldn't be a damn thing he could do about it.

Room 7, small but neat enough, had little on the budget motels in which he usually stayed. Still, he mused as he unpacked his bag and set the alarm for six, Seth Stepanski would have probably given up his prized collection of beer steins to be spending the night in this room rather than where he was.

Ben felt distressed at taking advantage of the man the way he had, and even worse at the discomfort he had to inflict on him to keep him immobilized where he was and yet alive. Whether or not Ben would have put Stepanski's life in jeopardy, he wasn't sure, but he did know that the moment he pulled his gun, he had stepped off a cliff. Now whatever he had to do to keep from crashing on the rocks below, he would do. In the end, with inspired imagination, a carefully chosen storage locker, a dozen padlocks and lengths of chain, and enough time, he had constructed a setup of which Rube Goldberg would have been proud.

The key was the steel supports that ran across the ceiling and around the walls of the locker, which was one of Budget's jumbo units—sixteen by twenty. Stepanski, undressed from the waist down, was fixed in the exact center of the room, chained to the ceiling and walls in such a way that he had only enough mobility to switch awkwardly from a bridge chair to the commode that Ben had purchased in a hospital supply store and attached to it. His hands were cuffed behind him, and duct tape was wrapped around his head, covering his mouth. A hole poked in the center of the tape made breathing easier and allowed him to drink by straw from any of a dozen bottles of water, juices, and protein beverages set up on a bridge table in front of him. The heat might be a problem, but Ben chose Unit 89 not only because it was one of the farthest from the Budget office, but because it was well shaded.

By eleven that night, Stepanski was secured and the setup checked and rechecked. Still, Ben made two more visits to the locker to look in on his prisoner and to replenish the beverage supply. At noon, just a few hours before he headed out to White-stone, he sat down on the floor and, arms wrapped around his knees, told the flight attendant in detail exactly what was going on at the lab and what he hoped to do about it. Stepanski begged to be released and promised to head home and say nothing, but Ben had gone as far as he dared to go.

"I have sent a box to a friend of mine," he said, "a professor at the University of Chicago. It contains the keys for these locks and a letter of explanation. In three days, she will either send the box overnight to the Fadiman police or drive down and release you herself. Hopefully, that will be enough time for me to figure out who and what Whitestone is, and to gather enough evidence to put whoever's running things out of business and into prison. I'm really sorry to put you through this, Seth, but I believe that what's going on with these people is way bigger than either of us."

He put a pair of earphones around Stepanski's neck and set a pocket radio behind him.

"I tried this out myself," he said. "With a little practice you can learn how to adjust the volume and change the station. You'll get three or four stations in here, but I sure hope you like country-western."

Finally, he set three nips of Jack Daniel's and three of José Cuervo Gold tequila on the bridge table, with straws in each.

"Because you're traveling first class with us," he said, "there'll be no charge for these beverages."

He set the earphones in place, then patted the man on the shoulder, and left.

From the moment he opened the door to Unit 7, Ben was locked in a debate as to whether it was worth the risk to try to make it around the Oasis, and ultimately to the Winnebago. If he went, it would have to be with his contact microphone. His particular model of the spy gear was low-end, but still serviceable for listening through walls. If he was caught carrying it, no amount of excuses would bail him out. Hoping against hope, he tried calling Alice Gustafson on his cell to discuss the situation. There was no signal whatsoever.

For a few hours, until darkness had firmly settled in, he rested and tried reading one of the magazines on his bedside table—a recent *People.* Usually for him, reading *People* was like drinking a chocolate frappe—absolutely effortless. Tonight, the celebrity-studded articles went down like ground glass. Somewhere out there a plane was being readied for a flight to someplace in South America. At the end of that flight, Ben felt fairly certain, someone with money, perhaps even one of the *People* stars, would be given life at the expense of someone like Lonnie Durkin or the chambermaid, Juanita Ramirez.

Wearing dark clothing, he stepped outside onto his room's small patio. The air was still quite warm and humid, but the vast, black sky was starless, and a hot wind had picked up from the west. Unit 7 was at the end of Building 2, not fifteen yards from the chain-link fence. Ben walked to the fence across a small corridor of grass. Beyond it, the blackness of the desert was indistinguishable from the sky, but in the distance, jagged spears of lightning pierced the night in a three-hundred-and-sixty-degree cyclorama.

The Oasis itself was not well lit, and the buildings were close enough together to offer some protection. Ben scanned the nearest structures for cameras, not really expecting to see them even if they were there. Then he carefully made his way back to the Sebring for his contact microphone and, he decided, his pistol. At this hour, any trouble he ran into might be with a single security guard. If the gun could help him make it to the car, there was a chance he could ram through the massive gate at the end of the drive. Just the idea of having his life depend on surviving that collision sent a jet of acid percolating into his throat. His fictional heroes never had trouble crashing through such gates unscathed, but he suspected that this particular gate might be more unyeilding.

Continuing his scan for security cameras, he crossed to the canteen in Building 3 and got a Diet Coke. Then, trying to stay under cover, he moved into the shadows of first one building, then another. The lightning spears appeared much closer now, and he swore he could hear thunder. The largest building, 5, had some pale light inside. Through the windows, he could just make out rows and rows of sophisticated laboratory equipment. It was neither difficult nor pleasant to imagine a tube of blood with his name on it being opened and processed by a tech working at one of those stations.

The streets of the Oasis seemed deserted, although in spots, the light from scattered windows washed into the night. Keenly on edge, clutching the case containing the contact microphone, and listening between every step for the sound of someone else, Ben maneuvered toward the Winnebago. Beneath his black, long-sleeved tee, he was unpleasantly damp.

The five minutes it took to reach the RV seemed like an hour. There was a faint glow from around the dining-area shade on the left side and the curtain pulled across inside the front windshield. Breathing heavily from tension more than exertion, Ben knelt just forward of the left rear tire and soundlessly unzipped the microphone case, which contained small earphones, an amplifier, and a thick, cylindrical receiver, about the size of half a roll of quarters. He worked the earphones into place and pressed the receiver against the side of the Winnebago. The quality of the reception wasn't great, but he could hear voices and make out most of what they were saying.

"Please, please let me go. I never did anything to you." The woman's voice, probably coming from the rear of the van, was quite clear.

"He's shooting the moon. For chrissakes, Connie, do you know how to play this game or not?"

Vincent! Ben was almost certain of it.

"Listen, Rudy, I have a kid, a son named Teddy. I told you all about him. Please, he needs me. Please let me go. Find someone else—someone without a little boy who needs her."

"Jesus, Connie, you dumb shit! You had to take a couple of hearts when you had the chance! Now he's going to get them all. Couldn't you tell that all he had was spades? Listen, Sandy, either you stop whining or I'm coming back there to put a sock in your mouth. And stop calling me Rudy. I hate the fucking name. I'm sorry I ever made it up."

The left earpiece was painfully tight. Ben pulled it out and was adjusting it when he heard the soft crunch of footsteps from his right. Pulling the .38 from his waistband, he flattened out on the ground and quickly worked his way under the van. Seconds later, a pair of cowboy boots appeared no more than two feet from his face, and only an inch, he realized, from where he had dropped the contact microphone.

For an interminable ten seconds, nothing moved except Ben's thumb, silently releasing the safety on his gun. Then the boots turned, passing so close to the microphone that one seemed to have brushed it, and headed toward the front of the van. Still frozen, Ben watched as the boots passed beneath the windshield and moved to the door on the far side. A moment later, two sharp knocks cut through the heavy quiet.

"Vincent, Connie, it's just me, Billy," a youthful voice said.

The door to the Adventurer swung open, bathing the ground with light. Instantly, from within, Sandy began screaming.

"Help! Please help me! For God's sake, they're going to kill me! I'm in a cage. My name's Sandy. Please, please help me. I'm a mother. I have a little boy! He's only eight!"

"Oh, I have had enough of this shit."

There was a brief scuffling of feet from directly above where Ben was lying, and instantly, the screaming stopped. Ben felt ill. He had to do something. Should he simply charge into the van shooting? He would have to kill the guard named Billy, Vincent, Connie, and someone else as well. Kill four people. Was there any chance he could do it? Would it be better to wait?

Clutching the pistol, feeling detached, almost dreamlike, he inched out from under the van. He wondered what John Hamman had been thinking and feeling just before he charged the machine-gun nest or whatever he did to earn a posthumous medal and a godforsaken road named after him.

Ben pushed himself upright. If he was going to move, it had to be now, while the door to the van was open. Was there any way to stop—any way he could just slip back to his room and let them proceed, at least for the time being, with whatever was planned for the terrified woman named Sandy? In exchange for leaving them all he would be keeping alive his hope of exposing the horror of Whitestone. He hefted the .38 in his hand and moved to the rear of the van.

"Hey, Billy, what gives?" another voice from within the van asked, as if the woman's outburst had never happened.

"Paulie, hey, whassapnin?"

"Nothin' much, Billy. Jes playin' a little

hearts with Vincent an' Connie t' pass the time."

Ben moved silently to the corner of the van. He had never fired a gun at anything but a range target and once a couple of bottles. Now he would have to take out the guard at the doorway and then climb over his body to shoot three killers before they could reach their weapons. Did he have any chance? At some level he knew the answer was no, but he felt unable to stop.

"You ridin' shotgun on the flight tomorrow?" the guard asked.

"All four of us."

"Oh, hey, Smitty, I didn't even see you there."

"Hi, Billy. Quiet out there?"

Five.

Ben lowered his gun as sanity took over.

"Must be big stuff," Billy was saying. "Put in a word for me, Vincent, will ya? Doin' security here gets a little wearin'. In case you hadn't noticed, nothing much ever happens."

"I gotcha. We'll do what we can. Well, back to the cards."

"You guys take care."

"See ya, Billy."

The door closed and was bolted from the inside. Ten minutes later, still badly shaken by how close he had come both to killing and dying, Ben was safely back in his room.

At midnight a violent thunderstorm swept through the Oasis, and then vanished as quickly as it had arrived.

At three, still far too wired to sleep, he was standing by the window when suddenly, out in the desert well beyond the fence, the blue lights of a runway lit up the vastness, stretching as far as he could see. A few minutes later, accompanied by a roar that shook Building 2, a huge jet, possibly a 727, landed smoothly, taxied to the far end of the runway, and stopped.

Stepanski's uniform had been taken in by a greedy tailor in Fadiman. Now Ben removed it from the closet and brushed some lint from the lapel.

The alligator was in his net.

CHAPTER 25

Women must be taught . . . the art of war, which they must practice like the men.
—PLATO, *The Republic,* Book V

Dom Angelo.

With only those two words to go by, Natalie commenced a desperate search through every phone book she could find. Nothing. She spoke with the desk clerk at her hotel, who questioned whether or not she might have misheard, and the woman actually said *Don* Angelo.

"Would that make any difference?" she asked, instantly buying into the possibility.

"No," said the man.

His Portuguese-English dictionary said that *dom* meant gift, or gifted one, and was also a title, specifically, lord.

Now, uncertain over what the anxious nurse in the floral print dress might actually have said, Natalie trudged up to her room, totally spent from the long day, the hills of Rio, the heat, and probably some lingering jet lag. She felt as isolated and alone as she could ever remember. She was an athlete with a single, damaged lung that there was little chance of ever getting replaced. Don or Dom Angelo, even if she ever did find him, wasn't going to change that reality.

There was no need for Brazilian whiskey to help her sleep this night, or in fact, for anything other than the white noise of the air conditioner. Tomorrow she would make two stops at Santa Teresa's—the first to vice president Gloria Duarte's office, and the second to the surgical ICU. If she was unsuccessful, it would be back to the police.

Don Angelo . . . Dom Angelo . . .

As she drifted off, the names generated an unending Mobius loop of questions. Was one of them a title of some sort? A first name? Why had the woman not even tried to explain? Did it seem that obvious to her that Natalie would understand?

One thing that their brief encounter had made clear to her: There was more to the assault in the alley and the subsequent loss of her lung than she had believed.

With time, the drone of the air conditioner rocked her into an uneasy sleep, but twice during the night, her exhaustion lost out to the familiar, vivid reenactment of her attack. As was the case so many times before, the horror was more intense than mere memory, and in many ways more real and detailed than any nightmare. After the second episode, she was too shaken to fall back to sleep. She was deceived by the cabbie at the airport, she was shot, she was operated on, her lung was removed, she was well cared for, and she was flown home as soon as her identity was established. All of that was completely and absolutely true . . . and yet, it wasn't.

At some point, Natalie reconnected with sleep. It was nearly eleven when she awoke. By the time she had showered, dressed, and made it back to the hospital, it was just past noon. Duarte was at a meeting, she was told, and would not be back in the hospital until the following morning. On a lark, she asked the woman's secretary if either Don or Dom Angelo meant anything to her. The woman smiled politely and suggested that her boss, who knew almost everything, would be the one to ask.

Certain that the way things were going, the nurse she sought would be out of the hospital, too, Natalie made her way up to the second-floor surgical intensive care unit— the SIC-U, it would have been called in most hospitals in the States. Following the removal of her lung in one of Santa Teresa's twenty-one operating rooms, she would have been taken there.

Please be here, Natalie begged as she stepped through the automatic glass doors. *Please be here. . . .*

She scanned what she could see of the busy unit and felt her spirit begin to sink. The SIC-U was state-of-the-art—ten high-tech, glass-enclosed cubicles, arranged around a central core nursing-monitoring station. Slowly, nonchalantly, nodding and smiling at anyone who made eye contact, Natalie strolled around the circle. She shouldn't have come during lunchtime, she was thinking. She shouldn't have—

Wearing blue scrubs, writing in a red looseleaf notebook, the woman she was seeking emerged from the last cubicle and headed away from her. Her bulk and her pronounced limp left no doubt that she was the one from the street. Her pulse racing, Natalie caught up with the woman at the nursing station. Her face was cherubic and quite pretty. She wore a thin gold necklace, but no other jewelry, and no wedding ring. Her ID read DORA CABRAL.

"Excuse me, Senhorita Cabral," Natalie said softly in Portuguese.

The woman, smiling, looked up at her. Instantly, her expression tightened. Her gaze darted nervously about. For Natalie, her reaction eliminated what little doubt remained.

"Yes?" Dora asked.

"I am sorry to come here like this, senhorita, but I am desperate," Natalie said, worried that her Portuguese might not be up to the task. "I believe that you are the person who spoke to me on the street yesterday afternoon. If you are, please help me know who Dom Angelo is. I have tried to learn who he is, but I have failed."

"Not who," Dora said in a harsh whisper. "*Where*. It is a village. It is—"

The nurse stopped abruptly, scribbled something on the margin of a sheet of paper, pushed it an inch or so toward Natalie, rose clumsily, and lurched into the corridor toward the cubicle where she had been working.

Totally flustered, Natalie was about to reach for the paper when something made her turn toward the entrance. A policeman wearing the uniform of the Military Police had stepped into the unit and was just turning toward where she was standing. His arrival was clearly what had driven Dora away.

Natalie didn't dare reach for the paper, but did risk a glance at it.

8 P.M. 16 R.D. FELIX #13

By the time she turned back, the police officer was coming toward her, grinning. With a dense, sickening sensation, she immediately recognized him. It was Vargas, the one-man welcoming committee who had approached her at the Pasmado Overlook.

Even though they had met in Botafogo, the same section of the city as the hospital, and likely where Vargas was stationed, Natalie felt virtually certain this second meeting was no coincidence. She also felt frantic to get the policeman away from the desk in the nurses' station where Dora had written her address.

"Why, you're Officer Vargas, aren't you?" she gushed, hurrying over to him. "The policeman with the wonderful English. I recognized you immediately."

"From the park at Pasmado, yes?"

"Exactly. Thank you for remembering."

He asked her name, and she told him, although she had little doubt he already knew. Had he seen Dora writing? The desk was five feet behind where they were standing. She somehow had to move him in the other direction.

"Senhorita Natalie," he said charmingly, "pardon me for saying so, but Santa Teresa Hospital isn't on the usual tourist itinerary."

Natalie's mind was swirling. What was he doing here? If he had been following her since Pasmado, he knew that she had lied about staying at the Inter-Continental. If he had been following her since her landing at the Jobim airport, something very terrible was going on.

Natalie had never had much patience for flirts—men *or* women—and had proudly never considered herself very proficient at it. But now seemed like a good time to try.

"The last time I was here in your city," she said, "I had the misfortune to run into an unscrupulous cab driver."

"Unfortunately, we still have a number of those," Vargas replied, "although we at the Military Police are trying to stamp them out."

"Well, this man took me to this alley and . . . I-I just can't talk about it very easily. I came here to the hospital to straighten out some insurance matters and to thank the staff for taking such good care of me when I was a patient here."

"I see."

Natalie took a small step forward and looked up at him, trying for an expression that was soft and vulnerable.

"Officer Vargas, if I was away from here, I think I could talk to you about what happened."

"Oh?"

"Do you have a few minutes, perhaps for a cup of coffee?"

"For you, I would gladly make time."

"Thank you." She touched his arm and sighed. "Something horrible has happened to me, and I would do anything to get to the bottom of it. *Anything.* Perhaps it is a blessing that you have dropped into my life not once, but twice."

"Perhaps," the policeman said as she led

him out the doors and toward the café. "Or perhaps I am the one who is blessed."

Dom Angelo, State of Rio de Janeiro, population 213.

The Botafogo branch library had that much information on the village, but little more. On some maps, it was located seventy-five miles north and west of the city, in what the reference librarian told her was the eastern part of the Rio de Janeiro rain forest. On other maps it wasn't listed at all. After an hour and a half of searching, Natalie had drawn a map that it seemed would guide her there—or at least close to there. Hopefully, at eight this evening, Dora Cabral would have more information on the place and what sort of answers Natalie could hope to find there.

It took most of an hour for her to disconnect from Rodrigo Vargas, a decorated veteran, he said, of fifteen years in the Military Police, long separated from his wife, but active in the lives of his two children. He knew Detective Perreira well, and described him as a man who spent far too much time sitting down. Throughout their conversation, during which Natalie said nothing of Dora Cabral or Dom Angelo, the policeman gave no indication that his appearance in the SIC-U while she just happened to be there was anything other than coincidence.

In the end, he said that given her unpleasant experience in Rio, he understood why she might have been reluctant to give the name of her hotel out just because a man was wearing a uniform and claimed to be a policeman. He then promised to go over some of the ground covered by Perreira, and gave her the name of a bistro where the two of them could meet tomorrow for lunch to update each other.

"I hope this is the beginning of a special friendship, Senhorita Natalie," he said earnestly as they stood to go.

"So do I, Rodrigo," she said, trying for a come-hither smile, and holding on for an extra beat when they shook hands. "So do I."

They parted inside the hospital, and Natalie got directions to the library from the information desk. She left, praying that Dora had taken advantage of the chance to destroy what she had written. Once on the street, she began moving through the city with absolute attention to whether she was being followed, employing every maneuver she had ever seen on TV or in the movies, plus a few she made up on the spot. She had four hours before she was expected at Dora's—four hours and a lengthy list of things she needed to get if she was going to drive into the rain forest.

By six thirty she had been to the library, hardware and outdoor gear stores, and several clothing outlets, taking some purchases with her, and promising to return for the rest once she had her car. If there was someone watching the Jeep, there would be no way she could retrieve it without being seen and probably followed, but she had no choice. A bigger fear was that the car would be gone, or in some way disabled, but it was right where she had left it, in a small garage two blocks from her hotel.

16 R.D. FELIX #13

With help from the reference librarian, she located Rua de Felix in the Gávea section of the city, three miles west of Botafogo. She loaded up the Jeep, covering everything with a canvas. Then, wishing it were darker, she began a serpentine drive from the shore to the hills and back again, racing through red lights, driving up alleys and through parking lots, and making any number of U-turns, always with an eye on the rearview mirror.

When she was reasonably certain she wasn't being followed, she locked up the Jeep in a well-lit spot, and with an unpleasant tension in her chest, flagged down a yellow cab. Gratefully, the driver was a weathered, gum-chewing woman, who reminded her not at all of the cabbie from the airport. Using a map, and ad-libbing when it seemed right to do so, she directed the woman up streets and back down, around blocks and through alleys. Finally, she asked to be dropped off a block from Rua de Felix. It was an indescribable relief when the driver simply complied.

The neighborhood was more run-down than Natalie had expected given Dora Cabral's occupation. Tenements, most three stories high, and few of them well maintained, were packed along dimly lit, narrow hillside streets, along with scattered, larger apartment buildings. Dusk was giving way rapidly to night, but there were a fair number of people on the streets, so Natalie did not feel particularly anxious about being alone.

It was exactly eight when she arrived at a featureless, four-story apartment building flanked by two alleyways, each about ten feet wide and modestly littered with newspapers, cardboard, and cans. The number 16 was painted in white on the redbrick facing.

There were two panels of fairly new mailboxes in the enclosed foyer, and a vertical row of doorbells. D. CABRAL was near the top. Natalie pushed the button once, then again. She peered through the glass of the inside door. There was a short staircase going up to the first floor. She rang the bell a third time. Then, sensing the first nugget of apprehension, she tried the door, which swung open without resistance. *So much for security.* Number 13, identified by gold numerals nailed to the center of the dark wood door, was on the right, at the far end of the hall. Natalie listened intently, then knocked—at first softly, then sharply. Silence.

8 P.M. 16 R.D. FELIX #13

There was no doubt in her mind that she had interpreted the written message correctly. It was now ten after. The nugget was growing with each second. Dora's plea on the street that Natalie not look back, and her reaction in the SIC-U to the arrival of the Military Police officer, underscored the woman's fear, but sharing the name Dom Angelo and the scribbled note suggested that she wanted to help.

"Come on . . . come on. . . ."

Natalie knocked again, then returned to the front hallway and tried the bell one last time. Her mind was racing through possible responses to this latest turn. One thing was certain—she wasn't leaving until she had done everything possible to ensure that Dora Cabral was all right.

Eight fifteen.

Natalie debated knocking on a neighbor's door to see if any of them might have a key to apartment 13. Instead, she went outside and, suddenly wary, walked to the end of the block and turned the corner before swinging around abruptly and heading back. Nothing looked suspicious, so she went to the edge of the alley and ducked in. Assuming the apartments were approximately the same size, the fifth and sixth windows on her left would be Dora's, but because the first floor was up four stairs, they were two feet or so above Natalie's head. There was dim light behind each of them.

Eight twenty.

The lights were not what Natalie wanted to see. A dark apartment could have meant that Dora had been delayed somewhere. Lights made the possibility less likely. Grimly, Natalie raced as best she could down the alley to a single, half-filled galvanized metal trash can. She carried it back, turned it over, and clambered up so that the lower sill was now at the level of her chest.

She was looking into a neatly kept bedroom with two twin beds. The light was coming from beyond—from the kitchen, it seemed. She blinked twice to assist her eyes in adjusting to the gloom. Now she could make out the sink in the kitchen and the back of a chair and part of the kitchen table. It took several seconds for her to realize that hanging off the side of the table was an arm.

"Oh, God, no!" she cried out softly.

Without hesitation, she slammed her elbow viciously into the pane, exploding nearly all the glass into the bedroom. There were several large shards still protruding from the frame. Rather than try to remove them, she reached up and unlatched the window, pushed it up, and found the strength to hoist herself up and inside. Mindless of the blood flowing from a gash just below her elbow, she raced to the kitchen.

Dora Cabral was slumped on the table, dead. Her head rested peacefully on one cheek. Her mouth was agape, her lips pulled back in a disturbing rictus, exposing her teeth. Natalie checked the carotid pulse in her neck and the radial pulse at her wrist, but knew there would be none. Then she noticed the syringe on the table, next to an empty multidose vial of what she felt certain was a powerful, injectable narcotic.

Nothing she sensed about the woman encouraged the belief that she was a narcotics addict, but if she knew nothing else, she knew that was always a hard call to make. In her heart, she felt that Dora's death was murder, and worse, that it had something to do with the two connections between them— the rain forest village of Dom Angelo and the Military Police officer Rodrigo Vargas.

Still numb and not thinking with much clarity, Natalie glanced down and noticed the blood dripping off her hand and forming a small pool on the linoleum floor. The gash by her elbow was two inches long and fairly deep, but she knew pressure would take care of the bleeding and in time, provided there was no major infection, all she would be left with was another Rio scar. She took a dishcloth from the sink and managed to tie it tightly around the wound. At that moment, she heard sirens approaching.

Was this a setup?

Fueled by a massive adrenaline rush, she was thinking quite clearly again. She had to get away. Using her shirt to turn the knob, she hurried to the hallway and immediately opted against the front stairs. Instead, she took a narrow flight down to a pitch-black basement. Virtually blind, she felt along the wall for a light switch. At the moment she was about to give up and head back upstairs, she found one and flicked it on. Just ten feet away was a small set of concrete stairs, leading up to a door. Opening it cautiously, Natalie stepped out into an alleyway between the backs of buildings, scarcely six feet wide, and permeated by the pungent odor of urine.

The sirens were close now, and she felt certain she heard heavy, running footsteps from someplace to her right. She *had* been set up. There was no doubt about it. It had to be Vargas. Sometime soon, very soon, she would be killed trying to escape arrest, and the loose ends surrounding Dom Angelo would be tied up.

Mindless of her breathing, she dashed to the end of the alley farthest from the foot-steps and then flattened against a wall as a uniformed policeman raced by. Finally, she slipped across the street and cut through another alley. Several more blocks, and she could go no farther. She was in an upper-middle-class neighborhood now, with single-family homes and lush gardens. Breathing heavily, and not all that success-fully, she sank onto the ground behind a dense grove of palms, ferns, and huge yuc-cas, and allowed herself to cry—not so much out of fear for herself or even horror over the death of Dora Cabral, but rather out of sheer bewilderment.

Somehow, she was either going to find some answers, or die trying.

Her search had to begin, and would hope-fully end, in Dom Angelo.

CHAPTER 26

**Have you never observed how invincible
and unconquerable is spirit and how the
presence of it makes the soul of any
creature to be absolutely fearless and in-
domitable?**
—PLATO, *The Republic,* Book II

Natalie spent the night in the back of the
Jeep, parked in a public garage north of the
city, using a duffel bag for a pillow and a tarp
for a blanket. For six hours her tension and
confusion battled with her physical and emotional exhaustion for possession of her ability to sleep. In the end, the struggle was
more or less of a draw, and she estimated
two hours of decent rest, maybe even three.

At five thirty, stiff and bleary, she climbed
out of the Jeep and paced around level two
of the garage. As far as she could tell, she
was fifteen or twenty miles north of Rio, just

a dozen or so miles from Route 44, a cutoff that would continue leading north and west, away from the coast. That two-lane would eventually become a winding, probably unpaved secondary road that snaked into the rain forest mountains for at least twenty miles before connecting, in some way, with a road to the village of Dom Angelo. It was going to be a hell of a trip, but that might be said for every inch her life had traveled since she stepped on board her initial flight to Rio.

She had a dreadful ache in her soul for Dora Cabral, and what the woman might have gone through before her death. There didn't seem to be any signs of torture on her body, but Natalie had little doubt that Rodrigo Vargas was skilled at the art of getting answers without leaving marks.

Natalie felt totally alone—more so perhaps than at any time in her life. She thought fleetingly about calling Terry or even Veronica to ask if they might fly down and join her in the search for answers, but one person who had reached out to help her had already died. No, this was going to be her game to win or lose. Actually, she acknowledged bitterly, no matter what, she had already lost. The scimitar scar on her right side attested to that. So now, the rules had changed. The game was no longer about winning or losing—rather, it was all about answers and, if possible, vengeance.

Answers and vengeance.

The second level of the garage was still largely empty, and the area, true to form, was awakening slowly. Natalie did some deep breathing and stretching. Her operation and the fire had taken their toll on her stamina, but she was still limber, wiry, and as always, deceptively strong.

Calisthenics in a grimy parking garage.

It was pathetic that a life with so much promise had come down to this, but that was the way it was. Most of her plans and dreams to become a great physician and a champion of the down-and-outers of the world had been sliced from her chest or seared by fire. Now, all that remained for her was the powerful need to know what in the hell had happened and why, and the even more overwhelming passion to find and punish whoever was responsible.

Answers and vengeance.

A small coffee shop across the street provided her with breakfast and a washroom, as well as a copy of the Rio edition of *O*

Globo. From what she could tell, the news-paper had nothing on Dora Cabral. Soon, though, she suspected, there would be a carefully crafted report, complete with the name of a chief suspect.

The wizened woman behind the counter looked as if she might not have taken a day off from working for decades. Natalie left an enormous tip under her empty cup, and headed back to the garage. At least, if she didn't ever return from this trip into the rain forest, someone would have benefited.

She straightened up her gear and gave passing thought to calling her mother or Doug Berenger. Regardless of the story she concocted, either of them was intuitive enough to sense there was trouble. They had already once been through the night-mare of believing she had vanished, only to have her resurface. What would calling them now accomplish except to make them worry? Besides, it was not yet seven and Rio was two hours ahead of Boston.

Instead, she wrote a long letter to Her-mina with instructions to share it with Doug. In it, she summarized the events since her return to Brazil, including every name she could remember. The waitress at the coffee

shop first tried to return some of the tip Natalie had left, thinking it was a mistake. Then,
finally convinced that her windfall was no accident, she provided an envelope for the letter and most gladly agreed to get postage
and mail it.

It was time.

The Jeep's fuel gauge was between
three-quarters and full, and under the tarp in
back were five-gallon stores of gasoline and
purified water. Throughout her career as an
international track star, she had always traveled well, and she could probably count the
nights she had spent in a tent on the fingers
of one hand. Now, she had survived her first
night sleeping in the back of a car in many
years. Whatever lay ahead for her, she knew,
was almost certain to include many more
firsts.

The morning was clear and pleasantly
warm, promising yet another flawless day.
Natalie swung onto the expressway north,
trying to get into the rhythm of Carioca driving, which did not often involve the use of di-
rectional signals or mirrors when changing
lanes, nor the use of brakes at almost any
time. On the seat beside her was the rather
crude map she had drawn to Dom Angelo.

Questions about the place continued racing through her brain with the speed of the cars whizzing past her on both sides. Most vexing of those questions involved the possibility that Dora Cabral was simply mistaken in believing that the village had anything to do with Natalie's ill-fated cab ride and the loss of her lung. It was too cruel even to consider that the poor woman had been killed in error. But if she really did know something, what could possibly be the connections between a med student from Boston, a nurse in Rio, and a tiny hamlet in the Brazilian rain forest?

Highway 44 west, located essentially where she had expected it to be, was a pleasant surprise—a recently paved two-lane road with painted center lines, soft shoulders, and not much traffic. If her estimates were right, there would be a cutoff fifteen miles up on her left, probably unpaved, that snaked through the mountains in the general direction of Belo Horizonte, the large capital of the state of Minas Gerais. A hundred miles this side of Belo Horizonte, what looked on the maps like a one-lane road would dive off to the left. And somewhere on *that* road was Dom Angelo. It was a long shot that she would make it without difficulty, but if determination mattered, she was going to find the place.

Five miles from where she suspected the road toward Dom Angelo might be, she slowed and began carefully inspecting and analyzing each turnoff. She was in the steep foothills of the easternmost rain forest. The two-lane road, no longer newly paved, and now pocked with potholes, rose almost continuously and turned sharply with little notice. Traffic was light, and it was often a minute or two before a car passed her in either direction.

Natalie slowed even further and rolled down the windows. She might have been imagining things, but the oxygen-rich air felt different in her lung. Deep, fulfilling breaths came easier and more frequently. Her pulse actually seemed slower. The forest came close to the road on both sides, shielding her from the late-morning sun. At various points, a broad, rushing stream appeared and ran parallel to the pavement for some distance before darting off into the dense underbrush and trees.

The paved road had leveled when Natalie

saw the cutoff. It was a well-worn dirt and gravel road, more than one lane wide, but probably less than two. A crudely painted sign that read CAMPO BELO had been nailed to a tree with an arrow painted beneath the words. By her estimate, Campo Belo was the nearest town of any size to Dom Angelo, but it was impossible to gauge the distance between them. Although she was almost certain she had found the road, Natalie checked the mileage and rechecked her map. At last convinced, she turned left and began a slow, roller-coaster climb through increasingly dense forest.

Excitedly, she began to allow herself to believe that she was going to make it to Dom Angelo without a major hitch. The going was slow, and six cylinders rather than the four the Jeep had would probably have made a big difference, but she was going to make it.

The first time she sensed trouble was when she pulled off to the side to stretch and have a brief meal of sliced meat, cold juice, and half a chocolate bar. She had been on this road for twenty or twenty-five minutes and had passed only one car coming in the other direction, but as she cut the ignition, just before the heavy silence of the forest enfolded her, she heard something. It seemed like the skidding of a car on gravel, along with the briefest noise of an engine. Then, in moments, there was nothing. Could it have been just an echo from her own car? Probably, she decided. Probably that was it.

She ate quickly, listening with a constant ear for any sound beyond the birds and insects of the midday rain forest. Then she pocketed her Swiss Army knife and shifted her hunting knife from her duffel bag to the front seat. Just an echo. That was all.

For the next mile or so, the road seemed to narrow as it went steeply uphill. To the left, rising from the edge of the road, was a nearly sheer, heavily forested hillside; to the right, an increasingly steep drop-off. If a car approached now, it would be impossible for them to pass, and someone would have to back up. Natalie drove with her attention equally divided between the challenging road ahead and the dusty emptiness behind. Her jaw was clenched, and her hands were white on the wheel, in part from the tension of negotiating the road, but also from the sound she had heard.

It was then that she was hit from behind.

She must have momentarily taken her

gaze off the rearview mirror, because the jolt, a substantial one, was a total surprise. Reflexively, she jammed on the brakes, causing the Jeep to be pushed toward the drop-off at a forty-five-degree angle. She would have gone over right there had she not switched to the accelerator and floored it while at the same time spinning the wheel back to her left. The side of the Jeep tore against the hillside, uprooting bushes and gouging the trunk of a tree.

Natalie knew, even before getting a fix over her shoulder on the driver, that it was Rodrigo Vargas. In the moment their eyes met, he grinned and waved.

Then his car, a large black Mercedes, dropped back a few feet and charged again. This time there was absolutely no escape. The Jeep was airborne before Natalie could even react, careening through the trees and dense brush for what seemed like an eternity. It hit the ground, still upright, with jaw-snapping force. The windshield shattered, the doors flew open, and the one on her side was immediately torn away. The Jeep bounced high enough to clear some underbrush. Turning partway over, it just missed a tree. Belted in and holding the wheel with all her strength, there was little else Natalie could do.

Finally, the car took a vicious hit on the left front fender, then pitched forward in a graceless cartwheel before coming to rest, wheels spinning, on the passenger's side, facing uphill.

The first thing Natalie knew with certainty was that she wasn't dead. She was strapped to her seat at a hideously awkward angle, and was bleeding from someplace above her left eye. The car was filled with a chemical fog, apparently from having the airbag deploy then deflate. Her right hip was throbbing, but her arms, hands, and feet all responded when she called on them to move. Whether it was from the tank or the five-gallon can, there was an increasingly strong odor of gasoline.

She unsnapped the seat belt and pulled herself up and out of where the door had been, stifling a cry whenever she moved her right hip. A contusion or muscle tear, she decided, but not a fracture. It would slow her down, but it wouldn't stop her. She noticed her hunting knife caught beneath the handle of the passenger door. Painfully, she leaned across, retrieved it, and slipped it into the elastic waistband of her pants. The Jeep had come to rest so far down the embankment that she could not see the road through the thick foliage, but she knew that somewhere up there, Vargas was preparing a descent to check on his handiwork and, if necessary, to finish the job.

She hobbled away from the Jeep and then knelt, head down, and listened. From not too far below she could hear rushing water; from above, nothing. Then the mosquitoes began—lone fighters and squadrons, attracted by her sweat, her breathing, and her blood, buzzing into her ears and nose.

No movement! she warned herself, staying in a crouch as the first wave began biting. **No movement, no sound!**

"Natalie!" Vargas's call pierced the forest. "Natalie, are you all right? It was stupid of me to have done that. If you're hurt, I want to help."

Natalie peered back up the steep, densely forested embankment, but could detect no movement. Six inches at a time, operating on all fours, forcing the intense ache in her hip from her mind, she worked her way par-

allel to the hillside, farther and farther from
the wreck. That Vargas had a gun, she had
no doubt. She had the knife, but her mobility
was limited, and her speed nonexistent.
Every movement of hers along the sodden
ground left crushed ferns and broken
branches. Soon, Vargas would be following
that trail. Her only chance, and that a small
one, was an ambush from above. Of course,
at the moment of truth, there had to be an
unencumbered willingness to use her
seven-inch blade.

"Natalie. I am sure you are hurt and in
need of help! I can help you. I can explain
everything. I can tell you about Dom Angelo."

He was slightly breathless, suggesting
that he was working his way down toward
the Jeep. Snorting some bugs out of her
nostrils, Natalie pushed on, searching for
just the right spot. From below, the sound of
the stream or river grew louder. Suddenly, on
her right, the forest broke away. The twenty-
five- or thirty-foot drop to the swirling
water—a broad stream—was not exactly
sheer, but it was damn steep.

"Natalie, I see where you are going. If you
want help, just stay where you are. I saw the
blood in your car. I know you are hurt."

There wasn't much time. Still on all fours, Natalie pushed ahead another twenty feet, then cut uphill for ten feet, and finally back toward the Jeep. If Vargas was following her trail, as he said, he would pass right beneath her. When he did, she would have one, and only one, chance.

She braced herself against the thick, squat trunk of a palm. There was no position she could shift to that didn't put strain on her hip, so she resolved to ignore any pain that didn't completely disable her. Somewhere she had read that there were more than 2.5 million species of insects in the rain forest. At that moment, she had no trouble believing that statistic.

To her right, she could see bushes moving. She pulled the hunting knife from her waistband and unsheathed it. The blade, unused except for slicing a piece of paper in the store, was frightening and intimidating. She hefted it in her hand, and decided to thrust it overhand, aiming for a target in Vargas's neck or chest. The image she had was of the attack by Norman Bates's mother on the detective in *Psycho.* As the rustling of the policeman's approach drew closer, she reflected on Dora Cabral, slumped on the table in her modest kitchen. Rodrigo Vargas, despite his charm and good looks, was a remorseless killer. She had to be strong and willing, she told herself. *Strong and willing.*

In seconds, she saw the top of the man's head above the undergrowth. He was moving slowly, aware of everything around him. There could be no hesitating. She crouched low and planted her right foot, clutching the huge knife, and working to ignore the electric pain in her hip. Vargas was coming into view. In three or four steps he would be directly between her and the drop to the river. The sound of the churning water was her ally, masking her last-second movement. He was holding a gun loosely and professionally in front of him. Two more steps.

Don't look up. Don't . . .

Natalie pushed off awkwardly and threw herself down at the man, flailing more than stabbing with the knife. She struck home just behind Vargas's right shoulder and thought she might have hit bone. The man screamed. His gun discharged ineffectually. Then her momentum took them both over the edge of the steep embankment, tumbling helplessly toward the river—two rag dolls slamming off trees and over bushes.

Ten feet from the bank, Natalie caught a woody shrub and stopped herself, the branches tearing skin from her arms. Vargas continued his near free fall, finally coming to rest facedown and motionless on the muddy bank, with his lower half in the water. Blood was soaking through his khaki shirt from a stab wound just behind and below his right armpit. Neither his gun nor her knife was anywhere in sight.

Natalie lay where she was, badly shaken, gasping for breath, and hurting in more places than she could catalogue. Below her, Vargas remained still, his legs dancing obscenely in the swirling stream. Had he broken his neck in the fall? Or accidently shot himself? Or had the wound she inflicted been mortal? Of the three possibilities, only the third seemed unlikely. The knife hadn't felt like it went that deep, but the thrust was wild, and almost anything could have happened.

Groaning from the discomfort, she rolled over and sat, bracing herself with arms that felt as if they had been assaulted with a bat. Below her, Vargas's legs continued their macabre dance of death. He was a bad man, she said to herself, and deserved his fate. In her heart, though, she still felt sick at having killed.

Painfully, she used a tree to push herself upright, then again stared down at the policeman, trying to focus in on what her next move should be. Rodrigo Vargas and the rental Jeep were probably where they would forever be. Her job was to get to Dom Angelo, and the most likely way to accomplish that was the man's Mercedes.

Where would the keys be?

The climb up the embankment was not going to be easy, and it would certainly not be worth doing if the keys were, as seemed likely, in Vargas's pocket. The notion of retrieving them from there made her queasy, but climbing up the difficult slope to check for them, then back down if they weren't in the car, then back up again made no sense.

Gingerly working her way down to the body, Natalie looked for a heavy rock to use as a weapon in case she was wrong about Vargas. What she found instead was something much better—his gun. It was resting in some mud against the base of a huge fern, about twenty feet from the water. It was a heavy, long-barreled revolver with a dark wood handle—something close to what

Jesse James might have worn. *No surprise there.*

She wiped off the barrel on her pants and carefully approached Vargas's body. His cheek was pressed into the mud, his face turned away from her, his arms outstretched. Cautiously, she knelt beside him, then hesitated before reaching into his pocket. Instead, she set her fingers on the skin over the radial artery at his wrist. His pulse was bounding!

Before Natalie could fully react to the discovery, a guttural scream issued from Vargas's throat. Snarling, he twisted over like a viper, latching on to the wrist of her gun hand. The once urbane policeman was an apparition. His upper lip was gashed through, and was bleeding briskly into the muddy mask that covered his face. His eyes were glazed by an insane fury, and his teeth, covered with mud and blood, were bared.

Natalie pounded frantically at his face with her free hand, and kicked him again and again with all her strength, hoping somehow to catch him in the groin. He outweighed her by fifty pounds at least, and despite all of her efforts, he steadily forced himself on top of her. His free hand got purchase around her throat, and his grip closed tightly.

Just as she felt she might be losing consciousness, one of her kicks connected, and for the briefest instant the grip on her wrist relaxed. Without a conscious thought, Natalie yanked her hand free, pointed the pistol in the general direction of her attacker, and fired.

In a spray of blood and gore, Vargas's form went instantly slack. The top of his skull, shot downward from no more than two feet, was gone, exposing what remained of his brain.

In near shock, crying out with every breath, her ears ringing from the ferocious blast of the revolver, Natalie wiped tissue and blood off her eyelids with the back of her hand. Then she whirled and plunged her face into the cool, silty stream.

CHAPTER 27

In respect of temperance, courage, magnificence, and every other virtue, should we not carefully distinguish between the true son and the bastard?
—PLATO, *The Republic,* Book VII

Dr. Sanjay Khanduri, swarthy, handsome, and very intense, weaved through the teeming streets of the metropolis of Amritsar, proudly extolling its virtues to Anson, who sat in the seat next to him, and also to Elizabeth St. Pierre, in back.

"We are in Punjab State, Dr. Anson," he said in his clipped, Indian-British speech. "Amritsar is my hometown. It is one of the most beautiful cities in our country, and is a spiritual center and pilgrimage destination of Sikhism. Do you know about that religion?"

According to St. Pierre, Khanduri was one of the foremost lung transplant specialists in the world. Now, nearly two months after his remarkably successfully operation, Anson had no reason whatsoever to dispute that claim.

"I know something of it," he said. "Very mystical, deeply spiritual. One God, no idols, equality of all, five symbols. Let me see if I remember them—no cutting of the hair, always wear four specific tokens: a comb, a steel bracelet, special underwear of some sort, and . . . and some kind of small dagger. Is that it?"

"The dagger is symbolic of a sword, and the underclothes are those of soldiers, symbolizing the Sikhs' constant readiness to fight for their beliefs. Excellent, Doctor. I am very impressed."

"But you are clean-shaven, so I am assuming you are not a Sikh."

"That is true, Doctor. Although I do share much of the philosophy of the Sikhs, I do not share all of it."

"Sanjay," St. Pierre asked, "is it very far to Mrs. Narjot's home?"

"Not too far, Dr. Elizabeth, but as you can see, the traffic is bad. We are on Court Road, which is always congested. We must go to Sultan Road. Three miles, I would say.

It would not take very long if we were actually moving."

Khanduri chuckled at his own humor. The mid-afternoon sky was an unbroken expanse of azure, and the sun was hot. With the surgeon's Toyota virtually motionless, beggars, chattering incessantly, were drawn to the windows beside the Caucasian man and the stunning African woman.

"I want to give something to each of them," Anson said.

"You are a very kind man, Doctor. Alas, there are many more beggars than you have money to give them."

"I suppose."

"And that is only in this section of the city. I am excited to see that you are breathing quite naturally. Now I get to appreciate firsthand that all of the positive reports Elizabeth has sent me are true."

"You did an amazing job."

"Thank you. I confess I was very nervous when the outbreak of *Serretia marcescens* pneumonia occurred throughout the hospital and we had to move you so soon after your surgery."

"To tell you the truth, I remember very little of those first few days after my operation. In fact, the hospital you transferred me to in Capetown is really the first memory I have."

"The *Serratia* outbreak was a dangerous one, Joseph," Elizabeth said, "especially with you on antirejection medication, however minimal."

"I was worried about transferring you to one of the other Amritsar hospitals," Khanduri added. "*Serratia* had already been showing up in some of their immunocompromised patients, and in addition they have been hit hard by staffing shortages."

"All's well that ends well," Anson said, sensing at that moment that he had never really analyzed the Shakespearean quote very deeply, and now wasn't at all sure he agreed with it.

"All's well that ends well," Khanduri echoed.

Traffic had begun moving again, and the beggars fell away. Anson sat quietly, marveling at the kaleidoscope that was Amritsar—architecturally sophisticated and opulent one block, tawdry and decrepit the next. It was a miracle that among this incredible mass of humanity, several million people in this city alone, at just the necessary moment, a lifesaving gift appeared for him in the form of a brain-dead man who was a virtually perfect tissue match to him.

"Whitestone has inquiries out quite literally all over the world," Elizabeth had explained when they were discussing his deteriorating health. "We are determined to protect our investment at all costs." She had punctuated the statement with a wink.

Indeed, thanks to the charming, unassuming man now serving as their guide, Whitestone's investment had been protected, and marvelously so. Now, as soon as he had finished making his peace with the widow and children of T. J. Narjot, Anson would complete the bargain and turn over the final secrets of the synthesis of Sarah-9.

Khanduri made a slight detour to take them past the gilded walls, dome, and tall minarets of the Golden Temple.

"The water in which the Golden Temple sits is called the Pool of Nectar," he said. "The Sikhs have been continuously embellishing and improving the structure in various ways since the fifteenth century."

"You seem very proud of the Sikhs," Anson said. "Why have you not embraced their religion?"

"I am Hindu," Khanduri replied simply. "I

believe strongly in the caste system, and the Sikhs don't outwardly espouse it."

Anson was still gazing at the temple, or he would have seen St. Pierre make eye contact with Khanduri in the rearview mirror and shake her head sternly and emphatically.

After three-quarters of an hour of driving, the surgeon pulled up before a modest, two-story dwelling on a middle-class street that was not nearly as busy as most of those around it.

"T. J. Narjot was the foreman of a crew that works doing repairs for the electric company," he explained. "His wife, Narendra, as is often the case here in India, stayed home with the children. She speaks no English, so I will have to interpret for you. This state, Punjab, has its own language, but both she and I speak primarily Hindi. Elizabeth, do you wish to come in with us?"

"Yes," St. Pierre said after the briefest hesitation. "Yes, I think I would. Is that all right with you, Joseph?"

"Absolutely. Dr. Khanduri, please tell Mrs. Narjot that we will not inconvenience her long."

They were greeted at the door by a slender, attractive woman in her thirties, unadorned, wearing a sari of subdued color. Her head was uncovered, and her ebony hair hung loose to her shoulders. She made no pretext at being demure, but instead shook hands with her three visitors, and maintained steady eye contact when speaking with them. The small living room was neatly furnished, with very little art on the walls or end tables. There were several photos of a lean, good-looking, mustachioed man with an engaging smile, whom Narendra later confirmed was her late husband. From somewhere in the back of the first floor came clatter and the sound of children's laughter.

After Anson extended his sympathy and thanked his hostess for receiving them, he asked about her husband.

"T. J. and I were married for twelve years," Narendra said through Khanduri. "Our children are nine and six, both boys. They miss their father terribly, and they still get very upset at even speaking about what happened."

"I won't disturb them," Anson said.

"That is much appreciated. Until his hemorrhage, he was in excellent health. The stroke was very sudden and massive—

bleeding, they told me, from tangled blood vessels that he had from birth."

"It was an arteriovenous malformation," St. Pierre interjected.

"I thought so," Anson said.

"My husband and I had spoken in general terms about what we would wish if something like this ever happened. Of course we never expected that—" Narendra began to weep. Khanduri motioned that it was okay to wait and allow her to continue, "—that either of us would need to make such a decision."

"I understand," Anson said.

"In the end, T. J.'s lung, corneas, and both his kidneys were transplanted. He then had a wonderful Shraddha"—a funeral, Khanduri explained—"and then his body was cremated."

"The Narjots are not Sikhs?" Anson asked, realizing as he asked the question that T. J. had neither the beard of a Sikh, nor the customary turban.

"No," Khanduri said. "Like me they are Hindu."

"But don't Hindus believe that organ donation is mutilation of the body, and therefore to be avoided?" Anson asked.

Khanduri did not turn to Narendra for the answer.

"In older days that was certainly so," he said, "but now there are an increasing number of Hindus who understand that organ donation is useful to others, and therefore most honorable. Fortunately for you, and for the other recipients of his organs, that is the case with the Narjots."

In all, the interpreted conversation lasted a little more than an hour, during which Anson asked about T. J. Narjot—his personality, interests, and personal history.

"He sounds like a very unusual man," Anson said when Narendra was through.

"Oh, he was," came the interpreted reply. "He was very special, and we shall miss him forever."

Finally, Narendra took her guests on a brief tour of her house that included a wave to her sons. In the hallway, Anson removed an envelope from his pocket. Narendra, immediately recognizing it for what it was, tried vehemently to refuse, but Khanduri intervened and, after a rather lengthy explanation, the woman accepted, then stood on her tiptoes and kissed Anson briefly on the cheek.

"Take care of yourself, Dr. Anson," she said. "My husband lives in you."

"My body will be a temple to his memory, Mrs. Narjot," Anson replied.

"So, Dr. Joseph," Khanduri said as they were driving back to the airport, "was the meeting with your benefactor's widow all that you expected it to be?"

"I do my best to avoid expectations," Anson said, "but it certainly was an enlightening experience. One that I shall never forget."

Anson's fists, held at his sides where neither Khanduri nor St. Pierre could see, were so tightly clenched that his nails nearly cut into the flesh of his palms.

It was three thirty in the morning when Anson slipped out the back window of his apartment. The jungle, cleansed by a light rain, was aromatic and mystical. Keeping low, and avoiding the security cameras, Anson took a long arc through the dense undergrowth, and then headed to his right, toward the access road to the hospital. The road was patrolled at night, but infrequently.

The flight home, with two connections, had taken most of a day. Anson had used his trusted friend, Francis Ngale, to set things up for him. Then he had showered, rested, dressed in clean, dark clothing, and finally set out through the window. After twenty minutes, he arrived at the road, paved by the government in gratitude for the work of the clinic. It took a few seconds to orient himself and determine that Ngale would be waiting a short distance to the south.

Anson was a brilliant man and loved solving puzzles of all kinds. The puzzle that was perplexing him now, however, was continuing to defy his logic. He did know that the journey he was taking to the village of Akonolimba would be a crucial step toward the solution. There were those, he knew, including Elizabeth, who considered him overly vigilant and suspicious. Now, it seemed possible that he hadn't been paranoid enough.

The rain clouds kept the unlit road quite dark, but there was some light reflected off them that sparkled on the wetness of the pavement.

"Francis," he called softly as he rounded a bend.

"Right here, Doctor," the security guard answered. "Just keep coming."

The massive man, as dark as the night, was waiting by the road, holding up the fourteen-speed bicycle that had once been Anson's, but now more or less belonged to anyone at the clinic or lab who might want to take it out for a ride. For Anson this would be the first time in two years, although his surgery had been so successful that he had no worries about using it now.

"You remember how to ride?" Ngale asked.

"I expect it will be as easy as riding a bicycle."

"Very funny. I have oiled the chain and the axles, as well as the gearshift and brakes. If you fall off, you will have only yourself to blame."

Anson patted his friend on the shoulder, and started pedaling. Ngale trotted beside him for a few concerned paces, then veered to the side of the road.

"I'll say hello to the mayor for you," Anson called over his shoulder.

"I already did that myself. Platini is waiting up for you."

As usual, the fragrances and sounds of the jungle were hypnotic, and twice Anson had to force his attention back to the road.

The five-mile ride to the village of Akono-limba, on the banks of the Nyong River, took just over half an hour. The dirt road that eventually bisected the town was too muddy to ride, so Anson walked the last quarter mile. Many of the huts were made of cinderblock and corrugated aluminum, but some were still reed and thatch. The village had running water and electricity as well as telephone service, but few of the inhabitants could afford to take advantage of them, and some of those who could simply didn't want to.

Platini Katjaoha, the mayor of the village, ran a general store, and lived in the most opulent house—stucco and cinderblock, two stories, with a carport, several rooms, and a cistern. There was also a satellite dish protruding off one of the outside walls. He answered Anson's gentle knock barefooted, wearing red Bermuda shorts and a button-up Hawaiian shirt that stretched tightly over his royal girth. His smile showed perfectly white teeth that seemed almost phosphorescent against the ebony of his skin.

"Mr. Mayor," Anson whispered in French, "thank you so much for doing this for me."

"You are always welcome in my home, Doctor," Katjaoha boomed, punctuating his greeting with a handshake and bear hug. "The door is closed upstairs, so you will awaken no one. My wife sleeps like a cow, anyhow, and the children are exhausted from getting underfoot all day. Can I get you some wine, tea, anything?"

"Just a phone."

"I heard that you had a successful operation. We are pleased."

"Thank you, my friend. I have a new lung."

"From someone in India, I heard."

"Actually, that's what I am here to find out. Did Francis tell you I would be making a long-distance call?"

"For all that you have done for the people in our village, you could call the moon if you wish."

"Thank you. Please write your number down. I will need my friend to call me back here."

"No problem."

"And I may have to wait for that call."

"Also no problem."

"You are a wonderful man, Platini Katjaoha."

"Then you are the idol of wonderful men. I will be upstairs. Call my name out if you need me."

Anson thanked him again, then settled into a frayed easy chair by the telephone and pulled a folded paper from his pocket. There was a five-hour difference between Cameroon and New Delhi, so he had some uncertainty as to whether Bipin Gupta would be at home or at his office. Knowing the head of the editorial page of the highly re-garded *Indian Express* newspaper as well as he did, Anson dialed the work number first. Not surprisingly, Gupta answered on the initial ring.

"Greetings from Cameroon, old friend," Anson said in near-fluent Hindi.

"Joseph, Joseph, what a pleasant sur-prise. You must call more often, though. Your South African accent is getting more pronounced."

The two of them had roomed together for two years during college in Capetown. Even though Gupta was quite fluent in English, Anson insisted from day one that they speak only Hindi to each other. He had al-ways had a knack for learning languages and quickly added Gupta's native tongue to his English, Afrikaans, Dutch, French, Spanish, and German.

He was surprised during the trip to Amritsar to realize that he had never shared the fact of his fluency in Hindi with Elizabeth. At first he was a bit embarrassed sitting by while Sanjay Khanduri translated language that he understood perfectly, but he was also amused, and he fully intended not to allow his humorous little deception get too far. However, that was before Narendra Narjot, or whoever she was, asked, "How do you like my performance so far?" and Khanduri shockingly replied, "Just keep your answers simple and straightforward, and I will do the rest."

"Bipin," Anson said after some initial courtesies, "I need you to check on two things for me. If it is possible, I will wait here for your reply. The first is a man by the name of T. J. Narjot, Sultan Road, Amritsar. About forty. He reportedly died at Central Hospital sometime during the week of July eighteenth."

"And the second?"

"Sometime around that date there was allegedly an in-hospital epidemic at Central Hospital and others in Amritsar with a germ named *Serratia marcescens.* I need to know if that epidemic actually took place."

The journalist had him spell the bacterium, then said, "You know that it is more difficult to determine that a person doesn't exist or an event didn't happen, than if they did."

"What I know is that my friend Bipin Gupta can do anything."

"Give me a number to reach you," Gupta said, "and an hour."

CHAPTER 28

**If they escape disaster, they will be the
better for it.**
—PLATO, *The Republic,* Book V

Rodrigo Vargas's black Mercedes was a powerful four-door sedan that smelled of cigars. Battered and slowed by her breathing and the deep bruise in her hip, Natalie had driven nearly a quarter of a mile before finding a narrow dirt spur cutting off into the dense forest. After she assured herself that the car was invisible from the road, she made four trips back to the Jeep to haul supplies up the hill. By the time she had transferred her compact tent, backpack, water, and food supplies into the Mercedes, it was late afternoon. During that time, not one car passed in either direction.

With no idea how far she was from Dom Angelo, she decided to drive, albeit slowly. In just thirty minutes, a road dropped off downhill into the forest to her right. A sign nailed to a tree at the fork had an arrow pointing to the left, along with the crudely painted directions, DA 2 KM. Less than a kilometer along that road, she found a pair of rough tracks cutting off into the dense growth to her left. She drove the Mercedes in until the tracks had all but disappeared at the base of a hill. This time she did her best to cover the rear of the car with tree branches, and then wedged the key tightly beneath the right front tire.

During the drive, she had concocted a reasonably satisfying story of a naturalist from America hiking the rain forest and, at the moment, searching for a relative who, last she knew, worked as a nurse in Dom Angelo. Part of her story would also be a nasty downhill tumble when the edge of the drop-off gave way.

Her backpack, with the tent strapped on, was heavier than she would have liked, but anything less might have drawn suspicion. The pain in her hip was an annoyance, but not unbearable, and served as a constant reminder that her continued existence was a threat to some person or group. She just had to find a way to keep the pressure on.

The early evening forest was awesome—rich with oxygen and the blend of a thousand scents. As she walked, she tried to conceive of how she might be connected to this place, many thousands of miles from her home. The road followed a prolonged, gentle slope before curving to the right. Then, with little warning, the forest fell away, and the road dropped sharply. Ahead and below her, nestled in a broad valley, was what she assumed was the village of Dom Angelo.

For a time, Natalie sat at the base of a thick palm and studied the scene below, which from this distance looked like a diorama. There were a number of structures—mostly residences, it seemed—aligned along a grid of dirt streets. The buildings were crudely built with clay and corrugated metal. Smoke curled from several of them. To her left—north, she reckoned—was what appeared to be the entrance to a mine, hewn into the base of a mountain that towered over the valley. To her surprise, there were electric lights on poles, scattered throughout the village. Beneath them, children were playing. Natalie guessed two hundred inhabitants, maybe two fifty.

A hundred yards beyond the mine entrance, a narrow waterfall, twenty feet high, filled a small pool, which then emptied into a fast-moving stream, coursing alongside the village. Natalie wondered if somewhere downstream, this was the water that was sweeping over the dancing corpse of Rodrigo Vargas. There were children in the pool, and at least two women washing clothes in the stream. Farther down, two men were working primitive sluices, panning for gems or gold.

Idyllic, Natalie thought, *quaint and absolutely peaceful,* and yet, she had been maimed because of the place, and another woman murdered.

With a soft groan, she pulled herself upright and headed down into the basin. Chickens were the first to greet her, followed by two generic brown dogs. Next were three women—all Brazilian Indians. The tallest of them was still well less than five feet. The trio smiled at her openly and without the slightest hint of suspiciousness.

"Boa noite," she said. Good evening.

"Boa noite," they replied, smiling broadly.

Natalie wandered casually along the hard-packed streets and stopped at a tiny store for some packaged meat, ginger ale, and some sort of small melon. The proprietress, another Indian, shook her head when asked about a woman named Dora Cabral. Several more citizens of the village gave her similar responses, including two miners just finishing a day's work in the hole in the mountain.

The altitude and long day were beginning to take their toll on Natalie's stamina. She was thinking about locating a place in the forest to pitch her tent when she spotted a chapel—whitewashed clay with a red tile roof and a stubby, square-topped steeple with a crude, six-foot cross on top. The canvases forming the top half of the walls and the door were rolled up and tied, exposing two rows of ten rough-hewn pews. The altar was unadorned save for an elaborate ceramic crucifix fixed to the solid wall behind it.

Although she considered herself spiritual in the sense of living in constant awe of the vastness of the universe, the wonders of nature, and the need to treat others with respect and some form of love, Natalie had never been religious in any organized sense.

Still, she felt a deep serenity in this simple structure and responded to it by sitting down on one of the benches.

Despite her attempts to relax and clear her mind, the horror of Vargas's attack on her and his violent death, along with the puzzle of Dora Cabral, simply would not let go. She had been in the chapel for, perhaps, fifteen minutes when a man spoke to her from behind in accented, though fluent, Portuguese.

"Welcome to our church."

His voice was gravelly and low, but somehow soothing. Before she even turned, Natalie breathed in the all-too-familiar scent of cigarettes.

Standing behind her was a priest in a plain, black, mud-spattered robe, white collar, and sandals. He was fifty or so, somewhat gaunt, with dark hair cut short, a day or two of gray-black stubble, and striking, electric blue eyes. A heavy silver cross dangled halfway down his chest, suspended on a thick silver chain.

"This is a very lovely place," she replied.

"You are American?" the priest said, in perfect English—or at least as perfect as someone probably raised in Brooklyn or the Bronx could have.

"Boston," Natalie said, switching to English and extending her hand. "Natalie Reyes."

"Reyes. So you are Brazilian?"

"My mother is Cape Verdean."

"I am Father Francisco Nunes—Frank Nunes of the Brooklyn Nuneses."

Natalie smiled as the man took a seat on the pew opposite hers. He had a magnetic presence that immediately drew her to him, but there was also an unmistakable aura of melancholy that she suspected might have something to do with the reason he had migrated so far from New York.

"This is quite a parish," she said.

"Actually, I minister to several villages in the rain forest, but primarily I am here. Call it penance if you wish."

Natalie declined the silent offer to pursue the matter. Father Francisco seemed anxious to talk.

"And here is?"

"Dom Angelo, a mining community— primarily emeralds, but also green tourmaline, topaz, opal, amber, and some sapphire. I have become something of an expert on the purity of these gems. And you?"

"I am a student, taking some time away

from my studies to reorder my priorities in life, and to hike the rain forest before it is all gone."

"It still has a ways to go, but I understand."

"I notice that most of the people here are Indians."

The priest laughed.

"Many of our residents are indigenous to these vast forests," he said, "but there are a number of others here who crave the anonymity of a place like this, where all transactions are done in cash, and people only have last names if they wish to."

"Do the Indians own the mine?"

Again an ironic laugh.

"These poor, pure people own next to nothing," he said, "and are probably the better for it. The gems they mine are quite profitable, and in Brazil profit often means involvement of the Military Police. It is they who own this place—at least a small group of them do. Think of them as the sheriffs and Dom Angelo as Tombstone in the once Wild West."

Natalie flashed on Rodrigo Vargas's hideous visage as he lifted his bloodied face up from the mud to attack her. Involuntarily, she shuddered.

"I . . . I have another reason for seeking out this village," she said after a time. "A relative of my family, a woman named Dora Cabral, originally from Rio, wrote my mother that she was working out here as a nurse. Is that possible?"

"Quite possible, yes," Father Francisco replied. "We have a hospital nearby, and that hospital employs nurses brought in from Rio, but although I know some of them, I know no person named Dora Cabral. I will ask around the village, though."

"I have already asked a few people, but no luck. It's hard to believe you have a hospital out here."

"Quite a modern hospital, in fact. They perform highly specialized forms of surgery, although I have never been privileged to know precisely what."

"Fascinating. So your parishioners go there for care?"

"Not for surgery. Operations are only performed by the nurses and doctors who are flown in or sometimes driven in from Rio, and then only on *their* patients. If one of our residents needs hospitalization, there is an ambulance we are allowed to use."

"Who runs this hospital?"

"The same people who run Dom Angelo."

"The Military Police?"

"Essentially. When they need help, they bring villagers down as cooks or for house-keeping or sometimes even to assist in the operating room. Once every week or two, a clinic is opened at the hospital so that a nurse or doctor can minister to the people from the villages."

"That's very good of them."

"It is all about control. The care the vil-lagers get they would not be able to get any-where else. Their gratitude may cause them to think twice should they consider trying to keep a stone for themselves. Not doing so is generally a wise choice. The police have a network of spies and informants, and mete out justice with a very quick and heavy hand. If you have spoken to any of the townspeo-ple, there is a chance the policeman cur-rently residing at the hospital already knows you are here."

"Well, if so, they will soon know that I am only passing through."

Father Francisco tapped a half-smoked cigarette from a crumpled pack and lit it, in-haling gratefully.

"I have decided that I have enough vices I

am doing penance for," he said. "The right to enjoy these, I retain."

"It is your right."

The priest hoisted Natalie's backpack on his shoulder.

"Come, I will show you a flat, protected plot overlooking the village where you can pitch your tent."

"That's very kind of you, Father. I wonder if there is any way I could visit the hospital. I fell down an embankment not long ago and injured my hip."

"I can clean and bandage your scrapes and cuts, and tomorrow I can inquire about the status of affairs at the hospital, but I can make no guarantee of treatment."

"That would be very kind of you. Tell me, where is this hospital?"

"A kilometer to the south. No more. I am sure if there is no special surgery scheduled, Dr. Santoro would be happy to care for you."

Natalie felt her blood freeze.

"Who did you say?" she asked, trying desperately to maintain a façade of nonchalance.

"Dr. Santoro," Father Francisco said. "Dr. Xavier Santoro."

CHAPTER 29

Then you will soon observe whether a man is just and gentle, or rude and unsociable; these are the signs which distinguish even in youth the philosophical nature from the unphilosophical.
　　　　　　　—PLATO, *The Republic,* Book VI

With the steepness of the hills and the height of the trees, night settled in quite quickly. The small plot of grass to which Father Francisco had led Natalie was beyond and above the stream, not that far from the waterfall. She politely declined his offer to help her set up her tent for fear that he would wonder why it was absolutely unused. Tomorrow, if she continued to be comfortable with him, she would share the real story behind her journey to Dom Angelo.

Meanwhile, she pumped the priest as hard as she could for information regarding

Dr. Xavier Santoro. What she learned was little. Francisco suspected that, like so many in
this part of the forest, Santoro had a past he
would just as soon forget. Eight years ago,
when Francisco took up residence in Dom
Angelo, the hospital and airstrip were already there, as was Santoro.

"A kind man," he said, "who genuinely
seems to care for the forest people."

If that's so, Natalie wanted to scream,
how did he end up operating on my lung?

In the gathering gloom, pitching the high-
tech tent was a chore that would have been
comical had the situation not been so intense. Finally, bathed in perspiration and
swathed in insect repellent, but victorious,
she sat outside her new home, reflecting on
her surprising lack of emotion at having so
violently killed a man just a few hours ago.
According to Francisco, the group of policemen controlling the mine and the medical
center numbered four, with at least one always present at the hospital. It was they who
maintained the church and meagerly subsi-
dized him, as much, he suspected, for his
skill as a lapidary as his ability to preach and
minister.

Tomorrow, Natalie decided, she would

probably share with him the news that the number of Military Police managers had been reduced by twenty-five percent. For the moment, though, all she wanted to do was sit still and wonder how she could have found her way from an alley in a *favela* just outside of Rio to a hospital in the middle of nowhere.

The vantage point from her campsite included a disarming view of the waterfall and pool, and of the town below, but of something else as well. To the south, in a valley visible over the tops of trees, the priest had pointed to a faint cluster of lights.

The hospital.

"That is where tomorrow we shall try and get medical help for your hip," Francisco had said. "I think you will find that Dr. Santoro has the answer to your problem."

Let us hope so, Natalie thought savagely.

It was nearly eleven before the nip of *cachaça,* sugarcane liquor, kicked in and Natalie retreated to the womblike interior of her tent. She slipped Vargas's gun inside her thin sleeping sack, and allowed herself to drift off, fully expecting the proximity to Dr. Xavier Santoro to trigger yet another flashback.

What she heard instead, after just a few minutes, was a soft scuffling from somewhere just outside the tent. Natalie silently slid the gun out, held her breath, and listened.

Nothing.

Astonished at how calm she was feeling, she aimed the barrel at the spot where she placed the sound.

"I hear you and I have a gun," she said in Portuguese. "Go away before I shoot."

"You do not need to do that," a man's harsh whisper responded. "If I wanted you dead, you would already be dead. It is what I do."

"Who are you and what do you want?"

"My name is Luis Fernandes. Dora Cabral is my sister."

With Vargas's gun still at the ready, and a high-intensity flashlight in her other hand, Natalie turned and crawled headfirst from the tent. Luis Fernandes was seated cross-legged, holding his hands palms up to show he was unarmed. He was slightly built, with an Indian's features, but definitely taller—much taller—than those men she had seen in town. A black patch, held in place by elastic, covered his left eye. Overall, he was quite menacing.

"You must speak a little slower," Natalie said, lowering both the gun and the flashlight. "My Portuguese is weak."

"Actually, you are speaking very well. Are you from Lisbon?"

"Massachusetts in the States, but my family is Cape Verdean. Are you really a professional killer?"

"I do what I have to, and some of the time I am paid for doing it. My sister works as a nurse in Rio at Santa Teresa Hospital. Is that the Dora Cabral you seek?"

For a time, Natalie studied the man's narrow, deeply etched face. He might have been anywhere from thirty to fifty, though she suspected early thirties. He was clean-shaven, with sideburns that came down below his ears, and had probably been handsome before the hardness of his life took over. Now, he simply looked rough. Natalie sensed there was no reason to be anything other than direct with the man.

"I am afraid I have some bad news for you," she said finally.

It was time, she decided, to share her story. Tomorrow, it would likely be with Father Francisco, possibly in the form of a confession. Tonight, it would be with this man, who, she strongly felt, was no threat to her. Luis listened intently as she recounted her two trips to his country, and the frantic events since she was approached by his sister at the crosswalk in downtown Rio. Outwardly, he seemed calm, almost detached, but even through the gloom, Natalie could see that his jaw was set, and his lips pressed tightly together.

"Believe it or not, there was a time when I was a teacher," he said when she had finished. "I taught music to schoolchildren. Then, one night, ten, maybe eleven years ago, I rose to the defense of the father of one of my students, who was being beaten by the police. During the struggle, one of the policemen fell and hit his head, and died. After a few years of running, and yes, killing, I ended up in this place. Even though the police run this village and the hospital, there are never any questions asked here."

"I understand," Natalie said.

"So now, after being a wanted man for so long, I am the head of security for the hospital. It is my job to bring people down from the village when there is an operation being done. I learned from some of the nurses how much they were being paid, and I talked my sister into signing up with Dr. Santoro. She only came here twice, and then suddenly decided not to come anymore. She never told me why."

"Perhaps something was going on at the hospital that bothered her. When was the last time she was here?"

"Two months ago, maybe a little less. You are sure it was Vargas who killed her, and Vargas whom you killed?"

"I am sure. This is his gun."

Luis took the weapon, inspected it, then hefted it expertly in his hand.

"It is Vargas's," he said. "He was a very hard man, with little respect for me or anyone else of stature below his own."

"Your sister was extremely frightened of him."

"It is not easy to resign from working at this hospital—maybe impossible. I owe you a great debt for avenging her."

"I believe your sister was killed because she tried to help me. She knew what was done to me at this hospital. Now, I need to know if I was really here, and if so, what happened to me."

Luis thought for a time.

"We are sworn to secrecy regarding the hospital and what is done there. The town depends on the hospital."

"Father Francisco tells me the mine is quite productive and could support the village."

"Perhaps," Luis said. "He would know better than I."

"Tell me, Luis. You know what they do there, don't you?"

The killer stared down at the ground. Natalie knew what he was contemplating. These people demanded loyalty, and were not the sort who allowed second chances. If he turned against them now, if they learned he had shared any of their secrets, there would be no going back for him.

"They do transplants," he said softly, "transplants of body parts. Many times the donors of the organs transplanted do not survive. In those instances, we are told to bury the bags containing their bodies."

"But . . . I was shot," Natalie said. "How could they transplant my lung when it had already been destroyed?"

"I do not know. I do not often see the patients—when they are alive, I mean."

"Luis, I am sure you are risking much by

telling me what you have. Please know how grateful I am. Do you have a family here?"

"A woman only, Rosa. She is the only person in Dom Angelo who is tougher than I am. She knows—knew—my sister, and will be very upset at the news she has been murdered. Rodrigo Vargas was not a man she liked or trusted. She will also be willing to help you in any way she can. You should know that something is scheduled to be happening at the hospital over the next few days. I have been instructed to assemble a squad of eight guards—two shifts of four—to keep watch on the hospital beginning in the morning."

"In that case," Natalie asked, "is there any way I could get into the place tonight?"

Luis Fernandes thought for just a few seconds.

"As a matter of fact," he said, "there is."

CHAPTER 30

The hour of departure has arrived, and we go our ways—I to die, and you to live. Which is better God only knows.

—PLATO, Apology

You may bring your torch," Luis said, "but do not turn it on until I tell you it is safe to do so. Unless there is something happening I do not know, only Dr. Santoro and Oscar Barbosa, the policeman, are at the hospital right now. If this is a typical night, each of those men will have a woman with him."

"I will do whatever you say."

The night was moonless, and the forest as black as it was noisy. Initially, even though there was no discernible path and he was operating with one eye, Luis moved through the dense underbrush with the vision and stealth of a jaguar. At first, Natalie was able to keep pace. Soon, though, the altitude and her injuries weighed in, and she had to ask him to slow down. He did so without comment. He was armed with at least one handgun and a long, slender knife, sheathed just above his right ankle.

They moved south, then west, then south again, over rolling terrain that in the main continued downward. The air was cool and incredibly clean. *How ironic to lose a lung in such a place,* Natalie thought.

It was after midnight when they ascended the steepest grade of their journey. At the top of the rise, with Natalie breathing heavily, Luis raised a finger to his lips and pointed ahead. Below them, much closer than she had expected, was the hospital, bathed in the light from half a dozen lamps set on tall poles. It was a single-story structure of pristine, whitewashed clay, sprawling across a plateau, surrounded by a four-strand barbed-wire fence. There was a long wing extending away from them to the right.

"As you can see, the building is shaped like an L. The wire does not extend all the way around it," Luis said. "Now, I must ask you a serious question. How badly do you want to get inside?"

"That depends on how much time I will have once I am there."

"Twenty minutes. No more. Maybe less. Try for eighteen."

The hospital was hardly small. There were ten windows along the wall facing them.

"How many operating rooms are there, Luis? Remember to speak slowly, please."

"Two. Right in the center. Those windows you see open on a long corridor that connects all the rooms. There are also two hospital rooms right inside the third window from the right. I think they are recovery rooms for those who have had surgery. Next, right where the wing comes off, are the dining room and the kitchen, and beyond them, in the wing itself, are two small clinic rooms and the sleeping quarters—maybe ten rooms in all, but I really don't know exactly how many. The dining room has some couches and soft chairs at one end where families wait for the surgery to be completed."

"And at the other end, after the operating rooms?"

"Dr. Santoro's office and one other for the surgeons who fly in."

"Do you know if those offices are locked?"

"I do not. When I am around they are always open, but there are usually doctors all over the place."

"Is that all?"

"Yes. No, wait, there is one more room, at the far left. It is a large room, at least as large as the operating rooms, filled with electronic equipment. In the middle of that room is a chair—an elaborate chair like the kind you might find in a dentist's office. And screens—several television screens on the wall. I have only been there once or twice. They do not like me or my security people to be inside the hospital unless there is trouble. They do not have uniforms for us, and we are not clean enough for them as is."

Natalie studied the structure, trying to visualize beyond the windows and imagine how, in twenty minutes or less, she might go about finding any information filed away about her. Tomorrow, there would be people arriving. Word might filter down from someone in Dom Angelo to Santoro or a military policeman that a woman was in the village asking about Dora Cabral. Tomorrow might be too late.

"You asked a question, Luis, about how badly I wanted to get inside."

"Yes?"

"The answer is I am willing to risk every-thing."

"By everything, do you mean your life? Because Oscar Barbosa is a powerful pig of a man, who has more brawn than brains, and who is truly poisoned by his power."

Natalie wondered what she would have ultimately done had not the phone call come in from her insurance company, raising questions about Santa Teresa. It didn't seem then, nor did it seem now, as if she had very much to look forward to in her life—except answers.

"As I said, I am willing to risk everything."

"You are a brave woman, Senhorita Na-talie, but I already knew that. In back of the hospital, some distance from where the res-idence wing and dining area come together, is a swimming pool. Beside the pool is a metal shed. In the floor of that shed is a trap-door covered by a reed mat. The tunnel be-neath the door was built as an escape route to the airstrip. I am not certain why. When you mount the staircase at the other end, you will be in a pantry in the back of the kitchen. Clear?"

"Clear."

"There are electric eyes guarding the rear of the hospital, where you will be. The diversion you want will come when I shoot out the control box for those electric eyes. One shot. The moment the shot rings out, an alarm will sound and your time starts. Barbosa and Santoro may have women in their rooms, or they may have sent them back to the village, but no matter. The women will stay in their bedrooms no matter what while the men investigate. Twenty minutes is the absolute most I can keep them occupied. Your way out is the same as your way in. The control box will be damaged beyond a quick repair, so the electric eyes will not be a problem. Wait ten yards beyond the pool until you hear my shot. We will meet back here. Do you think you can find this spot?"

"I do."

"I will give you time to get in place. Take a wide route around the hospital."

"Thank you, Luis. Thank you for doing this for me."

"I do it for my sister," he said.

As directed, Natalie took a track well to the east of the hospital. The forest was so dense that at times she lost the spotlights altogether. Finally, though, she saw the pool—a small, dark rectangle surrounded on all sides by a concrete patio, and separated from the hospital by twenty yards or so. Lights from several windows washed across the broad courtyard. The corrugated metal shed was just where Luis had said it would be.

I am willing to risk everything.

Natalie's bold pronouncement echoed in her thoughts as she crouched in the brush forty feet or so from the shed. If she was caught, she would die. There was nothing more certain than that. Did it make any difference? No matter what, her life was going to be led as a cripple, probably because of her unusual transplant antigen pattern and her low lung allocation score, but also possibly from the side effects of the powerful meds that would keep her from rejecting a lung that wasn't closely matched to her in the first place. She would gladly have changed places with Odysseus, facing the monsters Scylla and Charybdis.

I am willing to risk anything.

Did she really feel that way, she wondered now. Did she really not care to see her life play out—to learn her destiny?

Before the answer became any clearer, a shot rang out, and an instant later, a siren began wailing from not far away. Without hesitating, Natalie activated the stopwatch mode on her wristwatch and sprinted forward to the shed, slipped inside, and dropped to one knee, breathing heavily. In moments, the siren stopped. By then, she had located the heavy wooden trapdoor and swung it open. Eight stairs led down to a concrete floor that crossed over to the hospital— maybe a hundred feet, she estimated.

She followed the flashlight beam to the far end of the tunnel, mounted the ladderlike stairs to the trapdoor, and pushed it open, struggling to maintain control of it. Above her, she hoped, Santoro and the policeman Barbosa had left the hospital and, guns drawn, were cautiously searching the grounds and the forest beyond.

The heavy aroma of mixed spices and foods told her that Luis had once again been absolutely accurate. She cut the flash and pushed herself up into a rather large, cluttered space, twelve by twelve, stocked floor to ceiling with food and supplies, and faintly lit through a glass panel in the door. Closing

the trapdoor and replacing the mat that covered it, she crawled quickly across the dining
area and lounge. The room was airy and
comfortable, with seating for twenty-five—
ten more counting the lounge. For the moment, the entire area was dimly illuminated
from the corridor beyond the wide, open-
arched doorway to the hospital. When she
reached that arch, she paused just long
enough to listen, then moved ahead. From
what Luis had said, there was no sense in
checking either of the small examination
rooms to her right, so she moved down the
main corridor.

The two nearly identical recovery rooms
were small but well appointed with state-of-
the-art, wall-mounted monitors and electronic IV infusion pumps. One glance at the
crucifix over the door of the first room, and
the clock on the wall to the right of it, and
Natalie knew that she had been in that room
before. So much for Santa Teresa. There
were no filing cabinets in either room, nor
did she expect there to be.

Four minutes.

The first operating room was incredibly
large and technologically well equipped, with

a cardiopulmonary bypass machine and elegant operating microscope. Between it and the next OR was the prep room where the surgeons and OR nurses scrubbed in. The second OR had no bypass machine, and less sophisticated equipment. Natalie felt certain that this was the room where her lung was removed. The questions resonated louder and louder. How did she get here from Rio? Why was her damaged lung removed, and not the good one? And perhaps most perplexing, why was she allowed to live?

Seven minutes.

The solid doors of the two offices to the left of the second OR were both locked. One was labeled with a bronze plaque reading DR. XAVIER SANTORO, and the other DEPARTAMENTO DA CIRURGIA—department of surgery. Natalie felt herself sink. She had eleven minutes left, thirteen at the outside, before Luis feared he would not be able to maintain his diversion, and the records she was seeking, if in fact such records existed, were almost certainly behind one of those two locked doors. Was it worth trying to break one of them down? She hesitated, aware that the seconds were ticking past. Finally, almost in spite of herself, she moved on to the final room off the hallway—the electronics room, as Luis had described it. The door, like of the other offices, was closed. The brass plaque read simply, DR. D. CHO.

Ten minutes.

Expecting the worst, and prepared to race back to the pantry, Natalie tried the knob. The door swung open. She stepped inside and closed it behind her before turning on the flash. A quick scan showed no windows, so she found a switch on the wall by the door and flipped it on. Instantly, brilliantly bright fluorescent light filled the room, which would have been unlike any she had ever seen were she not suddenly and absolutely convinced that she had been there before— many times before.

Screens, electronics, and speakers were on every wall. In addition, there was a glass cabinet of medications. The focus of the room was the chair Luis had described— plush leather with a number of segments that were all adjustable. Hanging down over the elaborate setup, on a heavy adjustable steel arm, was a thick, square, full-head helmet made of some sort of metal. Attached to it was a smoky black plastic visor. Several cables, dangling down from the ceiling, were connected to each. Natalie pictured herself clearly, being transferred from a stretcher to the chair. She imagined, no, *recalled,* the helmet being slipped into place, and the visor being pulled down.

Virtual reality. Natalie was certain of it. The room was set up to create and implant situations that had never really happened. And since her scar, X rays, and diminished pulmonary function were all quite real, the scenario that resulted in her surgery had to have been what was manufactured.

Fourteen minutes.

Natalie rushed to the desk, which was strewn with papers and letters, all of which were addressed to Dr. Donald M. Cho at either a post office box in Rio, or one in New York City. She folded several of the more interesting-looking ones and stuffed them into her pocket. Then, one letter caught her eye. Actually, it was a fax to Cho, written in English, from Cedric Zhang, Ph.D., Psychopharmacologist, Audio-Visual Implantationist.

Transfixed, despite the crush of time, Natalie read the note.

Dear Dr. Cho:

I was so pleased to learn how successfully you have adapted my methods for the implantation of virtual scenes into the minds of your subjects. As you have discovered, the potential for my theories and equipment is limitless. We are clearly geniuses, you and I, and are now in possession of a technique that can quite literally change the world. Over a short course of treatment, witnesses can be programmed to testify that they saw or did not see whatever we wish. Agents and soldiers can relent in the face of torture, and give out implanted information they absolutely believe is true. The modifications you have made and tested, especially the addition of electrodes that produce legitimate sensations of pain, heat, and cold, are brilliant. I suggest we meet at your earliest convenience after your return to New York.

With deepest respect,
Cedric Zhang, Ph.D.

Seventeen minutes.
The circle of confusion was beginning to

close. Natalie knew now that she had never been shot. The last real thing that happened to her was the injection into the base of her neck. The recurrent nightmares were nothing more than glitches in the system created by a Dr. Cedric Zhang and modified by Dr. Donald Cho. She still had questions, piles of them, but some of the most disturbing ones had just been answered. Somewhere in the room, she felt certain, was a DVD or film of some sort showing, from her point of view, the attack and ultimately the gunshots that brought her down—gunshots that had never happened except through the lens of a camera.

Nineteen minutes.

Clutching her flashlight, her pockets stuffed with hastily folded papers, Vargas's gun in her waistband, she flicked off the light and slipped out into the corridor. It was foolish to have stayed so long. If she was caught now, she almost certainly would crumble under the weight of torture and drugs, and give them Luis Fernandes. It had been selfish and foolish of her to stay.

Crouching lower than the windows, she sped down the corridor toward the entrance to the dining room. She had just reached it when the main door to the hospital opened.

Without looking back to confirm her impression that it was Santoro, Barbosa, or both, she dove to her right into the family lounge area and flattened herself behind a sofa. The gun was partially pinned beneath her, but she dared not move to get at it. Moments later, the two men entered the room. They were speaking rapidly—too rapidly for Natalie to pick up everything they were saying.

Winded from her dash, and certain the men could hear if they but listened, Natalie pulled her shirt up over her mouth and breathed into it, forcing herself to pause for a few seconds after each breath. She pushed herself tightly against the back of the sofa as they walked past, less than ten feet away. From what she could make out, they were angrily trying to sort out who might have taken a shot at the hospital's security electronics. Once, she heard Luis's name, but she had no idea of the context.

The lights in the dining room were still off, but she could see both men clearly, and she knew that if they turned in her direction, they could see her as well.

Please, no. . . . Don't look. . . . Don't look.

Barbosa was an absolute bull, short and

solid with a surprisingly high-pitched voice. Santoro was as she remembered—smooth, slightly built, with glasses and a prominent forehead. He motioned the policeman to the lounge, and to Natalie's horror, Barbosa sank down onto the sofa behind which she was hiding. Fortunately, her breathing had begun to slow, and the policeman's respirations, by virtue of his size, were grunting and noisy. Natalie pressed her shirt even more firmly against her mouth. There was no way she could move to get at her gun.

"Who would dare shoot at us?" the bull asked.

"Probably whiskey," Santoro responded around words Natalie couldn't make out.

She had drawn herself into a fetal position. Barbosa's backside, through the sofa, was no more than a foot from her. The large pistol in her waistband drove painfully into her already injured hip.

Go! Please go.

There was more conversation, which Natalie could not completely decipher. Then finally, after what seemed an eternity, the two men stood.

"Tomorrow will be fun," Barbosa said. "I like this place when there is action."

"There should be plenty of that very soon."

"Tell me, Xavier, have you heard anything from Vargas? He was due here late today."

"Nothing."

"Must be another woman. Single, married, young, old, virgin, whore, willing, reluctant. They dot his landscape like cow plop. I tell you, Santoro, someday, one of those women is going to be the death of him."

CHAPTER 31

They see only their own shadows, or the shadows of one another, which the fire throws on the opposite wall of the cave.
—PLATO, *The Republic,* Book VII

Moving as little as she could, Natalie waited for two more agonizing minutes before she stretched out and, with no little difficulty, crawled to the pantry. Half expecting to be surprised by someone, she made her way back through the tunnel, past the pool, and into the forest, wondering if Luis would still be waiting for her on the hilltop north of the hospital. As best she could recall, she retraced her steps around the building, and then started up a rather steep incline. After a short while, perhaps halfway up the hill, she gave in to the altitude, her hip, the slope, and the tension of the past hour, and sank to the ground, hungry for air.

Luis had probably gone back to the village anyway, she reasoned, suddenly feeling immeasurably sorry for herself. The whole business of the hospital at Dom Angelo had been nothing but a scam—an organ-theft operation with a high-tech component thrown in. It had been her misfortune to have flagged down the wrong cab at the Jobim airport. As usual, pure and simple evil was purely and simply about money. An O-positive lung? Well, you're in luck. We're running a special on those this week. Next week, livers. The quartet of military policemen, now a trio, were into gemstones and organs—emeralds and kidneys, opals and lungs. Pay for one, pay for the other. Disgusting.

Natalie pushed herself to her feet and trudged upward, not really caring if she met up with Luis or found Dom Angelo or not. At the top of the ridge, with no sign of Fernandes, she turned and gazed back downhill at the hospital, glowing beneath the spotlights and what was now the first blush of dawn.

How many lungs? she wondered. *How many hearts? How many deaths?*

This wasn't trading in organs, this was simply stealing them—stealing them and implanting scenarios in the poor victims' minds. When Luis was describing burying the bags containing the bodies of donors, she had wondered why that wasn't her fate as well. Now, she knew. She was being kept alive as a test subject for the product and technique being developed by Donald Cho and Cedric Zhang—a new cottage industry for the enterprising military policemen to support, and ultimately, more money for their coffers. In all likelihood, someone had been checking up on her in Boston, maybe by rifling the records of her therapist.

It all hung together perfectly.

"Did you run into trouble?"

Startled, Natalie whirled. Despite the dense undergrowth, Luis had come up behind her soundlessly.

"God, do not sneak up on me like that— especially when I have a gun."

Luis's wry expression made words unnecessary. There was no way she would have ever gotten a shot off.

"Come," he said, "there is a better place for us to sit and talk."

In silence, they walked north and west,

rising up into some of the densest forest Natalie had yet encountered. This time, Luis seemed more mindful of her physical limitations, and actually helped her through some of the more difficult parts. At the top of a particularly steep rise, the forest suddenly opened up, revealing a solid granite plateau, fifteen feet across and eight feet deep, tucked against a hillside. To the south and east was a clear view of the hospital and the land beyond it. The spectacular vista, with the early morning sun washing across it, belied the evil that resided there.

"I nearly got caught," she said after her breathing had returned to normal.

"I thought that you had, and actually said a prayer for you. Do you need to lie down?"

"No, no, I'm okay."

Natalie quickly recounted her close call in the hospital.

"So, you were brainwashed into thinking you had been shot," Luis said when she was done.

"The techniques they are developing could be a source of great profit when they are fully perfected. I don't know the exact details of how it works, but I suspect that first they used hypnotic drugs to open my mind to suggestion. Then, using a visor that's like a TV directly over my eyes, and a scene recorded as I would have viewed it, they implanted a reality in my brain. They even used electrodes to add the sharp pain in my back as the bullets hit me."

"That is impressive."

"It is terrible. I wonder how many poor souls have lost organs there."

"They perform maybe one procedure every two weeks."

"How frightening."

"So, Vargas is dead, and you have the answers you were seeking. I guess we are finished, you and I."

For a time, Natalie sat, arms folded around her knees, gazing out at the lush panoply below, sorting through her feelings. Luis was right. She had battled her depression and her demons and come to Rio again because of unanswered questions. Now, there was nothing left but to return to Boston, continue with her pulmonary rehab, and await her position on the lung allocation scoreboard.

She had been at the wrong place at the wrong time, and as a result, life as she knew it had been destroyed. Still, the fire to end her life had, at least for the moment, been quenched by a sense of pride over what she had accomplished over the few days since her return to Brazil.

"Luis, what do you think would happen if I contacted the American embassy or the Brazilian police about what is going on here?" she asked.

"The truth?"

"The truth."

"There is an enormous amount of money supporting this hospital. You can destroy the building, but unless the people behind it are dead, it will simply be built up again. Besides, I don't know how you do things in America, but here we need proof that a crime has been committed before people can be convicted. Right now the only proof we have is that Jeep you rented and the dead body of a policeman in the stream below it. Oh, yes, I also believe you have the policeman's car."

Natalie nodded that she understood. For a time, as dawn brightened into morning, the only sound was the forest. When Natalie did speak, the words were from the woman who had stood up to Cliff Renfro and Tonya Levitskaya.

"Luis," she heard herself say, "these people have killed many and also have ruined the lives of many more—including mine. I am not satisfied with just answers, I want satisfaction. I want vengeance. If I die trying, then I die. The one good thing, if you can call it that, of all I have been through, is that there is little left for me to fear. I want to do whatever I must to close this place down for good—to turn it into dust. And I want Santoro and Barbosa behind bars or I want them dead."

"You know," Luis said, "more and more as I think about what was done to my sister, I have been feeling the same way. If it had not been Vargas who had murdered her, it would have been Barbosa or one of the others."

"I agree."

"You must be certain, though, that you are willing to risk everything for your revenge. What advantage we have will rest in that certainty."

"I am certain, Luis. The best I have to look forward to is not a life I wish to lead."

"Then we shall try."

Luis offered his hand and Natalie held it tightly.

"So, what can we do?" she asked.

"Maybe nothing," Luis said, slipping his fingers beneath his eye patch and rubbing at whatever was under there, "maybe everything. First we need some weapons, and then we need some help."

"Where do we start?"

"We start right here."

Luis walked to the hillside behind them and pulled some shrubs from the ground. Behind those, five feet from top to bottom and also across, was the opening to a cave.

"I never noticed that!" Natalie exclaimed.

"That is the point. Very few know this is here. Inside we have guns, explosives, and a place to hide should we need it."

"But why do you—?"

"In my line of work, it always pays to be careful and to plan ahead."

"Can I look inside?"

"You can, but first I suggest you look over there."

Natalie turned toward where Luis had pointed, toward the southeast, but she saw and heard nothing new.

"Here," Luis said, handing her a pair of high-powered binoculars he had retrieved from just inside the opening of the cave. "Look beyond the hospital, then listen."

Natalie saw immediately. A long runway, very long, lined with alternating blue and white lights, had been carved east to west into the forest some distance beyond the hospital. Nearly a minute later, she heard what Luis had heard some time ago, the drone of an approaching plane. Moments after that, she saw an airliner soaring in low from the east.

Luis and Natalie lay side by side on the rock shelf, trading off the remarkable binoculars, watching as the plane made a perfect landing, then turned at a cul-de-sac that had undoubtedly been created just for that purpose, and taxied to a spot midway down the runway. From somewhere in the trees, both Barbosa and Santoro, accompanied by four people carrying semiautomatic machine guns, materialized to greet the arrivals.

A hydraulic lift lowered from the belly of the jetliner, bearing an unconscious woman on a stretcher, along with an accompanying man and woman in surgical garb. Next trip, the platform bore three men, one of them a huge blond with a ponytail, and a woman. They were followed by a uniformed crew of two. As the procession neared the hospital, the lift made one more trip, bringing down a man dressed as the captain, wearing his uniform hat, and one other man, in shirtsleeves—perhaps, Natalie decided, the flight attendant.

Finally, Barbosa and two of his men entered the jetliner and began unloading luggage and other supplies.

"I make it eight men and two women," Luis said. "Plus Santoro, Barbosa, and four security guards from the village."

"It would seem that our odds of success have just dropped significantly."

"To some extent."

"Please explain."

"One of those men with Barbosa would give his life for me, and one of the other guards, the one with the red hat, is my Rosa."

CHAPTER 32

The best of all . . . is to do injustice and not be punished, and the worst of all . . . is to suffer injustice without the power of retaliation.
—PLATO, *The Republic,* Book II

Ben was pleased with himself—very pleased. He had rolled the dice and had it come up seven. Nearly twenty hours among the enemy, posing as a man he was not, performing a job of which he had no knowledge, and he had succeeded. In fact, he acknowledged, he was actually quite good at serving people cheerfully and obsequiously, and equally skilled at staying out of the way when he wasn't doing that.

The flight was long, but reasonably easy, with a stop in Venezuela to take on fuel, and another one someplace in Brazil, possibly to do business with an immigration official.

Never did he see an actual customs agent. It was amazing how smooth the water could be when it was blanketed with an oil slick of money. Ultimately, he watched through the small porthole in the forward door as the jet swept low over dense forest that went on for many miles, banked slightly to the right, and then dropped down on a well-lit runway that seemed to have materialized from the undergrowth.

The landing was textbook.

By far, the most distressing part of the flight had been the several visits he made to the compartment at the rear of the plane, where the woman who had been the prisoner in the Adventurer lay in what had to be a drug-induced coma. The night before, she had cried out that her name was Sandy, and that she was a mother. Now, she looked only like someone who was about to die. In a bizarre, horrible sacrifice, she would unwillingly lose a vital organ so that another—probably a totally stranger—might live.

A man and a woman in surgical scrubs with stethoscopes in place were tending to her. The man, swarthy and thick-necked, sounded and looked more like a longshoreman than a doctor, but the woman, silver-

haired and probably in her sixties, had a cultured manner and speech suggesting she
might well be a physician. They called for
soft drinks, then on two occasions for meals.
The woman on the stretcher had an oxygen
mask and IV in place, as well as a cardiac
monitor. She was a rather pretty redhead in
her forties, and looked serene and at peace,
but Ben was nearly overwhelmed by the
memory of her pathetic cries.

The chances were slim at best, he knew,
but somehow he had to find a way to help
her escape.

The man named Vincent was taller and
broader across the shoulders than Ben remembered. From the moment the killer
stepped onto the plane, Ben was searching
for any sign of having been recognized, and
replaying, as best he could, every second of
their encounter in Cincinnati. It was so dark
in the garage, and everything had happened
so quickly. It didn't seem likely the man had
gotten a solid look at him. By the time they
had been airborne for a few hours, Ben's
concerns had largely vanished.

For his part, Vincent spent much of the
flight asleep on the shoulder of his girlfriend.
Connie was most definitely not the girl of

Ben's dreams. She was a ferret-faced woman with a barbed-wire tattoo around her upper arm and a tight white tee that accentuated her huge breasts. She smoked throughout the flight, while the other two security guards played cards or slept.

"How're you doing, Seth? Almost finished cleaning up?"

The captain, a burly man named Stanley Holian, was as laid-back and nonthreatening as Vincent and the team of security people were menacing. Ben had been in the cockpit as much as he had been anywhere on the plane, and was grateful for every minute of *Sportscenter* he had ever watched. A few batting averages and an opinion as to who was going to win the National League pennant, and he was just one of the guys.

"One more minute, Stan."

While Holian finished up in the cockpit, Ben made a final pass through the now-deserted main cabin, and then entered the area at the rear of the plane, shielded from the main cabin by a curtain. He was looking for something, anything that might serve as a weapon. He found nothing that he could count on, which was probably for the good. This was not Seth Stepanski he was dealing

with. It was a trio of professional killers. That
he had succeeded against Vincent in
Cincinnati only lengthened the odds of his
succeeding again. Unless he found help in
the rain forest, it was wishful, fanciful thinking to believe he could free the comatose
sacrificial lamb and make it safely back to
civilization.

So, what next?

He still had the elements of acceptance
and surprise working for him, but that was
about all. Minute by minute he would just
have to assess the situation and search for a
scenario—any scenario—that had even a
remote chance of success. Was he willing to
stand by and leave Sandy to her fate? He
might have to, he acknowledged. Dying himself wasn't the answer to putting these people out of business. He felt ill at the prospect
of readying the plane for the flight back to
the States, knowing what had happened to
the woman—knowing that because of these
people, there was an eight-year-old boy who
was never going to see his mother again.

Stan Holian was waiting for him by the elevator to the hold. Was there a gun someplace in the cockpit? Ben wondered. He
glanced down the aisle. The door to that

room was closed and almost certainly locked.

"Where in the heck are we, Stan?"

"Brazil."

"Very funny."

"North and west of Rio. Seventy-five, maybe a hundred miles."

"I've never been to Brazil."

"Nice place. Truly beautiful women. I don't expect you'll get to do much sightseeing on this trip, though. Day after tomorrow, maybe the day after that, we'll be heading back."

"How long have you been doing this?"

Holian pointedly ignored the question and motioned Ben past the roughly dressed Brazilians who were transferring boxes of supplies to the hydraulic platform. As they were lowered from the belly of the plane, Ben caught a glimpse of a sprawling white building nestled in the forest. Then it disappeared behind the trees. Once on the ground, all he could see around them was the forest. The early morning was cool, and after so many hours in the plane, the moisture-rich air, laden with the sounds of insects, tasted especially sweet.

Vincent was waiting for them by a broad dirt path off the edge of the runway. Then the three of them—pilot, flight attendant, and killer—made their way in silence until the path emptied into a road, this one much wider and more gravelly, with well-established tire impressions.

"You go on ahead, Captain," Vincent said to the pilot. "Same room as always. Your bag'll be there soon. I have something I want to go over with Seth, here."

Holian did as he was asked. As the man disappeared around a bend, Ben, alone with Vincent for the first time, began feeling a nugget of apprehension.

"The hospital's just around there," Vincent said. "It's an amazing operation. You'll be impressed."

"I'll bet I will," Ben said, searching for any giveaway in the killer's tone.

"Do you know what's going to happen to that woman we brought here?"

The nugget expanded.

"Nope."

"Well, pal, we're going to cut her heart out. How about you, Seth? Do you know what we're going to do with you?"

"I don't—"

Before Ben could say another word, a long-barreled pistol materialized in Vincent's hand and whipped across the side of his face, sending him spinning to the ground.

"Did you really think you could get away with this, you stupid shit?" Vincent said. "I had to go to the operating room to have that damn paint cleared from my eyes. Did you think I wasn't going to remember you? You didn't fool Janet in the office for a second. She had a photo of you brought to me before you had even opened your suitcase." He kicked Ben viciously in the back. "How long before *you're* a candidate for the operating room?" Another kick. "I think we should find that out."

Huddled in a fetal position on the packed road, Ben was unable even to speak. He had eaten little for some time, but what there was in his stomach made a sudden, uncontrollable reappearance through his mouth and nose.

"Up," Vincent said, kicking him once more, this time in the back of the knee. "I'm going to show you to the hospitality room. When you and I are finished, you're going to envy that passenger of ours."

CHAPTER 33

But can you persuade us, if we refuse to listen to you?

—PLATO, *The Republic,* Book I

All right, let's do it again. Who are you?"

"Callahan. Benjamin Michael Callahan."

"What do you do?"

"Detective. I . . . I'm a private detective. For God's sake, please—"

"From where?"

"I-Idaho. Pocatello, Idaho. . . . No, please don't do that again. Don't—"

Vincent touched the electric prod to the side of Ben's chest. The shock, more intense than any pain Ben had ever experienced, exploded down his arm and around his back, sending every muscle in its path into agonizing spasm.

Ben screamed and then screamed again. He was absolutely helpless.

There was no place to go, no one to intervene, and no way he could get Vincent to let up.

Helpless.

The interrogation had gone on for hours, with the electric prod being the main source of pain, along with a device that screwed down on his fingernails. After being beaten, he had been dragged to a room in the basement of the hospital, stripped naked, and lashed to a high-backed wooden chair. A dozen shocks later, plus some work on his hands, he had wet and soiled himself, and from what he could tell, had passed out as well—probably more than once.

Twice, a Brazilian aborigine, short but extremely powerful, had dragged him to a shower stall and allowed him to wash off in cold water. Then he was shoved back onto the chair, and the torture and interrogation began again, with Vincent, reminding him over and over about their encounter in Cincinnati, relishing every scream.

"How did you learn about the RV?"

"S-someone in Soda Springs wrote down the license plate."

"Don't bullshit me!"

"Please stop! I'm telling you the truth. I swear I am."

Again the prod, this time on the inside of his thigh. Again the hideous nerve pain and muscle contractions. Again the screaming.

Ben knew from the moment Vincent had slashed him across the face that he was going to be tortured. He also knew that although it would likely be the last thing he did, he had to keep Alice Gustafson's name from them. Once she read the letter he had sent her and freed Seth Stepanski, there would be plenty she could do to make a dent in the Whitestone Laboratory's illegal organs operation—but only if she was alive. If Vincent and his people got to her, his own death would be meaningless. His focus, as they dragged him to the room, likely the last place he would ever see, was to concoct a story that was close enough to fact and held together well enough in the telling and retelling to be accepted as the truth.

"How did you find us in Cincinnati?"

"I'm a detective, for crying out loud. That's what they hired me to do. With the license plate number it really wasn't that hard."

"Who else knows about all this?"

"No one. No one. Just me. No one knows anything about this except me. . . . No! No more!"

Whether it was from being chilled to the bone or from the breakdown of his nervous system, he couldn't stop shaking.

There were some forms of pain Ben could handle—headaches, ankle sprains, viruses, strep throats, even the pounding Vincent had administered. But from the deepest memories of his childhood, he had hated and feared being drilled by the dentist. Even with Novocain or whatever they used for numbing, the anticipation of just the slightest touch on a dental nerve was almost more than he could stand. The prod in Vincent's hands was like a hundred drills into pulp, only there was no numbing medicine. None at all.

Again the killer shocked him, this time on the base of his neck. Every muscle in his body seemed to contract. His jaw viciously snapped shut, causing him to bite through the side of his tongue and snap off part of a tooth.

"Again, who hired you?"

"The . . . the Durkins. From Soda Springs. Their son was killed by a truck in Florida. . . .

The coroner there thought someone had stolen his bone marrow. It's the truth. I swear it is."

"I'll decide what is and isn't the truth, and if I decide you're messing with me, I swear I'll open you up from ass to eyeball with this thing. Now tell me again, how did you end up in Texas?"

Ben had no trouble making it seem as if he couldn't stand any more of the cattle prod. His situation was hopeless, and all he wanted now was to get out of his life with as little further pain as possible, and to take with him the ort of nobility that would go with not exposing Organ Guard and its devoted founder. He retold the story of the White-stone Laboratory in Soda Springs, and his almost inadvertent glimpse of the address on the case of blood vials to be shipped to Fadiman.

The shocks became less frequent, though no less terrible. Finally, after what seemed an eternity, Vincent motioned his helper to throw Ben into the shower stall again. His chest and abdomen were covered with bile and drool. Unable to stand on rubbery legs, he sat on the grimy tile and supported him-self against the wall as the chilly water beat down on him. He extended the shower as long as he could stand it, then unsteadily crawled back to his chair.

Vincent was gone. Beside the chair were a large, clean white towel and a pile of neatly folded clothes—a pair of chinos, a gray tee, thin white socks, and a pair of black, spit-polished high-cut boots. The aborigine motioned for him to get dressed.

Ben had wondered how, when his torture was no longer entertaining, he would be terminated. He had expected, even hoped, for a bullet to the brain. Now, he didn't know what to think. Dressing was an excruciating, slow process. His legs were almost too battered and the muscles too spent to bend, there were electric burns over most of his body, and his swollen, bluish fingers were too stiff to handle the laces. After watching him struggle for fifteen minutes or more, his guard tied him back in his chair and then laced the boots. Next he went to a small refrigerator in one corner of the torture chamber and brought over a bottle of water and a thick chocolate bar, and freed one of Ben's hands. Ben tried to connect with the man.

"Do you understand me?" he asked.

The guard stared at him blankly.

"I asked if you understood me."

There was no way Ben's bruised jaws could even make a dent in the cold chocolate. *Just as well,* he thought. His stomach, raw from retching, was in no shape to accept any food. Glumly, he sipped the water through cracked, bloodied lips. His body was throbbing, his vision blurring, then clearing, then blurring again. From time to time during the days when he was younger and more philosophical, he would ponder the unanswerable, wondering how old and where he would be when he died. It felt strange and more frightening than he could have imagined to have that moment actually arrive.

But why had he been dressed up?

Ten minutes passed. Then another ten. Ben, too dry even to sweat, felt himself slipping in and out of consciousness, and would have fallen over had he not been strapped to the back of the chair.

The opening and sharp closing of the door startled him awake. Even having endured pain that was beyond pain, even somewhat prepared for facing certain death, what he saw drew an instant band of fear around his chest. The man he knew only as

Vincent, his torturer, was about to become his executioner.

The apparition that was the man stood before him, feet apart, head erect, looking taller and stronger than a park statue. His face was expertly streaked with camouflage paint, which matched his shirt and pants almost perfectly. His long blond hair was tucked beneath a commando watch cap. But that outfit was not the source of Ben's fear. Across the killer's back was slung a quiver containing a dozen or so long arrows, and in his left hand, held just off the floor, was a complex-looking bow.

"Let me introduce you," Vincent said. "This is a Buck Fever Compound Bow with a seventy-pound draw and a PSE shoot-through arrow rest. These here are thirty-one-inch Epic carbon arrows. Straight and true all the way. We ain't got much time for tracking and hunting on these trips. And decent game is in pretty short supply here anyhow. So what's a hunter to do?"

"I . . . don't think I can even stand up," Ben said.

"In that case, this is going to be one goddamn short hunt. Now listen and listen closely. Rio is maybe eighty miles south and east of here. Belo Horizonte is almost due north, a hundred, maybe a hundred and fifty miles, but in that direction there's some powerful steep hills—mountains, some might call 'em. In between, there's any number of little towns and villages where you might find a friend. Personally, I don't think you're gonna make it, but you never know. First, you gotta get away from me, and I don't think folks would accuse me of bragging if I said I was a pretty good shot with this thing."

His free hand flashed out, grabbed Ben by the hair, and pulled his head back as far as it would go.

"I need some fresh blood of yours to keep the scent," he said. "I promise you, Callahan, if you don't make this a challenge for me, if you don't put up enough of a fight, I'm going to wound you someplace that won't kill you, and have you dragged back in here for a serious go-round with the prod that will make this last session seem like a carnival."

He released his grip, but before Ben's head could flop forward, Vincent hammered him across the face, reopening the gash his gun barrel had made.

Ben ignored the blow, and the pain, and the blood streaming down, soaking into his shirt. To his way of thinking, he wasn't being given a chance to live, but rather a chance to die outdoors and with a modicum of dignity. He had won the battle against this man and against Whitestone. Alice Gustafson and Organ Guard were safe. Now, it didn't matter that he was about to lose the war. He had long ago lost his faith in the church—in any church, in fact—but now he sensed that if his childhood priests and catechism teachers were right, and there was a heaven, he at least had a shot at getting there. He only hoped he could put forth a decent effort and that the end wouldn't hurt too much.

Hail Mary, full of grace, the Lord is with thee. Blessed art thou among women and blessed is the fruit of thy womb, Jesus.

"Untie me," he heard his surprisingly forceful voice say.

Vincent nodded to his assistant, and it was done. Ben clenched his teeth as best he could, and pushed himself upright. A wave of dizziness and nausea threatened to topple him, but he forced himself to remain erect, and even managed to take another pull from the water bottle.

Holy Mary, mother of God, pray for us sinners now and at the hour of our death.

With the Hail Mary reverberating in his mind, Ben took one painful, awkward step toward the door. Then another. He wondered what it would feel like to have a high-powered arrow pierce his body. These weren't summer camp archery arrowheads Vincent would be firing at him. They were the hunters—the ones with three or four metal sides coming to a lethal point at the tip.

Another step—this one somewhat easier. He took a deep, steadying breath, and passed through the door into the mid-afternoon sun. Vincent strode out after him.

"Straight ahead," he ordered. "I'll tell you when to stop."

Ben forced himself upright. He had won. Now it was time simply to play out the string. Just two months ago, if someone had told him he would be dying for a cause he believed in, he would have leaned back in his scarred desk chair in his tawdry little office, and laughed until he cried. Where was Madame Sonja when he needed her? The whole business of being tortured would have been so much easier if he had only known in advance he was going to make it—if he had only known in advance that he was going to safeguard Alice's name and mission to the death. He wanted so much to see Vincent's face when he told him that the game was over, and that Whitestone had lost. But of course, that would have to remain his secret.

He forced his chin up and trudged forward, one painful, unstable step at a time. Then he paused, took one last swig from the water bottle, and tossed it into the brush. They were on the gravel road, out of view of the hospital.

It was time.

"Let me get this straight," Ben asked, his voice raspy and not as strong as it had been, "if I kill you, I can just go free?"

"That's it," Vincent said, perhaps a little irritated. "Get away and you're free. Kill me and you're free. Get shot, you lose."

"Has anyone in this little game of yours ever gotten away?"

"What do you think?"

"Then I'll just have to be the first."

"You have a minute, asshole. Sixty seconds and *thwack!* My eyes will be closed, but my ears won't. Go any way you want. I

owe you big time for Cincinnati, so I'm only
going to wound you with the first shot—and
maybe the second one, too, now that I think
about it."

"Say when," Ben said.

"When."

When!

Just like that, Ben's life was on the clock.
Several precious seconds had passed before he moved. The brush to his right
seemed slightly thinner than to the left, so
he plunged in that way, not trying for stealth,
but rather to stay on his feet and put at least
a little distance between him and the man
who was about to kill him.

"Forty-five seconds!"

The voice seemed inches away. Ben
slapped aside branches, and pulled himself
ahead using the trunks of trees. The initial
pitch was mainly downhill, but the terrain
was rocky and uneven. If there was any path
or track that could at least partially mask his
progress, he didn't see it. Several large boul-
ders announced the beginning of an uphill
push. He should have gone the other way,
he thought. In his condition, uphill was an
enemy. Oh, hell, what difference did it make?
This wasn't a matter of life and death, it was

a matter only of death—only of when. He was in his last seconds on earth. His life, which had once held so much promise, was about to end painfully, and suddenly thoughts of what he had missed, of what had never happened, were shooting through his mind.

"Thirty seconds!"

Vincent's voice seemed marginally farther away.

The hill, much steeper now, would have been no problem for him if he hadn't been so battered. As it was, the dizziness and nausea were intensifying. Maybe he should hide—find a place of dense growth and try to burrow in and wait his killer out until dark. Ridiculous! For one thing, he hadn't put that much ground between them, for another, branches were breaking with every step, and finally, he realized, where he was, the undergrowth had fallen away. If he continued standing, Vincent would have a straight shot from many yards away.

At that moment, Ben stumbled and pitched forward, slamming heavily into a massive granite rock face that was four or five feet taller than he was. The rising ground around the monolith made Ben think he

could at least make it up to the top. Then
what? The best he could think of was throwing himself down onto the killer and trying for
one of the arrows. The best of no options.

"Fifteen seconds!"

Ben wondered how far he had gone. A
hundred yards? Probably much less.

On his hands and knees, he forced himself uphill and around the huge boulder. He
was light-headed and gasping for air, but
inch by inch, he moved ahead.

"All right, asshole!" Vincent called out.
"Time to die."

Ben flattened himself near the top of the
rock. He was probably at such an angle from
the ground that he couldn't be seen, but he
still felt exposed. He held his breath and listened. There was only the machine thrum of
thousands of insects. He glanced about.
There were some tall trees—maybe ma-
hogany or eucalyptus—and thick undergrowth, extending six or seven feet off the
ground, but his chance to run was gone. His
only hope was to stay out of sight and pray
that Vincent passed directly beneath him, or
that somehow, he had started off in the opposite direction.

Again, Ben held his breath. This time, he

heard something—a rustling of the brush not far to his left. Vincent was close—very close. Ben turned his head, but did not lift it. Instead, he pressed his cheek against the granite and peered in the direction of the noise. The underbrush was definitely moving, and the moving force was headed in his direction. If Vincent circled the rock to the uphill side, that was it. Hunt over. Ben knew he should have kept running. His only chance now, and not much of one at that, was to wait until it seemed the killer was right beneath him, then hurl himself down.

The noise of cracking twigs and shifting brush was even closer now. Just to the left of where Ben lay. Staying flat, he shifted his weight as best he could. At the movement from above, Vincent would be swinging his bow upward, trying to get off a quick shot. Ben would avoid the arrowhead, fall on him, and quickly go for the quiver.

Quiet . . . listen . . . look . . . Don't breathe. . . . Don't breathe. . . . Hail Mary, full of grace, the Lord is with thee . . . and . . . NOW!

Ben pushed to his knees, prepared to leap, but Vincent wasn't beneath him. Instead, an emaciated feral dog, tan with white legs and a long, narrow snout, was sniffing its way through the bushes. Ben felt a surge of hope. Maybe Vincent had gone the other way after all. Maybe there was still time to run. At that moment, he was shot from behind. The arrow slammed through the muscle at the base of his neck, glancing off his collarbone before exiting with the arrowhead and four inches of shaft exposed just below his jaw.

Stunned by the impact and the shocking pain, Ben pitched to his right, fell heavily onto the surface of the huge rock, and then toppled off. He landed on his side, air exploding from his lungs. Through the corner of his eye he could see the point of the arrow, and the part of the shaft that was protruding from his body.

Holy Mary, mother of God, mother of God, pray for us sinners now and at the hour of our death. . . .

But in that minute, death did not come, nor in the next. Ben lay motionless, beyond feeling pain, tasting the coarse dirt of the rain forest floor, the surrounding greens and browns a blur. Finally, there was movement from behind him to the edge of his field of vision.

"That was for Cincinnati," Vincent said.

"This one is for all the smart-asses in the world who think they're putting something over on the rest of us."

In a final moment of absolute clarity, Ben's vision sharpened, and he saw the camouflage-painted apparition, fifteen yards away, grinning as he raised his bow and drew back. Suddenly, Vincent jerked his head back and swatted at his cheek as if he had been bitten by a gigantic insect.

"What the—?"

They were the killer's last words. From somewhere in the forest, a long, thin blade flashed from the trees, and pierced his neck through and through. Blood from a severed artery was spewing from the wound before he even began to fall. Widened eyes, a muffled cry, and a graceless pirouette, and the behemoth slumped to the ground, dead before he even hit.

Ben, not being able to completely comprehend what had happened, felt blackness closing in. At the last moment, before total darkness, he felt a light touch on his shoulder, and heard a voice—a soft, reassuring woman's voice.

"It's going to be all right," she said.

CHAPTER 34

Our guardians, as far as men can be, should be true worshipers of the Gods and like them.
—PLATO, *The Republic,* Book II

Dr. Anson, please come quickly. It's Rennie. I think this is the end for him. He's still awake, but his blood pressure is gone."

Anson followed the young nurse to room 10—the quasi-isolation room at the far end of the hospital. Rennie Ono, a woodcarver in his early forties, was getting ready to die. He had battled his AIDS for a decade, but after years of quality living, he had lost out to a combination of infection and sarcoma. There was nothing else that could be done—at least nothing medically.

Anson pulled a chair to the bedside and sat down, taking the man's emaciated hand in his.

"Rennie, are you able to hear me?"

Faintly, Ono nodded, although he was beyond speech.

"Rennie, you are a good and kind man. It will go well for you in the life after this one. You have fought your illness bravely. Are you afraid now?"

Ono shook his head.

"May I read to you, Rennie? May I read to you? May I read you through the passage? Good."

Anson opened a well-worn looseleaf notebook—his notebook. It was filled with drawings, short essays, diary entries, and poems, and he added to it in some way nearly every day. There was no title to what he was about to read, only the words, carefully printed on a sheet that was whiter than the others:

The world can be hard, full of trickery,
Full of deceit,
Full of injustice,
Full of pain.
But there is an emptiness waiting, my
     friend—a great, glowing emptiness,
Soft and fragrant with the essence of
     peace,

The essence of serenity.
You are almost there, my friend.
The magnificent emptiness is the
  eternal harbor for your soul.
Take my hand, friend.
Take my hand and take a step, just
  one more step,
And you are there.

Anson felt Rennie Ono's grip go slack. The faint rise and fall of the sheet over his chest vanished. For several minutes they remained silent and motionless—nurse, doctor, patient. Finally, Anson stood, bent low, and gently kissed the man's forehead. Then, without a word, he left the room.

It was nearing dawn, the most cherished time of Anson's day. From the moment in Amritsar when he had realized the deception of the surgeon Khanduri and the woman claiming to be Narendra Narjot, along with the tacit participation of his dearest friend, Elizabeth, he had been sad and perplexed. Sleeping little, he had thrown himself as never before into his work and into caring for the patients in the clinic and hospital. All the while, he waited for understanding of what his response should be. Now, after several conversations with the nurse Claudine, who had been let go by Elizabeth, he was ready.

When Anson reached the lab, his friend Francis Ngale was waiting just outside.

"Dr. Joe, the laboratory is prepared," the huge security guard said. "Dr. St. Pierre has just arrived at the hospital."

"Good."

"Did Rennie pass on?"

"He did."

"Peacefully?"

"Very peacefully, Francis."

"Thank you, Dr. Joe. He was quite a good man."

"Now we have business to attend to. Might I have the remote control?"

Ngale handed over a small, rectangular box.

"Tested and retested," he said. "I hope you don't have to use it."

"If I do, I do. The chair is in place?"

"It is."

"You are a good friend, Francis. You have always been so."

The two men embraced briefly, and then Anson sent Ngale back to the hospital. A minute later, the man reappeared, leading Elizabeth into the room. She was wearing a loose, filmy white cotton skirt and matching blouse. Not even her expression of bewilderment and concern could mask her enduring beauty. Anson motioned her to the chair, and stood in front of her—sometimes pacing like a barrister, sometimes standing quite still and erect.

"Well," she said in English, "summoning me here at four o'clock in the morning is certainly a first."

"Yes," Anson replied, "it is. As you know, prior to your arranging our trip to India to visit the widow of my benefactor, I made you a promise that I would share the final secrets of my research on Sarah-nine with the scientists from Whitestone."

"That is correct."

Her bewildered expression intensified. Why would he be retelling something she knew so well?

"All you are missing is the identification of which of the ten strains of yeast in our vats we are actually using, and also one step in the process of stimulating the yeast to actually produce the drug."

"Yes?"

"Well, I have decided to renege on my part of the bargain."

"But—"

"You have been deceitful, Elizabeth. You built our friendship, and then abused it."

Anson had always been an extremely peaceful man, but his temper, once triggered, could be intense. He cautioned himself against going off at this moment. Not with the remote in his pocket.

"I don't know what you're talking about," St. Pierre tried.

Anson rattled off a few sentences in Hindi.

"I assume you recognize the language, even if it is one of the few you do not speak. I am reasonably fluent in it—at least fluent enough to identify that ridiculous charade in Amritsar."

"I don't understand," she tried again.

"Of course you do. Upon our return, hoping against hope that I had somehow misread the whole dreadful scenario, I contacted a journalist friend in New Delhi. There is no evidence that a T. J. Narjot ever existed, nor that there was ever an outbreak of *Serratia* in the hospitals of Amritsar."

"Wait," St. Pierre pleaded, now clearly beginning to panic.

"There's more," Anson said. "Ever since my operation and recovery, I've been mystified by the convenience of my respiratory arrest here in the hospital. I called the nurse, Claudine, who was here that day. At first she tried to protect you, or rather her future as a nurse, which you threatened. But ultimately her allegiance to me won out, and what do you suppose I learned? I learned that my dear friend Elizabeth, my dear old friend, nearly killed me out of her own self-interest."

"That was done for your own good, Joseph. You needed the transplant."

"You mean *you* needed me to have the transplant. My work wasn't going fast enough for you. Or was it that you were fearful I would die before your damn scientists had picked my brain clean?"

"Now, Joseph, that isn't fair. Whitestone built this hospital. We built these labs."

Anson withdrew the remote from his pocket.

"You know my friend Francis, yes?" he asked, motioning to Ngale.

"Of course."

"Francis is something of an expert in demolition. At my request, he has wired this entire research wing with explosives. Elizabeth, you have exactly fifteen minutes to satisfy me you are telling the truth, or this lab is going up in smoke."

"Wait, no. You can't do this!"

"Fifteen minutes, and all this will be rubble, including those precious vats of yeast, and my notebooks, which are piled right over there in the corner."

"Joseph, you don't understand. It is not my place to tell you anything. I-I need to make some calls. I need to get permission to share some things with you. My life is in danger if I don't. I-I need more time."

Anson theatrically checked his watch.

"Fourteen minutes."

St. Pierre looked frantically about as if searching for a rescuer.

"I need to make a call."

"As long as it takes less than fourteen minutes."

St. Pierre raced off.

"Shall I go with her?" Ngale asked.

"Her only option is to tell us the truth. The people who employ her are smart—very smart. They will see that."

In just a few minutes St. Pierre was back.

"All right, all right," she said, breathless. "I've been authorized to tell you certain facts, but no names. Is that acceptable?"

"You are the liar, Elizabeth. You are the deceiver. I will make no promises."

"All right, then, sit down and listen."

Anson nodded to Ngale, who brought over a chair, and then, with one final look at his friend, excused himself from the room.

"Proceed," Anson said. "Just remember, though, if I feel you are lying, I will not give you a second chance."

He held up the remote for emphasis.

St. Pierre straightened herself and met his gaze defiantly.

"A number of years ago," she began, "maybe fifteen, a small group of transplant specialists—medical and surgical—began getting together at international transplant meetings to discuss the awesome pressures of our specialty, and our dissatisfaction and frustration with the system of organ donation and allocation."

"Go on."

"Around the globe, restrictive legislation was essentially removing us—the internal medicine specialists and surgeons responsible for organ transplants—from the loop of decision making. Surgeons began lying about the severity of their patients' conditions to push them farther up certain lists. In addition, public apathy and a lack of involvement by organized religion have deprived societies of a reasonable supply of organs. And finally, perhaps most frustrating of all, again and again, people whose self-destructive behaviors—smoking, drinking, eating poorly—have caused them to need a transplant slide back into their self-destructive ways, and literally destroy the organ that could have saved the life of a more responsible, more deserving candidate."

"Were you part of this group?"

"Not initially. I was invited to join the Guardians about eleven years ago."

"The Guardians?"

"As you can imagine, the discussions the initial group of transplant doctors had were deeply philosophical. In this group were some of the greatest minds in medicine, facing some of the greatest ethical dilemmas."

"And also possessing some of the greatest egos, I've been told."

"These men and women—especially the transplant surgeons—are burdened with incalculable responsibility."

"The Guardians?"

"Gradually, in search of a philosophical center, the group began focusing more and more on the writings of Plato, particularly *The Republic.* His philosophy and logic made sense to everyone. Meeting by meeting, through readings and discussion, the basis for a highly secret society was formed."

"Dr. Khanduri is a Guardian?"

"I said no names."

"Damn it, is he?" Anson snapped.

"Yes, of course. Of course he is. Why do you ask?"

"Because he spoke about his disagreement with the Sikhs over their rejection of the caste system. Plato, as I recall, divided society into three castes."

"He didn't use that word, but yes. The Producers—laborers, farmers, and the like—are the lowest of the three; the Auxiliaries—soldiers, managers, and secondary leaders—are next, and at the apex of the pyramid—"

"The Guardians," Anson filled in, "the elite."

St. Pierre nodded proudly.

"Intellectually, athletically, artistically, creatively, altruistically, scientifically, and politically. Think of what would have happened if Einstein or Nelson Mandela, or Raymond Damidian, who invented the MRI scanner, or . . . or Mother Teresa, needed an organ to survive and they were mired down in some list or bureaucratic red tape or . . . or there were simply no suitable organs available. Think of yourself, Joseph, and all that you are about to bring to mankind because we were able to procure a lung for you—and not just any lung, a perfectly matched lung. As transplant specialists, it is the goal of the Guardians of the Republic to see to it that other Guardians around the world who need organs of any kind are supplied them."

St. Pierre's zeal and intensity were chilling. Anson could barely breathe. The word "procure" cut through him like a knife. For the first time, he began considering the possibility that the source of his new life might not have been someone legally dead.

"From where?" he managed hoarsely.

"Pardon?"

"Where? From where do these organs come?"

"Why, from the Producers and the Auxiliaries, of course," St. Pierre said. "Certainly not from other Guardians. That wouldn't make any sense. It is against our policies."

Anson stared at the woman he thought he had known well for eight years. His utter disbelief was directed not merely at what St. Pierre was saying, but even more at her absolute comfort in saying it.

"How many Guardians are there now?" he asked.

"Not so many," she replied. "Maybe twenty-five, maybe thirty now. We are very selective and as you might suspect, very careful as well. Only the best of the best."

"Of course," he muttered. "Only the best of the best." He held up the remote. "Elizabeth, I promise you that if you make one effort to move from that chair without answering my questions, I will press this button, and you will die, along with this lab."

"But you will die as well."

"My priorities are straight. Now, tell me about procuring this perfect match."

St. Pierre fidgeted uncomfortably and looked around as if expecting a knight-errant to ride in and save her.

"Well," she said finally, her composure now only marginal, "if a Guardian is to receive an organ, it must be a perfect or near-perfect match. Otherwise there would be emotional trauma, and medical issues around the high doses of toxic antirejection drugs they would have to take. Look at you, Joseph. You are barely on any medications at all. After your operation, you were back at your critical work in almost no time."

"I would imagine many of the Guardians who receive organs can pay for them."

"And they do. Such monies are used to forward the work of the society."

"Through the Whitestone Foundation."

"We are the Whitestone Foundation, yes. We perform philanthropic works all over the world on behalf of artists, healers, politicians, and scientists like yourself. We own Whitestone Laboratories, Whitestone Pharmaceuticals, and soon, if you are a man of your word, Sarah-nine as well."

"Don't you dare talk to me about being a man of my word. That entire trip to India was a fraud—a total charade."

"That was because you wouldn't let up in your insistence to meet the family of your donor, and the council of the Guardians of the Republic felt that for the time being at least, that was neither practical nor desirable."

"My operation wasn't performed in India?"

"I've cooperated with you in every way, Joseph. Now, will you please put that thing down."

"Where was my surgery done?" He brandished the remote for emphasis. "No lies."

"Brazil. It was done at a Whitestone facility in Brazil. You were kept sedated and then transferred from there to a Guardian surgeon in Capetown as soon as it was safe."

Anson took a deep, cleansing breath.

"Okay, now tell me, Elizabeth, who was he?"

"Pardon?"

"The donor. Who was he and where was he from?"

Again, St. Pierre cast about fruitlessly for someone to intervene. Her jaws were clenched in frustration.

"Actually," she said finally, "it was a woman—a woman from Boston in the States."

"Her name?"

"I told you, no—"

"Goddamn it, Elizabeth," Anson bellowed, "give me her name or be prepared to die on this spot! I mean it, and you know I mean it!"

"It's Reyes. Natalie Reyes."

"Okay. Now, step by step, you are going to tell me everything you know about this Natalie Reyes and how she came to be chosen to give me her lung."

CHAPTER 35

**When a man thinks himself to be near
death, fears and cares enter into his mind
which he never had before.**
　　　　　　—PLATO, *The Republic,* Book I

Ben reentered consciousness to a pungent,
though not unpleasant, aroma, and a
woman's voice softly singing in a tongue he
didn't understand. The arrow was gone. The
agonizing pain in his shoulder and the racking ache throughout his body were present,
but strangely muted. It was not the first time
he had awakened, he recognized, not the
first time he had heard the woman singing.
He was naked from the waist up, on his
back, on a pile of blankets and rags in what
seemed to be a cave. Sunlight was pouring
in through the entrance, ten feet or so away.
　Gradually, his vision came into focus,

along with his memory, beginning with the moment of Vincent's gruesome death— some sort of dart to the side of his face, then a knife through his neck. The lethal arrow Ben had expected was never fired. Instead, what he remembered was a woman, kneeling beside him, speaking English and reassuring him that he was going to be all right. Smooth, tanned skin; dark, vibrant, concerned eyes. Along with a man wearing an eye patch, she had gotten him to his feet and struggled to get him to walk. The rest was a blur, except for her face. It was a lovely, intense, interesting face.

Steeled against the pain, he tried to sit. The woman singing nearby, more ageless than aged, made no attempt to stop him. She was a tribal native. Her face, though deeply lined, had features not unlike the man who had helped Vincent torture him. Behind her, Ben saw the source of the scent that was filling the cave—a pot, boiling on a small fire, emitting wisps of gray smoke.

He managed to get upright and remain that way for a few seconds before a wave of dizziness forced him back. The woman caught him with one hand and lowered him down. Then she eased a small ladle between his lips and held his head as he drank the thick, aromatic liquid that was there. In just minutes, the pain was completely gone, replaced by a cascade of remarkably pleasant thoughts and images. Soon after, as she was replacing the dried poultice on his shoulder with a moist one, the light from the cave opening began to dim. The tumbling images slowed, then faded.

Minutes or hours later, when his consciousness returned, the woman from the forest was kneeling beside him. Her face made him smile.

"Hi," she said, "my name is Natalie Reyes. Do you understand me? Good. Here's some water. You must drink."

Ben nodded and took cautious sips from an earthen cup. Behind Natalie, the other woman worked away at her fire and pot.

"Ben," he managed after his lips were moist enough. "Ben Callahan from Chicago. Are you Brazilian?"

"American. I'm a medical student from Boston."

"Thank you for saving me."

"My friend Luis did the saving, not me. The people who run the hospital murdered his sister for trying to help me. Friends of his down there told him you were being tortured. We were watching from right out there when that man with the bow followed you out of the hospital and down the road. Luis knew what was about to happen and he decided to save you."

"I'm glad he did," Ben understated. "I never thought—"

"Easy," Natalie said. "There's time."

Ben again forced himself upright. This time, the dizziness was minimal. His shoulder was carefully wrapped in gauze that looked as if it might have been used before. As his thoughts cleared, his expression darkened.

"No, there isn't much time," he said excitedly. "There's a woman in the hospital. Her name's Sandy. She's going to be killed— operated on and then killed. I think they are going to take her heart. They—"

Natalie calmed him with a gentle finger to his lips.

"You are very dry and dehydrated," she said. "You need water. If we can't get enough fluids in you, you won't be able to help anyone."

"That woman behind you, she's giving me some sort of incredible drug."

"She's a shaman, and a friend of Luis's. Her name is Tokima, something like that. She speaks a mix of Portuguese, which I understand fairly well, and some kind of tribal dialect that I don't understand at all, but Luis does."

"Well, ask Luis to see if she wants a permanent job making me feel like this."

"The color just left your face, Ben Callahan. That's your blood pressure dropping off the table. In a few more seconds, you are going to start feeling rotten—very rotten. I think you'd better lie down."

"You can predict what's going to happen?"

Natalie checked his pulse, which was rapid and weak.

"Your cardiovascular system is under stress. You need rest and lots of fluids."

"And some more of that medicine," he said, just before he drifted off.

Ben awoke twice more. Each time Natalie Reyes was nearby, looking down at him with deep concern and caring.

"I saw you on the rock down there when that monster was hunting you," she said at one point. "You were so weak and you were so brave. Now that I know what brought you here, I think you're even braver."

She gave him water, and the medicine woman, Tokima, treated him with some of her mixtures. Each time he felt stronger and sat up longer. Piece by piece they were able to share the accounts of how they came to be in Dom Angelo.

When Ben opened his eyes for the third time, Natalie was still there as before, but crouching next to her was the man who had saved his life.

"Luis," Ben said, rolling to one side and extending his hand.

"Ben," Luis said, his grip incredibly strong.

"Luis doesn't speak English," Natalie said, "but he's kind enough to speak Portuguese slowly, so I can translate what needs to be translated."

"Tell him I'm sorry about his sister," Ben said.

"You're a very sweet man to think of that," Natalie replied. "Brave and sweet. I like that combination."

She had a brief conversation with Luis, who met Ben's gaze and nodded. Ben saw the intensity of a warrior in the man's good eye.

"The woman you are worried about," Natalie said, "is still unconscious in the hospital and on a breathing machine."

"She's drugged," Ben replied. "She was kidnapped, and now she's drugged. Back in Texas she was screaming about her child. She yelled that she was being kept in a cage. Then someone, probably Vincent, shut her up." He sat up with no assistance. "Is there anything we can do?" he asked.

"Tell us exactly who came in with you on the airplane."

"Three in the cockpit, four in the cabin—now three thanks to Luis. One of those is—was—Vincent's girlfriend. There were also two aft with the patient. One of them is an older woman—I think she may be an anesthesiologist."

Natalie translated for Luis and got some information in return.

"At the hospital we have Barbosa, he's a crooked policeman; Santoro, he's a crooked doctor; Vincent's assistant, whom apparently you met; plus a few kitchen, housekeeping, and janitorial people."

"Long odds," Ben said.

"They're going to get longer. Another group—the nurses from Rio and those others surrounding the recipient of that poor woman's heart, are due very soon."

"Somehow we've got to get her out," Ben said.

"What do you mean, *we?*" Natalie asked. "You are in no shape for battle."

"I'm going to do what I can. I've come too far not to. Here, give me a hand."

Ben reached out and was effortlessly pulled to his feet by Luis. For a few seconds, the cave reeled, but he braced himself against one wall and remained upright.

"Sweet, brave, *and* tough," Natalie said. "Nice. Okay. We've got the two of us, plus Luis, his girlfriend Rosa, and one other guy from the village that Luis says we can count on. How good are you at war strategy?"

"I got an A in it in college. Do I have time to get my notes?"

"Luis," Natalie said, gesturing to Ben, "I think we are five."

Luis did not reply. Instead, he crossed over to where Tokima was working, and spoke with her. She nodded, took a small plastic pail, and headed off into the forest.

"Tokima has been healing people for many years," he said. "Perhaps eighty."

Natalie translated for Ben, who merely grinned, nodded, and commented that although she had already worked a miracle for him, he hoped the medicine woman could give him something long-acting for the hours ahead.

"Does she know my insurance probably won't cover this treatment?" he asked.

Natalie translated for Luis, who actually smiled. Then the two of them spoke for some time, before she turned to Ben.

"As you probably know, there are many, many psychoactive drugs in the plants out there," she said. "Tokima has gone out to get the strongest of them all—a root. Luis only knows the Indian name for it, which is something like *Khosage.* Dried, ground, and smoked, it is a very powerful hallucinogen, but taken in excess, there is little time to enjoy the more pleasant and interesting effects. Violent vomiting and diarrhea, along with severe abdominal pain, disorientation, and even death will soon intervene. Assuming Tokima can find enough of the root, Luis thinks he can either get it into the food that is being prepared for lunch, or have one of the kitchen help do it for him. With any luck some of the people at the hospital with guns can be disabled, as well as those who are scheduled to assist with the surgery."

"Sounds like a plan," Ben said. "What about Sandy?"

"Assuming you can make it, you and I will cut through the forest to where I have left the Mercedes of the policeman I killed. Then we'll drive around to the access road and down to the hospital. By the time we arrive, there should be absolute chaos. Somehow, then, we've got to wheel Sandy out and get her into the car. Luis and his people will then just have to melt into the forest."

"He's ready to do that?"

"He loved his sister very much."

Ben patted the man on the arm. Then, unwilling to have either of the others know that his light-headedness was returning, and that both knees and his lower back were throbbing, he took a mug of water, shuffled out to the granite shelf in front of the cave, and sat, his back against the rock. Below him and to the south, sparkling in the late-morning sun, was the hospital. *Hospital.* Ben laughed ruefully. Aside from Nazi Germany, the word had probably never been more inappropriately used. The brutality of what had been done to him there, and to so many others, made him shudder. Now, hopefully, it was going to end.

We're coming, he thought savagely. *We're coming.*

A short while later, Tokima returned, her red plastic pail filled to overflowing with thick, gnarled, rust-colored roots, glistening from having just been washed. With hardly a word, she set about preparing the poison. Luis, moving like the predator he was, headed down the hillside. Natalie moved outside the cave, settled down next to Ben, and took his hand.

"A private eye, huh," she said. "Do you own a gun?"

"Of course."

"Ever had to use it?"

"Of course. Boot Hill in Chicago is full of the men I've put there—women, children, and pets, too."

He shot the hospital with his finger and blew the smoke from the barrel.

"Absolutely terrifying," she said, gently folding his finger back in place. "They don't stand a chance."

"Do you think we do?"

"Of course."

"We're both sort of living on borrowed time anyway."

In another fifteen minutes, unheard and unseen, Luis suddenly appeared at the side of the cave opening.

"People are nervous about the disappearance of Vincent," he said. "It is being assumed that Ben killed him. I am supposed to be out looking for his body right now."

He went into the cave and returned with a heavy clay bowl containing the root preparation, covered with leaves.

"You ready, Ben Callahan?" Natalie asked, helping him to his feet.

Ben clenched his fists and willed the dizziness to lessen.

"Ready," he managed.

"The kitchen staff is preparing lunch," Luis said, allowing time for Natalie to share the information with Ben. "I need to get the final ingredient down to them. The doctors are in with their patient, awaiting the arrival of the one who is to receive her heart. The flight crew is sunning by the pool. Santoro is everywhere, preparing for two operations. Barbosa and the other guards are ready for trouble. The time is now."

"The time is now," Natalie repeated.

"Come," Luis said, "I will point you in the

direction of your car. Plan on being outside the hospital with it in one hour. With any fortune, we will be bringing your patient out to you for a ride."

CHAPTER 36

Here is no path . . . the wood is dark and perplexing; still we must push on.
—PLATO, *The Republic,* Book IV

The trek through dense forest to the Mercedes was a bear. The heat and humidity were intense, and the journey was uphill nearly all the way. Using the sun as a marker, Natalie and Ben gave the town a wide berth, and continued to head due north. She was convinced that if they just stayed true to that direction, they had to hit the Dom Angelo road at some point. Then, a turn to the right, and she was certain she could find the dead-end path where she had hidden Vargas's car.

She and Luis had allowed an hour and a half for him to get the toxic hallucinogen into whatever was being served for lunch, and then to get it disbursed throughout the hospital, and for her and Ben to retrieve the Mercedes and drive it around to the rear entrance. It was, as Ben had said, a plan, but it was a shaky one. With timing tight and the hospital on red alert because of Vincent's disappearance, the chances for things to go wrong were many.

Natalie had only a rough idea how far away the road actually was, or how difficult the terrain, so she pushed ahead more aggressively than she would have liked. Now, after half an hour, the altitude and steady upward climb were taking their toll on her compromised stamina. But she could see that Ben, though he was keeping up and refused to ask any quarter, was having an even tougher time.

"Let's take a break," she said, breathing heavily as she handed him the canteen.

"You holding up?"

"I'm managing. It shouldn't be too much longer now."

She didn't bother to ask him the same question. He would say he was doing fine, but Natalie knew he wasn't. The pallor had returned to the area around his lips, and he had a disturbing glaze over his eyes. It was inconceivable to her what he must have endured before being set off into the forest to be hunted down. There were nasty electrical burns speckled over much of his body, his fingers were swollen and discolored, and both the entry and exit wounds on his shoulder, despite Tokimo's poultices, were showing early signs of infection. She wondered how he could possibly hold up much longer. Fortunately, she reminded herself, all they had to do was make it to the car. From then on he would be a passenger.

"Ready?" she asked.

"Lead on. I can do this."

"Have a little more water."

"If you say so, although I have the feeling that all this water I've been drinking isn't exactly from a Crystal Springs bottling plant. Dr. Banks, my doc back in Chicago, will have a field day trying to diagnose all the injuries, parasites, and other diseases I'm going to bring home from this trip. You better hurry up and finish med school so you can help him take care of me."

"No problem. Like many women, I'm cursed with the need to take in wounded, broken men and fix them up."

They stopped once more for rest and water, and just as Natalie was questioning whether or not they might have drifted off course, they hit what she felt certain was the Dom Angelo road. Ben was dragging badly now, and no longer able to disguise his weakness. Still, as long as they found the Mercedes without difficulty, they were doing reasonably well for time.

"Hang on, Ben Callahan," she urged. "We're almost there."

A right-hand turn toward what she hoped was the town, and five more minutes of walking, and she found the overgrown cutoff. Ben was so far behind that at some points after rounding a bend, she lost sight of him completely. She waited until he caught up, and then led him to the car. The moment she saw the branches she had used as camouflage lying on the ground, she knew there was trouble.

Rodrigo Vargas's Mercedes was right where she had left it, but it was not going to be driven—not now and probably not ever. All four tires were slashed and flat. The hood had been pried open, and much of the engine destroyed. The driver's side window had been smashed. As deflated as the tires, Natalie checked beneath the driver's seat for the extra ammunition she had left there. Gone.

"Trouble in paradise," Ben said, bracing himself on the trunk. "This damage seems too total and meticulously done to be senseless vandalism."

"I was thinking the same thing," Natalie replied, checking her watch. "Ben, I can make it down to the hospital, but I don't think you can."

"I don't know. I think—"

"Please. You look as if you're about to fall over. Either wait here with the water or try and make it into town. I told you about Father Francisco. You can find him there. Tell him what's happening, and what happened to you. He'll take care of you. I'm sure of it. Maybe he'll even have access to a car to drive you down to the hospital."

"But—"

"Ben, please. Luis is risking everything to help us. I need to get down there. It's mostly downhill, and I can take the road. I'm a runner. I can do this."

"O-okay."

"Keep the water, I won't need it."

"Don't you forget to come and get me," he said.

"Okay, I'll add it to my to-do list: Get Ben. See you soon, my friend. Promise. Give my best to Father Francisco."

She kissed him on the cheek, whirled, and for the first time since the fire in Dorchester, Massachusetts, five thousand miles and several lifetimes away, she ran.

In her biggest challenges on the track, Natalie never pushed her body any harder than over the next twenty minutes. She was running on a single, damaged lung, carrying a backpack containing Vargas's heavy pistol, duct tape, rope, and a Swiss Army knife. The downhill slope put a heavy strain on her ankles and knees as well as on her balance. The more winded she got, the more out of control her balance became. Twice she stumbled, once she fell, scraping skin off her palms. Her chest was on fire. At no time could she get in enough air. She slowed, then slowed some more. Still, she drove herself. Finally, unable to get a decent breath, she stopped, clinging to a tree trunk, gasping. Thirty seconds and she was off again, lurching down the steep grade like a drunk.

After one more brief stop, fighting for air and trying to ignore the explosive pounding of her heart, Natalie found herself on level ground. A long, right bend in the road, and she was in front of the same hospital entrance where, just a day before, Ben had been shoved out to meet what seemed a certain death. Hands on knees, she allowed her breathing to deepen until finally, one sweet breath fought its way to the depths of her lung.

Glancing around, she withdrew the gun from her backpack and began, warily, to circle the residence quarters, retracing roughly the route she had used to escape after her last visit. She stayed in the trees and gave the far end of the wing a wide berth.

As she neared the broad patio and the swimming pool, she could tell almost instantly that Luis had succeeded in at least one phase of his mission. Three men were around the pool, all of them in swimsuits, all of them giggling. On the tables near them were bowls of some sort of stew.

". . . So then she brings the tray out, filled with like a ham and pork sampler, trips, and flips the whole frigging thing onto the rabbi's lap."

The teller of the tale, a redhead in his late twenties, burst into uncontrollable laughter at his own humor, sloshing his drink onto his lap and making no attempt to blot it up.

The flight crew, Natalie quickly deduced.

One of the men—more mature-looking than the other two, and probably the captain—was on his hands and knees, violently vomiting into a low bush, while simultaneously continuing to laugh.

"I don't feel so good," the third man kept saying over and over again. "I don't feel so good. . . ."

There was no way Natalie could make it to the storage shed and the passage to the hospital without being seen by the trio. She lowered her backpack to the ground, then leveled her long-barreled revolver at the redhead.

"Okay, on your bellies," she snapped. "All of you."

The men, including the captain, glanced up at her, pointed, and howled. Natalie gave brief consideration to simply shooting each one of them in the leg, but knew she wasn't capable of it unless there were no other options. Instead, she moved quickly to the redhead and whipped him across the back of the head with the muzzle, instantly opening an inch-and-a-half gash. The man cried out as he fell, facedown, onto the concrete, but then he began laughing again, mumbling, "Jeez, why'd you do that?"

Natalie stared from one of the men to the others, wondering what her next move should be. Did they have weapons in their rooms? How long could she count on Tokima's preparation lasting? There was no way Luis could control the amount of drug they each ingested. Were they all going to die from it?

While she stood contemplating, the man who wasn't feeling well rolled from his chaise and retched into the pool. Natalie had decided it was safe to leave them where they were when a woman wearing olive military fatigues burst from the shed, her semiautomatic machine gun ready. She was five feet at the most, with a pleasant, russet face and broad hips. Quickly, she took in the scene.

"You are Natalie?" she asked in coarse Portuguese.

"Rosa?"

Luis's girlfriend smiled and nodded.

"We must tie them up," she said, gesturing toward the rope and tape. "Luis says everyone gets tied up."

The two of them, with no fear of resistance from the men, quickly bound their ankles and taped their wrists behind their backs. The patio and pool were now awash with whatever had been inside their stomachs.

The women wiped their hands on elegant beach towels, and hurried to the shed and down into the tunnel. In the dining room they found the kitchen help in one corner, bound and gagged in a way similar to the flight crew. Trussed up not far from the Brazilians, her glare threatening to burn a hole in Natalie's chest, was a narrow-waisted white woman with short, dirty blond hair and a barbed-wire tattoo around her arm. Natalie gestured toward her, silently asking who she was, but Rosa could only shrug.

It could be worse, Natalie wanted to say to the furious woman. *You could have eaten lunch.*

"Do you know where Luis is?" Natalie asked as they moved cautiously, guns drawn, from the dining room and past the lounge where she had hidden behind the couch so close to Santoro and Barbosa.

"He has been here," Rosa whispered, risking a peek around the doorway of the first recovery room and then gesturing inside.

Natalie flattened against the wall across from Rosa and looked inside the room. There on the floor, wide-eyed and trussed up in a manner that would have challenged Houdini, were a husky man and a silver-haired woman in scrubs. They were in obvious distress, due in large measure to the vomiting they were doing through their noses and around the duct tape pasted across their mouths. On the hospital bed beside them, blissfully unconscious and breathing with the help of a state-of-the-art ventilator, was a pretty, red-haired woman—*Sandy.*

"I think we should leave her be like this for now," Natalie said. "Do you agree?"

Rosa nodded and started down the hallway. Natalie, anxious to get clear of the fetid air in the room, made some minor adjustments on the ventilator, and followed. Three from the kitchen, three from the plane, the woman who was probably Vincent's girlfriend, and the two medical people—nine accounted for, but none of them a major source of danger. Those people were still out there someplace. Natalie caught up with Rosa by the main entrance. The corridor leading down to Dr. Donald Cho's macabre treatment room was empty. The fact that the

master of virtual reality and psychopharmacology had not been brought in for this case
spoke frighteningly of Sandy's fate. There
would be no need for a DVD brainwashing
her into believing a bogus reason for her
surgery.

Rosa stood beside the heavy glass double doors, put a finger to her lips, and motioned outside. There, facedown on the
ground, was a red-skinned man in fatigues
similar to Rosa's. There was no blood about,
and no obvious wound, but if he wasn't
dead, he was doing a praiseworthy imitation.

"Salazar Bevelaqua," Rosa whispered.
"He beats his wife. Luis never liked him."

"You don't have to remind me to stay on
Luis's good side," Natalie replied.

The odds were growing shorter. As near
as Natalie could count, it was Rosa and she,
plus Luis and one ally of his. Four. Against
them were Santoro, Barbosa, and two remaining security men from the plane. Suddenly, the still afternoon air was pierced by
volleys of gunfire. A man screamed out in
pain. Then, just as abruptly as it had begun,
the gun battle ended. From off to the right,
they heard moaning, and a man swearing
over and over again in English.

Handgun ready, Natalie followed Rosa in that direction. At the edge of the building, sprawled on his back, peppered with bullets, was the man from Dom Angelo. Rosa hurried to him, cradled his head in her hand, then quickly turned to Natalie and shook her head grimly. Nearby, writhing on the ground, clutching his abdomen, his white turtleneck jersey saturated with blood, was another man—one of the security guards from the plane, Natalie reasoned.

"Oh, God! Goddamn it!" he kept moaning. "Oh, please, help me."

Without a flicker of hesitation, Rosa stood and, from five feet, shot the man in the forehead. Natalie was no longer amazed at her own detachment and lack of emotion. The world of Whitestone Laboratories was a world of big money, of violence, and of death. She had been unwillingly drawn into it, and now she had adjusted.

Sharing their unspoken concern for where Luis might be, and if he had been hurt, the two women inched their way back into the hospital and turned toward the portion of the main corridor that ended in Cho's laboratory. Natalie stopped in front of the closed door to Santoro's office and tried the knob.

She was surprised to find it wasn't locked, and had taken a single step into the room when the door was viciously slammed, and Barbosa's powerful forearm slipped over her shoulder and tightened around her throat. He was nearly a full head taller than she was, with a bulging, rock-hard belly that pressed into her back. The hair on his arm was like sandpaper against her skin.

"Drop it!" he hissed. "Drop the gun!"

Gagging from the pressure across her trachea and larynx, Natalie immediately complied. Barbosa opened the door slowly and, using her as a shield, moved into the hallway and called out, "Drop it, Rosa! Drop it now or I will break her neck and kill you at the same time. . . . You know I can do it and you know I will. Good. Now, get on the ground. Facedown! Quickly."

Her lips drawn back in the snarl of a tiger, Rosa slowly did as the policeman insisted. At the instant she was prone, the outside door flew open and Luis lurched through. He was a disheveled apparition, wounded at least twice, once in the left shoulder and once in the chest on the right side. Blood, probably his and others', was smeared across his face and the legs of his khakis.

His right hand, clutching a pistol, dangled impotently at his side. Natalie sensed Barbosa smiling.

"So, traitor," he said, keeping his forearm tightly in place, "it is over for you. Drop the gun and lie down next to your woman, and I will have one of our surgeons see if they can save your life."

"That would be very kind of you, Oscar," Luis said. "I know I can trust you to keep your word."

The warrior's arm snapped up like a striking cobra—so fast that Natalie barely understood what was happening until it was over. Orange fire spit from the muzzle of his gun. At the same instant, Barbosa's grip across her throat vanished. She dropped to one knee and whirled in time to see the policeman stumbling backward. His hand, blood oozing from beneath it, was pressed over where his right eye had been. His vast bulk slammed heavily against the wall by Santoro's office door, then slid to the floor, macabrely held in a seated position by his massive girth.

"I told you I was good at killing," Luis rasped, before collapsing.

CHAPTER 37

Wealth and poverty; the one is the parent of luxury and indolence, and the other of meanness and viciousness, and both of discontent.

—PLATO, *The Republic,* Book IV

For a time, Ben sat there on the ground, leaning back against the Mercedes, sipping the last of what little water remained in the canteen. He felt feverish and weak. His shoulder was throbbing, and a pounding headache was evolving directly behind his eyes. Natalie had been right to leave him. He should have suggested doing so, himself. Now, here he was. He wondered what Alice Gustafson's reaction would be to his predicament. She had risked her life a number of times to expose those trafficking in illegal organs, so maybe she wouldn't think much of his putting *his* survival on the line when he drove through that gate to the Whitestone compound back in Texas. But then again, she probably would.

Thanks to whoever had vandalized the car, the plan he, Natalie, and Luis had settled on had come apart almost before it had begun. It still seemed possible that Luis could get Tokima's drug into the food at the hospital. It seemed possible that the guards and professional killers who were defending the place could be overcome. It seemed possible that Natalie could make it to the hospital in time to help, and that she could somehow get Sandy off the respirator, into someone's car, and back up the hill to whisk him away.

It all seemed possible, but not very likely.

Ben pulled himself up and battled back the resultant dizziness and nausea. He had come too far merely to sit here and wait. Natalie had said that he might be of help if he could reach the village and contact the priest there. If he tried and instead ended up moldering on the roadside, at least he would have died knowing he had gone for it. At least he would have made his return to the earth having cared.

As he pushed a step away from the car, his hand brushed across his pocket and the small revolver Luis had given him. He had actually forgotten that it was there. It was a .38—a snub-nosed Saturday night special, not unlike the gun still in the wheel well of Seth Stepanski's Chrysler back in Fadiman.

He took several more steps, then forced himself up straight and marched back to the road. The two classy women in his life, Alice and now Natalie, would be proud of his grit. So would Sandy if she ever knew. It was strange to think of her lying there medicated to unconsciousness in the hospital while so much turmoil swirled about, and all of it involving her.

He turned away from the direction where he and Natalie had come, and headed toward the town. One step, then another. Head up, shoulders back, he tried to ignore the pain racking his body.

**Keep going . . . keep going
Father forgive us for what we
    must do
You forgive us, we'll forgive you
Holy Mary, mother of God . . .
We'll forgive each other till we
    both turn blue
Pray for us sinners . . .**

The afternoon sun was intense now, and because of the hour, the rain forest road offered little shade. First John Prine, then the Hail Mary, then John again . . . line by line, verse by verse, Ben kept walking, stumbling from time to time, but never falling. He might have walked a mile or just a few hundred yards. He couldn't tell and it really didn't matter. The water was gone, and his hope of making it anyplace was dwindling. His head was down now, watching his boots inch forward one painful step after another. Then, a slight downward change in the road caused him to lift his head, and there below him was the town—a postcard photo of Lilliputian structures, nestled in a lush valley. He was nearly insane from the pain and the dizziness, but he had made it. His cracked lips pulled upward into a raw, defiant smile.

He was still dragging more than walking when he reached the actual outskirts of the village. Curious eyes followed him as he made his way toward the center of town.

"Agua, por favor," he said to an old woman, using his feeble Spanish and hoping it bore some similarity to Portuguese. *"¿Dónde está Padre Frank . . . a . . . Padre Francisco?"*

The wizened woman offered no water, but did gesture up the street to a quaint chapel. Down several of the streets, Ben saw vehicles of one kind or another. If anyone could borrow or rent or even commandeer one of them, it would have to be the village priest. What shade there had been on the road was gone now, and heat radiated like a kiln from the hard-baked clay. He shuffled forward, but sensed that he might crumple at any moment. The surroundings grew dim, and as he approached the church, he felt his legs beginning to go.

Hail Mary, full of grace, the Lord . . .

Bit by bit, life came back into focus. Ben's first major reconnection to the world was that he was on a bed—clean linens, a pillow, no, two of them. The aroma of brewing coffee helped nudge his consciousness along.

"So," a man's voice said in English, "my American patient awaketh."

"How do you know?" Ben asked.

"You have been somewhat delirious for nearly half an hour. What you said made absolutely no sense, but being from Brooklyn, I know American when I hear it. Frank Nunes—Father Frank if you wish, Padre

Francisco if you want to sound more exotic. You took some water—two glasses—just a little while ago. Would you like some more? Coffee?"

Ben's awareness returned with force. He pushed himself up and swung his feet over the bed, mindless of the cannon blasts between his eyes.

"Listen, please, Father. I just came from Natalie Reyes, she said she—"

"Ah, the missing vagabond. I helped her to a campsite, and then when I went to look in on her the next morning, she was gone."

"She's at the hospital," Ben said breathlessly. "There's trouble there. Big trouble. I need your help."

"My help?"

"There's a woman who's been flown in. I was on the plane. If we don't get down there with a car, she will die—no, not just die, she will be murdered. I've got to get a car and I've got to get down there right away."

"Is Senhorita Reyes all right?"

"I don't know, Father, she—listen, I really don't have time to explain. This is an emergency. Natalie is in danger, so are some people from the village here. Luis—"

"Luis Fernandes?"

"I never knew his last name, but he's trying to help us."

"Us?"

"Natalie Reyes and—please, you must believe me. People are going to die there. Maybe many people. If you can just get us a car, I can explain on the way. Maybe you can intervene. Maybe you can do something to—"

He glanced over at the kitchen table across the room and noticed a set of car keys lying there. Father Frank followed his gaze.

"My car is not very dependable," he said.

Ben was beginning to feel exasperated.

"Let's at least try it," he begged. "Or . . . maybe one of the other ones in the village. Surely you—"

"I'm sorry."

Ben stood up.

"Okay, if you can't help me, I'll find someone who can."

"Sit down," Frank said sharply.

"No! I need your car."

Ben reached for his revolver, but his pocket was empty.

"That little thirty-eight was dangerous," the priest said. "The barrel was filthy. No way to know for sure which way the bullet was going to go. Now a *Glock* is a different story altogether." He withdrew a glistening pistol from beneath his robe and flicked the barrel in Ben's general direction. "I polish this forty-five every Sunday, right after Mass. Parts of the rain forest can be quite wild and dangerous. There are times, even for a priest, when the shield of God may not be enough protection."

"You're no priest!" Ben snapped.

Furious and desperate enough to be mindless of the consequences of his action, he dove at the man. Father Frank parried his attack with little effort, throwing Ben back onto the bed.

"Easy," the priest said. "I have no desire to hurt you as I am, in fact, a man of the cloth— less pious than some, I would grant you, but far more pious than others. I just happen to believe that there is no great dignity or holiness in being poor. It is one of the few beliefs I do not hold in common with the good book. The people who run that hospital see to it that our church remains solvent and that I remain as dignified as possible."

"And all you have to do is keep these people in line."

"That and to let the powers at the hospital know when nosy strangers driving cars that aren't theirs come wandering into town with pristine boots, pretending to be hiking the rain forest."

"It was you who wrecked the car, wasn't it?"

"I do what I am told. Mercedes don't hold up that well here in the rain forest anyhow."

"So, here we have a priest who carries a gun, vandalizes cars, preaches to people he considers too poor for dignity, and supports himself and his church by taking money from murderers. Aren't you something. Makes me really proud I'm a Catholic."

"Xavier Santoro is no murderer. Nor, for that matter, are any of the others associated with the hospital. Mr. Callahan, so-called illicit organ traffic takes place all over the world. Money changes hands and kidneys and other organs change bodies. What can be wrong with that? One person benefits in one fashion, the other benefits in another. In fact, in my opinion, there is no reason for such exchanges to be illegal or to consider them immoral."

Stunned, Ben stared at the priest, trying to see whether or not the man believed what he had just said. Then he remembered saying almost the same thing to Alice not that long ago.

"Frank," he asked, regaining some com-posure, "do you know who that woman Na-talie is or why she's here?"

"Aside from the fact that she's searching for a relative, and posing to be someone she is not, no. I know nothing about her."

"Put the gun down, Father. I'm not going to try and leave. . . . Thank you. Now, I have just one more question for you, and then I'll do whatever you say, and tell you anything you wish to know."

"And what is that question, Mr. Callahan?"

"Padre Francisco, do you know what re-ally goes on at that hospital?"

CHAPTER 38

**In what manner does tyranny arise?—
That it has a democratic origin is evident.**
—PLATO, *The Republic,* Book VIII

The dining room was like a MASH unit. Rosa
and Natalie had moved the tables and chairs
to one side, and had dragged their captives
to the area of the lounge where a makeshift
enclosure of sofas, easy chairs, and dining
tables turned on edge kept them all in view.
For the time being, the jet crew had been left
by the swimming pool, but the rest of the
hospital workers and what remained of the
security staff were all present and accounted for.

Luis, though badly wounded, had been
able to direct Natalie to the virtual reality laboratory at the end of the hall, where she

found Xavier Santoro and a guard from the plane. Dapper, urbane Santoro had been violently ill, and now was cringing in one corner, swatting at the products of his hallucinations. Still, he was managing periods of lucidity, during which he kept telling Natalie that she was making a terrible mistake.

Not far away from the surgeon was a strapping young man with his gun in his hand, too disoriented even to function. Natalie relieved him of the pistol without a struggle and then helped him shuffle down the corridor to Rosa, before bringing a wheelchair back to transport Santoro. Chuck's surly girlfriend, who initially seemed to be the only one unaffected by the stew, had suddenly gotten sick and begun also to show other signs of toxicity. Luis and his medicine woman had done their jobs well.

In spite of their triumph, Natalie and Rosa were grim. Luis, stretched out on one of the sofas, was in trouble. Natalie had tended to his wounds as best she could and had begun an IV infusion of saline to keep his sagging blood pressure from dropping to critical levels, but there was no question he was bleeding internally—possibly from a laceration to his liver.

The mission now was to stabilize him as quickly as possible, wake Sandy, and get the two of them off to a hospital, stopping along the way for Ben. Natalie had seen two cars—sub-compacts—parked by the rear of the hospital. They might need them both to transport the five of them, and they would need them quickly. Somewhere out there, people were on their way—at the very least, nurses from Rio, one or more surgeons, and a patient in need of Sandy's heart.

"Luis," Natalie said after getting a blood pressure reading in the low eighties, "for the time being, I should move you into the room where there is a heart monitor."

The warrior shook his head and lifted the pistol he had tucked beneath him.

"Others are coming," he said. "We must get away or we must be ready."

"We have come this far, Luis. We will make it, but only so long as you are there to save our lives if we get in trouble again. You are my hero, and I have been so busy with everything, I have not thanked you."

She turned to Rosa, pointed to her own lips, and then gestured to Luis's. The woman grinned and nodded her permission.

"Thank you, Luis," Natalie whispered,

kissing him lightly on the cheek, then the lips. "Thank you for saving my life."

Luis managed a weak grin.

"It was nothing," he said. "In dangerous situations like this, there is often only one chance. I had to take it."

"The shot that finished Barbosa was amazing. You didn't even seem to aim. I think I felt the wind of the bullet as it went past my head."

"It was a lucky shot," he replied. "If I had hit you, I would have just pulled the trigger again." He punctuated the remark with a wink.

Leaving Rosa to guard their prisoners, Natalie went in to wake up Sandy. In fact, the morphine infusion had run dry, and the woman, already much more conscious, was actually beginning to fight the ventilator.

"Sandy, easy does it," Natalie urged softly, stroking her forehead. "Easy does it. Sandy, squeeze my hand if you understand me. . . . Come on, squeeze my hand. . . . Good. That's it. That's it. Sandy, my name is Natalie. I'm a medical student from Boston and I'm here to help you. Everything is okay. Squeeze if you understand. . . ."

It took just a few minutes for Sandy Macfarlane to wake up enough to have the breathing tube removed. She was hoarse, disoriented, and near hysteria, muttering about her son in Tennessee and also someone named Rudy, but to her credit, she was able to listen to Natalie's explanations and gradually to cooperate enough to roll onto a stretcher.

Natalie wheeled her to the dining room. There was little change in those poisoned. Most of them were still trying to cope with the effects and side effects of the hallucinogen. One of them, the husky man in surgical scrubs, either an anesthesiologist or possibly a surgical assistant, was tucked on his side in a fetal position, not moving and, on closer examination, not breathing. Exhausted and desperate to do something about transportation, Natalie was able to summon little more than a brief pang for the man.

She hurried over and knelt on one knee by Santoro, whose color was a ghastly gray-green.

"Santoro, I need a car or a van. What do you have?"

"I have nothing for you. You are making a mistake, a terrible mistake."

With no time to argue, Natalie forced the

muzzle of Vargas's heavy pistol into the surgeon's groin.

"You might not remember me," she said in English, "but I hope you do. Two months ago, you and your friend Dr. Cho helped steal one of my lungs. You caused me great pain and ruined my life and I will have no problem at all in doing the same to you." For emphasis, she jammed the pistol in even harder. "I'm going to count to five. If you haven't told me where I can find the keys to at least two cars or a van, I'm going to pull this trigger and blow whatever is there between your legs to bits. And you know what? I'll be happy to do it. Maybe you can become the first one on your block to have your privates replaced with a transplant."

"No, wait! Help me, I'm sick, I—"

"Five . . . four . . . three . . . two . . ."

"Wait, my desk, my desk. The keys to the hospital van are in the top drawer of my desk."

"Van? I didn't see a van, just two small—"

"It's on the other side of the hospital. Down that way. Now help me, I'm going to be sick to my stomach again."

Ignoring him, Natalie raced to the office

and located the keys, then hurried back to where Luis lay. His pressure was still in the low eighties and his color was poor. She was certain that he was in pain from his wounds—he had to be. Still, he gave no outward sign of it.

"Luis, we're ready to go. I've got the keys to Santoro's van. There should be room for all five of us."

"I do not think so," he said. "Leave me and Rosa. We have friends in the town. We can take care of ourselves."

"Absolutely not. We need to get you to a hospital. Ben, too."

Luis did not reply. Instead, he put his finger to his lips and pointed in the direction of the landing strip.

"A helicopter," he said. "It just landed."

"I didn't hear anything."

"It probably came in downwind."

Natalie motioned Rosa over.

"Rosa," she whispered, "Luis says he heard a helicopter fly in and land. Did you hear anything?"

"No," Rosa said, "but believe me, if he heard something it is there."

"Maybe we can force the pilot to help us take Luis and Ben to Rio."

"Let me go and check," Rosa said, changing the ammunition clip in her gun. "I will go out the back past the pool, and then move into the forest."

"Just be careful."

There was no time for Rosa to heed Natalie's warning. Her gun ready, she cautiously opened the door to the pool and patio. Before she had taken a full step outside, there was a burst of machine-gun fire, which nearly cut her in two, and drove her several feet back into the dining room before she dropped, lifeless, to the floor.

Natalie had taken no more than two steps toward her when two swarthy men in commando garb and Arab headdresses charged into the room, then two more. In seconds, moving with extreme precision, they stationed themselves strategically around the room, guns ready. One of them flicked his automatic weapon at Natalie, and issued a sharp order in Arabic. Natalie opened her hand and let her gun drop. Then she raised both hands and kept them up.

The soldiers scanned the room, looking for anything threatening, passing over Rosa's crumpled, bloodied corpse as if she weren't there. Then one of them marched back through the door. Half a minute later, he returned leading a man in an elegant robe and headdress.

Was this the patient ticketed to receive Sandy's heart?

Natalie felt as sick as any of those who had ingested Tokima's toxin. The four of them—Ben, Rosa, Luis, and herself—had tried the impossible, and only moments ago it seemed as if they had succeeded. Now, Rosa was dead, Ben was sick, Luis was gravely wounded, and she was standing helpless in the face of a team of professional soldiers. They had tried, they had lost.

"Please," she shouted across the room at the latest arrival, "please listen to me! Do you know what's going on here?" The man, taller than the others, and imperious in his manner and bearing, stared at her blankly. "Do you speak English?" she persisted. "Portuguese? I want someone who speaks English or Portuguese."

"Then you are in luck, Ms. Reyes, because I am fluent in both."

With those words, her mentor, Doug Berenger, strode through the door and into the room.

CHAPTER 39

When he obtains the power, he immediately becomes unjust as far as he can be.
—PLATO, *The Republic,* Book II

The moment Natalie saw Berenger, the missing pieces of her life began flying into place. Instantly consumed by a hatred more powerful than any passion she had ever known, she slowly lowered her hands and stood, arms folded, watching as he impassively surveyed the carnage and illness surrounding them. Then he turned to her.

"Our friend in the village, Father Francisco, radioed our friend Sergeant Barbosa here at the hospital that a beautiful, sexy tree-hugger with clean, new boots had made it out to Dom Angelo. When I heard Barbosa's description of the woman, I had a funny feeling that it might be you. You are to be commended for making it this far."

"Go to hell, Doug," she said, barely able to keep herself from leaping at him in an effort to claw his eyes out before the Arab soldiers cut her down. "You're a goddamn murderer— a killer."

Her mind was racing. Over their years together as mentor and pupil, then as friends, she had developed a strong sense of the man. Now, she struggled to integrate what she knew of him with his involvement in this place. There was little chance, she reasoned, that she was going to survive—no, she immediately corrected, there was no chance at all. But somehow she had to get at him. Somehow she had to take advantage of his arrogance, his love of power, and his enormous ego. Somehow she had to rattle him—ridicule and goad him into making a mistake. No matter what, she was not going to die passively.

"George Washington killed for a cause," he was saying. "So did Eisenhower, and Truman, and Moses, and Mandela, and Simón Bolívar. And Lincoln sanctioned the deaths of hundreds of thousands in the cause of what was right."

"Oh, please, spare me your feeble justifications for being an amoral monster."

The surgeon's eyes flashed, and she knew that she had stung him. It wouldn't be the last time, she vowed.

Berenger turned from her to the director of the hospital.

"Santoro, where's Oscar?"

"My stomach. I'm sick . . . so sick."

The surgeon began sputtering and coughing up bile and acid.

"Damn it, Xavier, where is he?"

"Don't . . . know."

"He's dead," Natalie said matter-of-factly. "I shot him. Right here." She pointed to her eye. "He was a pig and a murderer, just like you."

"And you, my dear lady, are an irritating, self-serving little bug, a gnat, aptly named and certainly not deserving of the status of a Guardian."

"Not deserving of *what?*"

"Tell me what you poisoned these people with."

"I don't know. A little shaman I met in the forest put together a special something for me." She glanced around the room. "He should have listened to me, though. I told him to make it a lot stronger."

Berenger crossed to where the silver-haired woman lay moaning and clutching her middle. He glanced down with some disgust at the body lying next to her and then carefully stepped around it.

"Dorothy," he said without a word of sympathy for her condition, "can you work?"

"I . . . I can't stop getting sick," she managed. "It feels like my stomach is about to tear in two. It was something in the food at lunch. I'm sure of it. I've been hallucinating, too. Poor Tony couldn't stop throwing up, either. How's he doing?"

"Not so well. Dorothy, I need you. I was counting on you to do the anesthesia for both cases. Is that the woman over there?"

At Berenger's gesture in her direction, Sandy began to shriek hysterically.

"No! Please no! I have a little boy. He needs me. Please! I beg you. Don't hurt me!"

"Oh, that's just sweet, Doug," Natalie said. "She has a little boy. Aren't you proud of yourself?"

"Shut up!"

Berenger quickly whispered something to

the man in the regal robe, who then nodded in the direction of two of his men, and issued a quick order. With Sandy continuing to scream piteously, the soldiers wheeled her away and into the farthest operating room. In moments, there was silence.

With Berenger's help, the anesthesiologist managed to get to her feet. There was no way to keep her from seeing Tony's corpse.

"Oh, dear," she gasped. "Poor man."

"Dorothy, listen," Berenger said, "we'll take care of Tony's family. Real good care. Now, you've got to pull yourself together. The prince will be here any minute. He's gone into congestive heart failure and may be in early cardiogenic shock. We need to move quickly, and to do that, we need you. When this is over, when you have helped give one of the most enlightened and powerful rulers in the world back his life, you will never have to work again if you don't want to. You will live in luxury for the rest of your days. Can you do it?"

"I . . . I can try."

As the woman headed unsteadily out of the dining room, holding her midsection and shaking her head as if trying to clear it, Natalie noticed that Luis, white as a sheet, had shifted position and was working his hand underneath him toward his gun. She shook her head in sharp warning, but he either did not notice, or else did not care.

"So," Natalie said, anxious to distract her mentor, "the paper I was supposed to deliver, the international transplant meeting—it was all calculated to get me down here."

"If there wasn't a meeting here, I modestly admit I would have found another way. You see, it wasn't mere chance and a passion for long-legged track stars that led me to connect with you when you were at Harvard. It was—"

"Let me guess. It was a blood test that was drawn on me at a Whitestone lab. A green-top tube, to be specific."

Berenger looked genuinely surprised.

"It appears that when the procedures here are concluded, you and I will have to have a little discussion as to who knows what about green-top tubes."

"I know that you are a murderer—a serial killer, no better than any of the rest of them."

"Think what you wish," Berenger said. "We prefer to think of ourselves as involved physicians who are righting a serious wrong in the system."

"Oh, please."

"You were a twelve out of twelve tissue match with a person we knew would one day need a new lung—a person whose work is about to revolutionize medicine as we know it. Twelve out of twelve, Natalie. That means almost no nasty antirejection drugs to slow him down. All mankind will be the richer for his work. Without your lung he well might have died."

"So you took me out to lunch and acted as if you actually cared about me."

"We needed to keep you on a fairly short leash. I ask you, who deserves that lung of yours more, you or him?"

"That's not your decision to make, Doug."

"Isn't it? You know, until recently, I actually tried to stick up for you. There was another candidate—a laborer, who was an eleven out of twelve match for our man. But then, when you showed how crass and arrogant you were by trying to stab Dr. Renfro in the back and subsequently getting kicked out of school and your residency, it was clear you had denigrated yourself, and lowered yourself far beneath any Guardian."

"Guardian? Guardian of what? . . . What in the hell are you talking about?"

"I wouldn't expect you to know."

"What kind of guardian? . . . Hey, wait a minute, are you talking about guardians as in *Plato's* guardians? The philosopher kings? Surely you don't think that you . . . oh, but you do, don't you? You consider your-self a philosopher king." Natalie knew that in her campaign to disrupt and rattle the man, she had just been given a weapon. "How many of you are there, Doug? How many philosopher murderer kings? Are you part of some sort of secret society—a Plato club?"

Berenger's expression left no doubt that he had been gored.

"You are in no position to be mocking," he said. "The Guardians of the Republic are among the greatest, most talented, most enlightened men and women on earth. By taking over the decision-making relative to the allocation of organs, we have done more good for mankind than you could ever imagine."

"The Guardians of the Republic! Oh, this is too much! Do you have an anthem, Doug? A password? A decoder ring? How about a secret grip and merit badges?"

"Enough!"

Berenger took a single step forward and

slapped Natalie across the face with all his strength, dropping her to one knee.

Natalie, her eyes watering from the blow, ran her tongue over the corner of her mouth and tasted blood.

"That was brave, Doug," she said, standing. "I hope you broke your hand."

"No such luck."

"Too bad. So, tell me, what harm did that poor woman in there ever do to anyone that would cause your precious Guardians to sacrifice her?"

"You'll never understand."

"Try me."

"She's a Producer—the lowest of all social groups. Compare the value of her life to that of the great man she is about to save. Either she must die, or he must. It's as simple as that. And I say it is no contest. Organs must be allocated to save the lives of those who can and will best serve mankind."

"You left out the part about being able to pony up a gazillion dollars as well."

"Wrong! Many of the Guardians we save don't have that kind of money."

"Such charity. And here I was so surprised and proud of you when you put Tonya in her place and treated that poor fellow who couldn't stop smoking so humanely."

"If you hadn't been standing there I would have kissed Tonya for being so right on the mark. I wanted to kill that bastard Culver for wasting that heart. I wanted to kill him on the spot. I wanted to open his chest with a dull blade, remove that precious heart I had been forced by the system to place there, and put it into someone who deserved it more and would take better care of it."

Out of the corner of her eye, Natalie could see that Luis had reached his gun and was slowly maneuvering it to where he could pull it from beneath his leg. His color had, if possible, worsened, and his eyes looked nearly lifeless. *Nearly.*

"So, Douglas the Great," Natalie said, "the reason you didn't just have me killed and buried down here is? No, wait, don't bother answering, Lord Philosopher King. I know. I'm alive just in case, by some fluke, my lung is rejected or fails to function for whatever reason, you want me incubating the other one."

"How long is this poison going to last?" Berenger demanded.

"I would say go fuck yourself, but I have high hopes of being elevated to the exalted ranks of Guardian once more, and I wouldn't want to say anything so crude that it hurts my chances."

Natalie could see that the corner of Berenger's eye had begun to twitch. Another hit. Turning his back on her, he ordered Santoro to his feet.

"Come on, Xavier, I need you in the OR."

Santoro tried to stand, slipped on the products of his own sickness, fell, and began to giggle and moan at the same time. At that moment, a helicopter swung low over the hospital, then off to the landing strip. One of the soldiers was dispatched to guide the latest arrivals in.

"Damn it, Santoro!" Berenger snapped. "Get up, get showered and dressed, and get ready to assist me in the OR!"

He grabbed the man by the back of the shirt and pulled him rudely to his feet. The cleansing shower would never happen. Luis raised his gun and, before either of the remaining two soldiers could react, fired from twenty feet away. The bullet caught Santoro squarely in the chest, knocking him back into an easy chair, an odd smile on his lips. A second shot, probably meant for Berenger, shattered a window.

"No!" Natalie screamed as the two soldiers riddled Luis with automatic fire from
their machine guns, causing his body to jerk
about like a marionette. "No!"

Natalie wanted to rush to him, but in truth,
there was nothing she could do, and the
Arab soldiers were extremely jittery. Instead,
she moved off to one side and satisfied herself that her hero was at least at peace, as
she, herself, would undoubtedly be before
too much longer.

Berenger was clearly unraveling. He
stormed over to where Vincent's girlfriend
lay, violently snapping her head and kicking
her feet at whatever hallucinations were ha-
rassing her.

"Who are you? What are you doing here?"

The woman glanced up at him and began
laughing hysterically. Then, without warning,
she threw up, spattering his shoes. Con-
temptuously, he wiped them on her pants
leg, and then turned toward the patio entrance where three soldiers rushed in wheeling a stretcher on which lay a young,
copper-skinned, mustachioed man, with a
portable monitor-defibrillator and oxygen
mask in place. His breathing was labored.
Behind him came an Arab physician in

scrubs and a white coat, and a young, lean, black man pushing a small, glass-front case, mounted on wheels, and containing a number of units of blood.

"You'll be working in OR one as usual, Randall," Berenger said to the man. "The bypass pump is just as you left it. You know where everything else is. Be careful getting ready, but do it quickly."

He patted the pump tech on the shoulder, hurried over to the prince, and listened to his heart and lungs.

"I don't like this," he said to the physician in English. "I don't like this at all. Where are Khanduri and the nurses?"

"We flew over them. They're in two cars, about five miles from here—on that winding road, half an hour, maybe. No more than that."

"You should have put them all on the jet and flown straight in."

"You heard the pilot back in Rio. He said the flaps weren't working right, and it was too dangerous."

"Christ. When did the prince start to slip?"

"At the airport, just as we were transferring him to the helicopter."

"Okay, okay, we can still pull all this together. Can you assist me in the OR?"

"I dare not leave the prince, especially when he is in this condition."

"All right. Get him into the recovery room and see what you can do to stabilize him until Khanduri gets here. Wait, what's the minister's name?"

"Minister al-Thani."

"I'm going to ask him if he can assist me in the operating room."

"I don't think that would be proper, no matter what," the physician said. "He is—"

"I need help, damn it! I need another pair of hands, even if the person they're attached to doesn't know anything about—No, no, wait. Never mind. Just get the prince onto the monitor in the recovery room and get him stabilized. I'm going to get started and have the heart harvested and ready when Khanduri and the nurses arrive."

"But who will assist you?"

Berenger actually may have smiled.

"She will," he said, pointing at Natalie.

CHAPTER 40

**An enemy . . . owes to an enemy that
which is due or proper to him—that is to
say, evil.**

— PLATO, *The Republic,* Book I

You're out of your mind!" Natalie cried out.
"I'm not going into the operating room to assist you. Not now, not ever. I'd rather die."

Berenger, almost invariably composed,
suave, and in control, was clearly rattled by
the sudden downturn of his patient, the violent death of Xavier Santoro, and Natalie's
constant sniping. She was pleased to see
that the tick at the corner of his eye had, if
anything, intensified.

"Actually, Natalie," he said, his teeth
nearly clenched, "it's not going to be you
who is doing the dying—at least not yet." He
bent down and picked up Vargas's pistol. "It's

going to be them." He gestured to the
kitchen and maintenance crews. "If you
aren't in clean OR scrubs, prepping your
hands within two minutes, I will begin at the
end of this row and will kill one of them every
minute until you comply."

"But—"

"There's more. If you don't assist me, I will
have to use Dorothy, my anesthesiologist.
And before I do that, I will have her strap the
patient down and allow her to wake up. Then
we will harvest her heart."

"Jesus, Doug, what are you?"

"Right now I'm a man who needs to get
things done in a hurry. Are you in?"

He casually aimed the gun at one of the
chambermaids, a pretty Indian woman who
couldn't have been more than sixteen.

"The Philosopher King," Natalie muttered
as she turned and headed for the operating
room.

Berenger followed her.

"There are scrubs for us in that cabinet,"
he said. "We can change in recovery room
two. I won't peek if you don't."

"Peek all you want."

"My second surgeon and the nurses
should be here any minute. Then I shall have

all the help I need, and you can return to the others knowing you have saved many of their lives."

After getting their masks and surgical hair covers in place, he led Natalie into the narrow scrub room, set between the two ORs, and nodded her toward the second of two stainless steel sinks. As they washed with antiseptic-impregnated sponges, her mind was consumed with finding a way to kill him. Antonio Vargas and probably Luis as well killed by their nature, but this beast and his fanatic Guardians killed by choice. Put a gun in her hand, and she would have no trouble pointing it at her former mentor and role model, and pulling the trigger.

"And so," he was saying, "at the very core of the Guardians is Plato's concept of the Forms—his determination that perfection is inborn in the Guardians. He used this concept to conclude that the soul of such as us must be immortal, because how else could the notion of what perfection is be present at birth?"

"It's been a while since I took philosophy at Harvard," Natalie replied, "but from what I recall, I don't think you've got it quite right. The only perfect thing you Guardians are doing is being perfectly immoral."

In the mirror, Natalie could see the tightness and tension in Berenger's eyes.

Keep jabbing, she told herself. *Whatever you do, keep jabbing.*

"The Forms tell me otherwise," he replied. "Our organization has prospered and has benefited millions and millions of the citizens of the world at very little cost. People will never know whose music is being brought to their ears because of us, or whose buildings they are marveling at that would never even have been conceived of. They will never know that the lifesaving drug they are taking was developed because we were able to supply its creator with the perfect organ at the perfect time. You see, dear Natalie, the Guardians are all about perfection and the Forms. Now, let us harvest our heart and place it where it belongs and where it can do the most good."

"How about we harvest yours instead?"

At that moment the door to the scrub room burst open and Randall, the heart-lung bypass pump technician, rushed in.

"The pump is ready, Doctor," he said.

"Any sign of Dr. Khanduri or the nurses?"

"None. Dr. al-Rabia says to tell you the prince is slipping."

"Damn it. Go have a chopper sent up to find out where the others are, and then get ready. If necessary, we'll put the prince on the bypass pump right now and just keep him there. Meanwhile, I'm going to get started next door. Come on, assistant, let's get cracking."

Berenger followed Natalie into the OR, where the anesthesiologist, having put their patient to sleep and intubated her, helped them gown and glove. Seeing Sandy Macfarlane looking so serene, Natalie felt a trickle of relief make its way into her profound sadness.

Just before her Achilles tendon repair, she remembered asking the anesthesiologist, only partly in jest, "How am I going to know if I didn't wake up?"

The man merely smiled down, patted her on the arm, and injected the preop meds. It was totally disheartening to possess that information about Sandy, and to be helpless to do anything about it.

Hey, Doc, tell me. How am I going to know if I didn't wake up from my surgery?

"Dorothy, are you all set?" Berenger asked. "We've got to move on this one."

"All set."

"Do you have ice ready? There's going to

be a delay between the harvest and the transplant."

"Always."

Natalie again looked across at Berenger's eyes. He was clearly frazzled, but for twenty years or more he had been the Man outside of and within the OR, and had successfully handled countless medical crises.

With no nurse to assist them, the anesthesiologist had pulled two large instrument stands across the operating table so that both surgeon and assistant could get at them. Doug Berenger was not only one of the most elegant, brilliant surgeons Natalie had ever seen, he was one of the fastest. Without asking for her help, he began rapidly swabbing russet-colored Betadine antiseptic over Sandy's chest.

"Let me tell you one last time, Natalie, if you make any odd or unusual moves, any at all, I will tell Dorothy over there to turn off the anesthesia before we proceed. Have I made myself clear?"

"Clear."

"Then just shut up and do as I say. Have sponges and hemostats ready just in case. Dorothy, we're opening."

As Natalie picked up what Berenger

asked for, she noticed three scalpels lying side by side on the far edge of the instrument tray. There was no way she could get at them without being seen, but there was also nothing else available that even looked like a weapon. A desperate situation called for desperate measures, and one way or another, she also knew that like the poor woman on the table, she wasn't going to wake up from her operation.

Without another word, Berenger snatched one of the scalpels from the tray and made a foot-long incision from top to bottom along Sandy's sternum. Blood instantly began oozing from a dozen or more small vessels, but unless one of them began hemorrhaging rapidly, Berenger would not bother to gain control.

There was no need.

"The bone saw is right there, Natalie. So are the spreaders."

Natalie felt sick as she reached for them.

The operating room door opened. Berenger turned to see the Arab physician, al-Rabia.

"Dr. Berenger," the man said urgently, "the prince's blood pressure is zero. I cannot bring it back up."

The few seconds Berenger was distracted were enough. Natalie swept her gloved hand across the two remaining scalpels and came away with one of them tucked in the sleeve of her surgical gown. Then she glanced over at the anesthesiologist to ensure that she, too, was focused on al-Rabia.

Now, her mission was clear—somehow to get close to Berenger, and then, for Rosa and Luis and Ben, and herself and all the other victims of the Guardians, to be fearless.

Berenger was clearly on edge—the juggler of balls, who had just reached a personal best when one more was thrown into the mix.

But he was still the Man.

"All right, Doctor," he said, "let's wheel him quickly into the OR, and I'll get him on the pump. Dorothy, just leave the gas on here and come with us. Natalie, let's go, we have work to do."

Berenger took a step toward the door, then another. Natalie, moving from the other side of the table, was now a pace behind him.

There is often only one chance.

With Luis's words resonating in her mind, she slipped the scalpel into her hand.

"Doug!"

Startled, Berenger turned toward her, exposing his jaw and the side of his neck.

Fearless!

With all the force she could manage, Natalie swung the blade up from her hip and swiped it viciously across Berenger's throat. Instantly, the opening of his severed trachea appeared where his larynx had been. A moment later, bright crimson arterial blood began spewing from a laceration through his carotid artery, splattering Natalie, and coating the floor.

Unable to speak, pawing futilely at his neck, the man called Socrates, one of the founders of the Guardians of the Republic, lurched backward and fell heavily, awash in the rapidly ebbing essence of his being. His last moments were spent staring up at Natalie in silent, absolute, wide-eyed disbelief.

"Come, Dr. Berenger!" al-Rabia cried from the OR next door. "The prince's heart has stopped! Come quickly!"

Natalie stripped off her gown and raced in to help, but she knew that unless the dysfunctional muscle that had caused the prince's heart failure could be replaced, there was nothing that drugs or cardiac compressions could do.

"Oh, dear Allah!" al-Rabia kept muttering. "Dear Allah, help us!"

Natalie continued performing CPR, but the cardiac monitor remained absolutely discouraging. She considered trying, with the help of the pump technician, to hook him up to the bypass machine, but her knowledge and surgical skill stopped well short of that. Al-Rabia, clearly a gifted physician, tried several shocks from the defibrillator, even though he knew that his master's problem was not fibrillation—a potentially reversible lethal rhythm—but rather, complete cardiac standstill—a virtually untreatable flat line. There really was no hope.

The minister, al-Thani, was standing just outside the doorway, only a few feet from Berenger's blood-soaked body. His eyes were narrowed and grim, his arms folded tightly across his chest. Clearly, he knew that the fate of his prince had been sealed.

Natalie, following al-Rabia's orders to the best of her ability, was waiting for him to stop the resuscitation, but the man desperately kept at it. Suddenly, one of the helicopter pilots appeared by al-Thani, trying at first to speak in Portuguese, than resorting to badly broken English.

"Lord. Two cars on road. Stopped. People on face on ground. Men, women with guns around them."

Ben!

The impassive minister actually sighed. Then he rattled off an order in Arabic to the physician, turned, and left.

Moments later the resuscitation on the prince was over.

Al-Rabia, his eyes glistening, looked dismally over at Natalie and shook his head.

"Allah will care for him," he said, "but he was such a good man, and would have made a wonderful ruler for our people."

"I'm very sorry," she replied. "For what it's worth, I think you did an excellent job. He had a heart infection that could not be treated."

"Maybe someday there will be such a treatment."

"Maybe someday," she echoed.

"Natalie, that is your name?"

"Natalie Reyes, yes."

"Well, Natalie Reyes, it means nothing now, but I want you to know that we were told the donor of the heart to our prince was brain-dead. Until we arrived here, that is what we believed. With Dr. Berenger in charge, matters simply got out of hand."

"I appreciate your telling me. Dr. Berenger and his organization were corrupted by their own egos and greed. They could not stand to be told by people they considered beneath them how to use their incredible skills."

"I understand. If the minister will allow me to leave the prince like this, perhaps with the anesthesiologist watching over him, I wish to come in and help you suture that poor woman's chest."

"I would like that, Dr. al-Rabia," Natalie said. "I would like that very much."

The two, Arab physician and American medical student, returned to the OR, where Sandy Macfarlane lay peacefully beneath the surgical drapes, being breathed for by a ventilator, and kept asleep by carefully metered anesthetic gas. The incision down her chest to the surface of her sternum was oozing blood, but certainly not enough to be a threat. Natalie electrically cauterized the largest of the bleeding vessels, then, with al-Rabia holding the skin edges together, she settled in and meticulously sewed the incision back together.

As she worked, Natalie flashed back to the Metropolitan Hospital emergency room just hours before Berenger would arbitrarily remove her as a Guardian for being suspended from medical school. Standing nearby was the nurse, Beverly Richardson, and on the table before her was the boy, Darren Jones, the last person she had sutured . . . until now.

Beneath her mask, Natalie smiled.

CHAPTER 41

You are lazy and mean to cheat us out of a whole chapter, which is a very important part of the story.

—PLATO, *The Republic,* Book V

With the anesthesiologist left behind to bring Sandy Macfarlane back to consciousness, Natalie headed excitedly to the dining room. The minister, al-Thani, was there, but all of the soldiers, save one, were gone.

"May I go out?" she anxiously asked al-Rabia. "There is someone out there—a friend. I need to make sure he doesn't get hurt."

"Is he the one who held up the arrival of the surgeon and all the others?"

"I believe so."

Al-Rabia shook his head in utter frustration and wordlessly checked with the minister, who clearly understood Natalie's request.

"Yes, yes, go ahead," he said. "They will not be hurt."

Before Natalie could leave, Ben and Father Francisco, hands in the air, entered the dining room, followed by three Arab soldiers and the man Natalie felt certain was Berenger's second surgeon.

Al-Thani barked out a brief order, and the soldiers lowered their weapons, then backed away.

"Where's Berenger?" the surgeon asked.

Al-Rabia pointed with his thumb.

"In the hallway," he said, not bothering to explain any further.

Natalie raced across and threw her arms around Ben, knocking him backward a step.

"Nice place you run here," he said, gesturing about the room. His gaze stopped at Luis's bullet-riddled corpse. "Oh, no."

"He was a warrior right to the end," Natalie said. "He always seemed ready to die. Before he was killed he did what was needed to bring this place down."

"Maybe his sister will be able to rest in peace."

"I couldn't believe it when the helicopter pilot said that someone had stopped the nurses and surgeon and had them lying on the ground. I just knew it was you. After Berenger told me that Father Francisco was on their payroll, I felt sick at having sent you to him for help. What happened?"

"Believe it or not," Francisco answered, "until Mr. Callahan, here, convinced me otherwise, I had no idea the donors who had come through the hospital had all been kidnapped. He told me the story of this professor from Chicago, and a farm boy from Idaho. He made the analogy between forcing the poor and downtrodden into prostitution and slavery, and forcing them to sell their body parts or, in this case, to give them away."

"Nat, Father Francisco, here, really came through when it counted. It took him just a few minutes to round up ten of the toughest men—*and* women—I have ever seen. We were fortunate to arrive at the hospital road just as the cars did. That man over there is a surgeon. He started bossing us around and telling us how important it was for them to get to the hospital. Next thing they knew, they were on the ground. Then, these soldiers came out of the trees, and all of a sudden we were on the ground, too."

Natalie turned to al-Rabia.

"What's going to happen to us and to these people?" she asked.

The physician received a silent answer from his minister before he responded.

"Contrary to what you might believe, senseless violence is not our way," he said. "Minister al-Thani is sad and angry, but not at you. The prince's body will be placed on one of the helicopters and flown back to the airport. After we return to our country, he will be buried as the hero he was."

They all waited somberly as the soldiers wheeled the prince out across the patio, followed by al-Rabia and the minister.

Finally, Natalie turned to Father Francisco.

"Once the flight crew is in working order, we'll hitch a ride with them back to Rio and get Sandy into a hospital. Then I'll get in touch with the American Embassy and set up a meeting with them and this Military Police detective I met in Botafogo. He didn't treat me with any great interest, but I sensed he took pride in his work and his position.

Plus Rodrigo Vargas disliked him, and that's recommendation enough for me. His name is Perreira."

"I will check with some friends of mine to see if he is someone you can trust."

"Thank you, Father Francisco. Today you behaved like a true man of God."

The priest shook her hand, then embraced her and thanked her for helping to free their town.

"You know," he said, "this man has some way with words. He wore me away—absolutely wore me down like waves pounding at the shore. Hey, you know what I think, Mr. Callahan? I think maybe you should consider becoming a lawyer, or maybe even a priest."

"No chance, Father," Ben said, putting his arm around Natalie's shoulders to brace himself. "I'm going to be too busy writing my first detective novel."

EPILOGUE

The soul of man is immortal and imperishable.

—PLATO, *The Republic,* Book X

I can see why you love autumn in New England so much," Ben said. "I'm really happy to be here again."

Natalie squeezed his hand and smiled up at him. Four weeks had passed since Dom Angelo, and this was Ben's second trip to be with her. Their embryonic connection, forged initially in the rain forest, was growing stronger and more passionate, although neither of them was anxious to push things too hard too fast.

"I have something to share with you," Natalie said as they passed the Esplanade where just a few months before she had

gone with friends to watch the Pops celebrate the Fourth of July, "but first tell me
about Texas."

"It was kind of a surreal trip," he said. "The
cops knew who I was and didn't charge me
anything for towing and storing my car. Then
I started out of town, but almost before I
knew it, I was heading out John Hamman
Highway to see the place one last time. The
gate was chained and padlocked, and the
Oasis inside looked totally deserted. I got
out and hung for a time, just taking in the
whole scene."

"That had to have been intense."

"Oh, it was. I stood there wondering about
how many. How many unsuspecting clients
were tissue-typed there? Millions, I guess.
How many perfect matches had they chosen? How many had died as a result?"

"Ben, you helped put an end to it all."

"I hope. So, how do you feel about taking
a leave from school?"

"It's the right thing to do. I'm not mentally
or physically in shape to go back yet, but I
will if I can. Maybe next year. Meanwhile, I'm
getting to spend some quality time with my
niece, Jenny. With her CP and my sister's
death, she's really had a raw deal of it and I

want to be sure she gets as much as life owes her. Plus I really am enjoying the time we spend together."

"And your residency?"

"First things first, Ben."

"I understand. I'm still angry and frustrated for you, that's all."

"I don't have a hell of a lot to look forward to in terms of my health, but at least I'm not walking around all day thinking about solving my problems with a bunch of pills and a plastic bag."

"I sure hope not." Mindless of the runners and rollerbladers passing by, Ben lifted her chin and kissed her gently. "Wanna sit down for a bit?" he asked.

"Why, am I breathing weird again?"

"Hey, hey, no touchiness, now. Remember our deal. You stay cool about your lung and I'll stay cool about having no career, no interests aside from you and the illicit organ trade, and no immediate job prospects. Job or no job, good lung or bad, we still have what everyone else has—we have today. Now, what did you want to share with me?"

Natalie didn't respond immediately. Instead, she rested her head on his shoulder, trying to purge any unpleasant thoughts from her mind. Finally, she reached in her pocket and extracted a letter.

"This came yesterday," she said. "You watch the boats. I'll read it to you." She was unable to cull the melancholy from her voice. "Sorry for sounding down. I'm still lacking closure in this whole business, and from time to time notions about the future just hit me."

"Hey, read and don't worry. My scars are almost gone. Yours is slightly more permanent." He ran his fingertips along her right side. "Anything that brings closure a little nearer, do it."

Natalie pressed his hand to her lips.

The letter was folded in quarters and already dog-eared.

"It's from Detective Perreira," she said, opening it.

Dear Senhorita Reyes,

This letter, like my first one, is being translated by an American friend who teaches English and can be counted upon to be absolutely discreet. I first want to tell you that the attorney you have hired here has been most active and seems to us all to be extremely competent. I believe that ultimately there will be no formal charges pressed against you in connection with any of the matters related to Dom Angelo.

I also wish to thank you and Mr. Callahan for referring your friend Alice Gustafson to me. I find her to be a charming, thoughtful woman, who only yesterday was a guest at our home for dinner. She and I have traveled together to Dom Angelo (my third trip) for picture-taking and for her to examine the hospital and the village. With the help of information from someone in the town, several bodies have been unearthed. It may be difficult if not impossible to identify them, but Professor Gustafson believes the answers to that mystery are in London, and she will be flying there when she leaves here. Scotland Yard has been investigating their end of this case and are eagerly awaiting her arrival. Although it will take some time to identify all of those involved, she believes that some arrests there are imminent. Professor Gustafson is, as I assume you know, a most determined woman.

We here in Rio de Janeiro have great respect for your courage and for the service you and Mr. Callahan have done our country. I hope our aggressive pursuit of this matter, and the arrests we have made, including two of our own, have changed your opinion of the Brazilian Military Police.

If and when you choose to return to our country, please accept my invitation to serve as one of your hosts.

"Power corrupts," Ben said.

Natalie's reply was cut short by her cell phone, which announced a call with its riff from Vivaldi. With no one around to disturb, she let the melody play through twice before answering.

"Hello?"

"Is this Natalie Reyes?" a woman's voice asked.

"Are you selling something? Because—"

"Please indulge me for a moment and I'll explain everything."

"All right, I'm Natalie. Now, what is this? Who are you?"

"Natalie, I know you picked up Ben Callahan at the airport earlier today. Is he with you now?"

"Look, either you tell me what this is all about, or I'm going to—"

"Okay. Okay. This has to do with Brazil."

Instantly, Natalie's irritation vanished.

"What about Brazil?"

"Natalie, if you're not already, you may want to sit down."

"We're sitting."

"Great. Can you put the phone where you both can hear?"

Natalie pulled Ben closer and did as she was asked.

"Okay," she said, "we can both hear."

"Natalie, my name is Beth Mann. I'm a private detective here in Boston. On behalf of a client, I have been investigating you since your return from Brazil. No Peeping Tom stuff, I promise you."

"An ethical detective," Ben whispered, pulling back for a moment, "must be a hoax."

"Go on," Natalie said.

"As part of my investigation, I have had a number of conversations with Dr. Rachel French—"

"My pulmonologist," Natalie whispered to Ben.

"—and also with your friend Dr. Terry Millwood. He is at White Memorial Hospital right now, awaiting your call. Those two physicians have spoken with the head of the hospital, and all necessary arrangements have been made."

"Necessary arrangements for what?" Natalie asked, absolutely nonplussed.

"Natalie, does the name Dr. Joseph Anson mean anything at all to you?"

"No, should it?"

"Not really. Dr. Anson is from West Africa—Cameroon to be more exact. He's a dedicated physician and a brilliant researcher in the area of neovascularization."

"Making new blood vessels," Natalie whispered to Ben. "Go on."

"At this moment, Dr. Anson is in or around Boston. I have no idea where. He has made a decision from which he has no intention of turning back. The decision was made after I told him about the fire at your mother's house and the damage your lung incurred in saving her and your niece."

"But how did you—?"

"Mr. Callahan, would you please take a moment and tell this woman what we detectives do?"

"We detect," Ben said.

"Please go on," Natalie said, sensing, but not yet believing, what was to follow.

"At nine o'clock this evening, just seven hours from now, Dr. Anson is going to peacefully take his own life. I will get a call from an attorney telling me the address where Dr. Anson's body can be found. Then I will receive a call from Dr. Anson. I have an ambulance standing by and will wait exactly thirty-seven minutes before sending it out to the location. By the time they arrive, Dr. Anson's heart will be beating, but he will be brain-dead. Believe me, Natalie, Dr. Anson is a genius, and is absolutely capable of making this happen. Once a neurologist has confirmed the brain death, Dr. Millwood and his team will be standing by to transplant Dr. Anson's lung into your chest."

"But . . . but why? Why not just donate a lung to me and keep one for himself?"

"Because, Natalie, Joseph Anson has only one functioning lung—yours."

Natalie felt her body go slack and wondered if, for the first time in her life, she was going to faint. Ben squeezed her hand so tightly that it hurt.

"Oh, God," she said. "There's already been so much death. Is there any way I could talk to this man?"

"Believe me, Natalie, I have spoken to him a number of times, and researched him thoroughly. Dr. Anson is at peace with what he is doing. All we need now is your cooperation."

Ben nodded vigorously at her.

"Then . . . I guess you have it," she heard herself say.

"In that case, Dr. Millwood is awaiting your call. He'll explain what happens next. I'm very happy for you. Be sure to stop by my office after your recovery."

"But what if—?"

Beth Mann had rung off.

Natalie, making no attempt to stem her tears, took both of Ben's hands in hers.

"Remember what I said about closure?" she asked.

The time is right, Anson was thinking. *The time is right.*

He was in a small, rented garage, just a mile from Natalie Reyes's apartment, sitting in a compact car in pitch-darkness. The passenger side window was open an inch. The opening was sealed with rags. Protruding inward from the rags was one end of a length of garden hose. The other end was sealed in the exhaust pipe. The heavy sedation he had taken at a carefully predetermined moment was beginning to take effect.

He had read and reread Beth Mann's two-hundred-page report on Natalie Reyes, her family, and even on the new man in her life. He had studied the numerous articles, dating back to Natalie's days as a student athlete at Harvard. He had watched videos of several of her races. And finally, he had walked beside her, close enough to brush her sleeve.

Oh, yes, the time was absolutely right.

Natalie Reyes, and possibly Ben Callahan as well, were perfect to oversee the bringing in of new management for the hospital, and to control the fate of Sarah-9. After she recovered from the surgery, she—and if she wanted, Callahan—would be summoned to his attorney's office to receive his notebooks and a detailed DVD he had recorded for her.

She would be under no obligation to stay in Cameroon indefinitely, but he suspected that once she breathed the wonderful air of the jungle and met the people, she might want to. She and Callahan were everything the would-be philosopher kings of Elizabeth's and Douglas Berenger's sad organization were not. They were true Guardians.

Anson flicked on the inside light and checked the time. Then he opened the notebook on his lap and read aloud.

The world can be hard, full of trickery,
Full of deceit,
Full of injustice,
Full of pain.
But there is an emptiness waiting, my
friend—a great, glowing emptiness,
Soft and fragrant with the essence of
peace,
The essence of serenity.
You are almost there, my friend.
The magnificent emptiness is the
eternal harbor for your soul.
Take my hand, friend.
Take my hand and take a step, just
one more step,
And you are there.

Anson lifted his cell phone and dialed.

"Ms. Mann," he said, "you may start tim-ing now."

Without waiting for a reply, he set the phone aside, shut off the light, turned on the ignition, and placed his notebook down on a well-worn copy of Plato's *Republic*.

AUTHOR'S NOTE

My goal in writing suspense is first and foremost to entertain my readers and to transport them, however transiently, from the stresses and cares of their lives to the highly stylized world of the novel. My secondary goals are to inform and to present, without resolution, issues of social and ethical importance.

I sincerely hope you have found *The Fifth Vial* thrilling and provocative entertainment. Now, I thank you for taking time to read this afterword note and for discussing its contents with your loved ones. It deals, as you would suspect, with organ donation, and the importance of your participation in an act that I feel defines humility and righteousness—that is, making your organs available to others in the event of your scientifically diagnosed, documented, and *re*documented brain death.

The subject might not be fun to think about, but it is crucial.

Almost every one of us would opt for a transplant to save our life or that of a loved one. Acknowledging that fact, it is nearly impossible to believe that the vast majority of us haven't registered to be donors in the event that illness or trauma renders us clinically dead—that is to say, irreversibly brain-dead according to the most sophisticated neurological testing available to physicians. Thousands of potential recipients currently wait for an organ. Many of them will die before one comes available. During that time, countless organs will have been lost to the casket or the flame simply because proper arrangements had not been made in advance.

The organs and tissue donated by just one person can improve or save the lives of up to fifty others.

Fifty!

It costs nothing to be a donor, and can

add meaning and majesty to what is otherwise a sad, confusing, tragic inevitability.

Becoming a potential organ donor is as simple as indicating your intent on your driver's license, or carrying an organ donor card, or contacting your state or national donor registry, or merely discussing your desire with your family members.

Here are some brief answers to frequently asked questions:

Who can be an organ donor?

People of all ages and medical histories should consider themselves potential donors.

What organs and tissues can I donate?

Organs that can be donated include heart, kidneys, pancreas, lungs, liver, and small intestine. Tissues that can be donated include corneas, skin, heart valves, tendons, and veins.

Can I sell my organs?

No. Federal law makes it illegal to sell organs and tissues as such buying and selling might lead to inequitable access, with the wealthy having an unfair advantage.

Does the donor's family have to pay any part of the cost of donating an organ or tissue?

There is no cost to the donor's family or estate for organ and tissue donation.

If I am a donor, will that affect the quality of my medical care?

If you are sick or injured and admitted to the hospital, the number one priority is to save your life. Organ and tissue donation can only be considered after you die.

Will organ donation disfigure my body?

Donation does not disfigure the body and does not interfere with having a funeral, including open-casket services.

Can I be an organ donor if I have a preexisting medical condition?

Your medical condition at the time of death will be assessed by medical professionals to determine what organs and tissues can be donated.

The Internet is a valuable place to get more in-depth answers to these and other questions, and to further separate myth from fact regarding organ donation and transplantation. Listed below are a few Web sites you will find helpful in this regard. After having your questions answered and your misgivings assuaged, I hope you will feel ready to do the right thing.

With thanks and warmest wishes,
Michael

United Network for Organ Sharing, www.unos.org

U.S. Department of Health and Human Services, Organ Donation Initiative, www.organdonor.gov

National Marrow Donor Program, www.marrow.org

National Minority Organ Tissue Transplant Education Program, www.nationalmottep.org

New England Organ Bank, www.beob.org

Coalition on Donation, www.shareyourlife.org

American Kidney Fund, www.afkinc.org

American Lung Association, www.lungusa
.com

American Liver Foundation, www.liver
foundation.org

American Organ Transplant Association,
www.a/o/t/a.org

And finally . . .

Organ Guard, Professor Alice Gustafson's
watchdog agency depicted in this novel, was
inspired by Organs Watch, and independent
university-based research and medical
human-rights project designed to monitor
justice and fairness in organs procurement
and distribution. Organs Watch documents
the global traffic in human organs and tissues; identifies medical human-rights viola-
tions and abuses in the procurement and
transplantation of organs and tissues; and
works with medical, governmental, and international entities concerned with ethics
and safety in organs procurement and transplant. For more information on ways you can

bet involved with and/or support this project, please contact:

Nancy Scheper-Hughes, Ph.D.
Director, Organs Watch
Medical Anthropology Program
University of California, Berkeley
232 Kroeber Hall
Berkeley, CA 94720
nsh@berkeley.edu
sunsite.berkeley.edu/biotech/
    organswatch/